COAST TO COAST

COAST TO COAST

Australian Stories 1965-1966

SELECTED BY CLEMENT SEMMLER

ANGUS AND ROBERTSON

First published in 1967 by
ANGUS & ROBERTSON LTD
89 Castlereagh Street, Sydney
54 Bartholomew Close, London
107 Elizabeth Street, Melbourne

Library of Congress
Catalogue Card No. 67-12696

Registered in Australia
for transmission by post as a book
PRINTED IN AUSTRALIA BY
J. C. STEPHENS PTY LTD, MELBOURNE

S867.

ACKNOWLEDGMENTS

THANKS for permission to republish stories in this collection are due to Barrie & Rockliff for "The Return", from *Road to Nowhere;* to the *Bulletin* for "Peck's Telescope", "Homage to Hymen" and "Say to Me Ronald!"; to *Honi Soit* for "Spoe"; to the *London Magazine* for "Odour of Eucalyptus"; to *Mate* for "Drift"; to *Meanjin* for "Four Sunday Suits" and "Possums"; to *Overland* for "The Swan" and "Pioneers"; to *Quadrant* for "The Discovery", "Preliminaries", and "The Road to Kuala Lumpur"; to *Squire* for "The Desert Flower"; and to Curtis Brown Ltd. for "The Full Belly".

"Say to Me Ronald!" also appeared in Hal Porter's *The Cats of Venice* (Angus and Robertson).

Published with the assistance
of the Commonwealth Literary Fund

Contents

PECK'S TELESCOPE   1
Hugh Atkinson

TREE WITHOUT EARTH   8
Marjorie Barnard

ONLY ON SATURDAYS   16
Don Campbell

THE METAMORPHOSES OF THE MISSES
McNAIR   27
C. B. Christesen

THE DISCOVERY   33
Manning Clark

PRELIMINARIES   45
Laurence Collinson

THE TINS   52
Peter Cowan

THE ROAD TO MADRID   72
David Forrest

THE RETURN   78
G. M. Glaskin

HOMAGE TO HYMEN   86
E. A. Gollschewsky

THE ROAD TO KUALA LUMPUR   95
Gwen Kelly

FOUR SUNDAY SUITS   106
Alan Marshall

DRIFT   122
O. E. Middleton

THE SWAN   126
Myra Morris

PIONEERS   133
John Morrison

THE CRABS   159
E. M. Noblet

SAY TO ME RONALD!   169
Hal Porter

POSSUMS   181
Katharine Susannah Prichard

THE DESERT FLOWER   189
Olaf Ruhen

SPOE   200
Hugh Storey

THE IDIOT BOY   205
Griffith Watkins

THE COMPOUND   211
Anna West

THE FULL BELLY   225
Patrick White

ODOUR OF EUCALYPTUS   243
Michael Wilding

Peck's Telescope

HUGH ATKINSON

WITHIN a month of his forty-fifth birthday, Peck had been divorced for the third time and had retired to lick his wounds. Figuratively speaking, he had no wounds to lick. ▃▃▃▃▃ adulteries had proved so flagrant that Peck's grievance was hopelessly distributed and after the first crushing realization that he had been a celebrated cuckold, he had felt neither jealousy nor pain and had dismissed her from the house and the memory of his flesh as though she had never existed. "What would you expect?" ▃▃▃▃▃ had asked scornfully. "He never loved me or any of his wives. There is no room in his ego."

Peck's other two wives had been as summarily forgotten. The first because she irritated him by the trivia of her interests. The second, he said, because the marriage had been perfect and he found himself without a reason to get up any more in the mornings. Lacking inner-direction and bored by the success of his business, Peck required conflict to provide an illusion of reality.

▃▃▃▃▃ had been contentedly married to a weak and dependent man when Peck met her at a suburban film evening. His settled condition represented a challenge which straightway absorbed him, and when he discovered that he no longer wished for a button to press which would disintegrate him on waking, Peck imagined himself in love and proceeded to wreck ▃▃▃▃▃ marriage with the kinetic energy and polemic skill which had made him famous in business.

The turnabout in the pattern by which he had moved through his previous marriages greatly upset Peck's partners in the city, who were accustomed to regarding him with awe.

Being decent, grey conservatives themselves, they had delighted in Peck's eccentricities, of which they counted his multiple marriages as being one. That life could play Peck a dirty trick, instead of the other way round, caused them alarm and confusion. Their suggestion that he should take a good long holiday was compounded out of affection and their own unadmitted embarrassment at the sight of their idol's clay feet.   Peck had not had a holiday, other than his honeymoons, in the twenty-seven years he had been working.   The furious hobbies in which he indulged: rare manuscripts, vintage cars, exotic orchids, meteorology, Siamese cats, finger painting, photography, tea blending, tropical fish, hypnotism and clock repairs, had absorbed all his time and interests.   Ordinarily, the idea of a good long holiday would have given Peck the horrors but the consideration exhibited by his partners, although unobtrusive and subtle, had begun to get on his nerves.   At least it will be a change from their silly faces, he thought, and wondered what one did on good long holidays.

He considered a visit to New Guinea, the Barrier Reef, one of the tropical islands off Queensland, trout fishing in the Snowy River, Alice Springs, a hunting camp in the Northern Territory, a cruise ship to Japan, or a solitary excursion into the country by motor caravan.   At the end of a fortnight's collecting folders, making enquiries in tourist bureaux, doing supplementary reading of reference in the Public Library and holding discussions in the Board Room, Peck was an encyclopaedia of onshore and offshore holidays and had thoroughly exhausted any interest he might have had in taking one.   He became excessively moody and not a little irritable.   At home he sacked the housekeeper for something to do and prepared his own meals, sinking into the silence of the house and moving about abstractedly through the litter of kitchen and bedroom, aimlessly fingering the paraphernalia of his discarded hobbies.   The wish to press a button which would instantly and painlessly disintegrate him, returned to haunt his wakings.   There seemed no point in anything and Peck's appearances in his office grew casual while he lay in bed for days recalling the memories of his life.

"I don't like it," one of the partners said, "He's in for a nervous breakdown."

"He's drinking a lot," another said.   "He never did that before."

A third said, "He needs a change.   We've got to get him out of that house."

"How about Rubinstein's place," the other asked, referring to a client.   "A local change would be better than nothing.   Rubinstein's going abroad for three months."

"It has a swimming pool and a yacht."

"He could go sailing."

"It's in one of the best situations on the coast."

"He could go swimming."

"He could lie in the sun and rest."

The partners rang for the company car and carefully put on their hats.

Rubinstein's house was on a peninsula, forty minutes drive from Sydney. On one side, the Pacific Ocean boiled against rock-footed cliffs, or rolled in green waves to the clean yellow beaches pocketing the headlands. On the other side, mountains of twisted trees locked long, calm reaches of water.

Peck looked each way, rather absently, after the partners had installed him and left. He walked on the terraces, reclined on the furniture and then retired inside and shut the door.

The housekeeper came from her cottage next morning and prepared breakfast for Peck. He listened morosely to her friendly chatter and was reminded of his first wife. Afterwards, while she clattered the dishes, he wrote a note on Rubinstein's stationery instructing her he would cook for himself, and when her husband left off gardening to take her to the shops, Peck went to the cottage and poked the note under a door.

At the end of three days he observed in a mirror that he had been neglecting to shave. There was a shock of grey in the stubble, which Peck had not noted before. He studied the grey hairs out of narrowed eyes and resolved to grow a beard. Not an artist's beard for decoration, but a Santa Claus beard for defiance. The growth absorbed his attention for a week. As the beard grew longer and greyer it accented the balding in his hairline. Peck had lost his teeth early and had forgotten that he wore a plate. Now he was reminded of it and removed the denture, except for eating. When he examined his greying beard in the mirror, he tipped his head forward to show the holes in his hairline and chomped empty gums at his image.

On a table in Rubinstein's study, a room Peck found depressing, was a long polished box with gold-plated clips, which he opened one evening while he idled there. Inside, on fixtures of baize, was a telescope and a tripod. The telescope was bound in leather and its eye winked faintly in the light. Peck's hands moved to lift the telescope but decided for themselves that they would not. He had no wish to be involved again in the pointlessness of pursuits. Peck went into the kitchen and put on a can of baked beans to warm. He ate with a spoon and his dentures grinned crookedly at him from the table. Peck reflected that one could do without teeth and prepared a dish of bread-and-milk, sucking it off the spoon. But his thoughts kept returning to the telescope and the wink in its glassy eye.

When it grew dark he put a chair by the window and fetched the telescope from the study. He fixed the tripod, adjusted the eyepiece and pointed the lens at the sky. The blistered moon looked surprising, a great pale ball in the heavens. He could clearly see that it had dimension and the mystery of another side. We usually see it as a plate. Peck thought it looked more like a pitted orange. He became uneasy, studying the moon, feeling its suspended volume and roundness. It depressed him with notions of the insignificance and the consciousness of mortality. Peck turned the telescope to the Milky Way and was impressed by its extravagance and beauty. He remembered that some stars had been gone for millenniums, burnt out or exploded to dust, that the light he focused on was the past made palpable, the living light of dead stars, journeying through infinity to twinkle now in his eye. It's a kind of immortality, Peck thought. Only when dawn approached and unwrapped the dyes of night did he remove his eye from the telescope and go sighing to his bed.

There came a dawn in which Peck sipped tea and watched the light on the water. Absently he tipped the telescope and focused on the seafront, where houses and flat blocks sprinkled. He saw a milkman making deliveries and sharpened the image to watch. Peck could see the milkman as clearly as though he was in the room and hear the clink and clank of the bottles by using imagination. He moved the telescope to the flat windows. Watching, he saw a glass go up in one of them and a man put his legs over the sill. The man turned to someone inside and for a moment there was long black hair at the window. Then he dropped to the ground, stood looking about and then nonchalantly walked away. Peck stared at the floor, remembering himself as he had been before his first marriage. Life had seemed so certain and exciting, and Peck had trafficked in windows. He had been breathless and gauche and easily startled, and once when there came a knock, he had jumped out of the window, thinking of the girl's father, forgetting they had moved to a better flat two floors higher up. In the fall he had badly sprained his ankle and hobbled on a stick for weeks.

He made tea and toast, lay down to nap and afterwards returned to the telescope.

The waves rose tall on the splintery blue sea, outside the tousled heads of the bathers. From high above them in the great white house Peck turned up the telescope's magnification. On coloured surfboards as slick as sharks, in the sculptured shapes of balance, the young wildly rode the racing walls with the water's flecked lip curled above them, and emerged from the loud crashing of white to ground on whirled sand and shallows. The mahogany stain of their strong, suntanned bodies glistened and dripped as they ran, to push the boards out again or carry them to the towels where girls in bikinis waited. A middle-aged man with hair on his shoulders lumbered a dropped stomach down to the water. Peck watched him wallowing and then thoughtfully went inside. In Mrs Rubinstein's dressing-room, he bared his gums at the long mirror. Then he took off his shirt, unbuttoned his trousers, and undressed down to the skin. For a long time he inspected himself. The flaccid muscles, the sickly pink skin, the womanish softening of chest, the sedentary calves, incipient stomach and unmistakable plumping of buttocks. Peck breathed deeply and drew himself up and then allowed himself to collapse. He distended his belly, made his shoulders droop and turned out his feet so they splayed. In that position he walked to the drawing room and stood while he mixed a martini.

When the partners rang, as they did each week, to enquire about his welfare, Peck was disturbingly vague and gave little satisfaction.

"What did he say about the new account?" one of them asked the other.

"He didn't say anything at all at first, and when I told him again he just said, 'That's nice', but very faintly. It must be a bad connection."

"I couldn't get on net with him either. He didn't seem to know who it was. Get the switchgirl to check and see if there's trouble with the line out there."

When they telephoned again Peck didn't answer. He was watching a schoolgirl in the magpie colours of blue tunic and white silk skirt. She was flirting with a lout on a bicycle. He scooped up her case and pretended to ride away with it and they wrestled when he came back. After a while he persuaded her up behind him and pedalled into the sandhills. Peck was remembering with an ear that still gave him trouble from a clout he had got at seventeen from a father after a dance at the school.

Watching the heavens by night and the humans by day was taking a toll of Peck. He was drinking too much, not eating enough and his eyes were inflamed from the telescope. The adulterous wife who had turned the tables on Peck had wounded him more sorely than he knew. Like many men, the licence which seemed natural and noble in himself was an utter confoundment to him in a wife, an earthquake in the order he had taken for granted. His sense of identity needed the sense of self-importance, and ▒▒▒▒▒▒ had graphically demonstrated that for her his existence had been blurred. It made Peck unduly conscious of his evident organic erosion, and the plays he witnessed through the telescope were a forcible instruction on the un-uniqueness of his life. In his fitful sleep he was disturbed by nightmares and after watching the stars, would wake with such aphorisms on his life as: "Nothing matters, except matter. Which does not matter." On another occasion he sat up in bed shouting: "Out, out, brief candle."

There was a bus stop on the road below the house, and he took to pointing the telescope there, morning and afternoon. A group of men of his own age climbed in and alighted at the stop. Day after day they materialized in the dreadful sameness of blue suits and grey hats. Day after day they returned from the city a little more crushed than they had left, to carry the badge of their brief-cases home to wives in time-payment castles.

The telephone rang and Peck continued to ignore it. The house-keeper and her husband came sometimes to the door which he had bolted against intrusion. They would call through the pannelling: "Can we get you something from the shops, Sir?" Peck would say: "No, thank you." There were tins enough in the pantry and drink enough in the bar.

He watched children for a time, finding it pleasant. He wondered why he had not had a family and remembered he had been too busy. Then he considered that they would probably have grown up to ride on a bus or wait at home with hands in the sink having more children to grow up like them. "Repetition, repetition," Peck said. "What in the world is the point of it?"

Peck gave his right eye a bad knock on the telescope and it came up in an ugly blue swelling. Considering it in the mirror he took off his clothes, drooped his shoulders, pushed out his stomach, brushed back his hair off the bald patches, chomped his gums, splayed his feet and toasted himself in the glass with a very strong martini.

The next day an ambulance came sirening to one of the houses. White-coated men hurried inside and came out bearing a stretcher. The siren whirred and the doors closed and the ambulance speeded off. Next afternoon a bow of black crepe went up on the door of the house. Peck wondered if it was for one of the men from the bus stop, but he couldn't be bothered to look. He put the telescope and tripod away and shut the case. Then he drew up a chair, put out bottles, and sat down thinking and drinking.

One of the partners said: "He's there all right. I rang the housekeeper."

"It's time we brought him back," said the second. "He's had a good long holiday."

"Doesn't do to get too much out of touch."

"He's probably been swimming, yachting, getting a suntan. It will be like the old days when he gets back."

"Next thing we know, he'll be married again," a third said and they laughed.

"I wish I were more like him, Peck really gets life by the throat."

"Let's all go out there now, and surprise him."

They got up and went for their hats.

In a sporting goods store, not far from the house, the salesman noted that his grey-bearded customer was drunk. He had caused amusement when he got out of the taxi in a turtle-neck sweater and top hat. He enquired if bagpipes could be bought in the area and seemed disappointed that they could not. Then he chose a repeating rifle in a canvas case which he slung unsteadily on his shoulder.

"Ammunition?" the salesman asked.

"Yes, please."

"How many rounds?"

"Just the one," Peck said.

Tree Without Earth

MARJORIE BARNARD

EVERYONE told Helen that she must make Christmas for the children's sake, or if they did not say it she could feel the pressure of their unspoken thought. They said it tenderly, urgently, secretly or with a false rallying brightness that did not deceive her. No more than Peter's steady quietness beside her did.

To Peter this Christmas was a test, a last call to someone almost out of sight and perhaps already out of hearing.

The children, not unnaturally, expected Christmas to be the same as it had always been, and digging in their short memories, like miniature archaeologists unearthing a long-buried city, they remembered what they had done last year and even the year before. Everything they had ever had they must have. Christmas was Christmas and nothing could change that.

Both Peter and Helen felt now a new deep awareness of their children; in her it was painful, swollen, sensitive; in him a strengthening of his sense of responsibility and of fatherhood. From different shores they saw the two small figures walking, not towards them, but upon a path of their own. Louise was nine, burdened with her grandmother's name and gold bands on her teeth, already precociously awkward and clumsy. Helen was moved and almost frightened to see in her so soon, in the midst of her childishness, flashes of a mature understanding and, as yet barely decipherable, traces of womanliness. Clare was just five and by a miracle had preserved her babyhood. By next Christmas that first blooming would inevitably be over, but it would last for this one. Clare was too happily, squarely, placed in her world, in her warm, milky health and sweet temper, to change ruthlessly in a night from baby to little girl. Everyone marvelled at Clare, but only her mother saw the budding woman in Louise.

Johnnie would have been two and this his first real Christmas. Helen decided suddenly: Yes, they would have Christmas, a real Christmas, a tree, a party, everything. Not a children's party but one for themselves on Christmas night. They hadn't had a tree since Louise was a tiny girl, before Clare was born. Since then Helen had been too busy for the extras. Now she wasn't, she had time on her hands, one moment full, the next empty. This would be the children's first real tree. Louise had been too young for the other one and no one remembered it now. Helen saw it as a tiny illuminated spot very far away, in another world, lost, dwindling to a point of light, quenched.

Helen's decision was made so late that they were all involved in a frenzied rush. But everything could be bought, even at the last minute, if you didn't mind what you paid. Helen didn't, and Peter was in no mood to cavil at bills. If only this sudden spate of energy, this Christmas fever, would break, as a thunderstorm breaks a heat-wave, the cold, dark, invisible night which had lain at the heart of the home now for months, it was all he asked.

The tree could not be decorated until after Clare was in bed on Christmas eve; it was to be a surprise for her. Peter thought it should be a surprise for Louise too. He'd had a vision of himself and Helen decking the tree in the sleeping house, then going upstairs hand in hand, together again. But Helen said no, Louise could help. That would give her more pleasure than a surprise. For some reason that Peter couldn't fathom, Helen seemed to want to make up to Louise for something; what, he couldn't imagine; always to draw her, their beloved little ugly duckling, into the light. It wasn't fair to Louise; let her be a child as long as possible. She felt things far too vividly as it was. He must talk to Helen about it for the child's sake, but not now. That would be too cruel. After Christmas.

So Louise stayed up beyond her bedtime and Peter brought in the tree, the sawn-off top of a shapely pine, from a neighbour's garden where it had been standing in the moist soil, waiting. Only the bread crock would hold it, so the bread was dispossessed, a big red bow tied round the crock's honest neck, a bucket of water set in it and the tree shored up with bricks and stones, and this engineering work finally bedded down in red tissue paper.

The tree stood silent, expectant, dark in the light, bright room. The resinous scent of its sap filled the air with a fragrance that was fresh and new but immemorially old. The waiting tree drew the household like a magnet. The neighbour who had helped to carry it in was unwilling to go though there was plenty for him to do at home; Carole came from the kitchen, loath, for once, to retire into her own life. She stood awkward but eager, hoping she would be asked to help. The neighbour was politely farewelled.

Helen flashed on Carole the smile which won and enslaved people.

"Aren't you meeting Harry tonight?"

"He can wait," said Carole with all the confidence of a girl who knew he would.

"Cruel girl. And on Christmas Eve too."

Carole, transformed into a heartless charmer by these words, waited with diminishing hope for another minute and then clattered off.

"Peter, you'd better get on with the other decorations while Louise and I do the tree, don't you think? We'd be falling over one another if we all tried to do it, wouldn't we? And we'd be so late. . . ." She put it to him charmingly and, of course, it was the sensible way to arrange the work.

Even Louise wasn't allowed to touch the tree. She could hand things, that was all. Helen worked with a withdrawn, concentrated expression, twining the red ribbon among the dark needles, hanging the stars, the bright balls, the miniature gold and silver crackers, setting the red and yellow candles on the ends of the branches, as if she followed a copy drawn deeply in her imagination.

Louise became more and more excited, jigging up and down. "This next, Mummy." "Oh Mummy, not there, *here.*" "This one, this one, *this one.*" But Helen took very little notice. She knew so well how it should go.

"Mummy, where's the fairy?"

"There isn't one, darling."

"But there was, I know there was."

"What fairy?"

"My fairy, the one on the other tree."

"But you don't remember that."

"Yes, I do. I *never* forget *anything.*"

She's too excited, Peter thought, she's worn out and she'll be a rag tomorrow. Helen must have been like that as a child, only pretty of course.

"*Whatever* will we do without a fairy? What happened to it?"

"Clare played with it when she was tiny and broke it."

Louise couldn't remember that. "Couldn't we get another fairy?"

"No, darling, we don't want a fairy."

"Yes, we do."

"We can imagine it."

"Can you?"

"Yes, so can you. Look, I'll put the big silver star on top."

"Oh Mummy, not the *silver* star, the *gold* one."

"I think it ought to be silver."

"No no no." Louise had burst into tears.

Helen dropped everything and ran to her. "Yes, darling, of course, the gold star. And look, the tree's finished and you must go to bed. Mummy will put you to bed."

She took Louise by the hand and led her, now docile with hanging head and gulping on every second step, up the stairs. She looked down at Peter, shaking her head in self-accusation and asking his forgiveness with her eyes.

Very gently she undressed the little girl and smiling tenderly washed the tear stains from her face. "Nothing to cry about, Lulu, we have a lovely, lovely tree, haven't we, darling?"

Everyone knew that Lulu was a frightful, terrible name for a girl to have, but it could be used secretly between them.

"Yes, Mummy."

Thin arms shot round her neck in fierce protective love. Lulu had let herself be undressed like a baby to please her. Helen gathered the child as fiercely into her own arms in the first passionate embrace. They were no longer mother and child but mother and daughter.

The moment was over. Louise relaxed, and with closed eyes nuzzled against her mother. Helen laid her down on the bed and drew the sheet up to her chin. "Happy Christmas, Lulu."

Peter fidgeted downstairs, uneasy, waiting to know where Helen wanted the holly wreath, waiting. Helen came down the stairs. She looked serene. "She's sleeping," she said, and went back to the tree.

It seemed to be finished but she still worked on it, adding a touch here and there, all of them right. The look of concentration was back on her face. When Peter came to admire her work, he felt that she invisibly shouldered him away.

Without a word Helen went upstairs and came back with something bright in her hand. It was a necklace he had given her when Johnnie was born. She twisted it along a branch and let it drip down half seen.

She said in a matter-of-fact tone, "It wanted something just there and that's exactly right. Don't you think so? The tree is ready now."

Didn't she remember? Her voice and manner suggested that she didn't. But she couldn't possibly forget. His mind was confused. Was this tree more than a tree, was the hanging of a necklace an atavistic rite? Something deeper and older than either he or she could understand?

Helen was looking at the tree impartially and critically as if she were assessing her work. "It is nice, don't you think?"

It was lovely, in all its decorations, rich but light and gay. It
was the Burning Bush, it was the Feast of Wan. He couldn't
speak. Had something happened? Had she found a way at last
out of the pain and grieving and silence? Was the hard core
mystically resolved? He dared not look at her.

But Helen didn't seem to want to know what he was thinking.
She was already going upstairs. She paused and smiled at him,
the smile that won people and enslaved them.

"I'm tired now, darling. Would you be an angel, do the lock-
ing up and bring me up just a tiny drink?"

They were as far apart as ever.

The night was a narrow dark canyon between the days. At the
bottom of it there was a thin trickle of sleep. When Peter woke
in the first light Helen was already awake, staring towards the
window, haggard and worn in the thin light. He wondered if she
were going to get through the big day. He felt all their elaborate
preparations, the decorations, the tree, piled suddenly into his
arms like funeral wreaths. The old feeling of despair, of being
able to do nothing for her, nothing, was back in its place. He had
tried too often. When he'd said, oh fatuously, and probably not
for the first time either, "I'm still here, darling, we have one another" she had turned on him in the ferocity of her grief. "Why
couldn't it have been you instead, or me?" She'd hardly known
what she was saying but it had come from somewhere just the same.
Here was Christmas morning, and if he couldn't say "Happy Christmas" what was there to say?

Now had come the most difficult moment of all, the moment
that struck at his heart with an almost unbearable sense of loss.
For now Johnnie, the early riser, the joyful, the uninhibited, would
have come running in to wake them. The moment was not to be
shared, for Helen would not share. She had shut herself from him
in her hoarded grief, but surely not for ever. If it were almost
unbearable for him, might it not be quite unbearable for her?
Would she not shiver like some frail, brittle glass vessel on some
such moment as this? Fear ran like cold water in his veins. How
could he ever explain to Helen the bleak reasoning that saved his
own sanity and supported him while it did not comfort? This was
the knowledge that to lose, to suffer, to die was as much a part of
living, as natural, as birth and happiness. Men and women took
on the human lot and when it could not be changed stood by it for
the dignity and integrity of their souls. Peter had never sought
after reasons or been a philosopher, but now in his need something

like a philosophy had risen out of himself. But he could not impart it. It lay dumbly within him.

Clare ran in dragging her full pillow-case. "Merry Christmas, Mummy. Merry Christmas, Daddy." Louise was behind her with her pillow-case, a little different because she knew the truth about Santa Claus now ("I'll tell her, no one else shall") and was unsure of her new role. But there was no trace left of last night's emotion and strain.

Helen was sitting up, laughing, holding out her arms. "Come in, darlings. Merry Christmas. Merry Christmas. Here you are Clare, get up on the bed and Louise on Daddy's bed. Let's see what you have there."

Treasure after treasure emerged from the pillow-cases. Helen had been lavish. Clare, her cheeks scarlet, ran from one to the other afraid of missing something, too excited to open her own parcels. Louise shone with happiness. When Carole brought in tea they wouldn't let her go. She had to sit down on the floor and share it all.

The father looked at the mother. She's wonderful, he thought, she's marvellous. With so much courage everything is sure to come right—how could I ever have doubted her?

Helen whispered at last, "We can't hurry them but there really is a lot to be done. . . ."

She had orchestrated the day and now she must conduct it. First the flowers; all the neighbours were stripping their gardens for her. She had so many she hardly knew what to do with them, and every spare basin, jug, and saucepan was cunningly converted to a vase. The decorations which had looked artificial last night were filled out and brought to life with flowers. The rooms were a work of art, everyone said so. Helen had the gift.

Only when the flowers were done did they open the door and let Clare in to see the tree. She ran and stopped. It was almost too much and there were too many people watching her, but when they encouraged her she looked at everything and was excited and happy just as they wanted her to be.

"Daddy," she said, pointing at the stars, the candles, the ribbons, "are those Johnnie's presents?"

"No darling," he answered, keeping his voice very even, "they belong to us all."

Clare often talked about Johnnie but Louise never did, never, and she was likely to be angry with Clare and slap her. Nothing like that happened today.

Then there was the arrival of the aunts and uncles and dinner which was a very handsome meal, and after dinner the children had to lie down and rest but could take just one Christmas present each into bed with them. It took so long to choose which that there was hardly any time for lying down. The mother encouraged as many uncles and aunts as possible to lie down too for she had to begin immediately after dinner to prepare the evening's party.

When Helen went up to dress it was late but everything was ready. She heard people arrive but that didn't hurry her. Peter was there to welcome them and give them drinks, and Louise, grave and important, was quite prepared to show any lady who brought a coat this warm night where to put it.

Helen dressed with great care in a long grey silk dress with a wine-coloured sash and shoulder knot. It was a long time since she had dressed like this and she seemed to feel her body unfolding like a tight bud softly opening to warmth, as she tended it. At last she was ready. They would be thinking that she was not going to appear, even Peter would be getting anxious, wondering if he should pop up to see if anything had happened to her. For a long time now he had kept that careful, anxious infuriating vigil.

At first no one saw her on the stairs, then Clare called shrilly "Mummy" and everyone looked. They surged towards her and those who held wineglasses raised them in a toast. She saw a blaze of light and colour, Peter's face, adoring. Other men's eyes. She took the party as a swimmer in the water, it carried her, buoyant. Her nerves as taut as the strings of a harp responded to every breath, but they gave out a sigh of music instead of pain. Her mind, transparent with fatigue and stimulated by it, yielded a new sharp awareness. She knew what everyone thought. Some "How could she?", others "How brave!", "How beautiful!", "It's for the children", "For Peter". A few that they did not like it at all, just a few.

It was the right sort of party, not wild, for this was Christmas night, but effulgent. Only the tree stood aloof, magical. The tree is my partner tonight, thought Helen. The necklace sparkled and was just exactly right in the place where it hung. Talk and laughter filled the room. Peter relaxed. All was well.

"Where's Clare?" someone asked, and they found her asleep in a corner as naturally as a puppy sleeps. A little indulgent laugh ran round the room, but when Peter lifted her up and stood for a moment with her in his arms there was silence, for the memory of the dead child was drawn slowly, like a barb, over every heart.

Helen whispered to Louise, "Go too and help Daddy put Clare to bed. It's getting late." She watched Peter and the children till the bend of the stairs hid them. "He's good to them," she thought, "and better for them than I am, even for Louise."

The incident had changed the quality of the party; it had grown quiet, as if the still warm night had stepped in through the windows to be one of the company. It was too early to go home yet the party was ended. Someone suggested that they sing carols. A strong voice began "Silent Night, Holy Night" and others joined in, steadying themselves on the selfless swell of the air. Beautiful and poignant beyond all reason they finished it because they had begun it. Helen stood like one frozen. In everyone there was now a longing to go home, to be in their own places on Christmas night. A guest with more initiative than the others pleaded an excuse and said goodbye. The others followed quickly. Helen gave each her cold hand in parting, and without waiting, or looking back or smiling, walked up the stairs.

In her room she began automatically to undress. A black wave of grief towered ready to engulf her. Christmas was over, tomorrow would begin again the succession of days that were all alike. Let the wave swallow her, she would still carry something precious with her, something she would never share. From the back of a drawer she brought out a phial of sleeping tablets. Her face as intent as a sleep-walker's, she cascaded them into her hand. She would be asleep before Peter came up. It was all she asked for, a little sleep.

Downstairs among the dying flowers, the wasting candles, and the broken food the immaculate tree kept its vigil.

Only on Saturdays

DON CAMPBELL

JACK laughs at me. "Sure you got enough clothes on?"

"It's cold, isn't it?" I lead my roan horse carefully around the yard. He's always girth-shy on a frosty morning.

"Well, you don't need two sweaters and the coat as well, do you? It's not a very cold morning."

"Well I do need them," I tell Jack. "I can take them off later when it warms up a bit."

"You shouldn't feel the cold at your age. Seventeen. You don't know what cold is."

"I know what a frost is."

He's a tall shadow in the sick light. He laughs at me again. "The horse'll have a job to lug you over the range with all those clothes on. Here, you can have this as well." He hands me a sugar bag full of tucker. "I'll take the billy."

I get on, gingerly. My horse jack-knifes when I hit the saddle and pig-roots around for a bit, slipping on the wet rocks. I get him reined up and wait for Jack to mount the big red stallion. He's a good rider, clips on like a peg on a clothes-line. The stallion snorts. He likes Jack. They've been together eight years. He puts his big head right over the gate, anxious to get outside. Jack opens the gate and we move into a flat disc of country where our horses' hooves break the crackling meringue of frost. My face and fingers burn with cold. The horses snap at each other, walking rapidly toward the ranges lying in their quilts of fog.

This is black basalt country, flat and rocky. Trees are crumpled out of form by too much light, washed white in past floods of wind. Netting fences hold the frost, blaze like Christmas decoration in the local store, looping out of distance into distance. We don't look back at the homestead or the yards as our horses slip on the iced ground, jerk at our red fingers, jangle the bits, leave pennants of white breath, fret at gates.

Jack says, "Fresh, the cows, aren't they?"

The ranges lie east of us. For an hour we ride up to their straight walls of shadow. Then it seems as if they've tumbled over in a broken mass of rocks and twisted gullies. And through their shattered fissures roars the sun, cascading westward, stirring trees and grass, breaking against our horses' knees and drowning us in light.

Jack says, "Sun's up."

We ride for three hours, moving closer to the ranges, rising on their foothills with the insolence of flies. When we're about a thousand feet up we get off, and I light a fire and boil the billy. Our horses stand quietly under a wattle-tree. They stamp at ants or twist their ears around for noises while we drink black tea and eat the mutton sandwiches.

Half an hour later we ride again, angling up the bald range itself, glancing back at the wide lake of country. Yellow earth, green-apple sky, rivers of white fog rising to the strong touch of sun. Houses, flakes of tin. Chimneys scribbling on the day with smoke. We rise on waves of earth, bare earth, unbroken, round, worn by rush of wind and streams of rain. Our horses root under us, hot and strong, lift us over the top and take us down the other side to the timbered country.

"We'll have dinner down on the river," Jack says, pointing where a silver thread of water draws the hills together. "Used to be an old hut down there."

"Old Baily's place?"

"Yeah. He hasn't been there for years."

When we get there and find old Baily's place I can see that the hut's in ruins. There's only one wall and a tin chimney left standing.

"I don't think much of his hut," I say.

"You can boil the billy, this time," Jack says.

"I boiled it last time, Jack."

"It's all experience, isn't it," he laughs. "Garn, you young begger; while I have a look around."

I can't see what's to look around, but Jack saunters down to the river, and I light the fire. Smoke rises in the windless air. I unsaddle the horses after they've had a drink at the river. They feed on white clover growing near the orchard that Baily planted many years ago. The Kentish cherry trees must be sixty years old but they're covered with tight, green buds. Jack comes back, and while we're eating he nods at the tangled orchard.

"Wants pruning," he tells me. "They'd come on all right."

"The pears'd be woody," I tell him.

"Yes, they would." He grinds tobacco in the mill of his big hands. There's a cigarette paper stuck to his bottom lip. "Know what happened to Baily?"

"No, Jack."

"He got killed at the war."

"I thought he was a real old codger."

"It was his father planted this orchard."

"Well, how the hell should I know that? You've always said, old Baily, so I thought he was an old codger."

"It's not a Federal case. I'm just telling you, that's all." Later, he says, "Better saddle the horses, eh?"

When I get back, leading the horses, I can't see Jack anywhere until he calls to me from the wall of the hut.

I go across to him. "What have you found, Jack?"

He's reading a newspaper. An old *Herald,* dated 1942.

"Lookit this old paper. I found it under the floorboards."

The paper is very old, leaves stuck together like a yellow board.

He squints eagerly at the faded type. "Bit of history here, boy. Picture of a Spitfire. Bit about Benghazi. I was at Tobruk. By Christ, eh. I think I'll take it home and read it when I've got more time. 1942. That's how many years ago? 1960. Two from ten leave seven. . . ."

"Eight, Jack."

His forehead corrugates. "Eight, then. Carry the two back down under the six. . . ."

"The one."

"The what?"

"You carried a year too many."

"I shouldn't be bloody surprised. How many years is it anyway? You went to school."

"Eighteen years," I tell him.

He stuffs the paper inside his coat and takes the stallion's reins. We get on and splash across the shallow river. The sun's warm paw comes down between my shoulder blades, from a long way off.

"Wasn't a bad sort of war," Jack mumbles. "If it hadn't been for those Italians running all over the desert looking for a compound we would've got rid of Rommel a lot sooner than we did."

"Who's Rommel, Jack?"

He looks at me as if I'd been sick in his lap, but says nothing.

We head off into the small hills, by clumps of wind-bent timber, under an eagle skating on a green rink of sky, wade through tussock flats flowing in a rush of silent straw. After four o'clock the sun flares nakedly against the winter air. Heat dies out of everything.

West is the colour of a lemon rind, and coldness settles into gullies
where we ride.

It takes us another two hours to reach the road that leads into
town. The horses are very tired now and we just let them walk
along. My legs are stiff. Jack has been riding with one leg over
the pommel for the last half mile. It's the one he got hurt at the
war. He's told me about how the cold gets into it in the winter.
It's dark now, and I've got the sweaters on again but the cold
penetrates right through. We cross railway lines already glistening
with frost, and Jack takes his leg off the pommel in case the
stallion shies at something in the town. I can smell smoke and
dinners cooking. The hills are blinking quietly with lights.

Jack laughs. "I'll bet I know where you'll be heading after tea."

"Bet I know where you'll be heading; to the pub."

"She's probably out of town," he teases me.

"Ar, shut up, Jack."

"Well, don't get up to mischief," he cautions me. "She's a nice
girl."

"Hell, what do you think I am?"

I hate Jack when he starts to talk about girls.

"I'm your father, aren't I? If I don't tell you who will?"

"But I won't do that, Jack. You said yourself, she's a nice girl."

"I know. But nice girls can feel just the same as bad girls. So
just be careful, that's all."

"Well, don't you get full, either. Not like the last time."

Our horses know they're heading for a feed, so they canter down
the main street and turn into a lane behind the pub. We take
their saddles off and lead them to the water trough and then into
the dark stables. The roan rubs his nose on my back as I empty
chaff into his manger. I can hear him snuffling for the grain before
his grinders go into action. I know he's happy, now.

Jack repeats his warning about controlling myself and the terrible
mess I'd be in if I did the wrong thing. He tells me what a powerful thing sex is and how nothing can resist it, all over again, just as
he's told me a hundred times before.

It makes me think about June. She's sixteen. Last time I saw
her was at the pictures at Delegate the night Jack lost money in a
pool game. She's got grey eyes and a big chest, but her stomach's
flat. A lot of sheilas with big chests are big all over. I suppose
I'm in love with her, as the saying goes. Her hair is very black.
I think about her a lot when we're back on the station taking
orders from old Thompson, the old cow. Jack reckons he wouldn't
know the difference between running a property and running a
brothel.

She's always lived in the town. She'll be at the flicks tonight.
I went to one of those learn-to-swim things in the river last year,
and that's when I met her. I suppose it's being in love when
you think about a girl all the time. . . .

"For Pete's sake," Jack laughs. "What are you doing there with
your hand in the manger? The horse'll chew it off. Let's go and
have some tea."

His shadow is twice as long as mine when we walk across the
gravel yard and go into the pub.

"Are you feeling tired?" I rib him. "Is that why I've got to
carry your hand on my shoulder?"

"I like you, Danny," he says quite softly, "We're mates, eh?"

"Just so long as you don't get full."

"Listen," he says confidently, "I know when to stop. It's you
and that girl. . . ." Then he whispers "Hey! We can't talk about
it here."

"I'm not talking about it," I say. . . .

But we're in the bar now, full of light and voices and the jungle
tang of men. Jack's bigger than most of these blokes. He's
flogged the ears off some of them, and a few of them have belted
him, but only when he was too full to care what happened.

I stand under his elbow at the bar and have a shandy while he
squares up to a schooner. I know he'll get full, of course. I just
hope the sergeant isn't in a bad mood tonight because Jack'll be
ripe pickings by the time that old buzzard comes around from the
police station to close the pub.

"I found this old paper today," Jack tells a few coves he's joined
up with. He lays it on the bar and strokes it open with his large
knuckles. The strong light shines in the black hair on his arms.
"It's all about the war," he says loudly. "Sally, there, you wouldn't
remember the war, would you?"

The barmaid's about fifty, a redhead with a fireball temper. She
pelts her green eyes at Jack and wipes the bar a bit harder close to
his beer.

"It's a bit of history, this," he says holding the paper down
stiffly. "This is the stuff they should teach the kids at school. Well,
my kid's been to school and he didn't even know who Rommel
was."

"I'll bet he never caught sight of you."

It's the barmaid, smiling. Her thin mouth is twisted like a piece
of pink string.

Jack says, "Which shows you was never in the western desert,"
Jack retorts. "If you had been we'd have all died of thirst."

The men laugh at this in a great gust of elbows and tobacco-stained dentures. I get shoved back from the bar like a pip being pressed out of a sticky orange.

"As for Rommel," Jack says seriously, "he was the cleverest bit of Hun they ever grew in Germany. And it was mainly the Australians who belted him out of Africa. What happened to him after they got him back to Germany? Any of you blokes know?"

"Hitler got . . ."

"Shut up," Jack tells me. "I told you on the way into town. Now I'm trying to find out if these other blokes know. And they should know. It's part of our history. Have a think about it." He drags down half a schooner of beer and winks at the barmaid. He's still got one hand on the yellowed paper.

"Let's go out and have tea while they're thinking about it." I tug at his trouser pocket, hopefully.

"You have some tea, Danny. "I'll stay here for a bit. These blokes . . ."

"You're gonna get full," I hiss, but he doesn't hear me. He's got the first signs already. "You shouldn't drink on an empty stomach, Dad."

"Go and have your tea, Dan," the barmaid says. She's standing right in front of me. "It'll be off in another quarter of an hour. And then go off to the pictures. He'll be here all night. I know him."

"I can't," I tell her. "He's got the money."

She blazes up at Jack like a lit patch of ferns. "Your boy's waiting to have his tea," she crackles. "The poor little devil's starving."

"All right. All right," Jack says, reaching into his hip pocket. "You needn't worry I'll . . . here . . . I'll . . ."

He puts his money on the counter, and she fingers the notes fast. She whips a fiver into the top of my sweater and tells me to scat. Jack gasps, but I'm at the door before he can turn round.

"A fiver," Jack says. "God struth!"

The men laugh loudly at this, and the barmaid waves gaily at me before I disappear.

I have tea at the café. It takes me half an hour to get outside the mixed grill and the ice-cream and coffee. Then I realize that Jack and I haven't even booked a room at the pub, so I do that first. Up in the pub room I have a good wash and do my hair. I've got a whole pocketful of notes, silver as well, and I don't feel a bit tired. It makes me think about June again, and about Jack and his warnings.

When I go downstairs and look at him through the doors of the bar he's worse than I expected. He's standing up to another bloke, jabbing him in the stomach with the rolled-up paper, which is wet with beer and a bit torn.

"Rommel was a good soldier, and you know it, buster." Jack's got him moving backwards with the paper. "Who the hell are you, anyway? You never got overseas, did y'? A bloody M.P. I suppose, that's what you were. I can smell you bastards a mile off."

The other bloke's face is red. He's pretty heavy; solid, like a sawn-off stump. He looks like a bit of a bruiser to me, and Jack's in no condition to fight. I jump straight in, wriggle through the excited crowd of men and arrive just in time to have Jack fall back on top of me. The other bloke's hit him fair between the eyes, a real king hit, so we both go down together. The crowd give a hell of a shout and then go very quiet. When I squirm out from under Jack's big carcass I'm looking right at a pair of black boots. It's old sourpuss, the sergeant. I'm only seventeen. Not old enough to be in the bar at all, and I know he's butchers on that, so I dive straight through his legs and race outside. I shoot, *splat,* into a crowd of sheilas on their way down to the picture show. June's there, too, but she keeps a poker face. The sheilas twitter a bit before they walk on down the street.

I wait around until the sergeant brings Jack out and leads him off to the station. I can hear Jack telling him that he wants a receipt for the paper because it's a bit of history.

I saunter down to the pictures looking at the shop windows. There's a sparkle of glass jewellery in the Greek's place, some beaut ear-rings there I'd like to buy for June. I wait there for a bit gaping through the window. Old Peter, the Greek, is glaring at me from the back of his shop like a suspicious pig, probably waiting to catch the brick I chuck through the glass. It's after hours, but he's still moving slowly around the shop sniffing at the shelves. I keep looking at the ear-rings. The cunning old cow always turns the tags over so you can't read the prices.

At the pictures I meet up with a red-headed kid I know, and while we're buying tickets I show him the ear-rings, real sparklers in a plush case.

"I had to knock old Peter up to get them," I say. "They cost a packet, too."

"What do you reckon she'll do for those?" he asks me. "Come on. They're standing up."

We crowd into the building just as the Queen's picture disappears and edge our way up to the front. We get in behind June and the other sheilas, and the bluey kid and I start teasing them.

They keep twisting round to tell us to shut up, so I hand the ear-
rings across to June. She hands them straight back. "No thanks,"
she says.

At half time I stay right with June all the way up to the café.
It's cold, and I offer her one of my sweaters, but all she says is,
"No thanks".

On the way back I draft her off the other girls and ask her
what's up. We're standing beside the second-hand car paddock,
and there's a doleful old truck with yellow headlights staring at us.

"Nothing's up, Dan. Why should there be?"

"We used to be friends," I say.

"Well, we're still friends," she says.

"Don't you want the present? I can't get anything back on it
from old Peter, and I'd rather chuck it away than give it to
someone else, so help me I would."

"What are you talking about?"

"The present I gave you in the pictures."

"Was that a present? I thought they were chocolates, and we
had some of those." She giggles at some other sheilas going past.

"Cripes, no. Here." I hand her the ear-rings.

She looks in the box and then snaps it shut. Her face is red,
and I know it's not just the cold air.

"June, I'd like you to have them."

"Why?" She's looking at her toes.

I can smell her hair and a trace of perfume, and I loose all the
words I ever knew. She hands me back the ear-rings and shakes
her head. Then she squeezes my hand and darts off to the pictures.

When the show's over I trail her up the street again, wishing that
she'd get rid of the other tarts, but they stick to her like glue. In
the café they giggle up together over their drinks, doing their all-
damn-best to uncreate me; but they needn't worry, I'm at the end
table, and they know it. That's when I get the brainwave. I know
where she lives, so I'll go there, because she's got to get home sometime tonight. But right then all the other girls leave her. They
giggle in my direction and fly off like parrots. I take three seconds
to join her.

"Can I take you home, June?"

"All right." She gets up quickly and heads for the door.

We walk up the main street and turn down a side lane. I'm
not hurrying, hoping that our hands will touch if I leave mine
hanging close to hers. When they do touch I remember what
Jack said about the terrible power of girls. He's dead right too.

But I love June. I wouldn't think of her that way.

Pretty soon we're closer together. She doesn't mind when I

put my arm around her waist. I lean down and kiss her hair, very cold in the black night. The quiet stars are bristling with frost, frozen grass stems break under our feet.

I look at her. She's the most beautiful girl I ever saw. Her eyes are like a wallaby's I caught in a trap when I was a kid. She's got the smoothest skin I ever saw. I could look down her front if I wanted to because I'm a lot taller than she is, but I don't, because I don't think of her that way.

"Danny, why do you want to give me a present?"

"I don't know. I just want to."

"I can't take them. They cost too much."

"Money's nothing."

"It's not my birthday. That's the sort of present you give to a girl when she's twenty-one. I won't be twenty-one for four years yet."

"A lot can happen in four years," I tell her. "It took us that long to belt Rommel out of Egypt."

"Who?"

"Some German character. It doesn't matter. It's history now."

"What's it got to do with the ear-rings?"

"Nothing."

"Well?"

"I'm crazy about you." I say it quickly before my throat closes right up. My heart's doing a hand canter.

"Don't be silly."

We stop in front of her gate.

"I never gave anything to a girl before. I haven't given a present to anyone since Mum died. I used to get her things at Christmas time."

"You must miss her."

"Hell yes, I do."

"I'd die if anything happened to my Mum."

"My old man's never been the same since."

"Is he . . .?"

"In the clink? Yes. I shouldn't be with a nice girl like you, the way my old man gets drunk every time he comes to town."

"It doesn't matter. You don't drink, do you?"

"No."

"Well?"

"I'm serious about you, June. I'm not just being a kid." My throat is closing up again.

"Who looks after you on the station now your Mum's dead?"

"Father Christmas, silly."

She runs her eyes over my trousers and shirt. I feel grubby.

There's hairs off the roan on my trousers too, but she couldn't see
them because it's dark.

She says, "Dan, I'll take the ear-rings. I think they're beautiful,
I really do."

I give her the ear-rings, and she kisses me. So I forget everything Jack told me about girls and I kiss her again and again. She
just stands there with her face turned up, not doing or saying anything. I'm kissing her so much she's got a job to stand up. Then
I stand there, stroking her hair, and she's holding my other hand.
Just when I want to kiss her again her mother shines a torch on us
from the bedroom window.

"June," she screams. "You come inside at once. Who's that
with you?"

The torch goes out and I can hear her mumbling inside.

"There's never a minute's peace. Where's my slippers?"

Her voice is about as gentle as a council truck dumping a load
of gravel, so I scat off when June tells me to go.

Jack comes into the hotel room next morning. He's very cranky
and sick, so I don't say anything. He takes his teeth out and lays
down on the bed. After a while he says, "How'd you get on last
night?"

"Not bad," I say. "How did you go?"

"Bloody awful. I got the cold cell again, right round the south
side. It's not a bloody jail's bootlace."

"No, Jack. What happened to the paper?"

"I had to use it," he says. "That old cow wouldn't provide
any, not that old cow.

"Well, I'm no blasted example for you." He shouts suddenly.
He jumps up holding his shaggy head. "I promised your mother
I'd be a good example. I'm just a bloody old drunk."

I want to tell him things. I work beside him all the week—
fencing, mustering, anything old Thompson cooks up for us to do.
I know how he can ride and swing an axe and sink a post-hole in
hard dirt.

When he's asleep his feet stick right out of the bed, he's so damn
long. He's never backed down from anyone.

I want to tell him things.

The snow and wind and sun that's beaten at his tough skin all
the years. His old army hat he looks at sometimes.

Waking me up early. All the cups of tea, and the porridge he's
made since Mum died. He shot my dog when it got crippled by
the mail truck, and I remember bawling into his chest about that.
But he never mentioned it again, about me being such a sis.

I want to tell him what a great example he is six days out of the seven, but I can't.

All I can say is, "Only on Saturdays, Dad."

The Metamorphoses of The Misses McNair

C. B. CHRISTESEN

THEY came aboard early, many hours ahead of the scheduled time of departure. Well before breakfast they could be heard pounding the promenade decks, their voices exclaiming excitedly like schoolgirls. Naturally we were curious about the new arrivals, but when we finally met them we (temporarily) lost interest. This story would not be worth the telling were it not for a rather curious incident which occurred as we were approaching Cebu in the Philippines.

Passengers who elect to sail on freighters are usually experienced travellers. I know of no statistics on the subject, but it would be fair to say they are for the most part middle-aged, comfortably placed, with a strong dislike of the inanities of crowded tourist liners. Above all, freighter passengers value privacy. They are not in a mad rush to go places—which is just as well, for the movements of freighters are entirely governed by cargo. The erratic departure and arrival times do not suit the majority of present-day travellers.

The S.S. *East Asian* (14,000 tons) was built in 1944 and registered in London. It usually plied between Australian ports and Hong Kong. We sailed from Melbourne a fortnight late and by the time we had reached Brisbane by way of Hobart and Sydney the capacious holds contained a truly enormous cargo of apples, jam, timber, meat, wool, flour, chemicals, machinery—even aspirin, malted milk, soap, paints, and electrical components. At Brisbane, stalls were erected on the forward deck to accommodate three racehorses and a black Angus bull.

These unfortunate animals were a constant source of interest to the passengers, particularly to the Misses McNair. They would stand for hours before the stalls, patting the beasts and uttering unbelievably moronic baby-talk. The yearlings took these indignities well enough, but the bull seemed sullen, resentful. He would lower his huge head and gaze fixedly at the two sisters with blood-

shot eyes. The bull's incivility spurred the ladies to ever greater
efforts. They would steal titbits from the galley, badger the Cantonese deck-hands to provide extra water and feed, even to draw
a canvas canopy over the stalls to reduce the glare of the afternoon
sun—a thoughtful gesture. But the bull rejected all offerings, all
advances. Oddly, he seemed to grow larger, more menacing, as
the days passed.

We were an ill-assorted group: a retired police inspector from
Mornington; a chartered accountant (and choirmaster) from Geelong; a newly-married Adelaide couple who had joined the ship at
Brisbane—the husband was an astro-physicist who had something
to do with the Woomera rocket range; a former bank manager and
his wife from Rockhampton—they seemed to be inveterate freighter-
travellers; a rangy American with a pronounced curvature of the
spine who had been working on research in Canberra for a Ph.D.
thesis on the poetry of William Woolls (1814-93); the ship's doctor,
who mostly kept to his cabin; a Sydney businessman who was "in
wheat"; myself, bound for Tokyo to sell a large consignment of
opals; and the McNair sisters.

Until we reached Brisbane shipboard life had been leisurely,
pleasant, uneventful, the passengers politely nibbling at the outer
crust of each other's lives. Now all was changed. Those who had
booked for the round trip became noticeably apprehensive; those
intending to disembark at Manila (the American) or Hong Kong
(the wheat-broker, who I suspected was bound for Peking), developed irritatingly smug expressions; and I too was grateful for the
prescience which was taking me on to Japan.

Physically, both sisters resembled caricatures of cows found in
children's "funny picture" books. Each was large, heavy breasted,
and their kindly faces were distinctly bovine. But their most not-
able feature was their buttocks. Viewed from the rear—and both
ladies were much given to *joggling* along the decks—the resemblance was quite extraordinary. The hams were placed quite high
and tended to be pointed by a slight downward curve at the small
of the back.

Both had jolly natures; obviously they had decided at an early
age to get the most out of life. Having been born and bred in
Gympie—which, after gold had petered out, became a rich dairy-
ing district—they could scarcely be blamed for the timbre of their
voices; but it did seem strange, for such beefy women, to have such
high-pitched shrilly discordant voices.

Trixie was the elder by a few years. (We had not reached the
Breaksea Spit before we were given a pretty exhaustive run-down
on their respective biographies.) It seemed she had taught in

various state schools for most of her adult life. Two years ago she had had a serious operation for a tumour of the neck. She was a vigorous advocate for church unity, though a "bit of a heathen" herself; kept a pet budgerigar; collected Norman Lindsay etchings; had once taken a minor part in a play in aid of spastic children; was a member of the Country Women's Association and a bush-walking club; liked an occasional gin sling; knew someone who had known Bert Hinkler ("a good Bundaberg boy"); had served in a Red Cross auxiliary during the War; was an avid television viewer; had published verse in the *Women's Weekly* and the *Gympie Times;* worried about Malaysia, Vietnam, and the pending change-over to decimal currency; was quite positive there was no oil at Roma; still liked jazz but drew the line at the stomp; thought Sir Robert Menzies was a dear; considered *The Group* and the Beatles a bit vulgar; disliked Pommies, Yanks, New Australians, and Santamaria; and every Christmas, "regular as clockwork", visited a guesthouse near Surfers Paradise. We gathered she was not particularly expert at surfing, playing the violin, bridge, and making her own dresses. However, she had always felt she got along well with most men. Some people had claimed she was too dogmatic in her opinions on vexed problems, but what was the use of having views if you didn't express them? As we were watching the lights of Cairns she declared she didn't think much of Patrick White.

At this point her sister Molly became agitated and surprised us by disagreeing with Trix. Some of White's short stories, she ventured to believe, were as good as anything she had ever read. Even Trix was nonplussed for a moment, but she quickly rallied and closed a potentially interesting literary discussion by saying, "P'raps."

Of the two, the consensus of opinion favoured Molly. For one thing, while her older sister was prone to utter a hideous hen-like cackle—'Ohoo-ukukukuk'—Molly invariably smothered her laughter in her handkerchief. And the way she bobbed her head to one side when spoken to, often clasping both hands over her smiling face, had a certain endearing quality. In most other respects, however, she was a kind of echo, or blurred carbon copy, of Trixie. When discreetly taxed on this subject while sun-basking by herself on the top deck, she was inclined to attribute her lack of confidence to lack of education. Trix had always been the clever one, she explained (though not without suffering obvious feelings of disloyalty). While Trix had been sent to Brisbane to improve herself, Molly had remained at Gympie to help her parents. However, occasional visits to Bundaberg to care for an ailing aunt had, she felt, benefited her enormously. It wasn't that she *wanted* to echo Trix; it was simply that whatever Trix said was exactly right, and that by repeating the end-words of her sister's remarks she (Molly) was (in effect) saying, "That's what I believe too." She often wished she could get in first to express her opinions, but she realized she wasn't as quick-witted as Trix.

Anyway, did it really matter? The main thing was, she carefully explained, that they were now able to be together. Upon the recent death of their parents they had inherited quite a tidy income. Trixie had decided to resign from the Education Department and to see something of the world. The trip to Hong Kong and back was to be the first of a whole series of exciting adventures. It was everybody's duty to visit other countries to see how other people lived. Didn't we agree? Surely it was obvious that world peace couldn't be achieved unless there was world understanding? The more we got together the more chance there was of the milk of human kindness to flow.

In the face of her compelling arguments some of us felt rather ashamed of our lack of brotherly love.

Molly's unexpected intervention while Trix was deciding the literary fate of Patrick White marked the first change we noticed in her behaviour. The sun-basking episode marked another. She had never before, we suspected, expressed her own opinions at such length or with such confidence. She began, too, to wear gayer frocks, and even shyly hinted she possessed a bikini.

Trixie at first seemed perplexed. It was as though she paused in mid-sentence, considered the portents, hovered momentarily, then swooped. Bathing togs, she let it be known, were to be used for purposes of bathing. Therefore—"Here we go, girls!"—she would "break the ice". She counselled the others to follow her excellent example.

The resulting splash caused much hilarity among the less sensitive passengers, and some degree of panic among the animals in their stalls further along the lower deck. The bull let out a dreadful bellow, which the wheat-broker rudely imitated. Certainly we all, including several of the ship's officers, manned the after-deck to watch the singular spectacle.

It was a smallish canvas pool, about six feet deep, filled to the brim, and it was said that the overflow which crashed to the iron decking like a tidal wave could be heard away up in the chartroom. When Molly joined her sister (again surprising us with her daring), there was really no space left in the pool for others. But Trix's shouted invitation—"Ohoo, ukukuk (gasp), come on in, the water's fine"—clearly indicated that this obvious point had entirely failed to register with her.

But the "ice" had in fact been broken. By the time we had reached Princess Charlotte Bay we were in the tropics; and the reactions of the McNair sisters also became increasingly tropical. All along the route they had joggled round and round the decks, heaved up companion ways, lurched theatrically at the merest suggestion of an ocean swell, until our nerves were mutilated, ravished, shot to blazes. Winifred Healing, the wife of the chartered accountant, kept uttering "Oh, my God!" until she developed a nervous hiccup. Wallace, the ex-police inspector, was heard to regret most bitterly his lapsed powers of arrest. The youngish couple from Adelaide courteously pretended nothing untoward was happening, though a certain tension in their attitude was noticeable, as though they were inclined to cast blame on us all. The tic in the Captain's left eye (I noticed but did not dare mention) increased in tempo—two rapid beats in keeping with some of the off-shore lights. It pained us that the Chief Officer seldom dined with us now. For no apparent reason the Yank would suddenly begin recounting stories he had heard of how water-buffalo were shot along the Zambezi. Only the wheat-broker, a conceptual lecher, seemed to appreciate the spectacle of pounding buttocks.

Now the activity of the sisters visibly quickened. They battened on to any officer who incautiously ventured abroad, asking a torrent of questions, admiring his white shorts, chaffing him about his hairy chest. Every answer given them was regarded as a possible leg-pull—"Oh you men!"—yet the questions continued. Who named Cape Tribulation? (Wallace's murmur was inaudible.) How and why did the *Endeavour* come to grief if James Cook was such an expert navigator? If we were so near, why couldn't the Barrier Reef be seen from the ship? Who was Princess Charlotte, anyway? Was it really and truly necessary to engage the services of a special pilot to guide us through these calm waters? Portland Roads—why "roads"? Who named Cape Desperation and Weary Bay? (This time I thought Wallace's side-comment was in distinctly poor taste.)

They were first down at mealtimes and the last to leave the table. The Purser was kept busy opening and shutting the library. A mutinous outbreak was feared among the Chinese stewards. The sisters physically forced us to play deck games by day and card games by night. They took to humming snatches of sea shanties —even bits of "The Volga Boatman". The monotonous drone of "yo heave ho" echoed from monkey-deck to engine-room. Molly began to smoke cigarettes, and then came the night when they both drank too many pink gins.

That was the night of the full moon. It rose in all its pristine glory into a peacock-blue sky, a huge orange-coloured Chinese lantern, and down the spangled pathway of light danced sea-nymphs and mermaids, white whales, mermen on prancing sea-horses brandishing tridents and blowing conch shells, and all manner of fabulous creatures of the deep surged and surfaced amid the molten silver-flecked arrowing lines of foaming waves—line upon line jostling and plunging as they kept abreast of the gliding ship —and opalescent sprays of flying-fish festooned the glistening bows, and the balmy air was spiced with cinnamon and nutmeg and the intoxicating fragrance of exotic flowers, and the songs of sirens could be heard, distantly, bewitchingly, calling calling calling. . . .

At about 4 a.m. the sky opened and lightning struck. We had been vaguely troubled by the presence in southern waters of "Henri-etta" and "Mamie"—two cyclones which were reported off the Queensland coast in the regions of Mackay and Brisbane. Radio reports were reassuring, so that it came as a shock when "Anastasia" struck somewhere in the Gulf of Carpentaria. The outskirts of this mighty disturbance hit us as we were passing through the Moluccas. The impact of gale-force winds was such that at first we thought the ship had struck a rock. Within minutes the oily sea was lashed to a frenzy. All was pandemonium. The crack of forked lightning, the thunderous roar of wind and wave mingled with the shrill screams of the maddened horses as their stalls were swept over-board into the raging seas. It was a night of awful *mystery* and terror and chaos.

We limped through mountainous seas toward Cebu with a dam-aged propeller. When a roll-call was made we found that the McNair sisters were missing. A Cantonese seaman had broken a leg and Lai Kwong the cook had lost his teeth. Most of the crockery, a starboard lamp and the wheat-broker's watch were shattered. All deck-cargo had been lost, except for the black Angus bull. And strange to relate, lying beside the bull were two cows quietly munching. The Captain was the least perturbable of men, but I noticed he kept tugging thoughtfully at the loose skin of his double chin as we slowly entered the harbour. We all went about our business that memorable day gravely disturbed in mind and spirit.

But perhaps the oddest aspect of this perplexing incident was that the cows were later found to be in calf.

The Discovery

MANNING CLARK

EVERY time Sebastian Sedgwick and his elder brother behaved outrageously their mother would cry in despair: "I don't know what
I'm going to do with you boys. Sometimes I wish I could send
you to a good boarding school. At least it would make men of
you." So it stood in their lives as a threat, a fate to be dreaded
as well as something outside the field of the possible, for as a
family they belonged to the genteel poor, till one day in November
of 1928 Sebastian won a scholarship to Batman Grammar School.
Then a bachelor uncle in New Zealand, who still retained some of
the wealth which all other members of the family had squandered
so wantonly, or lost so mysteriously in the bank crash of the 1890s,
came to the rescue with a promise to pay for the elder brother so
long as Sebastian held his scholarship. And Mrs Sedgwick began
to tell all who were prepared to listen that her Sebastian had won
a scholarship. That was the first discovery, this metamorphosis of
the prison-house, where they were to be flogged into being men,
into a place of honour, a place which all coveted but few could
achieve.

So one day in February of 1929 with the bags strapped on to the
running-board (they used rope because leather was far too expensive
for a family of their limited means) of a Morris roadster, with Mr
and Mrs Sedgwick in the front seat, and Sebastian and his brother
in the dicky seat, they set out from Belbird for the long drive to
Melbourne where with tears in her eyes, and a rather smothering,
mothering embrace, and that puzzling use of her two themes, ". . .
it will make a man of you dear, it will make a man of you . . .",
and, ". . . if you only knew how proud we all are of you", she and
her husband, who contented himself with an enigmatic "Good luck
to you . . .", adding a "you'll need it", were off, and Sedgwick and
his brother walked away from the car, away from the world they
had known, away from the friends of their childhood, away from

those with whom they had fished and trapped rabbits, and been
both betrayers and betrayed, walked away from all that into a new
world. Feeling like men about to explore a new world, and like
them, tempted to rush back to the familiar, to what they knew,
they looked back towards the car, but that symbol of their early
world they knew had disappeared. Before them were huge iron
gates through which they had walked and then down some steps
and over a brick quadrangle, and through a door, and into a great
darkness.

Everything that happened over the next few weeks was, for
Sebastian, like those pictures in the mind during a high fever, like
those grotesque distortions of life pictures, as it were, which never
seemed to fall into focus. And in the rare moments when the fever
left him, he did not feel that he could talk about what was happening to him to anyone else, because it was too shameful and humiliat-
ing to let anyone know that any other person would do such things
to him. There was that moment, for example, when he saw a wave
of pleasure sweep over the face of the assistant chaplain when he
showed the boy with whom he was to play tennis that they would
be using new balls—off-white, fluffy, bouncy balls and not those
smooth-surfaced, drunken-flighted ones which he could afford.
What was the meaning of that? Why was that the one thing
which could make the assistant chaplain become warm and friendly?
Yet if he, Sebastian, so much as smiled at the assistant chaplain,
he was greeted with a look of lofty disdain.

Within a few weeks, too, it seemed to Sebastian that the school
was not at all concerned with what it claimed to be concerned.
Every Sunday in chapel they all went down on their knees and
asked that the paths of true learning might ever flourish and
abound. Yet for the other six days of the week they seemed to be
concerned with something quite different. Masters seemed to
become much more angry if a boy spoke to them with hands in
pocket than if he misconstrued a passage of Latin prose: one
master, for example, had raged horribly in the first week when a
boy from the country wore a blue shirt with a white collar. Why
was that? And yet every time he tried to puzzle this out, the answer
eluded him.

He was just as puzzled by the behaviour of the boys to each other,
puzzled, that is, by what the few at the top were inflicting on all
the rest. For here again, as far as he could see, they were not
concerned with achievement, with subduing the passions, neither
with truth nor with beauty (he did not, of course, use such words
at that time) nor with the quest of the greatest and the best in their
civilization and their religion. What was very puzzling, neither that

aspiration to be like that precious One, nor that hope that one day, in some future time and place, there would be a happy issue out of all afflictions for the faithful servants of Christ, seemed to touch them at all. (I may say that for Sebastian, young as he was, it was just this promise which imposed order on the chaos.) What they seemed driven to achieve, what was for them the greatest good, was not that Christ figure, not that Greek ideal of "Know thyself", but a much more limited objective, something much less exciting, though, in its own way, quite terrifying, for they seemed to be driven on by some desperate passion to see that all boys had the same haircuts, thought the same thoughts, and were "true to our dark blue". Within the first few weeks disturbing stories were passed on from boy to boy about what happened to those who did not conform. It took Sebastian a fortnight to find out that if you used a brush-back, wore the hair long, or horror of horrors, had a *nana* haircut, *they,* the ones in charge of behaviour, sent for you in the middle of the night, and belted you with towels till you promised not to offend again.

But that was all the progress he made in those few weeks, because, try as he would, he could make no progress in discovering how he should think. The only times he had let slip what was in his mind in front of one of *them* had left a wound in his memory. He was in one of his cheeky, indeed one of his impish moods, and was staring fondly at the plate of peaches and cream which one of *them* had bought as an extra, an antidote to the never-ending potatoes, stew and sago pudding, hoping for a slice, for he had seen other boys in his group win a slice, and a peach, and some cream, and some of the juice by just being nice—so when one of *them* asked him sharply: "What are you staring at, *ickle man?*" he replied with a toss of the head: "I was wondering whether you would find that anticipation was a greater joy than realization." But *he,* the one of *them,* was not amused, nor, for that matter, was the rest of the table. *He* snapped, "Our ickle man's quite a show-off." The curious thing was that Sebastian only said it to give pleasure to others, and a mouthful for himself. I may say that over the next few weeks he made many attempts to win the regard of the same boy, but every move always ended in the hot flush of humiliation and defeat.

So by the time Easter came (it was very late that year) he was beginning to wear a puzzled, anxious look on his face, and when May came soon after, with the leaves from the plane trees rotting in the dungy, springy earth on the Domain, he began to wear a mask, to try to make sure the face, not even by the movement of a single muscle, betrayed to the outside world what was going on

within. He began to withdraw more and more, to find in solitude
the one priceless treasure of never being tormented by anyone except
his own thoughts, which, by the simplest act of the will, he could
preserve uninterrupted pictures of delight. It was not that the
outside world had ceased to beckon to him, or to offer him moments
of pleasure. Sometimes when the choir sang a verse from the
Psalms, such as "Lord, I am not high-minded, I have no proud
looks", the tears would come to his eyes, and his throat would be so
constricted that for a moment it was as though he could not talk.
And it was the same at nightfall when darkness descended over all
the land, and just before the stars came out, a luminous light
suffused the edges of the sky, and the wind stopped nudging the
trees, and silence descended, a great hush, during which the fever
and the fret of the world seemed also to be still. For a moment
neither man nor beast was tormenting each other, and he used to
think then of that other darkness inside him, that sensing of a great
mystery at the heart of things. I don't mean to imply that during
such moments any answer to the questions that were bothering him
was revealed to him, but only that here, in the great hush, there
was a promise that one day he might find an answer or at least a
promise that one day he might be able to live with it, and find the
strength to put up with what went on in the world, as though
all the humiliations, cruelties, torments were insignificant and trivial
beside such a mystery.

The odd thing was he could not speak to anyone about the things
that really mattered. So there had to be two lives—this secret life,
in which he was like one of the ancient mariners, setting out on a
voyage of discovery of the human heart, having taken a vow not
to tell anyone what he found, and that other life, that life of living
with the other boys where the cunning of evasion of trouble was
always warring with some darker passion, another voice inside him
which drove him recklessly on to contests with those who wanted
all boys to think little and alike.

But May, he used to say years later, he had stumbled on the
secret that he who wishes to enjoy the world must travel alone. I
am not sure that he had really reached such a gloomy conclusion
about human affairs within three months of going to Batman
Grammar. I know that he walked to the boat races alone that year.
It may be that was one of those ironies of chance—I mean that he
had fallen out temporarily with the other boys in his year, who, by
the way, were surprised to find that he was one of the very few
who ever comforted them when they were in trouble, not knowing
that he already believed there could be no sorrow like unto his
sorrow, as though loving kindness was all that human beings had

to put between themselves and those blows they were quite impotent
to stop raining on them from our coming hither until our going
hence.

Whatever the reason, he walked alone that year to the boat-races,
walked alone along those asphalt paths on the edge of the Domain,
at times shamed into some sense of inferiority by his failure to be
with the others, and at other time buoyed up by some feeling of
superiority, of being marked out, singled out from the others for
some purpose, some calling which, at that time, he could but
dimly perceive. When he arrived at the river bank he was glad he
had come alone, because anyone else would only have got in the
way of what he was about to explore. A great tide of people was
moving towards the finishing post for the races. There, small
knots of boys wearing the same coloured caps formed themselves
into a ring, and began to chant, as they jumped up and down.
When he arrived, one group began to shout:

> *"Who are we?*
> *Can't you guess?*
> *We're the boys of the G.G.S.!"*

Another group immediately began to form, and bob up and
down, shouting:

> *"Get your boat and lift her,*
> *Take your oars and shift her."*

and throw their caps in the air in a last moment of frenzy when
they shouted: "Wesley, Wesley, Ra Ra Ra." Then the boys from
his own school formed their ring and began to sing:

> *"Row the race, boys, swing together,*
> *Sinews tough as cords of leather,*
> *Strong yet light upon the feather,*
> *Lift her, make her go!*
> *Churn the tide in eddies spinning*
> *Now a spurt you gain you're winning,*
> *Grammar to the fore!"*

And he would have joined in with them, one part of him urged:
"Have a go—surrender . . . lose yourself with your own", but
another side of him said that to do so would mean identifying oneself with one side, becoming part of the show, and so ceasing to
be a spectator, ceasing, that is, to be an observer of life, and
becoming, as it were, a participator, and what he wanted then most
passionately was to see it all, to drink it all in, to be at one with
all the world before him and not be identified with any part of it.
So he stood a pace or two apart from the hoppers, and watched
with delight and wonder as the three boats rowed with a becoming
majesty up to the starting post—each causing one group to jump

and shout in frenzy—thinking that it should be given to such grace, such strength and beauty always to know victory, and then that moment ten minutes or so later when in spite of the uproar on the bank, the desperate shouts of encouragement, one crew alone swept on to victory, while the other two, the grace and majesty now gone, and fatigue, even weakness, appearing on their faces, slumped on their oars after crossing the finishing line. Then the crowd surged towards the boatsheds, where, once again the boys from his school formed groups and began to hop, and sing, and shout the question: "Who are we?" and the reply: "Grammar," just as the warmth began to go out of the day. And still he stood apart, watching it all.

He was so carried away, both by the poetry and the majesty of the afternoon, that he joined a group for the long walk back to the school, and began to talk about the four flashes of foam on either side of the boat as the oars dipped, of the bow cutting the water and the colour in the water, the sky, the leaves with their autumn tints and the city in the distance brooding untouched by all their sound and fury, until he noticed one boy nudge another and little giggles of derision pass from boy to boy, and one boy said: "Our ickle man's a poet," and another added sarcastically: "But doesn't he half know it?" So he held his tongue for the rest of the long walk home, though, in his pain and confusion, he wanted to tell them, he used to say years later, that that was the whole point— he never could be a poet because he never could find the words to describe what was inside him. Somewhere inside him he claimed he felt at the time that that was just another one of those unfair things in life, that being born with such sensibilities, such awareness, but not, alas, with the verbal gifts, the musical gifts to do anything about it. I don't believe he ever put it that way even to himself at that time, because it was not till much later that he even began to entertain the idea that any man who put his foot on the primrose path of pleasure in Australia risked provoking the conformers and improvers to terrible deeds of darkness. At the time he was like somebody lost is a great fog, convinced that there was a way out to the light, and at times he lashed out at those who did him great evil as every now and then he rushed towards that light.

Besides, on that day he was too carried away by the experience to entertain any dark thoughts about life or other human beings. He was looking forward to the treat the Housemaster had promised for them if Grammar won—a visit to the theatre to see *Good News*. So after the meal which ended with the singing of the boarders' song:

You ought to be a boarder,
For a week or two.

You work all day,
You get no pay
You're fed on Irish stew.
The potatoes they are rotten
And the meat it walks to you
You ought to be a boarder
For a week or two.

Then, for a few moments everyone was so caught up in the gaiety of the moment, that boys looked at each other tenderly. It was a time for moistness in the eyes, and a reaching out for each other and then away, the rush down the stairs, the agile and the daring taking four or even six at a time, the timid, the cautious and the clumsy not daring more than one, but all so caught up in the laughing, heaving pack that no frowns, no cries of "I'll get you for that" countered the mood of the moment. With a shout of "Grammar, Grammar, Ra, Ra, Ra", they were away, and on to the tram where, for the sake of that decorum which was even stronger, they became suddenly stilled. Then on to the cable tram in Bourke Street, where the movement up and down excited them again, and then the mad rush to the theatre, climbing the never-ending flight of stairs, rounding each corner with hope followed by the low moan as they saw yet another flight, till, at last, at the very top, they filed into the "gods" for a seat in the front row from where they could see deep below pearl-necklace-wearing women laughing at everything their male partners said. Sebastian wanted then one day to be as comfortable and witty as one of them, and then the light went out, and the magic began.

Up went the curtain, and while the orchestra played gaily, the drummer especially catching his eye for the frenzied way he fiddled with his sticks on the drum, suddenly young men and young girls appeared dressed in holiday clothes, the men wearing straw boaters and the girls straw hats, with lovely, fetching ribbons streaming from them as they moved, all of them swaying rhythmically to the music, till they reached the footlights where they sang gaily:
"Good news is welcome to me",
then glumly:
"Bad news is hell come truly"—
a mood which only lasted an instant, and was gone like thistledown before the winds of their gaiety, for that other theme came back, heralded by a gay trill on the cornet and a roll on the drums as they sang loudly:
"Oh Mister good news
That's what I'm waiting for
GOOD NEWS."

Then they all ran off the stage laughing and four men strolled on
and sat down at a table and began to play cards, and behind one
man, the most handsome of them all, who had a light in his eye,
and looked as though he could excel at everything, there was a most
beautiful girl who seemed to want this young godling to win—to
want that most desperately and possibly to want other things as
well which Sebastian did not understand as he was but thirteen at
the time, and still innocent of those other hungers, and that war,
and all the joy, and all the humiliation in those deeds of darkness,
and only saw then that for some inexplicable reason the young girl
could not take her eyes off the man, and seemed to want him to
succeed in everything, and every time he won she clapped her hands
for joy till he, standing up, faced her, but instead of looking happy,
a great darkness seemed to descend on him, as he said to her,
holding her two hands in his: "You know—lucky in cards, unlucky
in love", a mood of sadness which seemed to overwhelm the other
three players as well because they had no further stomach for the
game, and tiptoed reverently off the stage just as the man, the
godling, said "What else matters if you're lucky in love"—a question
which made the girl turn thoughtful too—her gay mood vanished,
and while she looked serious, but still very lovely, the man began
to sing:

> *"I don't mind if at poker I'm green*
> *If I'm satisfied with a beautiful queen*
> *I'll say I'm lucky in love.*
> *Lucky in love,*
> *What else matters if you're lucky in love."*

Many things happened after that, and I hasten to add that it all
ended happily, with the godling lucky in cards as well as in love,
marrying the lovely girl and everyone singing again:

> *"Good news is welcome to me,*
> *Bad news is hell come truly."*

But by then the magic had gone out of the evening for Sebastian,
or rather that chance remark by the man who looked as though all
human achievements were open to him that a man could be lucky
at cards but unlucky in love—a remark the rest of the evening
simply threw away — had started up something in his mind, something which had never occurred to him before. Without taking
thought he had assumed that the words meant what they said—
that unto him that hath it shall be given—but here, suddenly in the
midst of the excitements of the evening, the gaiety, the fun, the
jokes, the laughing, and the music, where life was held up as one
long round of pleasure, a beautiful young man had dropped the
remark that you could be lucky or successful in some things, but

not in others—say love—and the chill of it swept over him, engulf-
ing him so that once again, he wanted to be alone, to brood over
what the man had said, and puzzle it out. So after the play, he
waited till all the others had jumped on the tram, and then
hopped on the other end so that he could worry over the mystery
of it—wondering whether this meant that if a man strove after
some excellence, tried, say, to perfect himself as a pianist, a violinst,
a mathematician, a physicist, or a historian, that he may not be
lucky in love. Anyhow, what was luck? Was your luck your
desert? Was what happened to you what ought to happen. Or
was it all blind chance, just luck like playing cards. And if it
was all luck, all blind chance, what was the point of trying, what
was the point of effort? And why was it that the other boys did
not seem to be interested in such questions? If there were questions, the answers to which affected all that happened to them in
life, why were they not interested? Did this mean they did not
care? If so, were there any other people who cared? He began
to wonder whether any of the masters cared. He could not believe the assistant chaplain cared, because the only time he had
ever seen him look excited about anything was when he made that
whinnying noise when he took out new tennis balls. Perhaps the
headmaster cared because there had been that wonderful moment,
that never-to-be-forgotten moment that night late in April when
he had come out into the quadrangle and rested his hand on the
lamp-post—and indeed seemed to need to rest it there, as he was
swaying slightly before he did so—and four or five boys, of whom
he was one, looked up in awe and wonder, out of the pool of
darkness at his face, framed there against the great dome of the
sky, and heard him say in a voice, which seemed to express all the
beauty, the horror and the mystery, wretchedness, despair and
loneliness of life—"I went hunting, boys. . . . I can only hope one
day you will all find life as beautiful as I did today." What had
he meant by that? Had he meant that the moments of beauty
and happiness would be very few? Why did he, Sebastian, feel
so drawn towards him? Did he, the headmaster, care about the
things that were worrying Sebastian? The only time Sebastian
had tried to say anything to him, they had not got very far. That
was the time the headmaster had asked him: "Are you getting things
straight?" And Sebastian had said, not cheekily, or showing off
(because the headmaster conferred a dignity on others to which
they themselves were otherwise complete strangers) but shyly, and
very tentatively: "Sometimes I wonder, Sir, whether things ever
do become straight." To which he had replied with sympathy:
"Try hard and they will." But he did not try to persuade Sebastian

that the crooked ever did become straight—and Sebastian knew
from listening to those lessons in the chapel on Sundays that whoever had written those ancient books had had the same doubts—
"There is one event unto all." And sometimes in school they came
on a line in poetry which spoke about this subject of his, which
the master rushed over, and the other boys ignored. So, perhaps,
on this, he would travel alone through life, just as then on the
tram he travelled alone, haunted by those words: "Lucky in love
. . . what else matters if you're lucky in love?"

It was as though he felt the need of some protection, something
to stand between him and what other people menaced him with.
It was in this mood of foreboding disaster, and the panic of seeing that he knew of nothing, either in himself, or outside himself,
to prevent such disaster, that he went through all the routine of
going to bed. He cleaned his teeth—but what good could cleanliness do to still those fears of what *they* might do to him—and put
on his pyjamas and knelt beside the bed, like all the other boys
in the dormitory, and prayed while the prefect waited with his
hand on the light switch—but what good would that do him, was
it likely that that mysterious One, who had made the world, but
so far as mankind was concerned, had not been heard of since,
would rescue him from *them*? Besides, even if He rescued small
boys from their tormentors, what had he, Sebastian, done to deserve
such favours? And if the mysterious One either could not, or
would not stir on his behalf, perhaps He might give him the
strength to face his tormentors, and in his panic, he clutched at
the promise that He would not suffer a man to endure more than
he could bear—which must be precious little in his case, and
besides, *they* were not to know that, and anyhow the prefect would
soon stop that, because he must surely want to get down to his
special supper room, and there . . . he knew it . . . were the
words: "Hurry up! I can't spend all night while chaps like you
say your prayers" . . . and off went the light . . . and with it,
the reminder: "No more talking, or I'll belt the hides off you,"
and there he lay, waiting for *them* to call, and when the door
opened, he was so certain it would be for him that he was half
out of bed when the face came out of the darkness, and the voice,
"You're wanted in the Long Dorm", pausing just long enough to
see the terror and hold his ear and say: "What are you so scared
about? Anyone would think you were going to be murdered"
. . . and laugh in his face. . . . And he followed him down the long
corridor, between the rows of beds, the frightened eyes of the
others turning in relief when they knew that *they* had got Sebastian
for the night, till the closed door, on which he knocked, and heard

the question: "Who's there?" and replied, "Sedgwick . . . Sebastian Sedgwick", and the door opened and a boy, much older than he, and taller, much taller, taunted him: "Why don't you want Grammar to win?" To which he replied: "But I do want Grammar to win." And one of *them* said: "If you want Grammar to win, why don't you barrack with the others?" to which he replied: "I couldn't help it." And one of *them* then said: "We are going to teach you to barrack. . . . Climb on the piss-pot! And put your toes over the edge, and say as though meant it, 'Come on, Grammar!' " Which he did, while *they* struck his toes, and beat his back and flicked at his face with knotted towels, and shouted: "Louder, louder, louder . . . barrack as though you meant it." But not knowing how to pretend to such enthusiasm, not out of pride or obstinacy, because he was prepared to stoop to anything to get out of the flick of towel and tongue, but not having the power to do what his tormentors demanded, he tried desperately for that tone he knew *they* wanted, but could not find it, until, moment of panic, his voice seemed to get weaker just as *they* shouted all the more insistently: "Come on, louder, louder," until one boy, *their* leader, possibly out of tedium, said that was enough for one night, and they would go on with the lesson next sports night—"Let's finish off with unders and overs." So off he went, like a hunted animal, under one bed and over another, while *they* thrashed him with towels wetted and rolled into a kangaroo's tail—under and over the whole twelve beds, and then down the middle, and out again into that long corridor, between the beds, while the boys stared, but took no action, not whispering, or murmuring sympathy, or asking whether they could help, or do anything, not because they believed Sebastian had only got what he deserved, that *they* were doing that which they, the younger ones, secretly longed to do, but lacked the power, or from lack of sympathy with any victim of cruelty or bullying, but just out of self-protection.

Because that was what Sebastian had to face up to . . . that there was no one to turn to . . . that the boys who had seen were afraid to do anything . . . that he could not tell those who had not seen, because they would humiliate him . . . it would shame him to do so . . . and he could not speak to the masters, because you did not do that sort of thing . . . or not in those cases, and although they were told there were some cases where you should speak to the masters, without being a squealer, he, Sebastian, had never found such a case. Perhaps he could tell it to the headmaster. Perhaps, next time the headmaster asked him whether he was getting things straight, he could say there were some things

which were not coming straight for him, but when he tried, he
found the headmaster only exhorted him to get his declensions and
conjugations straight, and then those other things at which Sebastian had barely hinted would fall into place.   He wondered about
the chaplain again . . . and all those promising words he recited
every Sunday, which seemed to suggest that there was an issue
out of all our afflictions, but whenever Sedgwick saw the chaplain
his mind seemed to be on quite different things . . . and so again
the words that came up from inside him, the anguish and the
questions, returned to the place whence they came, unanswered.

One Sunday night soon after the towel bashing he noticed a
shaft of light across the flagstones outside the main door of the
chapel, and peered in. . . . Someone was playing the organ. Not
daring to go in, he stood in the darkness with his back to the door,
lost in wonder, because, as he listened, it seemed that the music
was saying very much what he felt . . . that, like him, it could not
put it into words, only images of sound, and yet as he listened
there, sensing some mystery, he found some words to make it intel-
ligible at least in part . . . that maybe there was no answer either
to our moments of suffering or our moments of joy . . . that maybe,
once you accepted that, this not looking for justice or desert, or
reward, that maybe some things were from eternity and would never
change.   But again, that was one thing the music did not give an
answer to—you could not tell that to anyone . . . and yet, the
music seemed to promise an end to that sense of being alone, a
grain of sand on an unending beach, to the terror of those never-
ending blows . . . the impotence . . . a promise of completeness.
And even if there was no one he could tell this to, some sort of
peace had begun to settle deep inside him . . . and, with it, the
end of that desperate need that someone must come to his aid,
or it would be too unfair . . . that hatred of others, because they
left him to a fate he was impotent to evade.   And he walked out
of the darkness into the shaft of light.   What did it matter if there
was so little light for a man to stand in?

Preliminaries

LAURENCE COLLINSON

ANNE awoke suddenly at 2 a.m. on Friday with the terrifying realization that Gray was unfaithful to her. That was surely the reason he'd called her up at school the previous afternoon and begged off their appointment for the evening. Her heart palpitated. She peered at her watch and immediately took the only practical step that would, for the moment, resolve her problem: she put a seconal capsule in her mouth and washed it down with her bedside glass of water. She hesitated over taking another, and then decided against it; two seconals would make it impossible for her to wake at seven. Even so, she could expect a fuzzy consciousness at least until morning break. If only she didn't have to go to work today. She could of course sleep in and ring up later to say she was sick. But as she'd arranged to meet Gray in town someone from school was bound to see her; it always happened that way; and even if her speedy recovery weren't reported to the head, her conscience or whatever people liked to call it would be uneasy. Besides, William would bang on her door at seven as usual to come and make breakfast for him and his father. William's row would penetrate the effect of even two capsules; in any case, she must give Bill no opportunity to be cynical at her expense. She would get up at seven.

When she looked again at the luminous dial of her watch, it was only five past two. She'd been sure that fifteen minutes had passed. That meant about twenty-five more minutes of wakefulness. The drug seldom took less than half an hour to act; often more since she had been taking it so frequently. Not, she told herself, that she was an addict; she could knock it off any time she wanted: if only a day or two would go by without some sort of upset; if only her mind could be in repose for just a day, she'd sleep at night like a babe, like William; she knew she would.

Just one day of freedom from anxiety. Auden had certainly been correct in his assessment of the times.

Had Gray been telling the truth? She mustn't think about Gray, otherwise she'd never get back to sleep. Perhaps she ought to take drinamyl in the morning: that would relax her. She'd be able to teach better; she wouldn't snap at the kids so much. But if she took one tablet in the morning, she'd have to take another two during the day or the effect would wear off; probably three; and her small store was rapidly decreasing. Perhaps Anita would give her another prescription: she'd call round to the surgery after school: the new rash would be a good excuse. Hadn't someone told her you could now get the stuff in spansules, one of which would have an effect lasting all day? She must ask Anita. Whatever happened, she'd have to take one pill before meeting Gray at seven-thirty; she must be at her best for him: no long silences, no stumbling, no depression: she must appear gay, alive, vital. She screwed up her nose and lips in disgust: she sounded to herself like one of the women in those cosy waiting-room magazines who wrote into somebody or other's column asking how to hold a husband. Or rather, she sounded like the advice that was given. Did all sex follow the same pattern—was it noble only to one or both partners and trite to everyone else?

The trouble was that drinamyl tended to loosen her tongue: she might talk too much, or say the wrong thing, or try too hard to be clever. Gray probably disliked talkative women. But she mustn't think about Gray: that way lay madness. Ten past two. Through the wall she could hear the dim snores of her husband. Again she wrinkled her face in disgust. When they had first been married, she had regarded his snoring with delight: an audible sign of their intimacy. Only *I* can hear him, had been her thought. The snore as a love symbol . . . love cymbal . . . cymbal . . . an interesting title for a psychology thesis. She must admit that Bill possessed one advantage over other husbands—during his periods of sexual quietus (lasting longer each year, thank heavens) he preferred to sleep in a separate room. Considering everything, though, it was remarkable that he visited her at all. Her other lovers hadn't snored; but then, she hadn't got to know any of them terribly well. Did Gray snore? So far, she hadn't had the opportunity of finding out. She'd only known him a week, and their one tentative episode had taken place in the car, and she'd dropped him at his flatette soon afterwards. Or was she fooling herself? Did she misread the signs? That was an easy enough thing to do. Perhaps he didn't want her at all. Perhaps at this very instant another woman was listening to him snore.

But she mustn't think about Gray. Quarter past two. She switched on her bed lamp and began to read.

Gray had asked her to fly with him to Paris, and Bill had just given his amused consent when William awoke her with his customary pounding on the door.

"Mummy, Mummy, Daddy says it's time to get up!"

"All right, darling, I'll be there in a minute or two. Ask Daddy to put on the kettle.

"He's in the lavatory."

"When he comes out."

"Can I come in, Mummy?"

"No, darling, I want to get dressed. Are you all dressed and ready?"

"Oh yes."

"Have you had a wash and brushed your hair?"

"Not yet."

"Well, go and wash and brush up, and then fetch in the milk and the paper."

William retreated, but Anne still lay there, unable to make the effort of facing the winter's bleak breath. Reality and her awareness of reality seemed to be slightly detached from each other. I'm getting a cold, she thought. Oh damn! and I wanted to be one hundred per cent for Gray tonight. Then she remembered the seconal, and presumed that to it she could attribute her instability. As well that she hadn't taken two. Her mouth felt dry and there were scabs of sleep on her lips. She picked them off and dropped them in the ashtray by her bed. She placed a hand over her mouth and breathed out. She sniffed quickly, repeating the process three times, but she could smell nothing. Could one smell one's own breath? She mustn't forget to take her toothbrush and paste with her so that she could duck into a Ladies' and clean her teeth before meeting Gray.

Now, the drinamyl problem. Before or after breakfast, or not at all till the evening? If she took one now, then she'd need another at morning break, then after school, then after dinner. But if she waited till after breakfast, that would mean another at lunchtime, and that would carry her through until after dinner. That would be four tablets as against five, counting the one she would have to take at supper time. Or should she take any at all during the day? They didn't seem to do her any harm. She sneezed. Was she getting a cold or not? Perhaps it was 'flu. She felt a tiny panic. Suppose she became ill during the day, too ill to do anything but come home to bed? She would definitely start the drinamyl after breakfast, and that would enable her to traverse the day in moderately good spirits, no matter what she was catching. Whatever it was, of course, was due to her neurosis. I mean, she told herself, that the disease might be caused directly by a germ or a virus or whatever they called it, but it wouldn't clutch me unless I were *ready* for it. How did that book put it? "Made susceptible to infection." I want Gray so desperately, and I suppose I feel a little bit guilty about it, too, and yet I'm pretending that it's all perfectly normal and trying to repress what I don't want to think about. Or is that carrying my meagre knowledge of psychiatry too far? She heard the toilet flush, and looked at her watch. Ten past seven. She must rise at once or she'd never make school on time.

"You'll be staying home tonight," Bill informed rather than asked Anne.

"No."

"No?"

Anne reached over and rescued the piece of toast that William had been trying to butter. Fortunately the table covering was plastic. She cut the toast in quarters and passed it back to him.

"I want some jam."

"Please," admonished Anne.

"Please," William repeated.

Anne recovered the toast, spread the marmalade, and passed it back.

"But I told you, I have a committee meeting tonight," Bill said calmly, his anger carefully hidden.

"It's all right. I've got a sitter."

Bill was silent. Anne restrained a victorious smile.

"It's the woman who came last time. I asked the agency for her especially. She seemed so pleasant. I prefer a middle-aged woman to a young girl: much more conscientious."

"Not necessarily."

"No, not necessarily. But I think this one is. She has to leave at eleven. I said you'd be home before then."

"I may not be. We're discussing Council elections." Carelessly he added: "I'll possibly be nominated."

"How splendid! Congratulations," Anne said, really wanting to be enthusiastic. "If you say possibly, it means for sure."

"Well, almost," Bill said deprecatingly.

"I'm afraid I won't be able to return before eleven."

"She'll stay an extra half-hour or so, won't she? We'll pay the extra. What's the earliest you're likely to be back?"

"Not before one. I may not even come home until tomorrow."

She concentrated on picking up her cup and drinking, waiting to look at Bill and not daring to. She ought not to be embarrassed at making such statements any longer, but she always was. "You should be able to manage with William in the morning. It's Saturday."

William seemed preoccupied with his milk, but he asked: "Are you going to stay with Aunty Celia again?"

"I may be, darling. I don't know yet."

"Just tonight?" William persisted.

"Just tonight."

"That's what you said last time," William scowled, "and you were away the whole weekend."

"Yes, I know, darling, and I'm sorry, but I'll definitely be back tomorrow. That's if I stop away at all."

Bill was determinedly reading the newspaper.

"Go and clean your teeth, William," Anne instructed.

William jumped down from his chair and ran to the bathroom. Anne rose and looked at Bill.

"We're running rather late," she said. "I won't stack the dishes. Mrs Meddows doesn't mind my leaving them occasionally. Will you be able to drop William at school?"

"Yes. You go ahead. I suppose Georgie's mother will bring William home?" He was being deliberately courteous, with just an overtone of reproof.

"Yes. And Mrs Meddows will stay till you arrive. I *will* run ahead, if you don't mind. I have to stop for petrol on the way."

"Why not get it after school?"

"I'm on the emergency tank as it is. Anyway, I'm going to see Anita this afternoon. And a few minutes makes the difference between a full and an empty surgery."

"Is something wrong?" His voice was sharp with concern, but Anne refused to be deceived. He doesn't really care, she insisted to herself. He doesn't really care about me at all.

"No, nothing important," she answered lightly. She kissed and said goodbye to William, who had returned reeking of peppermint toothpaste and with a white smear on his cheek. "Wipe William's face, please, Bill," she said, and hurried to the garage.

Anne stretched out her arm for a rigid right hand turn and drove into the service station she most often patronized near the school. She pulled up beside a bowser and waited, hoping for the owner's son to attend her in preference to the owner. It'll be a good omen for tonight if he does, she thought. She watched them both through the windscreen as they manhandled a heavy truck tyre. They were so intent they hadn't noticed her arrival. She pressed the horn button and they turned, then spoke to each

other, from this distance silently, as in an old film, and then the
son laid down his spanner and ran jauntily toward her.

"What'll it be today?" he grinned.

"Fill her up, please, and would you mind checking the tyres?"

"No trouble at all."

It's all an act, she scolded herself. Simply an act, psychologic-
ally designed to create a satisfied customer. The geniality, the
benevolence, your slightest wish is our command, sire, we *love*
you, do come again. They probably go to special schools to be
trained in breaking down consumer resistance. But this brute—
how old? twenty-four?—is so evocative of lust, even though his
overalls are loose and make no revelation: they're the dismal skin
of a delectable fruit. Is he aware of his outrageous masculinity?

"How's the oil?"

"All right, thanks."

He wiped the windows, took her money, gave her change, and
bade her a brilliant good morning. She drove away, sighing
ironically for apples she could never have the courage to attempt
to pluck.

A quarter of a mile from school, she realized that she had forgotten toothpaste and brush. She braked suddenly, earning an
aggrieved toot from the motorist behind her; she parked way out
from the kerb and rushed to a nearby chemist. The service station
having proved so auspicious, she couldn't afford to neglect anything.

The locker bell was ringing as Anne slammed the door of her
car. Chattering, shoving, gesticulating, giggling girls and boys
surged into the corridors and, with far more noise and energy
than each of them would have expended had he been alone, they
obtained their books and material from their lockers. Anne
pushed through them to the staff room. Although the caretaker
had cleaned the passage that morning, and although it had been
empty until a few minutes previously, it was already littered with
paper, orange peel, apple cores, squashed cakes, and bent sandwiches. Pencils, books, ballpoints, odd tennis shoes, handkerchiefs, even bags, caps, and coats, enough to stock a small bar-
gain counter, had already been mislaid and trampled underfoot
by the students. Some of the objects would be picked up and
handed in to the pound, a greater number would stay on the
floor or in the finders' pockets. Smells of floor polish, brilliantine,
soap, and scent disjointedly met with the odour of old clothes,
unwashed bodies, and the uncontrolled farts of the younger children. Anne scarcely minded. After twelve years of teaching she
had become inured to what, after all, was the traditional atmos-

phere of a school. Most traditions were foetid anyway. She took the cup from her secretaire, filled it at the basin, and gulped down a drinamyl. Why had she deferred taking it until now? It'd be almost a period before it started working. She wanted to feel its effect but at the same time to be innocent of swallowing it. Like a lot of other things she did, she guessed. Another bell rang. She grabbed the books she needed for her first class and made her way to Friday morning assembly.

The Tins

PETER COWAN

THE houses along the street were without fences, but the place into which the car he had been following had turned was the only one with a strip of lawn unbroken by any tree or garden. The square of grass, closely cut, deep in colour, the edges neatly clipped, extended to the pavement. It was marked only by the cement drive to the garage at the side of the house and the small branching path from the drive. Unprotected, stripped of pretence, the ugliness of the house seemed to Alan almost unfairly disclosed to those who passed along the street. He stepped from his car and walked across the bare lawn.

Jacobs opened the front door. From a small entrance hall they entered a room that looked out across the even square of lawn, and Alan was aware at once that this was of a piece with the bare facade of the house, the entire absence of garden or shrubs. All the real possessions, the small tokens of individuality, had been stripped from the room. The two chairs, the small square table, the heater in the fireplace, seemed left behind by some mistake. So that Jacobs could not see his surprise, he looked out through the thin curtains, and a dark shadow had dulled the grass. Low down over the houses across the street there was a heavy bank of cloud moving in from the sea. But his gaze had perhaps held too long on the few items of the room, or Jacobs had read his silence, for he said:

"I make do here. Sit down for a moment. The reports are here."

He went across to the table and began to sort some of the papers. The reports were in two piles, one of those it appeared he had finished, the other Alan supposed he had still to do. Jacobs said:

"I haven't actually finished—I seem to have more of them to do than I thought."

"If I take them tonight," Alan said, "it looks as though you won't finish at all."

"It is my fault. I know they're not supposed to be taken away from the school. I thought I'd be able to finish."

Jacobs stood by the table, something like defeat in his stillness, in the words that seemed to waver ineffectually. Alan reflected briefly that his own standing with Taylor, the first assistant at the school, was so low that perhaps the reports being overdue again would not matter. And for himself the job was something he used to his own ends, a fill-in, while for Jacobs it was a livelihood. On the evidence of this house, perhaps an inadequate livelihood. He said:

"Look—if you've not finished—leave them. It won't matter that much if I'm late."

"Oh," Jacobs said. He was looking down at the piles of paper. "It's my fault, really. I should have finished them."

"No, leave them. When I said I'd come round on the way home I assumed you'd done with them."

The rain hit the window with a suddenness that made them both look sharply away from the pieces of paper. The room had darkened. Alan said:

"If it isn't inconvenient, I could do them here, and then you could have them tonight. I won't be long—"

"That would be fine. I would like to finish them tonight."

Alan looked at the window. This could go on for ever, he thought. Like two people in a comic film deferring before a doorway. At any moment both would start forward and collide. He stepped towards the table, half expecting Jacobs to do the same, and opened the satchel he had brought to carry the reports. It held his record book. He took out the book, and his pen. Jacobs said:

"I'll turn on the light. It's quite dark in here now."

The light was from a single globe that hung in the centre of the ceiling, shielded by a plain white shade, but in the bare room the illumination was sharp.

"You have 3M only for art?" Jacobs asked.

"For which I'm thankful. But to be fair, at least it is something within their horizons. A few of them even like it."

The gutter outside the window made a steady sound that he was conscious of as he worked at the pieces of paper spread on the table. Brian Jacobs went out, and occasionally Alan heard him in some part of the house, but there was no sound of anyone else, and from the appearance of this one room he found it hard to imagine that any others lived here. He had assumed Jacobs was married, perhaps with a family, somehow he had that manner. And the

suburban house, however bare inside, seemed too big, too inconvenient, for a bachelor, even without the feeling Alan had of
something like the echoes of other lives still clinging to the place.
He filled in the columns, made the comments, offered the assess-
ments that suggested art was only another branch of mathematics,
and he knew the contempt he felt for himself when he attended
upon such rituals.

Jacobs came back into the room, and sat down to look at the
morning paper. Alan finished the reports, and as he tidied them
he stared at the single reproduction the room possessed, a small
print too high on the wall, above the table. A Corot, a typical
suburban piece, he thought, a bad reproduction, and in this bare
room holding no more relevance than a scene from a grocer's
calendar. So, he thought, it was perhaps for this one worked, to
be reduced to insignificance on the stark walls of some suburban
villa. Was it worse to be destroyed in a classroom? He felt
depressed, angry, as if somehow he had been tricked, whatever
optimism sustained him during the day denied here, in this room,
before this quiet, negative person.

"You've finished," Jacobs said.

Alan nodded, putting the papers in a single pile.

"Finished is right."

"It's still raining. Perhaps we could have a drink."

He had no wish to stay. But the painting he had been working
on had reached a stage where it was halted, unresolved, and he
did not particularly want to go back and confront it again. And
if he stayed he need not call for Ella. Yet he would have declined
the invitation, was about to find the conventional words, when he
saw that the other was watching him, seeming to anticipate the
refusal.

"After all your work—" Jacobs said. There was a hesitation in
his words, enforced by the uncertainty in the rather wide eyes
behind glasses Alan had never seen removed, which suggested something other than politeness. Alan was for a moment surprised,
and then he knew that the bare house should have prepared him
for the assertion. But the very starkness of the room in which they
sat had suggested a self-sufficiency. Loneliness was more likely to
exist among the gewgaws and trumpery of possessions that held
memory. This room, almost, cancelled the past. He looked at
the window, and there was the rain and the afternoon already
turned to evening.

"Well, yes," he said. "Thanks."

From what he supposed was the kitchen, Jacobs returned with a
bottle of whisky. Advertising had declared the brand's fame and

quality, its suitability for any occasion, and he imagined this might even have included theirs. But it was not a drink he liked. He wished he had gone back to the flat, and he began to worry about the painting again.

"I indulge myself to this extent in the evenings," Jacobs said. He smiled, as if excusing himself.

The room seemed, as they drank the whisky, to become more like some waiting room, stripped of personality and meaning. Jacobs began to speak, almost at once, of the school, and the inevitable shop-talk of teachers grew around them. Alan heard his own voice, the time went on, and he despised himself and the man whose words crossed his own. He began not to care that Jacobs was refilling the glasses, at first apologetically, then quite openly. Their voices reached the emphasis, the agreeableness, of their acceptance of one another and of the evening. Here, Alan knew the hiatus in his work could be kept at a distance, if it could not be forgotten, he need not call for Ella, and it began to be obvious that Jacobs was not going to do much on his reports. Jacobs observed the small clock on the mantlepiece, which at one point Alan supposed must have stopped.

"You'll probably have missed your tea at home. We seem to have been rather longer at this than we expected—I'll make something here if you'd care to stay."

"I haven't missed it," Alan said. "I get my own meals. I have what the landlord calls a flat. But it happens to be good to paint in—there's one quite large room with a decent light. And he doesn't ask questions about the mess. Or who comes and goes."

Jacobs seemed not quite to follow him. "That sounds—ideal."

"But I was going to say—about the tea—it doesn't matter, thanks. It's time I was on my way. I've enjoyed the drinks."

"No," Jacobs said. "It's no trouble. It won't take long. I'm by myself here." He looked about the room and then he smiled faintly. "I suppose you guessed."

Then he said earnestly: "It's no trouble. I'll put on a can of meat and vegetables—makes a very tasty meal." His eyes blinked behind the wide glasses with the seriousness Alan had noticed when seeing him explain something to a child at school.

"I have found one can live very well from tinned food. There is quite a satisfying variety today—inexpensive, and excellent quality. I can assure you there is no need to despise these products—"

"No, no," Alan said. "I don't despise them. And anyhow, I eat damn near anything. I'm too lazy to cook for myself—it seems good time wasted to me. I eat out, or bring something cooked in —fish and chips if all else fails."

"Not something I have any taste for," Jacobs said. "But you will stay. Get yourself another drink. I won't take long."

The meal justified Jacobs's claim, though Alan felt at that point perhaps neither of them was discriminating. He had begun to regret the whisky, and was glad to eat. But as they had left their drinks, their conversation seemed in danger of drying up also, and by the end of the meal they had returned to a rather muddled form of discussion about the school and examinations, neither of which were topics he would have chosen to taint leisure with. But in the small kitchen whose shelves and cupboards redeemed a barrenness reminiscent of the front room, he knew silence to be unthinkable.

When they had finished Jacobs made some coffee, and he seemed suddenly to have become tired, tired beyond the effects of the drinks and the end of a day. His talk had become spasmodic, he offered broken sentences, inconclusive words, helping these out with gesture of his hands and a strained animation of his features. Alan did not know how much whisky he usually drank in the evenings, nor what effect it had, but he began to feel Jacobs resisted a desire to allow his conversation to offer some personal revelation. He had yielded nothing in the time they had been in the house, and as if to protect whatever need it was that forced him to anonymity, to a complete impersonality, he got up and began to put the things from which they had eaten into the sink. He ran hot water, and commenced to wash up. Habit seemed to have gained on him, or an absorption in some thought, or reverie, which clearly did not include his guest.

As Alan took a cloth to dry the things Jacobs said: "No—let them drain. Thanks all the same."

Alan pushed some of the scraps into the tin that had been opened for the meal, and was about to put it in the kitchen tidy. Jacobs said suddenly: "No—sorry. I didn't see what you were doing. Don't throw it out."

"Don't? Right. I didn't realize you wanted it."

"I don't want to throw it out."

Jacobs's tone held querulousness, almost an edge of ill temper, but to Alan it suggested some issue he did not understand. He said: "I find empty glass jars handy myself for paints and brushes. That kind of thing. The tins are useful to mix a bit of enamel in. I can toss them out when they're no further use."

"I never throw tins out," Jacobs said.

"I suppose they do have uses."

"It's not a matter of use."

"Oh?"

"Not for me." He began to wash the tin, and as Alan watched him he saw that Jacobs preserved the paper wrapping, scouring the inside carefully with the dish-mop.

"When you look at this," Jacobs said carefully, "what do you see?"

"Well—rather pleasant shape, I suppose. Colour. Quite attractive if you simply let the colour work and don't try to take in the bloody weak advertising. I've never looked all that closely at one."

"Gay."

"Yes. I suppose so. Strong colour, anyhow."

"One might say—they have their own individuality."

He was wiping down the sink top. He lifted and replaced the tin.

"You mean—different brands—products?"

"Partly. But each one, even of the same brand, and the same product."

"I don't know about that," Alan said. "Though I have a friend who runs a sheep stud and he claims sheep are all different. If you can say that, I suppose you can say it of tins. Although it seems to negate the principle of machinery. I don't know I could detect the subtle difference myself."

The mild facetiousness seemed to stir Jacobs.

"Suppose each of these is an entity? And as unwilling as we are to be thrown away when we are finished. When we are no further use. Have you ever thought of it like that?"

"But they are made to be thrown away—it's their purpose."

"Oh? And are we made for some different purpose?"

"The bloody things are inanimate objects," Alan said. But the statement seemed, looking at Jacobs's somehow expectant face, the sudden seriousness of his expression, too harsh. "Or aren't they?"

"Could you prove such things do not have awareness?"

"It would be pretty hard to prove they have, surely."

"Sophistry." He smiled. "In any case, perhaps it doesn't matter. Whether they have or not may not be the real issue."

"I suppose, " Alan said slowly, "you would say that what matters is whether one likes to bestow such qualities on them. The way we think." He was reminded of the year he had spent at a university, and it seemed that in philosophy classes they had worked out all this kind of thing. But he was aware that unfortunately it eluded his groping words now. Jacobs was looking at him with a rather childlike earnestness, as if he trusted him, and was allowing this insight into himself because he felt he would not be mocked. Alan thought with sudden irony perhaps Jacobs misread the kind of indifference he, as a temporary art teacher, had towards the school

and those he worked among as tolerance. But he had no wish to
mock him. Jacobs's belief seemed in fact no stranger than many
which men organized their lives around.

"I will show you something," Jacobs said. "I think it may change
your point of view." His words had become more careful, enunci-
ated a little more clearly, perhaps, Alan felt, because he had over-
done his own whisky, or perhaps because of the importance this
revelation had taken on for him.

Jacobs opened the kitchen door that lead outside. The darkness
and the soft sound of the rain were like the statement of a reality
they had forgotten. The light on the small veranda seemed weak,
penetrating only a few feet beyond the cement strip to a narrow
path bordered by sand. After a moment Alan could see the out-
line of a shed, or garage, but the square yard itself seemed to hold
no trees or shrubs, to be denied even the neat lawn of the front.
In daylight it must have been an expanse of soft grey sand.

Jacobs stood in the doorway, his hand touching a second switch
on the wall just outside the door, and for a moment Alan thought
he was not going any further with this, that he would find some
excuse to bring them both back into the lighted room of the house.
But he seemed driven by the mood of self-revelation that the drinks
or the presence of a listener had initiated, and there might have
been then for him no escape. His fingers pressed the switch, and
he selected a key from the ring he carried.

"We'll make a dash," he said. "Only a few steps—we won't get
wet."

He stepped from the veranda, began to run, and then was fitting
the key to the lock of the shed. He opened the door only slightly,
enough to admit Alan, and with a curious movement slid around
the edge of the door even as he closed it.

The single globe close to the roof elongated the shadows of the
rafters across the corrugations of the iron sheets. As he stepped
inside Alan found the pattern briefly held his eyes, and then looking down, he knew a curious certainty that he had seen this before,
the moment of time simply recreated. At the back of the shed,
shelves held evenly spaced rows of tins. Along the sides and in
small neat piles and pyramids about the floor there were more.
Small squat cans that held cooked meats and vegetables: tall cans,
and some that were wide and heavy-looking that contained fruit:
the long flat shapes of fish cans, and the minute tins of cream:
many he could not name. And while his sense of familiarity faded,
and his first impression of numbers began to diminish, under the
light the colours held a glow, a richness, that reminded him of a
greenhouse filled with the blooms of potplants and orchids, exotics.

Save that there was here too much order, precision; these colours, the blues and golds, the clear reds and whites, the green of lettering, would not change or fade. There was something immutable about them that after the first impact denied his sharp sense of beauty and excitement. But their massed effect, the rows and pyramids, was striking, oddly satisfying.

So that at first he had no sense of strangeness that this should exist in a shed, or what might once have been a garage, in a suburban yard of grey sand. He could hear the rain upon the roof. He had a sudden strange conviction that Jacobs had stolen this food, that here were the proceeds of an infinitely magnified kleptomania, but even the most persistent pilferer of supermarts could hardly have gone so far without detection. He said:

"An atomic war won't worry you. You haven't got a shelter under here?"

"A shelter?"

The jest could hardly be sustained, but he felt that only in lightness could any sort of contact exist between them.

"You know—an air raid shelter. Some people used to make them—though I've never seen one."

He might have blundered on, but Jacobs said: "Oh no. You haven't seen what I mean. These tins are all empty."

"I see. Of course."

"So there it is," Jacobs said. "I do not throw them away."

It was perhaps no more, Alan thought, than a man showing his collection of stamps—pieces of paper with a price attached to them. Or a book collector his books that were merely the bindings and title pages, pleasant perhaps to look at along a shelf. People even collected beer bottle labels. Jacobs made no move to step further into the shed, it was as if he was satisfied seeing the groups of tins there. It might have been the kind of resignation of his stance, the perhaps illusory moment of self-satisfaction that came upon his features, but he appeared to have performed a duty, satisfactory in itself, necessary, something he could not evade. He said:

"You called them inanimate objects. That doesn't really mean anything. Not when you look at them. It is a matter of seeing them."

But he appeared to have become tired. His words, his body, the faint movement of his hand in gesture, had lost purpose. Alan felt that already he might have regretted going so far. Or that he had been so lavish with the drinks. Perhaps, simply, there was no more Jacobs wished him to know. His next words might have been spoken to himself:

"At least, it is something I can't do. Simply to discard—"

And then he was waiting, so that he could again close and lock the door. They ran through the rain to the house. From the front veranda, when Alan had entered the car, Jacobs waved once, standing at the top of the steps, and before the car had backed into the road, he had turned off the light and gone inside.

The next day Alan did not see him. Since the art room was detached from the main buildings, on some days he was scarcely in the staff room. He came up a little after four, having had a late class, and few of the teachers were still in the building. In the staff room Hector Johnson was speaking on the phone. An ex-army officer, he taught maths in the senior school, with competence but an almost total lack of interest. His enthusiasm for football made him popular, his lack of interest in his subject Alan suspected even gave him a bond with his students. He had been at the school long enough to know something of Jacobs, and since he put the receiver down almost at once, Alan said:

"I had a few drinks with Brian Jacobs last night. We exchanged reports, and by that time a grog seemed in order."

"Quiet fellow, Brian." Hector was obviously thinking of his phone call.

"I've never really seen much of him. He was here before your time, wasn't he?"

"Brian? Yes. He was here when I came. On his own now, I believe. Never says much, but I think his wife died. Some time back."

"There didn't seem to be anyone there last night. Or we mightn't have got into a session on his whisky."

"Somebody died. No, wait a minute. His wife left him. That's right. Not much was ever said about it. I remember now. She cleared out."

"I didn't know that."

"He may have divorced her. I don't know. She just simply up and out of the place, I believe. Chapter finished. You know women."

As though the subject had never interested him he picked up the evening paper from the phone table. He pointed to the front page. "They're getting up a petition against hanging that bastard who shot a policeman. It was cold-blooded, cowardly murder. I'd go back to the Middle Ages and draw and quarter the swine." He looked down at the paper. "I don't understand people. You'd expect to find some pity for the policeman's family—not a word of that—only for this bastard—"

He pushed the paper away, and gathered some books, looked at his watch, and walked past Alan to the door

"Late now," he said. He seemed always to dismiss some invisible squad with a couple of final words.

Alan drove round to the small house where Ella had a room. The streets were wet from the rain, but there were wide clear spaces in the sky, the clouds higher, white against the few heavy black patches to the east.

"You're very quiet," Ella said as they drove.

"I was wondering why a man would collect tins," he said.

"Tins?"

"Food tins."

"So that he can use them, I suppose. Hadn't that occurred to you?"

"These are tins he has used. Empty cans. And I'm not sure collect is the right word. Perhaps I should say, why would a man be unwilling to throw away empty tins?"

"Well—" Ella said, and then seemed uncertain that he was serious. A look of strain began to mark her features, the expression that seemed to him always exaggerated. Uncertainty worried her, small remarks could cause an almost childish withdrawal; her face, the small round chin, her wide dark eyes, the heavy lips, would compose themselves to a set of hurt that irritated him. It was like an unfair advantage, because though he suspected the pose to be deliberately assumed, to ignore it seemed too cruel.

He told her of the episode with Jacobs, not mentioning his name. She listened without speaking, and, by the time he had finished, they had turned into the drive of the house where his rooms were. She looked at the few thinly leafed shrubs along the fence, but made no move to get out of the car, and then she said:

"He's lonely."

"Perhaps," he said. "But there's not much consolation in a shed full of tins."

"Maybe not. But I think you'll find that's what it is."

"There's a truth in it somewhere," he said. "Like space fiction —you deny its reality, but there can be a truth in it."

"I think it's what I said—something simple—"

"That part of it is obvious. Yes."

Her thick lips puckered quickly as if he had hurt her. He said: "It doesn't matter now. Leave it."

He had expected her to ask the name of the man, but she made no further mention of the incident. She prepared a meal while he became more irritated at the painting he could not complete. He decided to ignore it, and begin something else he had in mind, in which he wanted to use Ella as a model. She posed, sitting on a rug and cushion on the floor. The light made her slender back show strongly in its curve to her waist, the slope of her shoulders, her body had a subtlety not obvious seeing her in her clothes; unsuspected, he felt, by those among whom she moved at the school. She taught in the Junior School, he had come to know her that year, attracted by her small, slight figure, she seemed to fit the somewhat twisted rhythms he had been evolving in his painting. But his sense that he was in some way discovering her had been short lived. He found she had been discovered quite adequately already.

He reached a point in the sketch where he did not need to concentrate, and he asked her about Jacobs.

"I don't really know him," she said. "But he's quite a nice person, I think. He was supposed to be quite seriously ill a while back. He seems all right now."

"Someone told me his wife had left him."

"Did she?"

"I don't know," he said. "It was only something I was told. Johnson mentioned it."

"I remember now," she said. "His daughter."

"He had a family?"

"Only the daughter. Rather a terrible thing happened. She was killed, I remember. She was walking along the road near their house, at night, and she was killed by a hit and run driver. They never found the person."

"Hector Johnson didn't tell me that. Did it happen after his wife left him?"

"I don't know," she said. "I didn't know she had left him. But I seem to remember they were both very upset, so I suppose it was before. Perhaps that was why she left him."

"I'm not sure I see the connection."

"Neither do I, really. But it could be."

"You can get up," he said. "I've finished this."

She came over to look at what he had done. Her hand indicated the series of planes against which he hoped she was both blended and contrasted.

"You make me suffer," she said. "Very turgid."

"There's an objective calm. Nothing turgid."

"A pity." She lifted her arms, stretching. "Was he the man with the tins?"

"Jacobs?"

She nodded. There was no point in denial. Her knowledge disturbed him, suggesting an intimacy which he had seen develop, and which had offered little chance of evasion. She was coming to know him too well, which he had not foreseen, and behind it all

there might lie the issue he had no taste for. Another person had
no claim on the pattern of his living, of his work, as far as he was
able, haphazardly enough, to plan ahead. He said:
  "Look—I wouldn't want him to know I'd ever told anyone. I
have some sort of feeling he trusted me."
  "And that would not have been wise?"
  "I'm a sort of outsider at that school—he may have mistaken my
indifference to the bloody place for tolerance—I don't know—
some sort of understanding."
  "Which you don't have, darling. Only indifference."
  "Oh?"
  "You'll leave that place when you're ready. The same as you'll
leave anything else. When you're ready."
  "Is that wrong?"
  "Oh—no. How could it be?"
  "You know I only want a year or two there to get enough money
to paint for twelve months."
  "Oh, I know."
  "He may have simply thought I was safe. Anyhow, I'm begin-
ning to doubt it ever happened. Perhaps all we did was drink too
much of his whisky. I was pretty blurred."
  "That could be," she said. "I had a night like that once. Or
I hope that's what it was. I'd die otherwise."
  He did not see Jacobs during the week until late on Friday
afternoon. His need to confirm the episode they had shared, to
rescue it from the imaginary quality it had begun to assume, had
caused him to look for opportunities of meeting the older man,
without effect, until they almost collided in the doorway of the
staff room. As they both stood aside, it occurred to Alan that
Jacobs had, from the wide windows, seen him coming across the
quadrangle, and had intended to avoid him. He looked tired.
Almost unwell. Alan did not think he was going to speak. He
said:
  "Quite an evening we had on the reports." He knew it sounded
weak. "You finished them all right?"
  Jacobs nodded. Suddenly his eyes reminded Alan of Ella's.
The same sort of private appeal, the plea not to destroy some
intimacy; what in her he had come to feel as stagy, the taking of
an advantage, as if she gave only to remind of it. And he was
aware of the same resistance to it in himself. Then Jacobs looked
down at the briefcase in his hand.
  "I don't remember," he said. "I don't recall—"
  Alan was going to make a joke of it, easing his embarrassment,
say something about them both enjoying the coming holiday of the

next week, but Jacobs stepped past him and went down the passage.

When he got back to the flat, so that he need not think about the big painting, he worked on a somewhat jumbled abstract that got further out of control. He had begun to feel that this too would elude him, when Ella came in.

"That's not bad," she said.

For a moment he was surprised.

"It started from those bloody tins."

"You and your tins."

"Not mine. But I've thought about them all the week." He indicated the painting. "Perhaps this will purge me. I may even take on pop art."

"They worry you, don't they?"

"Yes. Him living there by himself. And that fantastic shed full of empty tins—if it ever was there. Yes."

"He's—rather a simple sort of man, isn't he. Children are like that—they see all sorts of small inanimate things as quite lifelike. In fact, as alive as they are themselves."

"But they forget and outgrow. A thing they're crazy about one day is forgotten the next. No, to have the kind of feeling he has for inanimate objects must be more highly adult than I can quite conceive. Or I can conceive it, but not attain it myself. It makes me uneasy, as if I was ignoring a whole section of human experience—shutting it out—"

"Well, I suppose we have to shut some things out."

"I saw him this afternoon. I don't know—he was as worried as hell—"

She looked at him quickly. "Because you know."

"You think so?"

"I'm sure."

"I didn't want his secrets. I should never have gone round there."

She lifted her hand, placing it over his. "Darling, you'll perhaps get a good painting from it. There's no use worrying. You can't help him."

She knew when he wanted to work, and her awareness was as accurate for the times he did not. After tea she was taking off her clothes before the radiator in the slow, impersonal, almost absent-minded way she affected when she knew their routine was work. As he watched her, Alan smiled, and she said:

"Am I funny?"

"No," he said. "I was only thinking how differently you can undress at times."

"Is this one of them? I thought—"

"You're right. I have to work. Time," he said, "time—I get so little done."

"You work hard enough," she said. She smiled at him suddenly. "I'm glad the holidays have come. And that I'm here."

"Yes," he said, and he was glad of the supple beauty of her body, and the unresolved problems of his painting, the evening ahead of them.

She had brought her few personal belongings in her small, shabby suitcase. In the morning she wandered about, tidying up, looking carelessly at work he had been doing. She said suddenly:

"Alan—those bottles and jars on the sideboard—"

He said: "I use them for brushes—and enamel sometimes. You've seem them often enough."

"Not all those."

"What's wrong with them?"

"Some of those I thought I threw out—when I was clearing up. I'm sure I did. Or got them ready for you to take outside to the rubbish. Didn't I?"

"I don't know. You may have. But I need them. You can see that."

She did not say anything, and he worked through the morning, feeling his mind clear slowly of routine and the preoccupations of the school. He did not mind if for a day or so he did no more, savouring freedom, and letting his ideas form.

After lunch she was looking at the bottles and jars on the sideboard, and he waited for her to make some comment. When she did not he said:

"It's all right. They won't be in the way there."

"You're not going to throw them out?"

"I can use them."

"Are you serious?"

"I don't know why I shouldn't be. What's the matter with you?"

She said: "Darling—you don't think—that it's beginning in you?"

"Beginning in me? Have I got some kind of disease?"

"I don't know. But after what you told me about poor Brian Jacobs—"

"It's not that," he said. "It's nothing to do with that. We don't have to be stupid about this. It happens I'm a bit short of a few containers—"

"Of course. That's why they're all empty. You're not using them. I'm going to throw them out at once."

"No," he said. "No—I need those. Any others we have—you can throw them away as soon as they're empty."

"You don't need them at all—"

"Don't touch them," he said.

She looked at him curiously, the jars with their clean bright labels standing along the sideboard, he had a desire to touch them, affirm them. Her shoulders, whose slenderness he knew so well, and which her sloppy sweater could only partly hide, moved in her slight, expressive shrug. He reached across the table, letting his hand rest on hers, and he saw that she felt he was perhaps simply seeking to divert her from the clash of wills, minor, but definite enough, that had come so suddenly. Or that she was aware had come suddenly to the surface. But she did not say anything.

In the night he went to the kitchen for a drink, and as he turned on the light he could see in the living room the jars along the top of the sideboard. The reflected light softened their shapes, the labels glowed faintly, he noticed the curve of the glass, the sharp, flat capping of the lids. Then as he opened the fridge he saw the cans and bottles and containers in the clear white interior. For a moment he knew a sense almost of fear, and he felt that objectivity, detachment, was slipping from him. As if this was some dream, and he had not in fact walked in here for the prosaic purpose of finding a drink. Ella was perhaps right. The small containers, the products and servants of man, stood before him in a simplicity and pride, a sort of gaiety in their shapes and colours. As Brian Jacobs had said. And they stood defenceless, at his or anyone else's whim. He thought of the tops taken off, the contents drained, the containers thrown out. It was a nightmare. A denial of sanity. He banged the fridge door and then, in a perverse irony, was certain he had broken the light globe inside. He fought the compulsion to open the door and look, knowing it was the oldest of cartoon jokes. He went back to the bedroom. The light from the partly curtained window made a pattern of shadow across the bed, and the slight form of the girl was without substance. Deliberately he woke her, not speaking, and as she turned towards him the broken light from the window disclosed her face and its half-ironic smile.

In the morning she made no reference to what, the evening before, had brought them to almost open disagreement. But he saw that she had not forgotten, that she had begun to arrange affairs in her own way. She did not go out, beyond trips to the shops a block away. She prepared their meals, and he realized with a certain humour that they were not eating out of tins. There was nothing he could fairly object to in her solicitude.

But her presence, however she might contrive to be unobtrusive, broke the routine of work he had planned. She was there, he had to talk to her, meals occupied set times, above all he was aware of her in the flat. The solitude that renewed him was dispersed. His projects became broken off, sketches were unresumed, the big painting remained as defiant and elusive as it ever had been. He knew that his irritation was unfair since it was her concern for him that provoked it. At the end of the week, in a sudden annoyance that must find some outlet, he dashed off what he knew to be a crazy whim, a thing that might have come from one of his junior classes, or a remedial group in a delinquent home. But at least the paint was slashed about with an abandon that was some relief.

"That's—that's strange," she said, standing behind him. She had made a cup of coffee. "It's not—somehow—like you."

"It is me," he said.

"It's cartoon. See—a room—and like upside down—a man up this wall—"

"Driven up that wall," he said.

It was suddenly so childish he felt ashamed. And unwilling that it should hurt her. He said:

"Pure corn—a sort of study in frustration—erotic fustration."

"Oh," she said. Then she smiled and she put her hand on his shoulder and leaned her weight on him. "Is that all?"

Late in the evening he was lying in the easy chair before the radiator, and he thought that for a time he had slept, the warmth pleasant. He saw Ella moving about in the kitchen, she came into the living room, tidying some magazines on a table, then apparently aimlessly she picked up the jars from the sideboard. She went back into the kitchen, and he got up quietly from the chair. She had found a couple of tins and put them with the jars on the sink. She was looking for a piece of paper to wrap them in, and did not see him just inside the doorway.

"Leave them," he said.

That she avoided any show of surprise revealed clearly enough her intention. She said slowly: "I'm—frightened, I think, about you. A little. And—besides—I don't like this rubbish about."

"A tidy person."

"Well, yes. I always have been. You knew that."

"I did, I suppose."

She seemed to wait. He said: "You don't—feel there's some kind of attraction in those things? Even as immense pity—about inanimate objects?"

"Pity?"

"Strong enough to be a kind of supplication?"

"No—of course not—"

"Brian Jacobs said you had to look at them—it was a matter of seeing them—"

"You can't be serious—oh why did you have to take any notice of that man. He's an old man. A bit unbalanced from being alone. You are not like that—"

"Show me the artist who is not unbalanced. I don't scare at that word."

"I meant—not alone."

"How do you know?"

Whatever showed briefly in the sudden upward glance of her eyes was erased. "It is only because you choose to be."

"Not with much success," he said. The week was like a mockery, and he looked at the painting on the easel near the window, unwilling to admit the days had brought him no closer to its solution. He thought that because he was tired, and had no longer confidence, knowing the depression that failure to work always brought him, he had allowed himself to begin this argument they both wished to avoid.

But she smiled suddenly, as if aware of his reluctance to make an issue of their words.

"You are not alone," she said. "And if you were you could scarcely fill this place with old empty tins and jars."

"Let's just leave the whole thing," he said. He gestured towards the painting, and he realized she had not spoken of it during the week. "I've got to get that right. All the week, and I've done nothing."

"It will come," she said.

He remained awake, not moving, long after she was asleep. She lay curled, childish, he thought there was something pitiable about her frail body in sleep, as if it so little contained her, was perhaps so insufficient to achieve her will. She must rest utterly, asleep, that she might find strength to drive it further. Almost he touched her, in reassurance.

In the morning, as she was making breakfast, he was putting some cutlery on the table when she pointed to the neatly wrapped parcel of kitchen scraps set beside the tins and jars at the end of the sink.

"Darling—could you put them out for me?"

He picked up the parcel of scraps, damp in one part, the paper stained.

"You don't give up easily," he said.

"Give up?"

"You think something has got into me—like some damned disease. All right. Suppose it has. I could even have an outbreak of pity. It's a very pervasive illness. Something perhaps you can't localize."

"I'm not sure I understand you," she said, not looking at him.

"I've told you," he said, and he took the kitchen scraps outside. She said no more about the jars and tins he had left on the sink. She was deliberately pleasant, almost gay, as if she knew he had expected otherwise. But that evening she became miserable, and apparently for no reason cried. Then she said she was getting a cold. Next day, Sunday, she spent in bed, the cold developing more spectacularly than either had expected. In the afternoon, when she was asleep, he made some tea and went into the main room to sit before the big painting that seemed now to have halted him entirely.

The flat was quiet. He felt alone as he had not been able to all the week. Ella might have left the house, the rooms suddenly empty of her presence.

As he looked at the painting he was aware of the sense of failure that held always the newness of fear. He got up slowly, and standing by the easel blocked his hand before the areas of paint, assessing, measuring, his spread fingers and palm like the gestures of a sign language. Tentatively he began to prepare some materials, and started to touch up a dark crescent near the top of the piece of hardboard. It was like the start from desperation, from the bottom of the pit, that sometimes broke through to a development that was important. At least now he could make the gesture. He worked more quickly, altering, working over, building up the shapes and colours that he felt had begun to assume significance. The light was clear through the long windows.

In the morning Ella said she would stay in bed, and with the first day of the new term ahead he almost envied her.

"You timed this well," he said.

"Yes. I'll probably be all right tomorrow. It's just as well they don't know where I'm recovering."

"Just as well."

"We'd have to have a hurried wedding."

"I don't follow the logic of that," he said.

Outside, rain had left the paths, the black surface of the street, stained as if by shadow, the light gaining slowly.

When he came home she was sitting by the radiator, in her dressing-gown, and he thought she could not have been long out of bed. Her dark hair was drawn back, and her skin seemed very white, her face without make-up. She said, her voice faintly roughened:

"And how was the treadmill?" Then she said: "What is it, Alan?"

"Brian Jacobs," he said.

"Brian Jacobs?"

"He was found dead in his house."

She said: No—no, he couldn't—"

"It must have happened some days ago. People evidently thought he was away for the holidays. But a neighbour went in this morning—"

"That's hardly possible," she said. "How could it have happened?"

"I don't know. He evidently had a heart condition. You said something about him being ill a while ago—he apparently had heart trouble then. But they'll say it was that. Perhaps it was."

"Perhaps?"

"The rumour is he'd taken something anyhow."

"But," she said, as if it mattered, "won't that be found out?"

"It might be. In the circumstances he could take an overdose of sedative accidentally, I suppose."

He put his coat on a chair, and stood for a time before the easel looking at the painting he had worked on the afternoon before. It seemed remote, the vision of another person, without relevance or life, and again he knew fear. He looked beyond the painting to the pieces of hardboard stacked about the walls, some propped on the mantel, one facing the room from the fireplace itself where no fire had ever been lit. In the armchair Ella was sitting, huddled, her slight body almost lost in the blue dressing-gown, staring at the red core of the radiator.

He said: "I'll get some coffee. I haven't had anything—you stay there."

While the water boiled he set out the cups, and began to clean up some odds and ends along the sink. Then abruptly he took a newspaper and put the scraps in it. He went into the main room and with one hand scooped the tins and jars along the top of the sideboard into the paper. He bundled them all together, but the newspaper, damp from the kitchen scraps, began to split.

"Mind!" she said quickly.

The tins fell from the paper and then the pieces of scraps dropped about them on the floor. A tin rolled crookedly across to bump along one of the paintings against the wall.

"The bloody tins," he said. He kicked one so that it skidded into the kitchen. He looked up and she was watching him.

"All right," he said. "I know you told me."

He brought in a broom and cloth and cleaned up the mess from the floor. He wrapped the pieces into a full newspaper, and with the parcel in both hands kicked the back door open. The rain had stained the cement steps and collected on the dented lid of the garbage can. There was a faint cold wind, though the sky was without cloud. He slammed the lid down.

He took the two cups into the main room. Her wrist seemed frail in the wide sleeve of the dressing-gown that slipped back along her arm as she took the cup. The coffee spilled slightly, a faint stain down the side of the saucer.

"Alan," she said, "I—didn't mean those things I said."

"They're thrown out," he said. "Finished."

He walked over to the window, looking out into the late afternoon sunlight. Then he turned, as if something in her stillness drew him, and for a moment he thought she was looking at the painting on the easel, the light falling across the still wet pigment, the blocks of colour suddenly clear. But he saw she was staring beyond it to something on the floor, to one of the paintings against the wall where the tin he had forgotten had rolled and was lodged. She began to laugh quietly, unsteadily, her fingers moving the spoon rhythmically in the wide cup.

The Road to Madrid

DAVID FORREST

GENERAL Franco's troops were coming up the horse paddock.
They advanced with due care, a small mass of big fellers and
little fellers, big girls and little girls. They were led by General
Shirley Meisenhelter.

Waiting for them, deep in the Rhodes grass in the North, was
the Army of the Republic. The left flank of the Republic rested
against a strainer post on the railway fence. The right flank was
secured against the garden fence around the school. The position
had been taken up by General "Hisser" Giess and he smugly regarded the deep compact front that the Republic presented to the
rebel army.

The horse paddock fence bisected his front, and according to
International Law in the shape of Education Department by-laws,
the horse paddock was neutral territory. But General Giess understood his adversary very well. In his eight years at school, he had
learned that General Shirley Meisenhelter was terribly unscrupulous
and wouldn't be beyond ignoring the Department of Public Instruction.

When he saw the rebels coming up the horse paddock, General
Giess smiled very toothily, for he had a surprise waiting for them
between the two fences. He felt he was a brilliant person, having
anticipated and outwitted the Meisenhelter.

The Royalist army came on. It advanced behind a screen of
the Chasseurs d'Afrique, or maybe it was the Riffs, or what the
Republic called it, the Riff Raff. At close quarters the martial
bearing of the main rebel forces didn't look so hot.

General Franco had had recruiting trouble. All the available
troops had wanted to join the Republic. A meeting of the League
of Nations in the boys' lavatory soon fixed that. The Republic
was forced to send a consignment of nondescript and or unwilling
troops to bolster the Rebels' fortunes. One unprincipled conscript

declared himself a Sefenth Day Adventish and went off for a drink
of water. Then he went to visit the League of Nations where he
was given political asylum from two of General Meisenhelter's
female provosts.

There were no conscripts in the ranks of the Riff Raff. Volun-
teers to a man, the cream of the rebel army, they rode to gauge the
opposition. Terrible big fellers, eight foot tall, five feet wide, and
black as hell, average age six and a bit. They couldn't fight much,
but, in General Meisenhelter's evil plans, they served to disclose
any cunning plans of the Giess.

The opposing generals were both pretty sharp, and when it came
to close-quarter stuff they both weren't averse to clocking each
other good and hard. General Giess's eyes narrowed when the Riff
Raff rode into view. In the General's view, the Riff Raff weren't
very big at all, but they were well on the way to being a bloody
nuisance.

A six-inch shell in the form of an orange came screaming down
the sky onto the Republic. General Giess absently caught the
orange and ate it. Communists are very practical people.

"Forward the Republic," yelled a lance-corporal of the Riff
Raff and the rebel advance halted as though it had been shot dead.

"Clip him on the ear," ordered General Meisenhelter.

"The Republic," said a lieutenant patiently, "is over there. *This*
is the Royalist force."

"It's not fair. Everybody picks on me."

"Idiot," said the lieutenant and clipped him on the ear.

The lance-corporal ran him through with a *feu de joie* and
rode on.

A rash member of the Riff Raff rode into a stand of Rhodes
grass and disappeared downwards with a little squeak. It was
meant to be a yell, of surprise mostly, when a large strong hand
fastened on his ankle. But while the yell was still on its way up
the back of his mouth, the hand snigged him down into the grass
and he disappeared under General Geiss's secret force of Zeglers.
There were a terrible lot of Zeglers at any time and Donny Bishop
was buried under all of them.

He tried yelling, but nothing came out, and he tried squeaking,
but without any success worth mentioning. There were two Zeglers sitting on each leg, one Zegler on his stomach and one on his
chest, and there was a horrible, pimply Zegler face regarding his
evilly from three inches away.

"Catholic," said Herby Zegler.

"Who's a Caflic?" said the prisoner indignantly.

Commissar Zegler said evilly, "You know what happens to people
who bomb women'n kids?"

"I never did," said the prisoner.

"Did," said Commissar Zegler, "Women'n kids. First we pull
your toenails off. . . ."

The prisoner looked terribly worried. The Zeglers always made
him look terribly worried.

They were a wild lot, the Zeglers.

The Commissar said, "Then your finger-nails. Then your tongue.
Then your ears. Then we tearrrr you limb from limb and feed y'
to the pigs."

Private Bishop shivered all over and he was hauled into the gully
and taken before General Giess.

"Strip him," said the General, "Tack him out on an ants' nest
and pour honey all over him."

"P-p-please," said Private Bishop.

"Die like a man," said the General disgustedly.

The Royalist army was not very well organized and didn't miss
its forward scout for a while. When it did, General Meisenhelter
stopped looking clever and became stony. She realized that the
Giess had done the dirty on International Law.

She reviewed her dispositions, with the expendable Riff Raff
forward, one battalion of Strohfeldts as the leading formation, and
the crack diehard Civil Guard. The General had some doubts
about the loyalty of the First Strohfeldt Battalion. It was part of
the consignment sent her by the Republic on orders from the
League of Nations. It was also down one Strohfeldt, that one
serving in the ranks of the Communists.

General Meisenhelter had no particular aversion to Communists.
If the Giess had decided to be a rebel, then she would have become a Republican. The Giess was her aversion. Her secret
mission in the rebel army was to trim Hisser down to size.

While she was standing there considering the Giess she became
aware that the Riff Raff had dwindled somewhat.

Her eyes narrowed and gave the field a comprehensive sweep—
the high Rhodes grass that should have been the neutral and
open left flank of the Republic, the ostentatious display of regular
infantry where International Law required the war to be fought,
and the battle standard of the Republic flying from the pepperina
tree in the school garden, the battle standard being one of Billy
Beitzel's socks.

The General's eyes moved a bit further and looked thoughtfully
at the residential palace of the Big Powers. There was really only

one Big Power, but he was big enough for anybody, particularly when he was swinging on the driving end of a lawyer cane.

General Meisenhelter began to grin, sent the First Strohfeldt Battalion straight up the horse paddock at whatever the Giess had waiting there for her, hopped through the fence onto the garden front and led the Civil Guard out at the charge.

"Geesers," said General Giess and put himself at the head of his troops.

A great raspberry went up from the Republic, "Ya, ya, Cacto-blastis. Ya, ya, Catholic blasters."

And so on, with variations.

"Who's a Caflic?" said Private Bishop in his death throes on the ant-heap.

"For the Republic!" hollered General Giess, "For the Mother-land! Death to them there dirty murderers."

"Charrge," screamed General Meisenhelter, and the Royalists and the Republic collided in a wild threshing heap of bodies and heads and arms and legs.

The Rhodes grass in the horse paddock in front of the charging First Strohfeldt Battalion suddenly boiled with freckly, pimply, horrible Zeglers, male and female, big and little, all of them. They climbed all over the First Strohfeldt Battalion and cut it to ribbons.

Threshing around on the battle-field, General Meisenhelter succeeded in dispatching a diplomatic envoy to the Big Power to report that the Republic was breaking International Law. It didn't do her much good for a while. She got buried under half the Republic and the Communist Strohfeldt saw her leg sticking out of the shambles.

He knew a Caflic leg when he saw one, and he began beating on it with a gibber. A lone streaking rebel broke through the ranks and charged at the battle standard. He didn't see Trooper William Beitzel until it was too late. Trooper Beitzel wasn't having any unwashed Monaghan mauling his sock. He nailed the rebel in the professional-looking but largely accidental Rugby League tackle around the ankles.

The Communist Strohfeldt was beating his way steadily up the Caflic leg with the gibber. He was giving the knee-cap a series of horrendous knocks when the person growing on the top end of the leg suddenly slid out of the mêlée and the devoted Republican found himself regarding General Meisenhelter, the most horrendous female in the Burnett, twice as old as him, and three times as big.

"Geesers," said the Communist Strohfeldt and streaked for the League of Nations.

It didn't do him very much good. It was General Meisenhelter's turn to apply a Rugby League tackle. This one was not accidental.

"Herbie," screamed the Communist Strohfeldt, "Nancy! Snow!"

The First Strohfeldt Battalion defected to a woman and fell on the Republic's enemies, mostly General Meisenhelter. General Giess found her and kicked her in the ribs.

The First Strohfeldt Battalion turned again, on General Giess, and kicked him wherever it was convenient. They got him down on the ground and hammered him.

"Kick a bloody woman, would y'?" howled Herbie Strohfeldt virtuously and thumped him in quick time, one hundred and twenty to the minute.

Things would have gone badly for Hisser if half of the Zeglers hadn't arrived from the horse paddock and begun to go through the First Strohfeldt Battalion again.

General Meisenhelter took the opportunity to disengage herself and the Civil Guard and any odd members of the Riff Raff not tacked out on ant-heaps.

A great raspberry went up from the battered Republic and the rebel army looked evilly at the battle standard streaming from the pepperina tree.

Terrible abuse began to fly between the armies.

"I'll strangle you dead, you horror," snarled General Giess.

"It's nothin' to what I'll do to you, gutless," announced General Meisenhelter.

"Billy Beitzel! You tear your shirt, I'll tell Mum on you."

And so on.

"Hisser ain't got any guts," announced General Meisenhelter to the rebel and Republican forces and Snow Strohfeldt gave particulars of General Giess's upbringing and other relevant matters.

General Giess understood that he was being baited into deserting his impregnable front to attack on unfavourable ground.

General Meisenhelter was stalling for time, but she kept that bit of news to herself. She understood the mind of Big Powers, and she contented herself with abusing the Giess and making alarming manoeuvres across the Republican front. For once General Giess was a bit slow to catch on, and when he finally realized that the Meisenhelter was shifting the crack Civil Guard to his left flank against the horse paddock, it was too late.

The Big Power came out on reconnaissance, discovered half of the Zeglers guarding the Republican flank in the horse paddock and opened fire with the long-range stuff.

"The last person out of the horse paddock gets six of this."

The left flank of the Republic fell back at a very high speed.

Snow Strohfeldt noted audibly that the male Zeglers didn't let the women and kids go first.

"Charrrge," screamed General Meisenhelter and the Civil Guard crashed around the exposed flank of the Republic, captured Trooper Beitzel's sock, administered the last rites to Private Bishop on the ant-heap, permitted the Sefenth Day Adventish to leave the League of Nations, and gave the Communist Strohfeldt a hefty clip on the ear to go on with.

General Giess stood there looking terribly thoughtful.

"Tell tale tit," he chanted venomously.

General Meisenhelter smiled graciously with her teeth only.

The Return

G. M. GLASKIN

IF she moved her head no more than an inch to the left, she could
see through the long lean scythes of grass right down the river
to where the punt was usually tied up. But for some reason or
other the punt wasn't there. And when she came to think about
it a little longer, she realized that the jetty also wasn't there. It
worried her, until it occurred to her that perhaps the place where
she was lying was either too far up- or down-river for her to see
where the punt and the jetty should have been. But no; when
she turned round to look over her shoulder, the roof of the house
was exactly where she expected it, peering at her over the orchard
of almond- and apple-trees which, despite their age, were again
green and swelling with fruit this summer.

She turned back to the river again, feeling the sun seep with
such luxury through the back of her dress. Where could the punt
and jetty have got to? Had her father decided after all to build
a new jetty, and, while the old one was being demolished, had had
the punt taken up to the boat-house? That *must* be the explanation. And yet, if this were so, she should have heard about it.
Surely her sisters, even Flora, could not have kept so important a
project secret from her? When she would go back up to the
house, later on in this glorious day when the sun's warmth would
be gone, she'd have it out with them, mark her words that she
would. They couldn't put everything over Maisie Jane Matthews,
no matter how smart they all thought they were, all five of them,
especially Flora, even Elsie; hateful, they were at times, like when
they said in sing-song voices:

"*Maisie's the baby, you can tell by her dimple,*
  And also because she's a teeny bit simple!"
Simple? Simple? What did they mean by it? But whatever they
meant, they couldn't deny that not one of them was as happy as
she herself was. Father always said so; Father was always right;

so it must be so. Which meant that she in turn could be sorry for her sisters, poor miserable wretches who, no matter how good their eyesight might be, could never, any one of them, see all the joyous things in life.

Like the river: the waters gliding and glimmering over the reflected trees plunged down deep deep deep in the river's depths, far more fascinating and mysterious than those so much more substantial trees always upright on the banks. The long grass: the best bed of all, and with stems to chew and make whistles from, and sometimes shaking seeds into her hair and down the neck of her dress to—to tickle! Insects to study: ants always so methodically busy, poor things, just like her sisters; ladybird beetles, like herself, opening their little red carapaces with the black polka-dots to spread their wings and half flutter, half totter, from one stalk of grass to another, blissfully without method or purpose at all. Birds skimming over the water and arrowing among the trees, alighting on branches, plucking at their plumage with quite shameless vanity, and pausing, stiffening now and again, to take watch around them—something they'd heard? or smelt? or just sensed without really knowing, like she herself did? Calling to each other, always so happy. Except crows, carping and cavilling their endless complaints; and black, like her sisters had been for months, in mourning when their mother had died. The old grey-white horse with the shaggy lock of mane hanging forlorn over his eyes, and his look of mild reproach just like their father's. Crickets itchy in the grass. On the grass, the grass!—how she always loved just to lie there in its luxury. Especially today. For today was a very special day, a very special day indeed. . . .

Today was her birthday. Seventeen years ago today she had been born in the house just over her shoulder of the mother she had never seen because, so sadly, so tragically, the poor woman had died shortly after she herself, Maisie Jane Matthews, had been born; and consequently she had never known a mother's love and maternal ministrations, no matter how much her five elder sisters might proclaim that they all of them were "little mothers" to their poor baby Maisie. For try as she might, she could not look upon any one of them as a replacement for the mother she had lost, consequently being acutely aware all her life of a profound and sometimes insupportable feeling of "being deprived". Her sisters could remember their mother; she could not. And no sense of reality could seep through to her from the one daguerreotype photograph of her which their father kept on the large walnut desk in his study.

But today was her birthday. She did not want to think any

sad thoughts today. Today she was happy, and happy she would
stay, even if to remind her she must occasionally wriggle her body
full-length through the languorous grass till she could peer through
the water's gently gliding surface (where did it go? and why
should it want to leave the peaceful loveliness of this place?) to
where spears of sunlight revealed the rocks and sand beneath; until
the water became too dark to see through any more, but would
still occasionally gleam with sudden if minute brilliance from the
bellies of minnows as they would abruptly turn in their otherwise
so leisurely yet mysterious errands.   Would she see a tortoise?
Today, of all days in the year, being her birthday, she could expect
to see almost anything.

Turning on her back, she gazed up at the incredibly immense
blue reaches of sky with its flocks of near-luminous clouds scudding from horizon to horizon like herded sheep.   She hoped they
wouldn't turn malicious and menace her birthday with rain.
Perhaps if she turned on her stomach again, would they all go
away?   She would try it anyway; and this time when she turned,
her body complained with an ache and a creak from, she told
herself, lying a little too long in the grass.   And she said to herself: That's how old people must get to feel, with their grey hair
and wrinkled skin sometimes flecked all over with death-freckles.
And as though thinking of old people had invoked a manifestation
before her very eyes, there, deep down in the water, and yet not
quite so deep as the rocks and sand and little clouds of underwater
dust, the face of an old woman appeared suddenly in the depths
to peer sinisterly up at her, the mouth leering uglily, and the eyes
—the eyes—relentlessly seeking her own.

She started back in fright, and wished she had stayed on her
back looking up at the sky.   Yet when she searched around her,
there was no one to be seen, certainly no old woman with hideous
face.   There were only the birds and the horse across the river
and no, not even the punt and the jetty.   Ah, but the house was
still there, craning to assure comfort.

What would that house provide for her tonight?   A birthday
dinner, of course.   Flora and Elsie, perhaps even Mabel, would
cook it; Grace would set table.   None of Annie's "good plain
cooking" tonight; her sisters would give the cook a night off.
They had promised.   But Bridget would still serve; her father
would insist on that.   And perhaps, tonight, having turned seventeen, she might be allowed a glass of wine?   But no, that might
be too much to expect.   Fruit punch as usual, she supposed, and
pulled a little moue.   Girls, she opined, should be allowed to drink
wine, even sherry, when they first put up their hair.   Hers had been

up for a year now, but the only wine she had tasted, she giggled to herself, had been drunk surreptitiously down in the dark of the cellar. Somehow, perhaps because it was forbidden, it had seemed all the more delicious.

And for dinner? Chicken, she supposed; the last of the turkeys had been eaten for Christmas. Flora's vegetable soup first, and then almost the same vegetables fresh from the garden to go with the main course. Unless, unless—unless Father rememberd how she adored asparagus and brought some home from the city. Dared she hope? Dare she hope, also, that he might give her the gold watch he had given to each of his daughters when they had turned eighteen—"My daughters are all becoming little women," he was always saying—or would he still refuse to make an exception of her and she must wait yet another year for her very own watch? Oh the agony of it all! She could almost guess what would come from her sisters: a scarf, handworked handkerchiefs, a pair of gloves that might or might not be of silk, a pair of stockings that certainly wouldn't be silk, a book on housekeeping from Flora when she just longed for a novel by Marie Corelli. Oh well. . . .

But afterwards, that was the main thing! Games in the parlour? Would they ask anyone in? The Jackson girls and—oh the wickedness of her!—maybe the Whittaker boys? Which would mean . . . and she writhed in the grass at the sheer wilfulness of her craving, sucking in her bottom lip and giving it a nip with her teeth, as though it had already been guilty of inviting a kiss . . . which would mean that they would have to invite—dared she mention his name?—the Whittaker boys' cousin . . . Septimus. There, she had said it! Dancing, Mabel at the piano, Milly on the violin, Flora always frowning! But she wouldn't care, she wouldn't care! She'd dance all she wanted to on her birthday, especially, especially—dared she say it again?—especially if Septimus should be the one who would ask her.

Ah, how she could dream here, deep in the grass and with the river whispering so many conspiracies.

That ache again, the cramp and creak in her back. Flora was always saying that she's give herself rheumatism, lying like that in the grass. But she didn't care, she didn't care! All that she did care about now was that, incredible as it seemed, she must have fallen asleep; for now, when she lurched up suddenly into a sitting position, she found the sky waned into golds and greys and the clouds scudding faster and thicker and the wind chill on her cheeks. Lord, what time was it? Then the blasphemy made first her hand fly to her mouth, then her offending mouth require the stifling of a titter. As if anyone could hear! But she must hurry,

she must run, or else she would be late for her own birthday,
and there was her new white muslin frock for her to change into
. . .

Up through the apple- and almond-trees, lurching with stiffness
from lying in the grass, her limbs feeling idiotically like those of
an old crone until she made them work all the faster. No rheumatism for her, especially not tonight. Through the arbour of grape-
vines with the carnations and gaillardias planted by Jenkins. Up
the path of the vegetable garden with scarcely a glance. If she
tried to squeeze out reality as she ran, a game she still loved to
play with herself, she could almost see what a wilderness of weeds
and horror it could all become if ever they should leave it. But
that, of course, they would never do; Father wouldn't even contem-
plate such a thing. And why should they leave, with all this peace
and beauty around them? As though her own silly daydream
would not be dispelled, she decided to dismiss it by calling Flora
to let her know she was coming.

"Flora, Flora!" she shouted, still running and running, panting
for her breath, laughing helplessly to herself and thinking: If I
don't reach the house soon, I'll be bound to collapse. "Flora,
Flora. . . ."

And then she stopped dead.

Oh yes, the house was still there, but what on earth could have
happened to it? The door was not only open, but *gone*. What
could have happened to it? And what was all that *dirt*, all that
dust and dry dead leaves doing all over the veranda . . . and . . .
and . . . how could the veranda itself have rotted and fallen in
as it had?

And the windows! The windows! Smashed, every one of them!
Panes gaping and jagged or gone altogether. No paint on the
frames; only chars as if from a fire. Even some of the frames were
gone from obscenely nude brick. Above her, rafters sagged and
rotted and, even more unbelievable, supported only a few rem-
nants of roof. Great gaping holes in it exposed malevolent sky.
And inside . . . *inside* . . . where there should have been curtains
and carpets, pictures and furniture, her sisters flitting bird-busy
from one room to another—there was . . .

Nothing! A charred, blackened wreck of a house, a mere shell,
as though it had been blasted to smithereens. She shrank back,
stunned, incredulous, horrified, barely stifling her sobs and possibly
a scream.

. . . Until it occurred to her: Of course, she had come up to
the wrong house. She had gone to some other part of the river,
for wasn't it true that she could no longer remember how she had

come there at all? *That* was why the punt and the jetty had been
missing. That was why the river itself had been somehow different
today. That's what she had done: she'd come back to the wrong
house. Now, instead of sobs, she couldn't help laughing at herself.
Flora was always saying she was a fool. Was that what they
meant when they said she was "simple"? Well, she didn't care,
she didn't care, just let them see if she did. And just to defy them,
she'd sing that song she had heard their Aunt Bella once sing, until
their father had stopped Aunt Bella, saying such things were unfit
for his young daughter's ears:

> *"Take me in your arms, love,*
> *Fan me with your fan;*
> *Kiss me and caress me—*
> *That's a nice young man!"*

But then, although she tried hard to laugh and be happy, defy-
ing also the dusk which frightened her so, she found herself sobbing again, sobbing and running she didn't know where, hadn't
the faintest idea any more, because the bend of the river, the trees,
the shape of the banks, all told her that from where she was running was where the house *should* have been. But something had
happened, she didn't know what, except that it must have been
some dreadful catastrophe, some horror that wouldn't bear thinking
about. And now the house was all, all of it gone—her sisters and
Father and Bridget and Jenkins and everything. All, all gone.
There was only herself left, fleeing from her terror in this horror
of wilderness.

From the river to the road, and then the next horror assailed
her. Some sort of machine, some monstrous and inconceivable
thing, all glass and metal glinting evil in the last light from the
sun, had baulked her path and was threatening to devour her. She
screamed; screamed all the louder when she saw the two figures
—a man and a woman, she thought, in some kind of uniform,
black—somehow emerging from the monstrous machine like the
two demons they were. She wanted to run from them, but couldn't.
As in a nightmare, her legs failed her and she left herself sagging,
sinking to the ground, falling and flailing, and all she could do was
moan her despair. When they reached her, the monsters, she
hadn't the strength even to struggle against them, but could only
fall limp with her weeping. The devil's advocates had sought and
seized her for her wickedness, and it was too late, too late; it
could never be undone.

"Flora!" she moaned. "Oh Flora, Flora! Don't let them take
me. Don't let them take me. . . ."

The devil's chariot throbbed and roared with mechanical monstrosity, and his advocates gripped and strapped her inside some kind of device so that she couldn't free or even move her arms behind her. And they leered at her so, leering and jeering:

"Now, now, Maisie Matthews. Come along quietly and we'll soon have you home again. You'll be all right, dear. We'll soon have you home. . . ."

And the she-demon jabbed a poisoned dart into her arm, filling it with venom.

Home? Hell, they meant. They were taking her *away* from her home; they had even, now that they had drugged her, taken away her home itself. Nothing, nothing of it was left. She could only cringe and quiver in horror, too terrified to think what might still be ahead of her.

Hell was a street of buildings like cliffs, all concrete and glass of incredible height and hideous taste, the street an inferno of hell-bent contraptions that hooted and hissed. Lights like molten suns glared in the night around her, making it garish as day never was. Voices boomed at unbelievable volume from what she thought must also be some kind of machines. When roof-tops could be seen, they bristled with contraptions like enormous paper-clips.

"We'll soon have you home," the demons beside her kept saying, over and over, as though they could fool her, "We'll soon have you home." And they half dragged her out of the contraption that at last had stopped throbbing and roaring and led her across that terrifying canyon and into one of the cliffs with stone floors and incredible slashes of colour where pictures should have been. They took no notice of her whimpering or of what she was trying to tell them, but dragged and pushed her to the fresh horror of a machine in the wall that carried them upwards, upwards, when they'd always told her that hell was *below*. It stopped, and they led her out, too terrified to say anything more, and she found herself at what she supposed was a door, where the man pushed some kind of button that gave a shrill little shriek.

When the door opened, she was confronted by some apparition of an old woman—could it be the woman she had seen at the river, come to claim her at last? But no; there was, she had to admit, something familiar about this one, as though she had seen it before, or had known she would encounter it some time in the future. Yes, that was it; for the apparition was a crude, a cruel parody of her sister, or what Flora might be like when she would be seventy, perhaps even eighty years old. Its face had a scar livid as a fire-brand on one of her cheeks. And as though the demons who had captured her knew what they had conjured, one of them said:

"We've found her, Miss Matthews. Yes, in the usual place."
And then, as though this wasn't torment enough, they had to go
on and say: "Come along now, Maisie. Be a good girl. Here you
are home again, safe with sister Flora."

"Oh Flora, Flora," she heard herself whimpering. "If only it
could be. . . ."

Could it be Flora? Older than Aunt Bella, older than old
Grandmother Matthews? This old haggard apparition, such a
parody of what Flora had been? This old, old woman saying:

"You've given her her tranquillizer? Good. You may be right:
perhaps we just *can't* cope any more. . . ."

And then, suddenly reminded of something that she simply must
announce, she found she could at least compose herself, stiffening
her body with its last shreds of dignity, despite her arms bound
behind her, and, no matter what they might think of her for it,
managing to say:

"You may all have the felicity of wishing me happy returns. It's
my birthday, you know. My seventeenth birthday."

But this seemed only to infuriate the apparition before her, for
this phantom of Flora was almost spitting when it said:

"Oh you fool, Maisie; You're *seventy,* not seven*teen*! And I've
told you and told you, you're not to go out alone. Never! They'll
put you away if you do, and *then* you'll know all about it. What
did you try to do, burn the house down again? And all of us
with it?"

At which the apparition raised a hand to the scar on her face.

"It's my birthday, Flora," she persisted; it was all that she *could*
say. "It's my seventeenth birthday. Don't deny me my party,
Flora, just because Milly is ill. Please don't deny me my birthday
party. I warn you, I'll do something you'll all be sorry for if you
do. . . ."

But then, some vague recollection—or was it something she had
forgotten?—reduced her to laughter.

Homage to Hymen

E. A. GOLLSCHEWSKY

EVER since Ettie had been awakened at seven to drink her morning cup of tea she'd been crying her eyes out. She vowed she'd not shut an eye, she'd heard the after-pictures traffic; the stomp crowd breaking up down at the Junior Citizens' Hall; then the early service churchgoers backing their cars out; and finally the bells from all directions, near and far, proclaiming it Sunday morning.

She believed this. Though he knew she'd been asleep when he rose at midnight to go and stand down the yard. He preferred to go outside and empty his bladder, if driven to it at night: the sky was so vast, the air pure and scented, the earth under his feet damp and firm. It gave him a satisfaction he never experienced in the neat little tiled toilet where Ettie kept some sort of breathing deodorant he loathed.

He'd had to shake her in order to wake her up for tea. But he guessed she *felt* as if she'd spent a sleepless night, and let it ride. He did himself. His dreams had been disturbing ones, when he did sleep. Which was unusual for him.

But everything about this Sunday morning was strange. Painful. Scarcely to be endured if you stopped to think. But to be lived through somehow and the other side of it reached, so better not to think too much. Get through it, even if not by familiar ways. He wouldn't be bathing the dachshund today, nor changing the indoor pot-plants for fresh ones from the fernery. The dead leaves under the azaleas and the fallen white stars under the clematis would have to stay until next weekend, spoiling the garden's neatness. He usually went down to the corner store right after breakfast and collected the morning papers, a packet of peppermints, and his week's supply of pipe tobacco. It wasn't to be thought of now. The very idea of the peppermints seemed a sacrilege. Still, at the back of his mind it was reassuring to know they'd keep the papers for him and he wouldn't miss his favourite sections.

He sat despondently on the back steps of the split-level house, shoulders humped, listening to Ettie's shuffling footsteps (she walked so briskly, so sturdily, so *decidedly*, with a resounding thump of the heels, and the vehement nose-blowing, the hawking and sniffing and hiccuping that marked her progress from room to room. He had no doubt that through a veil of tears she would set the house to rights and present it immaculate, shining, redolent with polish, when the Farleighs arrived after lunch. (No scent of flowers inside—the plastic ones were so "real" you couldn't tell the difference and saved a lot of work. Not that Ettie did anything different with the time saved from picking up fallen petals, removing the film of yellow dust scattered by pollen dropping, or scouring soured vases, but she had more time and energy for other chores.)

At the bottom of the yard the red rooster crowed with a peculiarly Sunday morning *bonhomie*. It was a sound to be associated with distant church bells, fresh-cut grass sending up a green pungency, and a roast dinner cooking. It sounded incongruous this morning.

Jenny stepped carefully past him, black hair tied up in a scarlet ribbon on top of her pert head, bottom round and young in old jeans, faded pink in color. Her feet, in scuffed leather thongs, were none too clean.

"Mum said I have to go over to Auntie Carole's today. Why? And what's wrong with Leonie? She's got the sulks." Tennis ball thwacked against the side of the house and expertly caught.

Thank God *she* wasn't old enough for boys yet! Though these days the young louts were on to everything before they left school —beer, cigarettes, girls, gambling . . . why, Joe Adams said at the School Committee the other night that in his shop the biggest buyers of those things (he didn't even think the words "french letters") were high school kids. Pity that bloody swine of a Farleigh hadn't been one of 'em, that's all *he* could say? Though Ettie'd be horrified if he said so; her principles were higher than his. Her ideas of right and wrong more clearly defined.

"Has she, now?" answering Jenny, who was still catching the ball with careless ease. "Doesn't sound like Leonie. She's no sulker."

"Well, she's locked in her room. And I heard her howling last night. And Mum's in a state. I thought at first . . ."—bright flick of glass-green eyes—"maybe somebody related to us had died."

If only it were a matter of simple, unashamed death! It didn't bring down all the fury of family gossip, condemn your parents, arouse excited curiosity in your circle of friends, and bring the

shine of sheer pleasure to the eyes of those you'd never liked if
somebody just up and died. Which wasn't to say he didn't feel
bad about Sam, on his last legs and five hundred miles away.

"No, love, we haven't heard any more about Sam. You get on
your bike now and go over to Auntie Carole's. We'll pick you up
later this evening. You had breakfast?"

"All I want. Cornies and an orange."

"All right then, off you go. Oh, and Jenny—if she asks you any
questions—anything about Leonie or anything—just say straight out
you don't know a thing. You know her, wants to know everything."

"OK, Dad."

His side would be satisfied about this when it came out. They'd
reckon it ought to bring Ettie down a peg. Think they hadn't seen,
all these years, how damned condescending she'd always been?
Handled right, they'd have clubbed in and given Leonie a slap-up
wedding, loading her with presents which they would cheerfully
add to their already heavy load of t.p. commitments, cracking
off-colour jokes about the situation, but facing the world united on
the girl's behalf. Now they'd only gloat.

Jenny wheeled her bicycle out, a thin, clean-scrubbed girl with
the morning sunlight diamond-bright about her. Ettie must be
preoccupied not to have noticed those dusty feet! "See you, Mum
and Dad," she called, mounting, to spin away down the drive on
her glittering new bicycle. Leonie, too, had been twelve. Such
a short time ago—you took your eyes off them for a minute and
they grew up. But she'd been more studious than Jenny, quieter,
docile, and affectionate toward her parents so that in your mind
and heart you rested easy about Leonie. She was your first-born,
and somehow closer to you than the brilliant son now at university
or the quicksilver, madcap Jenny, so like her mother with that
flashing brightness, that shrewdness. His gentle Leonie, dove soft,
unwilling to hurt anything. How could she bear the hurt she had
inflicted on her parents? He longed to tell here there was no hurt,
no pain. But she knew better.

Ettie appeared on the back porch. He couldn't remember to call
it a patio, as she did. He was shocked at the way her always
immaculate grey hair hung in drab wisps about her face—she
hadn't as much as put a comb near it. And her face was bloated
from crying.

"Well, the house is straight at last. And precious little help
I've had. All right for others to drop their bundle—but somebody
has to keep up." She sank into a patio chair of plaited nylex. His
own old squatter's chair of mildewed canvas and wooden armrests

plastered with cigarette burns, kids' scribbling, stains from innumerable cups of tea and coffee, spots of paint, and bits of transfer which had only partially adhered to the woodwork had been moved out to the toolshed. He'd never accepted the new chairs.

Ettie gave her red nose a final blow and tucked away her handkerchief. "Jenny gone?"

"Yes. She called out goodbye to you."

"Well, that's her out of the way, thank goodness."

In the next-door garden somebody played a spray of water over a bed of dahlias, dark red. Their astringent scent seemed to seep heavily into the air, weighing it. As the quiet and the silent suffering and Ettie's weeping had already done.

"I've been talking to her. I said this will just about kill your father. Men are funny about their daughters—nothing but the best for their daughters, never mind the wives. You should have thought of Dad, I said. How can he ever forgive you?"

Ettie was wrong. He felt no different toward Leonie, whose flesh and blood had leaped with life, as his had done. He only wished, with a secret guilt, that he could make everything easier for her. Forgiveness didn't enter into it. *He* would, if he could, save her the interview with Ivan's parents, her mother's tears and reproaches, this public pawing over her secret love, her most intimate feelings. If most fathers did feel humiliated and outraged when their daughters got caught, then he was a strange and unnatural father.

"I'll resign from the Ladies' Auxiliary. They'll know why, of course, but I won't give them the satisfaction of sympathizing with me. And somebody will have to write and tell Dennis. We can just say she's married, nothing more. The neighbours will just have to be faced, brazened out. Let them think what they like. They won't *say* anything." But her defiant voice cracked betrayingly.

He smoked in silence, hand curved over his pipe. Poor Ettie. She who had said so often, "Well, nobody can point a finger at *me!*" now saw pointing fingers everywhere she looked.

"When the Farleighs come I want you to look decent, Dad. Give them no advantage. Whatever Leonie's done they're not getting a chance to look down on her family. You know what cane farmers are—think they own the town."

"Don't worry about them, Ett." Pipe gone out again. He tapped it against the step, sending a shower of ash over the red cemented flagstones below. Ettie didn't even notice. "Old Farleigh's up to his ears at the bank, everybody knows that."

"Still and all." Her eyes gazed unseeingly down the length of

the backyard into the one adjoining it back to back where a man
and a woman were washing a car. "By next Saturday every
woman at the butcher's will have heard. How shall I order the
weekend meat with them all watching me? The tennis club will
be worse . . . they're such snobs, and it was a long time before
they asked me to join. It's not as though we were rich, or business-
people, or owned property—engine-drivers do all right, but it's not
what you could call big money. To think that Leonie—"

He stopped listening. He'd heard all about the shame, the girl's
heartlessness, and endless whys of it. He wondered if it would go
hard with Leonie, giving birth. She was a slight little thing, no
hips at all, thin as a sandpiper. When you thought of child-bearing
women you pictured stout thighs, wide hips, full breast, straight
back. Not a wisp of a girl with no chest at all to speak of, though
she was nearly twenty.

Ettie'd been taking long enough. "What about lunch?"

"I'll open a tin of soup. Fetch Leonie while I heat it and put
the kettle on."

He felt clumsy and awkward, an intruder, going into his
daughter's room. He hadn't seen her since last night, when, holding tight to young Farleigh's hand, she'd stood in the doorway of
the lounge and told them. But she wasn't lying, an abandoned
heap of misery, on the bed, as he'd thought to find her. She was
sitting by the casement window, her bed neatly made, her hair
softly brushed out, dressed in her usual Sunday morning outfit;
shorts and loose flyaway shirt. She looked no different that he
could see.

"Mum's got lunch ready, girlie."

"Yes Daddy." Her face still had its velvety softness, its mauve
shadows, its big brown eyes. Her neck was still fragile as the stem
of a wineglass. Unchanged.

He touched the straight, light thickness of her hair, feeling for
the bony skull beneath. He wanted to tell her something, to show
his love, to reassure her, but the serenity of her eyes put him off.
Should a sinner look so *innocent*, after all?

"Come on, well. You had no breakfast."

"I do feel more like eating now," she admitted.

He looked rueful. Morning sickness, yet! "Well, anyway."

He gave his pants a hitch. "The placket of your shorts is undone.
You should have told us sooner—surely you knew you'd be needing
new clothes and things?"

"It closes." She zipped it in a trice.

"We'd better not keep Mum waiting."

Lunch was a dreary meal. Then it was cleared away, Leonie unnaturally deferential to her mother, *she* silent in a resigned greyness of the soul. Only later did her spirit pick up its skirts, as it were.

"Put on your new blue suit, Leonie," she commanded. "And your corselette, of course. The Farleighs will be here soon. And take some pains with your face—you always look so wishy-washy if you don't use enough colour. Off you go, Dad, and have a bath. A shave, too, mind."

When he saw her again she was his familiar Ettie. Grey hair drawn sleekly into a false chignon, rose lipstick, the new striped linen sheath frock that had been bought for a happier occasion. No sign of defeat in her straight back. She was ready for the Farleighs.

Their big car turned out to be dilapidated, after all, dusty and dented as it growled into the drive and stopped. But a late model. Used a lot and driven hard, he thought, following Ettie out to greet them. For some obscure reason he was glad to see old Farleigh's collar was frayed and none too clean. The shirt had probably been worn once already. Somehow that helped minimize the feeling of subservience he couldn't help feeling toward these people, parents of the boy who had landed them all in this mess.

Farleigh was a big man with red hair, ruddy complexion, loud voice, and a strong smell of spirits. He boomed acknowledgment of Leonie's nervous introductions. Best place for him was indoors where his voice wouldn't carry to the neighbours.

Ivan, they knew already. A tall, thin young fellow with a residue of pimples from a late adolescence on forehead and chin, the white hands of a bank johnny (Catch him on the land? No sir!), the cool, indifferent eyes of modern youth, and a wide mouth full of white teeth. Leonie's father conceded that he "might develop into something." At twenty-two what could you expect?

He saw from the beginning that he was going to get along best with Mrs Farleigh. She was short and plump, over-painted, her hair rinsed a bright gold so that it emphasized every contour of middle age in her face and neck, bust so tightly constricted, so prominently poised, that he felt as if she had two pistols concealed there with muzzles pointed at him. But he saw with what warmth she embraced Leonie.

"Well, this is a terrible shock, isn't it?" Ettie said in the hall, leading the way to her temple, her pride, her security in a world of threatening change: her newly-done-over lounge.

"Terrible?" Mrs Farleigh paused beside the big TV lamp with its fibreglass shade like white linen, and didn't even notice it. "Yes,

in one way I suppose it is. Ivan isn't making much money yet.
However—" her smile, revealing translucent dentures, embraced
them all. With hope. She hadn't glanced at the feature wall
which Ettie's friends all exclaimed over.

"Oh, money!" Ettie disclaimed it. "No, I meant the disgrace. I
never dreamt, I'm sure . . ."

Ah, yes, you did, Ettie. You feared it, day and night it preyed
on your mind. Always at the girl—"Don't let him touch you
intimately. You know what I mean? Nor put his hands on you
at all. It cheapens a girl and leads to all sorts of things. You
could get into trouble. A man isn't going to pay for what he gets
free, is he? And the wedding ring's a kind of payment." You
tried in your own way to prevent this, Ettie. Because you dreaded
it so.

"It happens often enough." Mrs Farleigh's smile was easy as
she crossed her legs. "But you'd think it wouldn't, with this pill
and everything. I suppose they never will make a pill to alter
human nature."

"Not in my family." Ettie heard only the first sentence and
what she took for implied criticism. Her hands had clenched in
her lap, hands worn and reddened from long years of service to her
god, The Home. No, he corrected himself sadly, The House.

Mrs Farleigh shrugged, releasing a scent of carnations in the
closed room. The smile became a slightly wicked grin. "You're
lucky," she said. "We've got five sons. Take a bit of controlling.
If it's not one thing it's another. Then I was never one to deny
them their wild oats—sowed some myself, you know." The slight
movement of her body lent the last words a certain Mae West
suggestiveness. He almost laughed outright before suddenly remembering what a serious occasion it was.

Ettie's lips tightened. Wild oats indeed! You could see it plain
in her eyes: a pity he didn't sow them somewhere else, then.

"Thing is," boomed Mr Farleigh, call me Tom, before Ettie
could speak, "does she want to go through with it?"

"Go through with it?" Ettie stared at him uncomprehendingly.

"That's right. Have the little bugger. These days there's no
cause to make a helluva fuss—I know a doctor who will take care
of Leonie here as good as if she was his own daughter. If that's
what she wants."

"You mean bring on a miscarriage?" Outrage in every line of
Ettie's disbelieving face.

"Abortion, it's called. I'd pay for it."

"Mr Fairleigh, what sort of a woman do you think I am to risk my own daughter's life just to save *us* pain and disgrace? I wouldn't dream—wouldn't *dream* of it!"

"I was thinking of Leonie," Mrs Farleigh intervened; giving a distressed, embarrassed laugh. "Not us. Or you. There's no danger. We wouldn't suggest—it's not like the old days with those hole-in-the-corner dens run by predatory old witches with filthy hands—"

Ettie put her hands over her ears. Making herself look quite absurdly dramatic. "No, no, your son doesn't shelve his responsibilities like that, Mrs Farleigh. Not while I have breath and she has a father to protect her."

Shocked flush empurpling Mrs Farleigh's cheeks. Anger sparking the merriment from her eyes. "I'm sure we didn't mean—"

"An immediate marriage will be best."

Ivan nodded eagerly. He and Leonie had scarcely looked at each other until now. Nor spoken. Their hands touched, reassuringly, at last. "That's what we came for," he said, "to arrange everything. I'm not trying to get out of anything. My parents just wanted to be sure Leonie wasn't being forced into anything."

"Leonie has no choice and you know it. She's made her bed." That seemed to remind her of something. "Dad and I have decided to give you a bedroom suite for a wedding present. So you'll have something to start with. She lifted an inquiring eyebrow at Tom Farleigh.

He coughed. "Yes, yes of course. Harrumph. Got a block of flats in town here—they can live in one of them till they save enough money for their own home. Broke, myself, unfortunately. But still own a bit of property. Milk, eggs, a dressed chook now and then—all helps. They won't starve. We'll see to that."

Ettie was nodding. Fair enough, her grey chignon said austerely. After all, it's your son's fault.

"Ivan's a fine boy," Mrs Farleigh insisted, interpreting that nod correctly. "She'll have a good husband. Some boys would simply clear off and leave a girl who hasn't the sense to look after herself." Ettie had got under her easy-going skin at last.

"The kettle's boiling," Leonie announced. "Shall we have a cup of tea?"

Sight of the tea-table set in the dining-room plainly restored Ettie. Wink of sunlight on silver service; gleam of snowy napkin peaked above hot scones; sponge cake tempting with strawberries and whipped cream; china fine as eggshells; twinkling cake forks.

"Milk and sugar, Mrs Farleigh? Ivan?—" driftwood, and plastic bottlebrush burning scarlet as a centrepiece. The tiny cup, ridiculous in Mr Farleigh's big farmer's hand. This was showing them.

It was settled then. Leonie and Ivan whispered together, heads close. Ettie was strict about her religion, the Farleighs rather vague. Ivan would change. It would be a quiet wedding. But nice. White satin for Leonie, dinner at the Royal by way of a reception.

It didn't take Ettie long to settle matters.

Privately, he liked the Farleighs. Especially her. That sharp smell of carnations every time she moved, the concern in her eyes when she said, "But your father hasn't eaten a thing, Leonie," as if it really mattered.

The big car with its battered mudguards like a prizefighter's ears was gone at last. There remained only the smell of call-me-Tom's cigar—accepted from a Christmas gift pack—the spicy fragrance of Mrs Farleigh's scent, the echo of all the words that had remained unsaid.

Ettie surveyed the tea-table. It was still fairly orderly. No butts in empty butter dishes, no tea-slops in saucers. Half the sponge layer gone. A few spots of tea on the crocheted cloth. The peaked napkin empty of scones.

Leonie looked tenderly after the disappearing car, leaning against the closed window. *He* was there and he'd be back. They'd be together. Her father thought that for Leonie the worst was now over. She'd always wanted just to marry and have babies.

He sat down and began to unlace his best shoes.

Ettie was gathering china with careful hands. "I think it all went off rather well, don't you? I think I put them in their place well and good. They know now what kind of people we are. Even if he does own a cane farm, I bet her house isn't anything to write home about. Or her cooking. Didn't he wolf those scones, but?"

He didn't have to answer. She went on, "I can't imagine why any man would want to marry a woman like that, can you? Common as a cat's fur. I'm afraid our Leonie will have a vulgar mother-in-law."

He thought of the laughter bubbling good-naturedly out of that deep breast; the scented warmth her flesh exuded, and the kindly understanding in her eyes when she looked at Leonie. And he was silent.

The Road to Kuala Lumpur

GWEN KELLY

THERE were so many teachers by now that some had never really met, but everyone knew Jeremy Stanislaus Whittaker, Stan for short.

Bill Beatty leant across the table, his cigarette dangling casual style from his fingers. His teaching was also casual: no late nights bent over exercise books, no refresher courses in vacation; but he was a natural actor and the rostrum of the school was his stage. Once a year he produced, acted, and directed his own show for the benefit of inspectors. To these men, bored and blunted by the repetitive pattern of the annual trek around New South Wales, Bill's lessons were an oasis in the desert of overprepared or under-done pedantry. Bill could afford to be sympathetic. His progression up the ladder of seniority would be as automatic as his union could desire.

He placed his hand on Stan Whittaker's shoulder, feeling the bald surface of the brown suit, trying not to see the aggressive more-proletarian-than-proletarian flannelette shirt, and the star-spotted tie that bulged untidily through the jacket. "It's a cinch, old man, if you say nothing. Just 'yes, Sir', if he asks you, or 'most interesting, Sir', if he shows you how. And Stan, take a friendly tip. Steer clear of the girls."

Stan Whittaker rubbed nervous fingers around the ring of ginger hair that straggled over the edges of his skull like the remnant of surf on sand. The skull was bare, shiny like his suit. "Thanks, Bill, but you may as well save your breath. The authorities don't like me. Never have. No one gets better passes in this school than I do. Four honours last year. Four honours. Did the kids get them? Not bloody likely. I was the mind behind the paper. Little me. Mark, mark, mark—eighteen hours a day for twenty years. Blokes my age are sitting on their rear-ends ordering the rest of the bunnies around. But me? An assistant teacher." He scratched a ginger curl with one finger. His eyes darted back and forth over Bill's face. "Yes sirring and no sirring won't help me. You know why? I buck the establishment. They don't like it. 'Personality unsuited to teaching.' That's what the bastards write on my reports. Personality! What am I supposed to be, a ballet dancer?"

The door opened; Mr Beston, boss teacher, in whose face the chalk had worn a line of indents, came in, followed by a rotund little man with alert expression but dead-pan eyes. His clothes epitomized neatness. "The symbol of the New South Wales Education Department," murmured Bill. "Awful to think we're all headed that way."

Mr Beston motioned vaguely. Perhaps this year there would be a school in the city. If only—he averted his eyes from the belligerent fringe of red hair rising militant at the centre table. He could not bear even to think about Whittaker. But he did think about him. Constantly. At night he rose brown, shiny, like an octopus from the slime of his subconscious ocean to haunt his dreams, and then his prayers. Every night he, Beston, reproached the Almighty, vaguely resentful. What sin of his could possibly deserve Whittaker? He mentally reviewed his assets: Rotarian, church deacon, president of innumerable charitable and cultural institutions. There was no reason for God to send him Whittaker.

"This is some of my staff, Mr Cumming." He giggled nervously as the fringe of red hair began to rotate. "These days there are so many teachers, we need three staff-rooms. Not like the old days." Mr Cumming rubbed his hands outwardly and his mental lobes inwardly: "Those were the days, Beston," he said. "Nothing today like the good man-to-man relationship we had with the boys." Stan's cackle cut across the room. "Not to mention the girls, old man. Especially the girls."

For a second the silence eddied around the teachers. "I don't think we've met, Mr . . ." Beston's eyes rested in chilly waves on Stan's shaking shoulders. Stan laughed in disbelief. "Aw come off it, Inspector. Everyone in the Department knows me, Stan Whittaker, I'm the boy they send to all the lousiest schools; the hack who works the skin off his fingers marking books to midnight, but who never gets promotion. You must know me."

Cumming drew back. His blue eyes were distant. "I fear, Mr Whittaker, your fame has passed me by. But it is not too late, I assure you." His voice carried the inflections of practised irony, sharpened on the sensitivity of helpless children in those endless lines of wooden rooms plus veranda in which his manhood had been incarcerated. Beston took Cumming's arm. "I'm sure you'd like to see the classrooms. Only this year we have acquired a new dressmaking room, a new . . ." The door closed; verbal diminuendo.

Bill Beatty leaned back in his chair, his eyes following the line of his long legs into infinity. "That's torn it, old man," he said. "If he didn't know you before, he'll never forget you now." The physics master, billowing into a waistline of centrifugal pressures, shook his head sadly. "Why don't you keep your silly mouth shut, Stan. Keep it clean. This is a mixed school, you fool. It does not matter if you are not pure, but you must at least appear to be pure." He looked at them, bewildered. "I didn't say anything. Just a little joke." Mary Enderby, chemistry mistress, settled her glasses a little more firmly on her practical work nose. "With you, Mr Whittaker, there is only one subject. The Department is quite right. You should not be in charge of girls."

Girls, girls, girls, girls, girls. When had he ever asked to be in charge of girls? He hated them. They spoilt his classes with their airs and graces, their innocent guilty insinuations, their blonde, black, red, dandruff-dripping bouffant hair.

Right in the front seat she sat, gazing at him with melting eyes, blonde so blonde, her brown-stockinged legs stretching beyond the desk, while she passed notes to her boy friends under the desk. The thought of her made his clothes uncomfortable. He could feel the sweat run down his back at the closeness of her. He hated blonde women—sly-eyed, breasts gently undulating above her clipped-in-at-the-waist tunic. She was Margaret too, they were always Margaret.

At home, Mum, good old Mum, had worked her fingers to the bone. Wasn't her fault he'd left at the Inter, when he was thirteen. They needed money, that was all; but he had always wanted to go to university. The weatherboard cottage was simple: two windows at the front, a tin-covered veranda, four rooms placed symmetrically in twos off a linoleum hall. Not big enough for seven kids. Six boys and he was the eldest. He liked his brothers, but he had never liked his sister, not much. When he first saw her, she was the scrawniest, ugliest, reddest-haired little brat imaginable. "Like you, son," said his father, as if it were funny. She grew into a whiny kid, who sauced Mum and sucked up to Dad. He was glad when Bobby arrived to complete the family. Put her in her place.

As the eldest he worked hard, up in the Normanhurst clay pits, but the pay was a pittance. The prospect of university seemed at times far away, but he saved bit by bit, year by year, working weekends, clipping lawns and hedges with the old man, who was supposed to be a gardener, but never got very far with it. When he was twenty, he laid down his knife and fork at dinner one day, and said, "Guess I'm going back to school next week."

"Stop kiddin', son" said his father. "I ain't kiddin'. I got a job on the nightcart. We finish at dawn." "God," said Bill, "You must be out of your senses, Stan."

The old man looked at him with hostility. He had always resented his intelligence, because he knew it came from Mum. He hacked his knife into a hunk of home-made cheese. "Time you got married," he said. "School's kid stuff. Time you did a man's work and raised a few kids." His scalp beneath the red hair pricked. "Plenty of time for all that," he said. "That's why the working class never gets anywhere. Basic wage and kids." "Aw come off it, Stan," said Michael. "You don't have to marry, I grant you, but Dad's right. School's kid stuff. With that red top, you could be havin' a regular go with the sheilas."

He felt his adulthood rise to stifle him. Girls. They worried him; their legs, their hair, their skirts. "No bloody girl's going to stop me gettin' places," he said. His mother's black eyes snapped approval. "Jeremy Stanislaus Whittaker. I told your Pa, when you was born, we had to give you a decent professional monniker. Just in case." "Guess I can't stop you," said the old man. "But no reneguin' mind. That cow out there has to be milked, and you can take your turn in the garden with the rest." His throat felt dry. "I ain't the one to sponge," he said.

"Gee," said Bobby, "Nightcart." He held his nose. And then Mavis began to bawl. "I ain't goin' to school if he's comin'," she said. "What'll the kids say? He ain't goin' to make a fool of me in his smelly old clothes." His mother smacked her. "Keep your mouth shut," she said. "You'll do as you're told." The girl turned to Dad. She was twelve. Just beginning to grow. A first-year with snooty ideas. She flung her arms around the old man's neck, sobbing. "The other kids won't talk to me," she said. "He don't have to come to school. He's twenty." Dad stroked her hair, muttering "there, there", and she nuzzled up to him, just as she always did, the little tick. "Bit 'ard on 'er, son. Nightcart a bit —well hardly suitable for a school kid." But he saw his mother's mouth tighten, and he knew no lousy girl-child was going to louse up his education. "She can leave at fourteen," snapped his mother. "Till then, she'll have to lump it."

Once a month they went down to the local tip. As his Dad said, "What some folks throw out ain't nobody's business." They had plenty of odds and ends at home from the tip. A couple of chairs they had fixed up as good as new, a couple of pots, a real lovely vase with only a bit of one side missing. Right near the top too. But this time he looked for books, ties, pens, pencils, anything to save his money, to stock him for school. He found a blazer. A little ragged it was true, but the crest was still good. When Mavis saw it, she bawled again, but Mum cleaned and patched it, and one way or another, it was pretty nifty.

He knew it would be difficult, but it was more difficult than he expected. He could hit it off with the fellows, up to a point. He was a good boxer, a good footballer. They thought his age a bit of a joke, but he soon got used to the everlasting "Grandpa", and if his job was a bit of a joke too, the amusement petered out in time. The staff was more difficult. It took weeks to learn again. He had never been slow, but six years dedicated to brick pits had eroded his balance of knowledge. He had not even seen it go; he merely became aware of its absence. And he was tired. Worn out by night work and the steady round of house chores. He sat staring vacantly, not hearing the questions, let alone the answers, while the masters wrote on the boards. Yet he could endure the masters. They had what he wanted. Success.

The girls were another matter. They moved away from him, they held their noses as he passed, they sniffed significantly when he was near them. Only ▬▬▬ was different. She came from another school, halfway through the year. Like him she was an alien; allowed to make a fool of herself with a nightcarter, because it was such a lark. He sensed their smirking joy in keeping his occupation hidden from her, and he connived at their secrecy.

She had fair hair, turned smoothly under, page-boy style, and held neatly in place by a net. He imagined her in a world, Jane Austen in style, playing a spinet. She sat with the other girls, but her eyes turned sideways towards him in the classroom. Once, after he had endured a particularly vicious bout of sarcasm from the maths teacher, she had pressed his hand in passing. He thought of her as his girl.

At the end-of-year social he sought her out. He overheard them, as he walked across the floor, his grey pants too short for his black socks. "Gee, look at his cute hairy legs." "Gosh, ▬▬▬, he's going to ask you to dance. Fancy him able to dance." "I hope he does," she said. "You wouldn't want to dance with him. He smells." "He doesn't." "Ooh, doesn't he? Don't tell me you don't know where he spends his nights. Right until dawn too. Noisiest of the lot." The heads came together, brown, fair, red, black, nondescript. He could only catch the whistling sibilance of a whisper. "He don't," he heard ▬▬▬ say. "I don't believe you."

He took her from them. He had picked dancing up in the dance halls, those Saturday-night-after-the-sport-and-pub-affairs, where Mum and Dad had undulated in unblissful escape to *Lily of Laguna, Come Back to Erin* rhythms, while he sat on the side benches, hugging his scrubby knees, and keeping the rest of the kids in check.

The smell of her passed under his nostrils and his hands grew hot. He was not a baby like the other boys. He took her elbow and propelled her outside, behind the shrubbery. He kissed her and she kissed him back, her tongue stabbing at him like the quick flicks of a blue-tongue lizard. He was aware of knowledge. "You don't," she said. "Don't what?" "Work on the dunny cart like the girls said." "Does it matter?" Her hands pushed him away, and he stumbled, then grasped the tip of white lace petticoat moving in disdain away from him. He pulled her down to him, crushing her as he kissed her. She screamed, kicking at his chin. "Don't touch me, you lout. Don't touch me." He felt a hand on his shoulder. "See me in my office on Monday, Whittaker." . . .

The office smelt of old maps and cigarettes. "You see," said the Head, "If we take a boy of your age into the school you must respect their womanhood. You are a man. They are still innocent. Think of your mother, boy. What would she say if she knew you had insulted her sex?" He thought, Leave my mother out of this, you silly old goat. She'd laugh if she knew. Innocence my eye. That chick ain't innocent. But he merely said, "Yes, Sir, thank you, Sir. It won't happen again, Sir."

There was one gain. There were no longer any distractions. The feel of work came back; he passed his examination; he won his scholarship. At university, whenever a girl appeared more than friendly, he merely patted her arm, laughed merrily, oh so merrily, and said, "Bet you can't guess where I work." He had no problems with them after that, no close ones; but the smell of them lingered, the thought of them continued to oppress him.

He had one breakdown during his course. After months of lying on his bed looking at the ceiling, while his mother worked a little harder, and his father nagged and nagged and nagged, he managed to rally and finally graduated. He failed, however, to get his teaching mark. He entered the Department all right, but his report carried the stigma of non-qualification. And because it seemed a good policy to unload the odds and ends that drifted into the teaching profession on to odds and ends that involuntary parents discarded in their wake, they sent him to one of the girls' orphanages, church-run, but dependent on Departmental teachers.

Their adolescence spilt from their clothes, exuded from the roots
of their piled hair, culminated in the United States armed service
badges that were pinned, avoiding the eye of authority, on the
underside of their blouse collars. Their knees were rounded, black-
clad beneath their new short skirts; their bodies rippled volupt-
uously, encased in the skimpy materials, straight up and down,
that the authorities demanded. He had been trained to teach
Latin, but they did not take Latin, so he taught them English.
Not "amo" but "I love", not "puella" but "girl".

"Please Sir, this book Sir, this play, something-Dream. It's
impossible, isn't it, Sir?" "It's the work of the greatest English
playwright, William Shakespeare." "Really Sir. You wouldn't
guess, would you Sir? But Sir, it is impossible, isn't it Sir? I
mean Sir, a fairy couldn't, not with an ass." Their limpid eyes
gazed innocently back at him. He felt the ginger spots on his
hands glow with embarrassment; his neck grew warm; his scalp
grew pink, red, to the edges of the shiny patch, so minute, imping-
ing on the ginger curls. Their amusement enveloped him, sweep-
ing his authority away.

"Stay in, Mary, and finish that work." She stood beside his
desk. Her hair was fresh washed, but over-long, dangling in the
white blouse of her shoulders. "I thought I'd better see you alone,
Sir." "Yes, Mary?" "I don't want to stay in, Sir." He pressed
his nose, pinching his nostrils to oust the smell of her. "You should
prepare your work then, Mary." She leant over him. He could
feel the warmth of her breath, Wrigley's Spearmint, on the hollow
of his shoulder. "You know what I'll say to the superintendent,
Sir, if you keep me in." "You wouldn't dare." "Just try it and
see, Sir."

He did not try it. Not that time. And weaponless against them,
he became the victim of their gum-chewing, note-writing, hair-
combing inattention. In vain he stood in front of them, begged
them, ordered them. When he finally rebelled, they carried out
their threat; not directly, merely hints and whispers.

"Mr Whittaker has complained of your impertinence, Jean."
Red hair fell thickly around thick cheeks downed with pink. Sly
eyes, and white lashes. "Yes Sir, I was impertinent Sir, but it's not
easy Sir." "Not easy, Jean?" "It's the things Mr Whittaker says,
Sir." "Such as, Jean?" "I wouldn't like to say, Sir. Not to you.
It's embarrassing Sir." They could prove nothing. His word
against a batch of lousy, teenage, potential delinquents; but they
sent him to correspondence school for five long years.

In the last of the five, he married Ruth, eighteen, whom he had
met at a W.E.A. weekend. Ruth, in the throes of academic con-

version, convinced that anyone who diverged from the normal was
the soul of creativity, and, hoping subconsciously from the bottom
of her unacknowledged bourgeois heart to supply a good woman's
help, married him a week after the first meeting.

For a month they lived in a tiny weatherboard cottage on the
edge of the Parramatta line. In the glow of her new unconven-
tional way of life, she willingly tramped a mile into town to pick
up groceries, necessities. So private in their out-of-way corner, so
much alone. But the first afternoon, she waited until 7.30, with
the spaghetti dying in the pot, the new lemon-scented tea stewing
in its own exotic savour, the rare French sweet dissolving in the
cloy of its meringue.

She met him at the door, distraught. "There was no need to
visit your mother on our honeymoon." "Mother needs someone to
milk the cow," he said. "I have always milked the cow after
school. What difference does it make?" She pressed her fingers
across her eyes and screamed and screamed and screamed. "Let
your rotten little brothers milk the cow." He fingered his ginger
curls, first in amazement then anger. "My brothers work too late,"
he said. "You have no right to speak of my family like that.
We're not ashamed to be workers. Mother's been a saint all my
life, sacrificing herself." She cut in: "Oh go on. Brick pits, night-
carts, rubbish tips. A fat lot of sacrifice anyone ever made for you."
He left the house.

They made it up, but six months later she left him in a flurry of
accusations in which the word "inadequate" recurred, in favour of
a new apostle of freedom, who was not balding and ginger, but
black and bearded, addicted to toeless sandals, dirty shorts and
life in boat-houses on the fringes of the Georges River, where shore
could be reached at high tide only by means of a rowing boat, and
at low by sinking through oyster-sharp succulent mud in grey sandshoes. He was undoubtedly a step nearer to Parnassus than Stanislaus, who now appeared a somewhat shoddy sample of unconven-
tionality. And he was adequate.

Stan spent the night of her departure in a head-beating state of
sentimentality. To his bosom he clutched her dainty, if somewhat
underwashed, garments, which she in her haste had overlooked,
bundled in a corner of the room where they had lain for two
weeks; but he rallied on the second day, and went back to Mum,
who passed over the cow with relief, and threw in the hens for
good measure.

For all that, Ruth had done him some good. Under her pressure
he had succeeded in getting away from correspondence in one of the
boys' technical schools. It was true the term "inadequacy" rankled.

He looked at it from every angle, emotional, sexual, physical, spiritual. He worried at it like a dog with a bone. He asked Jack Bessaway, big, paunchy, on the same staff. "Forget it, man," said Jack. "All these females are the same. Insatiable. Everyone of them." He felt happier. He was also happier at school. Quite obviously the boys thought him a bit of a queer. Infantile manifestations of sex which other masters repressed he greeted with a leer of delighted recognition; but they hit it off in a rough and tumble sort of way, and the boys passed their examinations.

He placed one hand on his still graceful hip, rubbing it from pocket to knee, so that the shine on his brown suit deepened. The battered text of *The Tempest* swayed, tremulous with long usage, in the other. Shakespeare for the Leaving. Every word. He looked over the top of the book and read:

"*If thou darest break her virgin-knot before*
  All sanctimonious ceremonies."

His quick eyes darted significantly across their faces. They looked back at him, wooden, unresponding. He read the passage again, throwing the emphasis on the chosen words. The third time they began to snigger, as it dawned on them that they were being invited to raise their voices in unrestrained merriment. "Dirty minded little bastards," he said to the staff room. "Can't even read Shakespeare without their finding some smutty meaning in the most innocent lines."

He did not get promotion. Neat, puny-mouthed little teachers, crimp-crimping at the niceties of English grammar, moved up; beefy, cane-wielding he-men, effervescing and exploding over the intricacies of chemistry, won promotion; but never Stan. The headmasters tried surreptitiously to move him on, the inspectors passed him over.

The growth of the multilateral school sealed his doom. There they were again, the sisters, cousins, even children of those blonde, red, black, nondescript, whispering, giggling little snobs he had endured in his Leaving year; the rock and rolling, twisting counterparts of those monsters in the girls' class at the home.

He read them Catullus. He repeated the lines, and in time the boys, just like the boys in his technical school, roared. But the girls smiled faintly, or looked at their hands, or raised their silken, plucked, possibly painted brows, and whispered behind their fingers.

He looked at the blonde beauty in the front seat, the dazzling fall of her hair, the long, dark, curling lashes, and he thought with hatred of the shrubbery outside the school. "Don't touch me, you lout, don't touch me." The past surged tingling through his ears. "Well, Miss," he said, leaning over her shoulder, feeling his heart

ticking against his ribs, his tongue clogging his throat—after twenty
years, "Don't you see the joke, or are you too superior?" She edged
away from him, drawing her so neatly pressed tunic tighter round
her. "Was there a joke Sir? I'm not very good at Latin Sir." He
looked at her eyes, while iris merged into light blue, blurred into
condemnation, deepened into purple, and blurred again. He drew
away. Little hypocrite; little Miss Touch Me Not.

"Watch her, Stan," said Bill Beatty gently, "Watch her, boy. Her
uncle's a Federal Minister, and daddy runs the local drink factory.
She's dynamite." Stan's head nodded, dummying back and forth
on his now stringy neck. "The local capitalist," he said. "The
local smarty boys, the privileged class. I understand. But we
don't recognize class distinctions in my room." Miss Enderby
stabbed at the book she was marking with red, annihilating-all-
nonsense Biro. "~~Margaret~~ is a lovely girl," she said. "Listen to
that," said Stan, "Just listen. You ruddy women all stick together.
Lovely girl, my eye. She's no more innocent than I am."
~~Margaret Naylor, Margaret.~~ She had to be called Margaret.
Blonde, seductive, lovely, hateful ~~Margaret.~~

The inspector came and went. There was no promotion.

"I told you to keep your mouth shut," said Bill wearily. "I'd
have got it," he said jumping up and down the staff room like a
grasshopper. "But that ~~Margaret~~ Stanton had to play dumb.
Decline 'puella' says the beak. A joke. First declension, first year
word. And she gazed soulfully at the old jerk and says, 'We've
never had that, Sir.' She did it on purpose, I tell you, on purpose."

He marched into the room, his usual mountain of completed
work, normal quota of corrected books and exercises, piled in his
arms. They rose to meet him but not ~~Margaret.~~ She was busy
reading a note, one of those grimy, befingered missives that they
passed gaily from one sex to the other, thinking he did not see
them. "Puella," he said, "come here." She looked at him,
unmoving, limpid eyed. "Come here," he said. "You can
sit near me for this lesson. I don't write notes." Some of the girls
sniggered. The boys laughed. She looked at him, hatred in her
blue eyes. He felt excited. She pulled her chair two feet away
from him. "A little closer, ~~Margaret.~~" She moved an inch closer.
"Right here," he said, "Next to mine. I can see what you're doing
then."

She placed her chair next to his, her head averted. He began to
read. It was Livy Book I, the rape of Lucrece. "Unpleasant," he
said to the class, avid for just this lesson, since they had read their
cribs in advance. Some teachers leave it out, but we're adult here,
aren't we?" They nodded, giggling, excitement lifting the fur on

their necks, in their armpits. "So we won't be silly now, will we? Just good, sensible, adult boys and girls." He leant forward in his excitement. His hand brushed the girl next to him. Hastily she pulled her chair away. "Take your hands off me, you dirty old man."

They stood facing one another. The shrubs flowered, heady, scented, and the smell of canvas maps in the headmaster's office closed around him. He smelt of the nightcart, and they had to protect the girls from fellows like him. He measured her with his eyes, his shiny brown suit clinging to his frame like armour. "I wouldn't touch you, ▬▬▬▬," he said. "Not for the world. Not even with a ten-foot pole with a skunk on one end of it."

There was a fuss of course. Cabinet Ministers and drink manufacturers and headmasters and district inspectors. So he resigned. There was a job in Kuala Lumpur. An English teacher for a Malay school. Catholic. The inspector wrote him a fine reference, and the Malayan Government paid his fare.

A month later, Bill Beatty received his first letter. "There's a conspiracy against me here," he wrote. "The Malays are all right, nice friendly little people, very natural. But Father Hellicon, the principal, doesn't like me. It's all this chastity business. I felt his mistrust the moment I landed. 'Father,' I said, friendly-like, you know how I am, 'If the Church runs the education system, no wonder the Indonesians want to take over.' That's the point, Bill. No sense of humour. He's one of these repressed types who can't take a joke. There's a job going in Ankara. I think I'll apply. Perhaps I'd be happier there. The Turks, after all, are Moslems."

Four Sunday Suits

ALAN MARSHALL

BEYOND the township stretched the saltbush plain, a dry sea without movement, without sound, canopied by a sky bleached pale by sunlight. Through this empty immensity hawks drifted aimlessly, swinging their shadows across mobs of kangaroos grazing far back from the sandy track linking the township to a vague horizon.

The township confronted this still spaciousness, shrank back from it behind the broken fences, the heaps of rubbish and the bleached grass surrounding the unpainted hovels that marked the town's outskirts.

Protected from the brooding hostility of the plain by the homes of half-castes, the main street held the life and energy of the township between veranda'd shops, offices and hotels. Saddled horses drooped at hitching posts. Sometimes a drover's wagon with chained dogs straining at the axles moved slowly past the shops, ignored by the coatless men yarning at doorways. A few trucks and cars stood askew on the sloping kerbs that fronted the hotels.

The town was an oasis in a loneliness of earth and sky where men found a need of company and where the destination of all who walked was the submerging group. In hotel bars, in stores they gathered. No man stood alone in this street; another always joined him.

The women who in mid-morning shopped along the street were products of an isolation with which they had either come to terms or from which they longed to escape. The warring ones had brown, unsmiling faces, bare of cosmetics. They were burdened with responsibilities. They pushed prams or were followed by clamouring children. They wore floral frocks, puckered and strained over bodies in which they took no delight. The contented ones were proudly clad. They were held erect, established in confidence by a background of brick villas and carpeted floors, tangible evidence

of their husbands' successes in the drab business premises of the
street.

But Edna was different. She was the daughter of a rabbit trapper who lived in a shack on the town's outskirts. Her mother was
dead. She was eighteen years of age and had shy eyes and a gentle
manner. Her expression never criticized; it reflected a wish to
please and in some hidden way, an obeisance. She was slender with
full legs and walked with an unstudied freedom and looseness of
movement that suggested a body resenting the confinement of
clothes. Men considered her pretty, but her appeal went deeper
than that.

The business men along the street liked Edna. Each morning she
walked the street's length with her shopping bag. Each man greeted
her:

"Good morning, Edna."

"Good morning, Mr Johnston."

Her voice contained a quality that increased a man's respect for
himself. It established him as a superior person in whom age had
failed to destroy a charm for women. It stirred him into romantic
dreaming, and as he watched her pass he was seized with a desire
to hold her body in his arms, to carry her away to some idyllic spot
where, free from the eyes of all who knew him, he could ravish
her or reveal an unselfish devotion that would make her cling to
him for ever.

Mr Carpenter, the stock and station agent, was sure she had a
mind of great purity and sweetness. They were terms he considered seriously. He believed in purity and sweetness. He often
pondered on the implications he felt sure were evident in the tone
and emphasis of her morning greeting. Sometimes he was quite
sure he attracted her strongly. At other times he was seized by
the conviction he was a most unattractive man and that it was
impossible for any girl as beautiful as Edna to love him. He com-
pared her with his wife who treated him as a likeable child to be
humoured. He was certain his wife was unaware of the fine qualities he possessed yet he was equally sure she loved him. And he
loved her. Of this there was no doubt. Say she discovered Edna
in his arms! How could he explain it? He shrank to a nucleus
of suffering at the thought.

But each morning found him standing at the doorway of his
office waiting for Edna to pass.

"I really have a pure and beautiful love for this girl," he told
himself.

Such an estimate of his feelings gave rise to exalted moments
when he had an urge to protect her from evil advances of other

men. But there were times when he wanted to seize her and fling
her on a bed and savagely take her. Because of the intensity of
his passion he concluded he was a man of great virility, much
greater than that of other men, and that his desires were desires that
established him as superior to most men. He was sure the men he
knew were incapable of any sex emotion other than an animal lust.
The same feelings in himself were looked on as admirable manifestations of a noble, unselfish love.

He wished he had read more and could appreciate poetry. Formless poems of love strove for intelligibility in his mind as he sat at
his desk recording the sales of sheep and cattle. Under the spell of
his reveries the forms upon which he wrote dissolved and vanished
and in their place was a long beach and the sea and Edna in his
arms as he strode to meet the waves.

One morning, under the influence of a sudden compulsion, he
asked her if she would come for a drive with him that night. It
was summer and a full moon.

"I'd like to, Mr Carpenter," said Edna.

Mr Johnston, the ironmonger, did not love Edna in this way.
Sometimes he disliked her. He was a stout man, abrupt, overbear-
ing and dogmatic. These qualities formed the shell beneath which
he quivered and palpitated with uncertainty.

The men who gathered in his shop to talk were quite sure he
was a well-educated man who could settle any argument provided
the answer was to be found in a book.

"I read every night before I go to sleep," he sometimes told a
customer. "No matter how late I get home I must read for a
little while. I'm always reading."

He had explained this habit of his to Edna as she stood before
his counter making a purchase.

"It's a good way to send you off to sleep," said Edna.

Edna is a fool, thought Mr Johnston sourly.

But he wanted her to like him. He wanted all women to like
him. Those women who showed pleasure in talking to him seemed
to him desirable women, and he strove to increase their regard for
him. Sometimes he enumerated them in his mind, concluding there
were five women he could have married had things been different.
Musing on the figure gave him great pleasure. Not many men can
say they've been loved by five women, he told himself.

He would not have liked to marry Edna but he would have liked
to humiliate her. He felt she really didn't admire him and he would
have liked to punish her for this. He imagined brutally rejecting
her pleading to be possessed then relenting and enjoying a conquest

sharpened by a God-like contempt. To seduce her would be so easy. She was completely unguarded by experience.

He went through a fortnight of indecision. He was restless in his home. He felt a need to travel and meet lots of girls. But Edna haunted the pleasure resorts his dreams fashioned.

"What's wrong with you?" asked his wife, who was dieting and eating a lot of lemons. "Why don't you do something round the house? Paint the laundry; it's got to be done before Christmas. The way you're going on you make the house feel like a jail. I've had it. I'll write to Mum and ask her to come up and stay for a few weeks."

The next day Mr Johnston asked Edna if she would like to drive out as far as Single Tree Bore with him; he had to deliver some parts for a mill out there but would not be able to leave until after dark.

"I'd like to go, Mr Johnston," said Edna.

Mr Salisbury, the farm machinery agent, was not troubled by his conscience when he asked Edna if she would like to go for a drive with him along Emu Creek. His intentions were honourable. Edna was a girl with many outstanding qualities, he had concluded after watching her each day as she walked down the street. She should be "given a chance". What exactly this "chance" was he had never quite worked out. But he was determined to give it to her. He prided himself on having a great understanding of people. ("It comes natural to me.") He often thought he should have been a psychologist. Or a sexologist. He was at home in either field. He had once read a book called *Studies in Sexual Aberrations,* and the knowledge he had thus acquired made him feel superior to all the men that he met.

"The average man knows nothing," he told Edna on their first drive together. "They don't know what's going on. They live all their lives in this joint and the people they meet know nothing either. They all lead dull lives, going to work and going home again. As for sex, half of them don't know it exists. They have children and that's the end of it. If they knew what goes on in the minds of people in big cities an' that they'd drop dead. I could tell you things about men and women you'd never believe. Not that I would tell you. I wouldn't. You've never come up against the hard facts of life. Part of your charm is your innocence. But I can tell you this, Edna," and Mr Salisbury placed his hand on her knee to give emphasis to his pronouncement, "innocence can be a danger."

Edna agreed that innocence could be a danger. As if in proof of the claim she made no attempt to remove Mr Salisbury's hand from her knee. Mr Salisbury placed a different interpretation on her forbearance. She trusts me completely, he thought, and reluctantly withdrew his hand. A feeling of humility had come over him. I am really privileged to be in this girl's company, he thought sadly. There is not an evil thought in her.

"I'd like to take you out often," he said, lighting a cigarette with a hand that trembled and drawing the smoke deep into his lungs, "but I can't do that. I'll meet you once a week. I'd like to put you on the right track."

Mr Salisbury had always kept on the right track. He attended his church regularly and had seven children. He didn't believe in birth control.

"What greater thing can a man contribute to his country than children," he was in the habit of saying when someone commented on the size of his family.

His wife didn't believe in birth control either. "Abstinence is the only answer," she informed her husband after the birth of their seventh child. Mr Salisbury was going to dispute this, but his wife had just had a blood transfusion and was too confused to appreciate such an argument.

When she returned to their home she had to work very hard, work that Mr Salisbury came to regard as an accusation. He decided he must also work very hard and he began returning to his office after evening meal. It also left his wife free to look after the children. ("Belle has enough to do without me getting in the way.")

Edna's company took his mind off the worries of supporting a large family. It also, so he told himself, introduced into his life a sense of purpose and a joy in living that would in the end make him a happier and more tolerant husband.

And, besides, no one knew about it. One thing about Edna, you could trust her.

Mr Simpson, the postmaster, trusted her completely.

"You see, Edna," he explained to her, "you can't rely on people in a town like this. They would take a delight in ruining a man. If I was seen out with you my wife would hear about it in no time. My friends would go out of their way to tell her. So you must understand how careful we must be not to be seen."

This protest against the duplicity of the townspeople did not disturb Edna's pleasant reverie. She sat relaxed in Mr Simpson's fat car, fleeing with it from responsibilities. She had stepped into it from a disintegrating, three-roomed house in which disorder gazed

steadily at her with hypnotic eyes until will vanished and helpless-
ness came. Two of the rooms were bedrooms. The third room
was a portal to the world outside, a world of conflict, of pressures
composed of rabbit traps, pleading men, the price of skins, cars and
searching hands, beer, tired muscles and hope. In this room the
first steps to survival were taken. To this room Edna and her
father returned to replenish their strength with unspoken com-
munion.

It contained a soot-encrusted, cast-iron kettle, hanging from a
chain that disappeared up the chimney above the open fireplace.
On the hearth littered with charcoal sat a huge frying pan, its
inner surface gleaming from the rubbing of a crushed newspaper.
A camp oven stood beside it. Rabbit traps and harness hung from
nails in the walls. The table in the centre of the room, its stains
still evident beneath a scrubbed surface, bore open tins of jam,
their jagged lids bent upwards, smeared faces on cylindrical bodies
clothed in coloured labels. Amid the eating utensils scattered
upon it was a tin of rivets, a hammer, a pair of pliers, a brass door
knob and a coverless copy of *True Love Romances*.

Her father, sitting before the fire mending harness with copper
rivets at which he hammered intently—he too represented confinement and frustration, even though she loved him. But at this
moment she existed in another world, not here where trees leaped
from darkness into the beams of the headlamps, gave a momentary
acclaim, then rushed into the past forever.

Mr Simpson's worries were his own. She could not accept them
as hers. "Yes," she said. "I suppose they would talk."

"I would like to meet you more than once a week," he said,
moving his shoulders as if adjusting them to a weight. "I've got to
think of everything—my wife. You have no idea what I go through.
I'm always thinking of you. I just can't push you out of my mind;
you're always there."

He said it resentfully, as if Edna's responsibility for his state was
reprehensible and should be censured.

It pleased Edna that he was always thinking of her. His tortures
appeared before her as a variety of facial expressions, all suggesting
longing, desire and hopelessness. The picture gave her a feeling
of contentment, achievement. She loved his love for her and
wanted it to continue so that she could comfort him when she
needed comfort.

She wished she had beautiful clothes. It seemed to her there
were frocks that would so transform her that her conversation
would improve with the improvement in her appearance and she
would become charming and irresistible. Then men would become

awkward and shy in her presence and she could bestow love upon them, a gift from an inextinguishable store.

"I don't know," said Mr Simpson hopelessly, increasing his grip on the steering wheel. He could not imagine Edna as his wife. She was not suitable. He could not see her moving efficiently around a kitchen or acting as hostess to his friends.

His dreams of Edna pictured her as his mistress, his home life still unchanged. He could put her in a flat, he thought, not here in this dead town but in Melbourne to where he imagined himself transferred and made postmaster of a suburban post office. After he had left with his wife and family she could follow by train. He would meet her at Spencer Street railway station, drive her to the flat he had acquired for her, then dash back to his own home. She would have to get work, of course—keep herself occupied.

He spent long periods at his desk working out exactly when and how he would visit the flat. He worked out on paper the cost of keeping her, then in sudden frustration went off on a dream of winning a lottery after which there would be no problems, only a life of happiness.

Mr Simpson, Mr Carpenter, Mr Johnston and Mr Salisbury always picked Edna up by a clump of mulga near her home. The house was situated on a back road along which, after dark, there was no traffic. Here she would never be observed moving from the shadows of the mulga trees towards the car door held open from the inside by either Mr Simpson, Mr Carpenter, Mr Johnston or Mr Salisbury.

That is, no one but "Curly" Martin, who didn't matter. Curly was never likely to meet the friends of Edna's lovers socially. He was young, twenty-two, and didn't own a suit. He was a rabbiter like Edna's father with whom he was friendly and with whom he shared the same problems of existence. He lived in a tent within sight of Edna's home. He cooked for himself, sang maudlin songs with genuine emotion while preparing his meals, and often visited Edna's father for a yarn. They respected each other's trapping areas and enjoyed each other's company.

The older man, whose name was Ben, liked Curly because he was a good "ear". Curly listened intently to Ben's tales, his mind stirred to attention by the sentimental nature of their content, by the actions and exclamations that accompanied the old man's unpunctuated flow of talk.

"I knew a bloke who lived in Yarrawonga by the livin' Harry he could scrap though I say it myself and I'm not talkin' but he sold horses my sister was dressmaking up there and this bloke could

handle colts but bless me soul he got taken crook something to do
with his guts doctors shut up when they reckon you're going to slip
your bridle but I'm tellin' ya a better bloke never swung his legs
across a horse and there he was with the sweat on his face and me
beside his bed and a slab off the side of his hut where the cold
wind came through God bless me I've never seen the likes of such
a place to die in which he did with his dog howling outside between
times ah I was sorry for him in his trouble the poor bastard."

Tales featuring love and death when told with feeling always
blurred Curly's eyes with tears. He was a cheerful man who
laughed and sang more than most. He thus swung easily to tears.
As a sad tale unfolded he became the recipient of poignant knowledge he imagined was denied to other men.

On such evenings Edna sat with the two men before the fire.
She had heard her father's tales, so never listened to his words but
sat in the shadows looking at Curly's strong unwrinkled neck or at
his hands resting on his knees. His hands suggested an ability to
lift and hold and grip with power; and looking at them her blood
became alive, proclaiming its quickening in her flushed cheeks.

Curly looked at her only when her father became silent for a
space and then his glance was an amused one. He looked at her
with tolerance and affection as if from his high seat of knowledge
he reached down to pat her.

He had watched her meet all her lovers. The opening of his
tent faced the mulga clump. They were men who on the street
regarded him as of no importance. It did not disturb him. His
knowledge of their secret life lifted him out of their reach and he
smiled as he passed them at their doorways, secure in a feeling of
independence and freedom.

Curly had broad shoulders and brown eyes. His dark hair was
curled into a cap on his head. When he laughed his cheeks puckered and his eyes became cradled in radiating wrinkles. He wore
a grey polo-neck sweater and blue denim trousers faded from many
washings.

Knowledge of Edna's easy surrenders stirred in him an awareness of her body's curves and warmth and roused in him dreams in
which he imagined her as he would like her to be, free of desire
for any man save himself.

He didn't ask her out. Her experiences with married men gave
her the power of making comparisons, and he shrank from offering
himself to her judgement. He became awkward and uncertain in
her presence but sought to conceal this by an attitude of indifference. It was this attitude that attracted Edna. The more he withdrew from her the greater became her desire. His apparent lack

of emotional response to her presence gave her a feeling of inadequacy. The gestures and movements that stirred her married lovers to action had no apparent effect on Curly. But there were other ways.

She always placed the cups of tea and plates of scones on the littered hearth in front of the men. This evening she had left the top button of her blouse undone. As she lowered herself into a crouch to find a place for Curly's cup, her elbow pushed the hem of her frock high up on her leg. For a second Curly glimpsed the white inner skin of her thigh and her breasts drooping in the shadow of her blouse. His eyes grew still. Edna raised her head and looked into them. Her tranquil glance, held with strain, changed to one of comprehension.

"Oh God!" thought Curly in sudden distress. "She'll think I'm a dirty bastard."

Edna pulled her skirt down, rose to her feet and clutched her blouse closer to her in a gesture she hoped would suggest an innocent girl in confusion.

Curly always went round his traps about midnight collecting those inexperienced rabbits caught from the first lot to leave the burrows. He then reset the traps for the dawn catch, gathering these rabbits when the first long beams of the sun lay flat on the tops of the saltbush.

Edna was always delivered back to the mulga clump by her lover of the night long before Curly set out on his midnight round. He was often sitting with her father when she entered the door, meeting his glance of comprehension with a quick lowering of her eyes.

On one occasion he was setting off on his round when she came walking along the narrow track to the house.

"Come on for a ride," he called to her. "I'll be back in an hour. You can carry the rabbits."

"I'd like to, Curly," said Edna.

He walked ahead of her round the traps. He hummed and sang and she followed behind him carrying the limp rabbits. She looked up at the sky. Great happiness had suddenly swooped down upon her, and she rose to its embrace as if it were a lover.

That night, her bare arm enfolding the pillow, she wafted into fantasy dreaming made exciting by the conviction that the world she now created was attainable. The dreaming of past nights had left desolate mornings in their wake, since these dreams could never be reconciled with the reality of her home. Dramatic entrances into night-clubs on the arm of a favoured lover, the applause of well-dressed audiences to her singing, beautiful clothes, jewels, worshipped, loved, adored, needed—such dreams had comforted

her even while they tortured her. Harnessed to them for support
she yet found their weight intolerable.

To have wings, to rise out of her home, lift herself up, up to the
stars where she could shed this house like a constricting garment
and find herself held in arms that were a protection! At times these
desires racked her into tossing and turning or sent her curved arms
up into the darkness where they paused in a tense, quivering appeal
—"Make it happen! Make it happen!"

But now her dream was of a tent and her face upon the pillow
was relaxed. No lines of tension surrounded her closed eyes. The
corners of her lips curved gently upwards. Picture after picture
wavered before her, eager for selection. Curly lay ill upon his
bunk, his head on her shoulder. She leant over him, gripped by
the beauty of every feature. She nursed him with devotion. She
washed him, fed him. He had called out for her, only her. "Don't
leave me! Don't leave me!"

But the morning presented him differently. His need of her was
uncommitted, denied involvement, and this she felt in a wordless
oppression. He always smiled when he looked at her or when
listening to her answering one of his questions, a smile that disturbed her since it made her feel like a child.

This feeling persisted when in the following weeks she sometimes
accompanied him on his trapping rounds. It subdued her, drained
her of power.

"Why do you go out with these men?" he asked her one night.

She hardly knew, but a remark of Mr Johnston's came to her
mind and she repeated it as if it were an expression of her own
conclusions. "When you are loved you are never lonely; any sort
of love is better than loneliness."

Curly pondered this. "Yes," he said at last, "I can understand
that."

Edna became pregnant. She told no one. She walked down the
street each day, her lifted face untouched by guilt. Even when her
figure proclaimed her condition to all who saw her she still carried
herself with the same unconcern, the same detachment.

The realization of her pregnancy came as a shock to Mr Simpson, Mr Carpenter, Mr Johnston and Mr Salisbury. They were
beset with suffering. They withdrew from their doorways to the
shadow of their premises when they saw Edna walking down the
street. Each was unaware of the part the others played in Edna's
life and each was certain that he alone was responsible for her
state. They ceased asking her to go for drives with them. They
carried on their work in a continual state of worry and distress

made more oppressive by the knowledge that their wives did not suspect them.

"I see Edna is in the family way," Mr Simpson said to Mr Johnston, believing that this statement was convincing evidence of his innocence.

"Yes, I've noticed that," said Mr Johnston, introducing into his voice a tone of indifference. "I never thought she was a girl like that."

"No," said Mr Simpson, "neither did I. It just shows you. You never know what they're like underneath."

They parted, each having lightened his burden for a space.

Though Edna was now ignored by these men Curly continued taking her on his midnight round of the traps. Though aware that she was expecting a child he was quite incapable of mentioning it to her, and she remained silent. He was certain he was not the father even though that possibility occurred to him. He had so conditioned himself to a pattern of thinking regarding Edna's affairs, a pattern in which he moved on the periphery, that his relationship with her seemed incidental to the forces that were shaping her. He had no part in her joys, her sorrows, her hopes. They were reasons for his compassion, not demands to bear responsibility. In his passion there was no involvement, therefore no obligation.

Yet there were moments when he wished that only he mattered and her affairs with others were of no consequence.

When Edna's time grew near Curly shifted his camp to another trapping area twenty miles away. He was not fleeing. From what did he have to flee! Let them settle it among themselves.

The baby was born and grew. Edna carried it down the street each morning, trailing behind her the clean perfume of soaps and powders and laundered baby clothes. She didn't have the money to buy a pram. Though Mr Simpson, Mr Carpenter, Mr Johnston and Mr Salisbury, freed from worry by her silence, did not now avoid her on the street they avoided looking at the baby. They were afraid of what they might see in its face.

Curly had not seen the baby. He had moved his camp several times, but he had no reason to return to the area near Edna's home. Rabbits were more plentiful in other places. But he returned when he received a lawyer's letter stating that Miss Edna Green was claiming maintenance for his child and that her claim was to be heard before a visiting magistrate in the local courthouse in a month's time.

"Listen," he said to the lawyer in whose office he found himself the day before the hearing of the case, "she's putting one over you.

I'm not the father; there were other blokes. She's trying to hang it on me because I'm the only one who's single. She's not going to get away with it."

The lawyer was not helpful. "She says you are the father. You slept with her, didn't you?"

"Sleep's hardly the word," said Curly, "but I'll go along with that." He paused, then added abruptly, "All right; I could be the father but I'm not. And I'll draw in a few others before I'm finished, see if I don't." He was feeling an angry resentment against authority, which seemed to be threatening him from the silent dusty books bound in leather that leaned askew on the office shelves. The law was his enemy, not this unsmiling man in front of him who, captive beneath a roof, had never known the freedom under stars. Arguing with him was a waste of time.

"Who's your lawyer—Bradbury?" asked the lawyer, naming his rival in the town.

"I'm handling this myself," said Curly, who had little knowledge of court procedure and saw the hearing of the charge against him as an opportunity for discussion in which he was free to make counter accusations without hindrance. "I'll show the bastards."

Out on the street he stood looking around him for a while. He had no feelings of resentment against Edna. She had picked on him because he was the easiest mark, that's all. She wouldn't want to put the boots into him out of revenge. He could imagine her naming him almost with pride while at the same time being sorry she was getting him into trouble. She would think he had shot through out of fear. He wished he could convince her he hadn't, that he had gone away to leave her settle it with those other four bastards who had started all this. He wondered which one was the father.

Anger rose and fell within him like a tide, flung itself against the images he had created of the four men who had seduced her. These images had little to do with reality. He did not see them as lonely frustrated men wrenching at bars. Loneliness to him came from isolation and had no part in the lives of men with homes, wives and children. It was not being unneeded that motivated them as it did him. That age calculated by years brought no change in dreams and was not empty of a longing for future fulfilment was incomprehensible to him. He saw these men as ruthless, coldly calculating, untouched by longings to serve or feelings of devotion. He wanted to humiliate them, bring them down just as a pursuing dog would a kangaroo.

He walked down the street until he stood before the doorway of Mr Carpenter's office. He waited until a customer had left, then stepped in and beckoned Mr Carpenter to the entrance where he awaited him, his face expressionless.

"Good morning, Curly," said Mr Carpenter.

"Mr Carpenter," said Curly, speaking softly as if the information he was about to convey was sinisterly secret. "Edna Green is taking me to court tomorrow. She is having me up for maintenance of her baby. I am not the father, Mr Carpenter, you are. I am going to name you in court. I think it would be a good idea if you were there."

Curly turned and walked out. Mr Carpenter had not spoken. He stood completely still even though his body was suddenly occupied by a formless panic that writhed and struggled to free itself from his shell and drag itself upwards to the wide security of the sky. He slumped into a chair and stared at the desk.

Curly entered Mr Johnston's store. Mr Johnston was explaining to an attentive and deferential man that the local council was composed of men whose only concern was to get something out of it for themselves.

"If I get in I'll stir things up," he said, emphasizing each word by the tap of a finger on the man's shoulder.

Curly called him aside and spoke his piece in the same conspiratorial tone he had used with Mr Carpenter.

"Mr Johnston, Edna Green is taking me to court tomorrow— maintenance of her baby. I am not the father of the child, Mr Johnston; you are. I am going to name you in court. I think it would be a good idea if you attended."

Mr Johnston received this information with startled indignation. He had just created himself a councillor and the feeling of power he had thus acquired remained with him just long enough to give force to his reaction. "Get out of the shop," he said savagely, thrusting his head towards Curly as if it were a weapon.

But Curly was already on his way to the door. Mr Johnston stared after him, his feeling of power quite gone.

The reaction of Mr Salisbury to Curly's whispered revelation was one of astonishment. He was so honourable. He was so certain of the right track. He knew so much about sex. After this long time it was incredible; all that was in the past.

"Good God!" he exclaimed in bewilderment.

Mr Simpson, after Curly finished speaking, suddenly realized with great clarity that the idea of a postmaster on his salary having a mistress was ridiculous and impossible. He felt he was surrounded by lying people out to ruin him. Here he was confronted by one of them, a man who would go around telling his friends, his enemies, everyone, that he was the father of Edna Green's baby.

"If you as much as mention . . ." he began savagely, but Curly had gone.

Mr Simpson, Mr Carpenter, Mr Johnston and Mr Salisbury came to breakfast in their Sunday suits next morning. This extraordinary departure from custom had an irritating effect on their wives, who were suddenly reminded of their wedding days by these relics of past pride and promise. The dark blue suits bought for that occasion seemed to have shrunk upon the men they had married, squeezing from them the rich full life their appearance had once promised.

"Why are you wearing your Sunday suit today?" each asked her husband.

Mr Carpenter explained he had an appointment with an important Melbourne agent; Mr Johnston had to meet a wealthy customer, he told his wife. Mr Simpson and Mr Salisbury were also meeting men they wished to impress. It was going to be a busy day for all of them.

Yet none of them left for work with the optimism and confidence a day of such appointments would have usually created in them. They were downcast and irritable and waited in their offices for the opening of the courthouse at ten o'clock with feelings of despair.

Edna was also waiting. She stood before the courtroom door impatient for it to open yet dreading the sound of it being unlocked. She was carrying the baby, now six months old, and she stood there clasping him close to her and feeling that in all the world only he needed her. In the tumble and sway of thought that held her motionless beside the heavy door, vague pleas for help struggled upward through this formless milling and poised captive behind her closed lips.

Once she said aloud, "Please love me," then hearing her voice she glanced around her with sudden fear, feeling she may have been overheard.

Mr Carpenter, Mr Johnston, Mr Salisbury and Mr Simpson were standing on the edge of the pavement and could not possibly have heard her. Among the casually clad people collected there the four Sunday-suited men introduced a funereal note. They had greeted each other with pretended surprise, each striving to conceal the burden of guilt each felt he alone was bearing.

"There's a few interesting cases today," observed Mr Johnston, speaking down as if to pupils. "I really shouldn't be here, but these local squabbles are really an entertainment."

Mr Carpenter was doubtful about their entertainment value. He felt that people standing trial for whatever offence should be pitied. Mr Simpson and Mr Salisbury didn't agree with this.

"All these cases are really slices of life," said Mr Salisbury.

"That's so," said Mr Carpenter.

They all imagined they were demonstrating a common interest with those surrounding them, but their Sunday suits removed them from these people waiting out of curiosity or in search of entertainment just as effectively as did the loneliness of their solitary sufferings.

Curly awaited the opening of the door with no such despair. He had created a confidence independent of facts. This he clung to tenaciously. He paced the kerb with the nervous tension of a racehorse within sound of a baying crowd. He kept away from the group. Every now and then he paused and looked at the door. When it opened he sprang forward and quickly mounted the steps where on the entrance level Edna had bent to pick up her bag. He paused to allow her to enter.

She did not look at him. She raised the baby to her shoulder from where, as she walked through the doorway, it looked back at Curly walking behind them.

The baby had curly hair and brown eyes and looked steadily at the young man with an expression that suggested he had stolen it from this follower, such was the resemblance between them. Curly, looking into those eyes, was suddenly robbed of purpose. For a moment he was incapable of any emotion other than a hunger for this child so obviously his son. This love, kindled in a flash of recognition, grew to immense proportions as he gazed. It quickened his breathing, became almost a pain, then rolled within him, transforming itself into anger and determination. He suddenly felt the victim of a plot to deprive him of his son, a plot in which Edna played no part.

He moved quickly up beside her. "Here!" he said. "Wait a minute!" He spoke in the tone of one taking full responsibility for a situation that demanded resolution. "We're not going on with this; he's mine. Come on."

He kept looking at the baby as he spoke, moved by a sense of fatherhood, a longing to shelter and protect him.

"We'll fix this up all right. Come on over to your lawyer."

He raised his head and for the first time looked at her face. "It's all right," he said gruffly, disturbed by the expression it bore. "Everything will be all right. Don't worry." Her face regained its composure. He took her arm.

The lawyer shuffling papers at a table before the entrance of the magistrate looked up at the couple in front of him.

"Look!" said Curly, not waiting for him to speak. "We've talked it over. She wants to drop the charge. It's my baby. I'm marrying her."

The lawyer looked surprised. He rubbed his chin with a nicotine-stained finger while he mourned the loss of prepared eloquence.

"It's all right," said Curly. "Ask her."

"Is that your intention Miss Green—to drop the charge."

"Yes."

"You are quite satisfied with his offer of marriage?"

"Yes."

"Good," he said. "Sit down over there. I'll tell the magistrate you are dropping the charge, that this man has admitted parentage and that you intend getting married."

Mr Simpson, Mr Johnston, Mr Salisbury and Mr Carpenter had already seated themselves. They awaited their destruction, laced and bound with a last desperate dignity. Case followed case but their expressions remained unaltered.

When, finally, Edna's lawyer announced she had dropped the charge and the magistrate had dismissed the case their relief for a moment deprived them of strength. But it returned as they rose, bringing with it a heightened sense of the day's beauty. The street they faced from the courthouse steps was wide and spacious and comforting in its promise of security. They thought of Edna with kindliness.

She followed Curly down the steps as he strode ahead of her, carrying the baby. There was a flush on her cheeks and shyness in her eyes.

Curly passed the four Sunday-suited men without a glance. But Edna looked at them—proud now.

"Good morning, Edna."

They all greeted her.

"Good morning, Mr Salisbury. Good morning, Mr Johnston. Good morning, Mr Carpenter. Good morning, Mr Simpson," said Edna.

She followed Curly down the street, her head up.

"I'm glad he did the right thing by her," said Mr Carpenter.

"I suppose he did," said Mr Johnson. "You never know with people like that."

"I'm sure it will turn out all right for both of them," said Mr Simpson. "She's a girl you can trust."

"Well, she's on the right track anyway," said Mr Salisbury.

Drift

O. E. MIDDLETON

HONE stopped the truck on the firm black sand and he and Grandpa Tapa got out. Dust from the road had drifted onto the back of the truck, settling on Grandma Tapa's head-scarf and on her old black dress, powdering Rewi's hair and face.

The boy helped the old lady to her feet, picked up the kit and jumped down. Stiffly, she followed him and they all stood looking out at the hazy, sparkling Tasman.

"You all set, Mum?" Grandpa Tapa asked gruffly.

"Yes, all set. Got the gear and the knife and the tobacco. Got my boy to look after me, too . . . eh, Rewi!" She put her free arm around the boy and gave him a hug.

"Take care of her, Rewi. We won't be long."

"OK, Granpa."

Hone and Grandpa Tapa got back into the truck. Hone started the engine, Rewi and Grandma Tapa waved, and soon the truck was a dwindling speck on the endless stretch of beach.

The old lady shook her head as they turned towards the water. "I hope they'll be all right."

"Granpa said not to worry."

"He always says that. The rocks are slippery up there. You have to watch out one of those big waves doesn't sweep you off."

"They'll be OK, Granma."

He would much rather have gone up the coast with Hone and Grandpa. At dead low tide the sea fell back, green and sullen, baring rocks that bristled with mussels. As you tore off the close-packed shells, your eyes kept straying to the heaving, swaying kelp. All at once, someone would shout a warning and there was barely time to scramble clear before the sudden swell swept up. Later, there was the hard climb up the rocks with the heavy kits, the race back against the tide. . . .

The old woman put down the kit. She took out a fishing-line,

baited the hook carefully with a strip of eel, and rigged up the kontiki. When all was ready, she set the little raft adrift and began
paying out the line.

For a long time the boy and the old woman stood at the water's
edge, watching the pale square of sail carry the tiny craft further
and further out. At last the trip worked, letting down the sinker
and bait and Grandma Tapa walked backwards up the line, spread
out the sugar-sack and sat down.

Further down the beach, two parked cars twinkled in the haze.
Fishermen in brightly coloured shirts, shorts, and caps stood in the
sea, casting with long surf-rods. From the cliffs and sand-hills
came the dry, incessant scraping of cicadas.

If I had a fine big surf-rod, I wouldn't be sitting here like
this, Rewi thought.

"Granma, can I take the knife and look for a stick?"

"Yes, take it. Don't be too long though."

He sped up the beach and searched the litter of driftwood along
the spring-tide-line until he found what he wanted.

Among the tangle of bleached sticks and dried kelp lay a clump
of tropical yams, driven by wind and current from some far-off
shore. Not knowing what they were and inwardly curious, he
stirred the strange, shrivelled tubers a moment with his foot.

As he dawdled back he trimmed the straight manuka stake and
sharpened one end. He glanced up and saw that Grandma Tapa
was puffing one of her home-made smokes. Her still, dark shape
seemed to merge into the beach. Only the pale thread above her
head seemed to have life.

Away down the beach, the surf-fishermen leaned out over the
shallows, lunging into deeper water with their long rods.

Rewi fell to paring the hard point once more. He dropped his
eyes and saw a stunted shadow transfixed by a spear, drifting over
the sand at his feet.

The next time he glanced towards her, Grandma Tapa was
standing upright, feet braced as she handled the line. As he
reached her side, it began to hiss through her fingers as the thing
on the other end struggled to break free.

"It's no baby, anyway!" she said with a chuckle.

"Maybe it's a shark?"

She made no answer, but kept a steady strain on the line, hauling
it in or letting it out with the movements of the fish.

After one extra-long run, the surging died down.

"He's gone to the bottom," she said. She drew the old line as
taut as she dared and plucked it sharply several times. Once more
it grew slack, then began to sing through her fingers again.

Rewi looked up and saw that his grandmother's lips were moving. Although the cool sea kept creeping over their bare feet and up their legs, sweat stood out on her cheeks and forehead.

Far down the beach, a lone figure still leaned out over the surf. The crumbling, grey-brown cliffs and high dunes hung in the haze like the coast of Africa. Over everything flowed the ceaseless, dry crackle of the cicadas.

Although the fish was slowly giving ground, Grandma Tapa dared not risk its full weight on the line. Rewi stayed close beside her, moving back from time to time as the tide crept up. As he stared out over the sea, a small ship came in sight. It moved slowly down the coast towards them until he could make out the small figures on its decks.

Grandma Tapa saw it too. She screwed up her eyes and watched it in silence.

"Do you know what that is?" she said at last.

"A coaster, maybe? Or a trawler?"

"It's a Jap boat. A big one too. See, there are no birds following it." She gave a chuckle: "They know better."

"It's very close," Rewi said.

"Yes. *Too* close." She bent her eyes to the line once more.

The big fish went on struggling. Though steadily weakening, it kept making sudden runs that strained the line and cut into the creases in the old woman's fingers.

Every so often, Rewi's eyes strayed to the Japanese fishing boat. With an uneasy, guilty feeling, he gazed after it as it slipped out of sight down the coast.

There was a sudden flurry in the sea eighty yards out and the snout and one curling fluke of a big ray broke the surface.

"It's a sting-ray!" Rewi cried.

"I see him," Grandma Tapa answered quietly.

The tide flowed strongly now. Spray wet their faces and the sun cast soft shadows on the sea.

Grandma Tapa stared up the coast. "Why don't they come now? How are we going to bring him in on our own?"

Rewi gripped the manuka stake. "We'll do it! Try to ease him up where it's shallow." He cocked his head, waiting for the ray to surface again. He felt deaf from the interminable murmur of the surf, the harsh shrilling of the cicadas. The waves broke more and more strongly, making endless patterns of white and green before his eyes, hiding the movements of the tiring ray. The sun stared straight into their faces now like the head-lamp of a great motor-bike.

"I'm going to try to bring him in. Take care, boy. Mind his sting!"

As she hauled in the last of the line, he grasped the spear in both hands and went out to meet the ray. Twice he dashed forward, ready to strike: each time the ray threshed the water and plunged away, narrowly missing him.

At the third try, he stabbed it twice through the body. Waiting his chance, he drove in the spear once more, with all his might and dodging the swinging tail, dragged the ray onto firm sand.

Still holding the spear with one hand, he took the knife from his grandmother, planted a foot on the slippery back, and hacked off the tail. Next he cut off the huge meaty flukes, washed them and dropped them into the sugar-sack.

All at once, a man appeared beside them. He wore a coloured shirt and shorts and a cap with a long peak. He carried a fine, long rod and was panting after his run.

"Oh!" he said, catching sight of what was left of the ray, "I thought you had one of those great big snapper . . ."

"No. Just a sting-ray. Very nice though if you cook it right," Grandma Tapa said simply, with a polite smile.

"You don't mean to say you *eat them!*"

The old lady fell silent, confused by the brash manner of the stranger.

"Yes, *we* eat them," Rewi said coolly. He looked straight at the fisherman. "Would you like the sting?"

"No thanks! You wouldn't catch me touching one of those things. I'd sooner cut my line!"

The boy laughed, but it was no longer the laugh of a boy. It was a sound full of scorn and of a deep, inner exultation.

Quickly grasping the tail beyond where the sting stuck out, he heaved it out into the surf.

"Well, guess I'd better be going. . . ." The man shouldered his rod and turned away. He drifted slowly down the beach towards the solitary car, a vaguely forlorn figure in his coloured clothes.

Grandma Tapa rolled up the line, carefully put away the kontiki and picked up the kit. A murmur that was neither surf nor cicadas came from far up the beach. She put her hand on the boy's arm and they stood still listening.

"It's them!" she said at last, unable to keep back the joy from her face and voice. ". . . And about time too!"

The Swan

MYRA MORRIS

THEY sat by the kidney-shaped pond, the three of them, Vicky, Mrs Bloomfield, and Cousin Ada in her battered wheelchair. Two of the women were elderly, carrying the tell-tale signs of age in their faces and figures—the crêpey eyelids, the blurred chin-lines, the clumsy contours of flesh that emphasized the youth of the girl so that she looked with her bony shoulders and small innocent face less than her twenty-two years.

She sat stiffly on the ground, feeling her hair pale as a primrose, fine as a spider's thread, lifting in the wind, watching the wind take shape in the patch of shivery-grass, leaving dents in its surface as a person leaves dents in a feather-bed. It's lovely here, she thought dreamily, and saw the black-brown waters of the pond freckled with frog spawn and the irises breaking their silvery sheaths at the edge. High above the pampas plumes of the island there hung a trembling cloud of gold.

"The wattle's early," she said in a flat, colourless voice.

"It isn't," retorted Cousin Ada. "It's just that people get into the habit of saying that year after year."

"Well, blowies are," said Mrs Bloomfield triumphantly. "Put one out this morning. Hole in the fly-wire door."

They looked at one another and laughed their gusty, crackling laughter. It was astonishing how easily they laughed, the two old dears—Cousin Ada with her gnarled, arthritic fingers and legs like twisted tea-trees, and Mrs Bloomfield who looked, with her raddled face and bronze-green mossy hair, more like a pantomime Dame than the vicar's widow she professed to be.

But there was something warm and comforting about that laughter. It had reassured Vicky when she had come two years before to make her home with Ada, her father's cousin. She had come because it was the only thing to do, because her stepmother had remarried and gone to Queensland, because she was, with her sketchy convent education, her lack of specialized training, lack of confidence and ambition, unfitted for anything better in the way of a job. No typing, no cleverness with figures, no beauty of face or form to put her on the quick road to success, only the memory of life in a dreary little township with an ailing father who had died almost penniless, and a long, drawn-out friendship with a plain good-natured girl (Mabel, left over from convent days), who had tried in vain to help her.

The easiest way out had lain with Cousin Ada, frightening at first with her get-up of sooty eyebrows and clown-like mouth, and deliberate vulgarities ("If I'm rude it's because I want to be rude, not because I don't know better."), but kindly and not tyrannical like the elderly people in novels who happened to be relatives and employers at one and the same time. And there was, as well as the kindness, those little tributes to her youth that were so gratifying.

"But lovey, you're young," Cousin Ada would say, nuzzling her deformed hands together. "It's divine to be young." "You're young, my dear, you can do it," Mrs Bloomfield would shout, watching her edge the wheelchair over the gutters without making any offers of help.

Every afternoon when it was fine Vicky would push the wheelchair across the tiled veranda, up the cracked asphalt path out into the road, and Mrs Bloomfield, emerging from a cottage lower down, punctually and precisely like a cuckoo from a clock, would join them. It was a pleasant walk to the Public Gardens past sleeping little houses sunken deep in piled-up flower-plots, past leaning backyard fences and the grassy vacant allotment where there were swings and slides, and except in winter time an old-fashioned merry-go-round with wide-nostrilled, painted horses that hung disconsolately, their arching hooves transfixed eternally in air.

The gardens, neglected now by the people of the sprawling country town, were entered through a once imposing gateway that still bore, rain-blurred and tattered, the printed notices from some long-gone local improvement society, but deep inside was an enchanted place of fine tall grasses that were pricked with black-headed soldiers and milkmaids as the sky is pricked with stars, great, shaggy pines that dropped their incense-smelling needles, and narrow flower-beds flung like flounces of chintz along the sides of the pond.

It was the pond that inevitably drew the three women day after day, day after day. Here the fat little ducks dived nimbly under the ribbonweed, and the single black swan drifted soundlessly like

a ghost swan in a dream, a creature of grace and beauty in the
water with its curving breast and ruffled wings, but clumsy and
grotesque on the bank, waddling on its ill-spaced legs like an
ungainly, pregnant woman.

Vicky wooed the swan with a dogged patience, but it resisted
her overtures and always moved away contemptuously from the
scraps of bread she offered, so that she envied the gardener's
friendly association with the bird.

Today the swan, red-eyed and angry, hissed and flapped his
great wings when Silly Sid, the gardener, left his mower and urged
it towards the water. He was a massive-shouldered, middle-aged
man with a strong neck that ran straight up to the crown of his
skull, and a large, flat face that wore, except in those moments
when he smiled a sweet, fumbling smile, a look of vacancy.

Now he tipped his hat further over his forehead and shambled
back to the antiquated hand-mower on the lawn.

"Swan's cross," he said simply, like a mother excusing a spoilt
child. He pointed vaguely to the empty sky. "There's been going-
ons at night now the moon's at the full. Cor blimey, I hear them
passing over the back, wild swans down from the north, squawking
and fighting and trying to get her to go."

Vicky nodded. Often she talked to Silly Sid, who told her in
his slurred, hesitating speech about the swans. Royal birds, he said
they were, kings' birds, both black and white. And it was something to see a swan's reedy nest floating like a bitty island on the
water. And it was something to hear them flying high at night, far
up, honk-honk-honk, flying away to the swamps by the sea for
food. There were some that went and some that stayed comfort-
able-like at home—like her on the water now. She'd never went—
not like the others . . . not yet—

He stood there leaning on the handle of his mower, drawing the
two elderly women as well as Vicky into his rambling talk.

"But it's spring—it's the urge making her restless now. It's the
urge."

"Tom cats," said Mrs Bloomfield cryptically.

"Men," said Cousin Ada with a snort of laughter. It was a
slightly obscene laughter, and it made Vicky blush until her sharp
little nose went pink at the tip. She watched Silly Sid lumbering
off with the mower.

"He's not so silly," she said.

"An old felt hat and sleeves too long would make even a university professor look cuckoo," Aunt Ada said briskly. She pulled the
afghan up over her knees, and adjusted her woollen scarves with a
tinkle of bracelets and brooches that made Vicky remember the

Chinese joy-bells that hung at Cousin Ada's front door. "Let's go! I'm hungry as a maggot."

They went out through the gateway, and Vicky, pushing the chair that ran easily on its rubber-tyred wheels, thinking back to the gardens settling down now into a rising tide of shadow, mauve and umber and purplish black under the great shaggy pines, felt a weariness dragging at her feet. I'm sick of it here, she thought, I've been sick of it for a long, long time. She looked at the back of Cousin Ada's head nodding now as the wheels of the chair wobbled over a stony patch, and was touched by a feeling of guilt. Some day she would leave Cousin Ada. Quite soon, perhaps, she would abandon Cousin Ada and the comforts of the solid white stone house snug behind its screen of crisp pittosporum trees. There was only the matter of making up her mind. There was only the matter of that letter to write, the letter she had almost written a dozen times in the past, secret-haunted week, the letter to Mabel with every word shaped and ready, only waiting to be put down— "Dear Mabel, I hope I'm not too late, but this is to say definitely that I'm taking your advice and coming to the city next week to apply for that job in the warehouse you mentioned. Now that Ellie has got married, I could, as you say, have her room and board with your family for a start. You have always been so kind to me—" Yes, she had always been kind, poor old Mabel with her long sheep's face and common-sense advice that was based on experience, but it was hard not to cringe away from the thought of Mabel's awful background, that grey industrial Melbourne suburb, that airless little back bedroom that she had once for a week shared with Ellie, now happily married—not to cringe away from the thought of a job with strangers who would find her inept, slow, terrified—

"Stop!" boomed Mrs Bloomfield, breaking into her muddled thoughts as they approached the vacant allotment. "Look, the merry-go-round's going."

Sure enough it was, for a man with grease on his face was pushing it strongly, his heels leaving holes in the grass, and a faint, choked, wheezy melody stuttered from somewhere under the roof. There was no one in the scallop-like carriages, no one riding the painted horses which had gone into motion, their bridles hanging uselessly, and the man with the grease on his face leered hopefully at the standing trio.

"Want a ride, ladies, sixpence a ticket."

Vicky stayed unmoving, her arms crossed over her thin immature chest, her skirt flapping about her ankles.

"No," she cried aghast. "No, no thank you!"

"I've never been on a roundabout since I was a child," said Cousin Ada wistfully. "Do you think it could be managed if we got Silly Sid across to give me a bit of a heave?"

"No, no," repeated Vicky, who thought it could be managed quite well if Cousin Ada wanted it sufficiently, since Cousin Ada could hobble round the house comfortably, and used the chair for going out only because it was simpler to be pushed than to walk. But those two grotesques capering around on a roundabout, those two whom she must humour, pander to as if they were children —"No," she cried again, sick with shame, "it's late, and the wind's getting fearfully cold."

"Cold as a fish, dearie," shouted Mrs Bloomfield. "Cold-blooded as a fish you young girls." She waved energetically to the disappointed man. The hurdy-gurdy music came to a stop with one long sobbing sigh, and the three moved on. "I once saw a wagon piled with merry-go-round horses," added Mrs Bloomfield with an enchanted backward look. "Funniest sight in the world! All those faces looking over the sides, grinning. Like a bit of Dante's Inferno made into a comic strip. I laughed till I was sick."

The two women began to laugh gustily, and Vicky, pushing the chair roughly across the gutter, felt a surge of sickening hatred. Those two old fools, she thought. Always laughing. She was tired of the laughter that had in the beginning delighted her. You have to be old to laugh, she thought with a piercing clarity. I am too young.

By the time she had edged Mrs Bloomfield into her garden she knew that she had made her decision. By the time she had opened the front door of Cousin Ada's house and set the joy-bells tinkling in the draught, she knew beyond the shadow of a doubt that she would write the letter that night and post it in the evening mail.

The house had settled down into a cold, breathless silence before she bent to her task. There had been the tea to get—only a snack since Mrs Scobie, the daily woman, always served up a substantial midday dinner—the fires to be seen to, and Cousin Ada to be shuffled off to bed in the front room opposite her own. There was no sound at all but the refrigerator treading a gay little tune on the kitchen tiles, and the pittosporum branches scratching against the windows.

Vicky sat at the little table under her window, her back to the bed that was draped with one of Cousin Ada's endless afghans. There was something oppressive about the chilly room that smelled of lavender and mothballs, and it seemed that time itself had stopped and the clock on the dressing-table, ticking away in a stealthy, hurrying murmur, had nothing at all to do with time.

A straggle of pale, straight hair fell over the girl's forehead as she reached for her Biro pen, and she pushed it back impatiently.

"Dear Mabel," she wrote in her childish script, "I hope I'm not too late, but this is to say that I'm taking your advice at last and coming to the city next week to apply for that job that you—"

Then the pen wandered off the paper and Vicky sat staring into the mysterious moon-washed night beyond the window-glass, thinking of Cousin Ada in her room across the passage with her glass of milk ("And a little something in it, dearie, to keep me warm!"), thinking of Cousin Ada, her kindness, her robust fun, the comfortable house, the games of cribbage, the good books from the library, the easy food on the table, the walks to the gardens—the days that slipped away quietly, peacefully like beads slipping over a string. . . .

I'll have to hurry, she thought, and looked at the ticking clock, her eyes slewed sideways. To get the letter written in time and posted at the corner pillar-box—to put the milk bottles out before she forgot them altogether; perhaps she'd do that first—in case—

With a feeling of escape she tiptoed down to the kitchen and came back clutching the milk bottles in her arms. One, two, three, to put down on the asphalt just inside the gate.

The night was brighter now outside, brighter and at the same time darker, the road marbled with black and silver, the sky like a depthless polar sea strewn with floating icebergs. And something was happening in the sky that had suddenly found a voice. Birds were flying over backwards and forwards and backwards again. There was a crying and a fluting high up, a thin unearthly singing on the wind, and the rush of beating feathers.

Vicky stood breathing fast, her hands at her throat. Sid's birds, she thought. Sid's birds, "wild swans from the north, squawking and fighting and trying to get her to go". Terror touched her. The whole windy, moonlit, jangled night was charged with menace. With her hands over her ears she hurried inside and shut the door of her room. She was safe here, enclosed away from the evil of the dark unknown. With a fierce gesture she swept her unfinished letter to the floor and stamped it under her heels.

The gardens next day were bright with sun. Mrs Bloomfield and Cousin Ada knitted far back in the shade, but Vicky sat at the edge of the pond, staring with glassy eyes. The pond was empty. There was no swan there. But, of course, she told herself half angrily, she had known that it was gone. Gone in the night. . . .

And then she saw it drifting slowly from behind the papery

island-stems, a black swan drifting idly in a dream, and Silly Sid shambling along the edge, clicking a pair of shears in his fat, unshapely hands.

"The swan," said Vicky pointing. "The swan! I thought it had gone in the night."

Silly Sid smiled his sweet, fumbling smile.

"Not her! She'll stay. She takes no count of going-ons! She likes her little place. She's happy captive-like."

Vicky looked at the swan. It rested motionless on the water, head bent over, seeing its reflection above the underworld that wasn't there. The swan, a happy captive caught in its own dim dream. . . .

I am the swan, thought Vicky, and she scrambled to her feet. I'll never write that letter, she thought, not that one or any other.

Pioneers

JOHN MORRISON

He was a farmer in a lonely out-of-the-way stretch of country between—let's say—Dinsdale and Weebah in central Victoria.

I got bogged on an unmade road outside his boundary fence one wretched winter evening. I should have loved every hair of his head from the beginning, because he represented my only chance of getting out that night, or even possibly the next day. It does me little credit, I know, but the truth is that I was angry with him before we came together.

His house wasn't far away. I could see it plainly, with its clustered outbuildings and a few trees, only a few hundred yards away across the darkening paddocks. Once, when several noisy bursts on the engine had only taken me in deeper, I looked over and thought I saw a figure on the veranda. But by the time he did decide to investigate I was well and truly planted, and in no humour to give him the kind of welcome he was entitled to expect. His own manner also didn't improve matters.

Eagerness and satisfaction fairly oozed out of him as he lumbered up and laid his great arms casually along the top wire. He was easy to read: he wanted company. Traditional bush hospitality is based on this need as much as it is on kindness. I understood that, but this fellow was just a little too uninhibited about it. He made no move to duck through the fence to take a proper look at the situation. He didn't even bother to sympathize with me. I was bogged, and I was his for the night. He made me feel less like a rescued mariner than a struggling fly for which the spider has just arrived.

"Too close to dark now, Mister, but we'll have you out of that in two ups in the morning."

He gave me to understand he had a horse that would walk off without even knowing there was a car on the end of the chains.

I hoped he was right. For the rest, there was nothing to do but thank him, express the hope that his wife wouldn't be inconvenienced, and go along.

If a neurotic is a person totally obsessed with self then I suppose he was a neurotic. But at least he was a cheerful one. He must have been closing seventy. There was a tell-tale stiffness in all his movements, but his energy was terrific. In spite of the raw evening he was wearing only a flannel shirt with the sleeves cut out at the shoulders, like a League footballer. He worked his arms like paddles, and had the long reaching stride of a countryman, setting his big boots down as if he were crushing something at every step. He just couldn't get me to the house quick enough. The exertion was making him blow a bit, but it didn't stop him from talking. Everything he said was a complaint, but whenever he turned his great bomb of a head towards me I could see the small eyes twinkling below the flopping brim of his hat. His face was coarse, ruddy, and big-boned. He had a trick of twisting his mouth to one side that called to mind a snarling dog. All in all he went well with the bleak landscape and falling night. His property was flat and almost treeless, limited on one side by a low range of fading hills and on all the others by walls of grey-box forest.

By the time we reached the homestead I felt I had the measure of him, and was wondering how I was going to last the night without quarrelling. Three times in less than ten minutes he'd put me right in my place.

The first time was when I offered him a cigarette, and he told me he'd never smoked in his life.

"I never could see what any man gets out of it. Spare me days, you go and toil your guts out to get some money, you take it into a shop, you buy a bit of dried herbs wrapped up in a tissue, and —you come outside and stick a match to it! It never made sense to me, Mister."

The second time was when, a minute later, I ventured to suggest that the weather might be taking up.

"Taking up?" He strode on for several paces in silence, giving himself time to digest this further evidence of my folly. "It'll take up at the end of the month, not before. The moon come in on its back. If you've been watching the weather as long as I have, Mister, you'll know what that means."

The third time was when, not far from the house, we came to two eagles crucified on the fence-wires. I'd got the whiff of the stinking carcasses as we approached.

"Wedgetails," he announced laconically as he undid a gate. "I got four of 'em last week."

To have spoken my mind would have been provocative, and therefore rude in the circumstances, so I just nodded.

He was too sharp, though, and after closing the gate behind me and going only a couple of steps he suddenly swung his head at me again.

"You wouldn't be one of them naturalist blokes, would you?"

"Naturalist? No, I'm not a naturalist."

"I thought you was a bit quiet about them eagles."

"I don't like to see dead eagles."

"I don't like to see dead lambs!"

"What about dead rabbits? Young rabbits. Eagles . . ."

"The myxo'll look after the rabbits. Tell you what, Mister, you could walk right across this propety and never see a rabbit."

"Since the myxo?"

"Since the myxo. Them C.S.I.R.O. blokes did a good job there."

Yes, I thought, but when the same people tell you to spare the eagles you won't listen to them.

Dignity, however, was satisfied, and I let it ride there. I'd become irritated by his persistent "Mister".

"Anyway," I said, "it's time we got around to names. I'm Bob Johnson."

He came to a dead stop and thrust out his hand. He had the grip of a wrestler. "Bob Johnson, eh? A good plain name, like mine. I'll settle for the Bob if you don't mind. I'm Roy Davison —Roy to you. Anybody round here'll tell you all about me. They say they'd know my hide in a tannery." He pushed his face close to mine. He had the smell of a strong and healthy man. "Mind you, Bob, I'm not offering you much. We live plain, just me and the Missus."

"I've never lived any other way. I'm a stranger, and you're taking me into your home."

"That's it!" He gave my hand a last powerful pump before letting it go. "No man can do more than share what he's got."

He started off again, and a few seconds later we were at the homestead.

I'd been watching it all the way from the road, looking in vain for lights. I hadn't expected electricity, but was a bit chilled now by the faint glow that came from one lonely window. I was, indeed, taken aback by the entire aspect of the place. He left me for a minute or two to "lock up the chooks", so that I had time to take stock.

From a distance it had seemed just an average small farmer's homestead, most of it obscured by a few trees left for shelter. I remember that the first impression it made on me, on close inspection, was of deadness.   It was like looking at a miniature ghost-town setting for a Western film.   In the half-light it was eerie. Just the usual conglomeration of outbuildings and yards grown up over the years in the slapdash tradition of the Australian bush. But too tidy, too clean, too silent.   A dog was barking as we came in, but had stopped at a sharp word from its master.   Now there wasn't a sound.   I'd have welcomed the snuffle of a feeding horse, the squabbling of fowls settling down for the night, or the sight of some vehicle standing in the yard.   There was nothing. I felt myself surrounded by the sad and unmistakable quietness of old age, of exhaustion, of labour completed.   And of decay.   A working homestead should be full of rich odours: fresh milk, cow-dung, dry feed, hempen bags.   Here there was nothing like it. The prevailing smell was one of stagnation, of dust and rust and moulding leather.   The odour of things no longer used creeping out beneath doors no longer opened.

More depressing than any other part of the scene was the house itself.   It was the smallest and most primitive I'd ever come across on an old-established farm.   What kind of woman was it, I wondered, who had never attempted to create a garden?   What kind of man who, even in this dry country, had never enclosed a small piece of ground for her to do so?

It was little more than a skillion-roofed shack.   Double-fronted, with a doorway set fair in the middle, and four naked posts supporting a veranda from which you stepped down only six inches on to the trodden earth.   The kind of shelter a selector would rush up in the first bitter years of struggle.   I knew the plan of it without going inside; the bush is full of them.   Four rooms, the two front ones cut by a tiny passage leading into a living-room.   Perhaps a back veranda with a sheeted wash-house at one end—perhaps.   It was in one of the rear rooms that the lamp was burning.   One window at the far end of an otherwise dreary wall.   It stared straight out at the equally dreary wall of the barn only a few yards away.

He came back.   No doubt he guessed I'd been doing a bit of sizing-up and decided he had better help me get my ideas into order before going inside.

"There's nothing much goes on here these days, Bob.   But I tell you what"—head thrust forward again, eyes narrowed, and the dogmatic voice coming out of the distorted hole in his face—"this used to be one of the best farms in this district."

"Did you select it?"

"Yes, I did.   I suppose I'm what you'd call a pioneer.   I broke it in myself." He put out his hands, palms upwards. Long years of heavy toil had given all the fingers a permanent inwards curve so that I could have laid a pick-handle in them just as they were. "With these two hands. When we come here first all this was grey-box forest. It was just being thrown open."

"And no bulldozers in those days!"

He gave me a pleased slap on the shoulder. "No bulldozers! Axe, monkey-grubber, and trawalla-jack—and fire. Head down and bum up and go for your life from dawn till dark. Young blokes these days don't know what work is. No wonder they've got no guts."

"You're pretty well retired now?"

"You can call it retired. I'll never stop as long as I'm on my feet. All the same I don't do much. Years ago all this was under wheat, with a little dairy herd on the side. I just run a few sheep now to give me something to do."

"No cows?"

"No cows. Just one for the house. I've got a son-in-law only a few miles away. He's a bit of a no-hoper, but he sees we've always got a milker."

"Your family has all gone?"

"Three daughters. All married and gone. There's just me and the Missus left. She never threw me a bull calf."

There was a note of bitterness in this last bit that he seemed to regret as soon as it was out. He was in the act of leading off towards the house, but he pulled up again.

"Not that I'm saying she could help that. She's a bit crook these days. Not wearing as well as I am, if you know what I mean. I'm beginning to have to look after her a bit. Get up and get me own breakfast of a morning, and that kind of thing. Nothing fresh to me—I've had women on me back all me married life." He had begun to walk again as he talked. "Look out for the step, and keep right behind me as we go in."

Four rooms—the two front ones cut by a passage leading into the living-room—

The woman turned out to be commonplace enough, but my first sight of her was not without impact. Lamplight dramatizes things that electricity only illuminates. I was struck first by her smallness; it was in such contrast to her great bear of a husband. Waiting for us to appear in the doorway, she was standing quite motionless on the far side of a table on which an ancient pedestal lamp was burning. Stooped, grey-haired, and with a pinched worried little face, she looked much older than Roy. She was slightly flushed and breathing heavily as if she'd just been exerting herself.

I had no means of knowing how she usually kept herself, but guessed that she had been hurrying to titivate herself up. She was wearing a dress of some dusty hue that could have been either green or blue in that weak light. It seemed to be well-cut and of good material, but sat on her in the crumpled and slovenly way of a garment that has just been dragged out of the bottom drawer. Her freshly brushed, glistening hair explained the faint odour of coconut-oil that hung in the room. An odour that mingled appropriately with the mustiness of a wooden house built too close to the ground and beginning to go in its foundations.

In all this, however, there was nothing particularly surprising. What did disconcert me was the way in which she was looking at her husband. Head lifted, eyes widened, lips set in that tight straight line that betrays clenched teeth, she was staring at him as if he'd just done something altogether outrageous. By bringing me in? I saw it for only a split second. She didn't realize how close I was behind Roy. She knew I'd caught her, because she was thrown into confusion when the introduction came.

Whatever was behind it, Roy showed no reaction. Rather maliciously, I thought, he added to her embarrassment by remarking on her toilet: "Spare me days, Ada, you didn't have to go doing yourself up! We've got a visitor for the night—Mr Johnson. This is my wife, Bob."

She smiled instantly, but it wasn't very successful. The smile of a woman who is not only upset, but is unaccustomed to meeting strangers. It was I who had to go round the table. Her hand was thin and dry, but it took mine firmly and held on.

"We was listening to you," she said in a faltering old woman's voice. "We could tell somebody was in trouble."

I expressed the hope that she wouldn't go to much bother over me. She began to make excuses for the poor fare I'd have to accept, but Roy didn't give her a chance to finish.

"I've told him all about that. Good gracious me, he knows we wasn't expecting him! Tell you what, Bob—it might be plain, but it'll be good. We'll give you the best bit of cold lamb you ever sat down to."

"You'd better make him comfortable first, hadn't you?" Her smile had vanished. "He'll want a wash. . . ."

"Of course he'll want to wash. Come on, Bob. I'll show you where everything is."

I'd been prepared for a bit of polite conversation, but he brushed her off with less consideration than one would give a housekeeper. He'd lighted a hurricane lamp, and as we moved away I could only excuse myself and throw her a glance that I hoped she would find sympathetic.

Roy's great bulk, and the poor illumination shed by the lamp, emphasized the smallness of the place. In the space of a few minutes I was shown passage, living-room, front bedroom, and bathroom; it was like moving about in a partitioned box. I kept thinking of the three girls who had been raised here.

Up to four feet the walls of the bedroom were stained lining-boards, as was the ceiling. The upper part of the walls was papered in one of those pretty-pretty floral designs that went out with antimacassars and button-up boots, and now faded and smoky. On the floor was a worn linoleum, with a fringed drugget mat alongside a brass-knobbed iron bed. There was a wardrobe, a dressing-table, a wicker chair, and a cretonne-covered stool which might have been a cut-down barrel. Nothing matched. Over the bed hung a framed text: "I am the Light of the World". There were two photographs. One, of a family group, was on the wall facing the head of the bed. The other, a bust of a young woman, stood on the dressing-table, with a small polished casket, and an oyster shell in which was an assortment of pins and brooches.

Everything indicated that I'd been given the main bedroom, but when I protested to Roy he brushed me off with that finality which I knew by now to be characteristic.

"You leave me to worry about that, Bob. We're all right. We're only too glad of a bit of company. Did you ever sleep on a featherbed?"

"Never."

He reached out and patted it. "Then let me tell you you're in for a treat. I wouldn't give you five bob for them kapok things. I'll just light this other lamp and then show you the bathroom."

He'd apologized for the modesty of his hospitality, but it was amusingly evident that he didn't really see it that way. He was thoroughly enjoying himself.

"You wouldn't have had much to do with these things either, I'll bet." He was bending over a little tin lamp on the dressing-table, adjusting the flame in the fiddling and exacting way of old people.

"Very little, Roy. They're just an emergency in town."

"No wonder they're all nerves and spectacles down there. You know what, I wouldn't have that electricity on, not if they was to bring it to my very gate."

"There's more to it than just lights."

"And that's the very thing that turned me off it! Years ago I very nearly put in a little generator of me own. I was thinking

of a milking plant. The girls was leaving, and Ada and me was
beginning to find it a bit hard. And d'you know what? The
minute I mentioned it she started on me. First she thought it was
going to be nice having an electric iron. Next it was an electric
jug—it was going to be beaut not having to light a fire of a morning just for a cup of tea. Then it was a toaster. Lights outside,
back and front, so we wouldn't have to creep about with lamps
after it was dark. Nothing big, mind you. Not a word about
stoves or fridges. Just a few little things to make life easier."
Roy picked up the hurricane lamp again, ready to lead off. His
eyes were narrowed to wrinkled little slits. And the lips were
snarling. "You know what—that's what's wrong with the whole
world today. They're making it too easy. People's getting that
way they don't know what to do to fill the time in. Anyway, I
saw the writing on the wall, and I put my foot down. No electricity
—no arguments. I settled for a little petrol engine for the dairy.
That got her out of the milking, anyway. I was able to do it all
on my own. She still moans about it, though—you know what
women are."

Yes, I thought, and I know what men are.

I took a few toilet things out of the small bag I'd brought from
the car, and followed him out again. We had to go through the
living-room, but Ada didn't speak. She just looked round to give
me a shy smile from where she was busy at the stove. The table
was laid, and there was an appetizing smell of hot scones.

It turned out that the bathroom opened off this room. It was
so small that Roy had to go in first, place the lamp on a bracket
evidently there for the purpose, and come out again before I could
go in. There was no pedestal basin and no tap. A bucket of
water stood on the floor, and out of this he filled a tin dish standing in a galvanized-iron bath from which white lacquer was flak-
ing. Everything, however, was scrupulously clean, including a
towel that smelled of moth-balls. I kept thinking: three daughters
were reared in this house—where did they sleep? And where now
are the signs that they ever were here?

Roy returned to the other room while I washed, uncomfortably
bent over the side of the bath. I could hear him and his wife
talking only a few feet away:

"Aren't you going to give him some hot water? There's plenty
of it."

"For goodness sake, Ada, stop fussing. He doesn't want hot
water to take a bit of mud off his hands."

"It would be decent to ask him, anyway. It's a cold night."

"He's young. Stop worrying."

"What time is he leaving in the morning?"

"Soon as we get the car out. He wants to be in Melbourne by noon."

"Will you be able to get it out?"

"It'd better come out once I hook Captain on to it! He'll pull it in two."

"D'you know where Captain is? It'll be dark."

"Spot'll flush him out for me. Where'd you put that linctus?"

"It's still on the back step where you left it this morning."

All this dialogue was carried on on a surly note, in the way of two people who don't really want to talk but have to keep essentials moving.

A sudden silence fell just as I re-entered the room. I found both of them frozen in an attitude of intent listening, facing each other but completely concentrated on something else. You could have heard a pin drop. From far away on the main road—the road I should never have left—there came the faint hum of a truck.

"Sounds like the Carsons," said Ada thoughtfully.

"The Carsons went through an hour ago," declared Roy.

"It might be George Mills coming back. He went in this morning."

"That isn't the Bedford. Sounds more like Andy Ferguson to me."

"The Jensens!" Ada snapped the words triumphantly, and to make it clear that as far as she was concerned the subject was closed, she turned again to the stove, adding in a flat voice: "Shirley was saying they all had to go in some day this week."

Roy became aware of me standing there, and promptly urged me to come through. "You know your room now, Bob. Give yourself a brush-up or whatever you want and then come right in here. We're all ready to sit down."

No secrets in that box of a house. The minute I was gone Roy returned to the subject of the passing truck. Every word came to me clearly.

"Did Shirley say what they was going in for?"

"I couldn't make it out. The line hasn't been too good lately, you know that."

"Who was she talking to?"

"May Rodney. She was telling May not to go over this afternoon because they was all going out. . . ."

"Shirley wouldn't say much anyway if she thought there was somebody listening in."

Eavesdropping over a "party-line", probably the only real con-

tact they had with the outside world. I seemed to have come a
long way from my car.

I was looking at the family photograph on the wall. It fascinated me. Six men, three seated and three standing outside a slab
hut against a background of tall timber. Everything in it dated
and strictly formal: the composition of the picture, the theatrical
attitudes of the subjects, their attire. All dressed up in their
Sunday best: blue suits with short jackets and narrow-cuffed crease-
less trousers, shirts buttoned at the necks, bowler hats. Bushmen
to a man, and tough. I don't think I ever saw a tougher-looking
bunch. Not a hint of a smile among them. Six closed mouths,
six jutting jaws, six pairs of cold eyes staring sternly at the camera.
It was like facing a firing-squad. They were all big men, and all
similarly featured. Brothers. I held the lamp up for a closer
inspection, but couldn't pick Roy.

Straight from this formidable gang I picked up the photograph
on the dressing-table. And this, I thought, is the woman I just
heard say: "You can start cutting the meat."

It was a most successful picture of a very charming girl. She
was wearing a blouse, or frock, of what appeared to be black
velveteen, cut well out on the shoulders—I think "scoop-cut" is
the word—and totally devoid of collar or other adornment. The
angle of view was inspired. I'd like to have seen another photograph of the same girl in profile and looking upwards. Such a
portrait would have emphasized dramatically the lines of a neck
rising with unusual length and grace from the exposed shoulders.
It would, no doubt, have caught an expression of dreamy innocence, of youthful anticipation. But it would have missed something better. As it was she was looking down at you, and turned
just sufficiently to show both eyes. The expression captured was
a delightful blending of surprise and friendliness, as if she'd just
realized you were there and had instantly taken to you. Eyes
widened, brows slightly lifted, lips barely touching in the begin-
nings of a smile. Every feature childishly rounded, like those of a
doll. But there was something in the firm little chin that pointed
straight to Ada. She would be led, but not driven, defeated but
never quite vanquished.

What was it Roy had said? She never threw me a bull calf. . . .

Without realizing I had moved, I found myself looking down
at the bed. Where she had "thrown" the three heifers. Three
times she had lain here in this stuffy room while Roy went out into
the night for doctor or midwife. What must it have been like at
each announcement that it was a daughter? That firing-squad of
brothers glaring down from the wall . . .

I could hear her now, still battling on in the kitchen: "Aren't you going to put a shirt on?"

And his arrogant, low-voiced reply: "You just get the tea ready, Ada. Just get the tea ready. I'll look after my shirt."

She did her best, and it was a good meal, but there was no getting away from him. And little I could do about it. He began to talk about horses as soon as we sat down, and kept on them.

The best bit of cold lamb I've ever tasted, green tomato pickles and chutney, good bread, good butter, hot scones, and—Captain.

"The best horse I ever had, and that's saying something. Know anything about the prices of horses, Bob?"

"Very little, I'm afraid."

"I gave ten pounds for him. Ten pounds at a time when any buggy horse would fetch up to thirty."

"What was the catch?"

"Badly broken, that's all. And in the hands of a bloke that didn't know the first thing about horses." Roy chewed a little faster, then gulped. "I'm in the main street of Weebah one day when I see this fellow holding the horse outside a store. Fair dinkum, standing at its head like a new-chum, and there's a good rail alongside that everybody tied up on. It sort of got me in, because this thing looked as if all it wanted to do was go to sleep on its feet. It wasn't even fidgeting. I was a bit curious, so I went over and chatted the bloke. And he told me it wouldn't stand. And it wouldn't tie up. It was what we call a pull-back. I'd seen them before. You can tie them up all right, but as soon as you go near them again they just lie out on the rope or reins so tight you can't get them loose. No struggling, mind you. They just stretch back as far as their necks'll go and prop like that. One of them things you just come across now and then in horses. Anyway, I finished up buying this one. The bloke had had a gutsful of him. . . ."

There was a lot more before Roy got to the point. He was sitting facing me, with Ada on the end of the table between us. Her eyes were on her plate, her expression one of bleak resignation. But for her I think I would have enjoyed the anecdote. Roy had a good sense of narrative, despite the note of egotism that ran through it all. At least I knew it was true, and he finished up by evoking a scene that was as Australian as it was amusing.

"I fixed him. I fixed him for keeps in less than thirty minutes." He stopped while he cut a few pieces of meat and collected them one by one on his fork. "About half a mile up the creek there's a greasy clay bank with a gum-tree set back just a bit from the edge. Well, I put a good halter on this horse and I walked him out there, and I tied him to that tree with his back to the creek. There was just enough level ground for his four feet. I walked away a few yards, turned round, and come back to him. Sure enough, out he stretches. He's a big lump of a horse, but there was plenty of tree too! Pull?—so help me God, you could have laid a ruler from the tip of his nose right down to his tail. Fore-legs away out in front, hind-legs slanted forward under his guts, and his backside hanging out over the creek. All you could see was the whites of his eyes. You could have strummed a tune on that rope. Well, I had a sharp knife handy, and I let him stop like that till he had every ounce of his weight in. Then—one quick slash . . ."

I was glad of something to chuckle over, but Roy's eyes didn't as much as flicker.

"Bob, may I never move from this table if that horse didn't turn right over three times before he hit the water. He must have thought he'd pulled the tree on top of him. He wasn't even game to come out on my side. He went clear across the creek and didn't stop till he was fetched up by the first fence. By cripes, that cured him! You know what, you could have hitched that horse to a baby's pram after that."

No doubt.

There followed more horse stories. Captain—Cigar—Tug—Ginger—

Good stories. They could have made pleasant entertainment if only he had allowed his wife to come in. It was her life, too, that he was talking about, but there was hardly a mention of her, never a shared smile, never once a comradely appeal for verifica-tion. As far as he was concerned there were just the two of us. She, on her part, made no attempt to intrude. She was evidently conditioned to it. But there was always dignity in her isolation, a subtle scorn in the lowered face. I felt she was drawing strength from me, knowing that I understood and was on her side. I recalled Roy's words: "Axe, monkey-grubber, trawalla-jack, and fire."

And Ada? When *we* first came here—

I got interested in Roy's knife and fork. The one, long-pronged and handled in black bone, might have been a worn-down carving fork. The other was a skinning-knife, the handle neatly bound with string and only a little pointed triangle left of the blade. He must have been using them all his married life. A careful man, who would look after things, the obvious things. I didn't like the thorough way he mopped his plate with a piece of dry bread, pushed it away from him, straightened himself up in his chair, squared his shoulders, and scanned the table for what was next. It was all too possessive and self-satisfied.

For an old woman Ada also ate heartily. A trifle noisily, perhaps, but with a certain fumbling daintiness.

More than once I tried to bring her into the conversation—if conversation it could be called—but each time Roy headed her off. I congratulated her on her scones, and received a melting glance of gratification. But before we could make talk on the subject he shouldered both of us out of the way.

"You know what, Bob—them scones have taken prizes at every show from Weebah to Dinsdale. And where it wasn't her scones it was my cattle. Only a small herd, mind you, but it was a good one. I had a jersey bull . . ."

Once, though well aware that I was taking chances, I seized an opportunity to ask her about the daughters.

"Yes, they're all married and away," she said quietly.

"Grandchildren?" I smiled, searching for a safe line of inquiry. I didn't look at Roy, but knew he was watching her.

"We've got eleven," she replied, "but we don't see much of them." She was going to add something to that, but again Roy took it away from her.

"There's only one of the girls in the district, Bob. The other two went to live in town. I never hear from them." There was no emphasis on the I, but it was significant.

"You did say there was a son-in-law not far away." I spoke quite without design, just to keep things moving. It was all so difficult. Something was lurking between them—

Ada picked up her empty plate and left the table. Roy flicked the cloth in front of him with the backs of his fingers.

"To tell the truth, Bob, he's not much chop. Too fond of bending the elbow, if you know what I mean. There's two things I've got no time for, that's boozers and drones. This fellow's both. Always either in the pub or hanging over a fence stopping another bloke from getting on with his work. I don't know, I can't make him out."

"Everything in moderation," I said cautiously. "I take a drink myself. . . ."

"I never tasted it. Wouldn't know what it was if you was to blindfold me. . . ."

"I know some good men who like a beer!"

"And I know some good men who don't! Beer and race-horses —they've been the curse of this country."

"I say! We haven't done so badly. . . ." It was time to challenge him, but I was startled at the way he took me up.

"We haven't done so badly?" The wrinkles around his narrowed
eyes were quivering. "You fair dinkum? I broke in six hundred
acres of good land—on me own. And I've met blokes that never
swung an axe all their lives. This country—look, Bob, can you
tell me how it is that in a country like this men go about looking
for work?"

"Oh yes. . . ."

"You reckon they want to find it?"

"My word they do!"

He fixed me with an exasperated stare. Ada had sat down again
and was buttering a scone. He seemed at a loss to know where to
begin on the great mountain of my studipity. I was wondering
how far I could go when he made up his mind.

"Hold on, Mister, I'll tell you a story. I get them coming
through here, you know—these blokes looking for the lost axe.
And scared stiff they might find it. Well, I'm out there along the
track one day doing a bit of fencing when one of them slouches
up. I'd had my eye on him all the way in from the road, and I
know the form before he ever opened his mouth.

"Good-day, boss!" he sings out, cheerful as you like. "Any
chance of a job?"

"There's plenty of work," I says, "but no job."

"What d'you mean?" he wants to know.

"I'm not an employer," I tell him. "A farm like this doesn't
run to paid labour. But I'll tell you what—I'll give you a bit of
work for your tucker."

"And his head come up—believe me, you'd think I'd made an
indecent suggestion to him.

"No wages?" he asks.

"No wages," I say.

"Stone the crows, mate," he says, "I'll give *you* a better job
than that. You come along with me and carry me swag and open
the gates, and I'll feed *you*!"

I began to chuckle, but Roy was in deadly earnest.

"You can laugh, Bob, but that's the form, take my word for it.
Mind you, he wasn't boasting. He looked as if he was living off
the fat of the land."

However, the story had taken some of the nip out of the air,
and one way or another he got back to his horses. When Ada
got up to clear the table he also rose. I asked if I might smoke,
and she immediately placed a saucer in front of me.

"We don't have any ash-trays, Mr Johnson." The shy smile that
went with this was a secret little message.

"Never been such a thing in the house," added Roy with mani-
fest pride.

He went out and brought in a bucket of water, from which he
refilled the kettles on the stove. Then, to my astonishment, he
took up a position alongside Ada at the sink and began to dry the
dishes. It was done so casually that it must have been routine.
No doubt one of a number of little things by which he preserved
an image of himself as a thoughtful husband. Not so casual was
his remark on the fact that no water was laid on to the house.
It had been too long in coming, it sounded defensive.

"I bet it isn't often you get into a house where you can't turn
a tap on, Bob?"

"As a matter of fact this is the first." To make sure he got the
point, I added: "And I get around the bush quite a lot."

A movement of the woman's head was arrested just in time. I
think she was going to give me a glance of approval.

"I know, they will have their little taps." An undisguised sneer.
"And they squeal like stuck pigs when a dry spell sets in and their
tanks run out. You know what—I've never once run out of water
all the years we've been here. That right, Ada?"

"Yes, that's right." I couldn't see her face, but she might as
well have added: You damned fool!

I couldn't tell how, but we had begun to communicate with
each other, and Roy was quite unaware of it.

"Carry your water in as you want it, and you'll treat it with
respect, that's what I say. Taps make it too easy. You forget
about the tank outside. But you go out and stand there waiting
for the bucket to fill, and you'll think of it then! It becomes an
instinct to reach out and tap it. I was brought up in the
Mallee. . . ."

He was getting the dishes away as fast as she put them out. Every
article in its appointed place in a cheap open-fronted dresser. Plates
standing edge to edge along the backs of the shelves, cups swinging
from hooks underneath. Knives, forks, spoons—each in its narrow
cell forever laid—he seemed to be counting them. The context in
which I was seeing it made it fiddling and childish. If only Ada
had been allowed to talk—

She never was. When all was done we sat down again. I knew
by the way he checked the trim of the lamp that there was to be
a session. One might have thought he was setting the stage for a
high-stakes card game or a seance. It was, indeed, becoming more
and more unreal as the minutes passed. Not a sound came to us
from outside. There wasn't even a breeze to make the house

creak. I'd have given much for a homely sound such as the purr-
ing of a cat.

Ada brought out some knitting, and I made what was to be my
final effort to draw her into the company.

"For the grandchildren?" I asked her.

"One of Moira's," she replied, looking at me with smiling eyes.
"There's always something wanted, and things are so dear to buy."

"And never as good! There's nothing to beat a hand-knitted
article. I'd say that's for a girl?"

She held it up. "A boy would look funny in it, wouldn't he?"

But at this point Roy decided she'd had a fair go. Leaning over
the table to make sure he got me away from her, he pointed a
thick forefinger at the knitting. "Bob, I'm never done telling her
she's a fool. Night after night she sits there straining her eyes, and
they're all a darn sight better off than we are. They don't even
thank her for it."

"You know as well as I do they're thankful," she said sharply.

"They don't go far out of their way to show it!"

"What d'you want them to do?"

"Come over and see us sometimes, Ada. That's all, just come
over and see us."

She was going to say something else, but changed her mind. She
just lifted her head, gave him a defiant stare, and went back to
her knitting. It looked like a brave effort to keep the family
skeleton in the cupboard, but Roy wouldn't meet her.

He sighed, puffed, shifted the saucer ash-tray out to the middle
of the table then back again, licked his lips—all the bogus fidget-
ings of a patient man driven beyond endurance.

"Look, Bob," he got out at last, "it's a sore point, this matter of
the daughters . . ."

"Let it ride, Roy," I urged. "Every family . . ."

"Every family hasn't! Mine are all women. D'you know what
—two of them girls has never set foot in this house since the day
they left. Moira comes once in a blue moon. She wouldn't come
at all if she didn't have troubles."

"The husband who drinks?"

"It isn't only the drink. His old man left him a good farm, and
he's letting it go down the drain. He doesn't know the first thing
about horses, to begin with."

The temptation to point out that we had moved into the age of
the tractor almost got the better of me, but I controlled myself,
satisfied that the talk was drifting into a safer channel. All his
attention was on me again.

"D'you know what that man did on me once? I'll tell you. I

had a horse here I used to use for breaking-in. A little bay mare with black points. One of the best deals I ever made. Picked her up for next to nothing. Another one of them blokes that couldn't solve his own problems. She'd been badly mouthed, and he couldn't do anything with her. Well, I got her, and I went to work on her, and she turned out a beauty. There wasn't much of her, mind you, but she was as game as Ned Kelly. And she had brains, I used to talk to her. I had her so she'd come to me at a whistle no matter where she was. And she'd hold anything in the brake. One day I had a colt tied on the side, and it reared up and come down with both forefeet inside the shaft. Work that out for a mess! And she got me out of it with only a bit of paint scratched off."

There was a lot more before he got to the heart of the story.

"I wouldn't have taken eighty quid for that mare. And d'you know what happened? That bright son-in-law—he wasn't the son-in-law then—he foundered her on me! Killed her just as surely as if he'd taken an axe and knocked her brains out. He borrowed her to go in to Weebah. I wasn't in the habit of lending my horses—I don't believe in it—but I was having a bit of trouble with the girls at the time," Roy shot a swift glance at Ada, still placidly knitting, "and I let him have it for peace' sake. And d'you know what that half-wit did? He drove that mare full bat for fifteen miles on a stinking hot day, turned her loose in the paddock of a bloke he hardly knew, and went off to the boozer!"

He knew very well that I hadn't yet got the point, and, good story-teller that he was, he waited, giving me time to do a bit of futile guessing and build up for the shock that was to come. His prolonged stare made me uncomfortable.

"He just couldn't get to that pub quick enough. I'm not saying it didn't enter his head that my little mare might be thirsty too. He thought of it all right. But he didn't think far enough. He just decided he'd have a few beers and then come back and give her a drink when she'd cooled down. It never entered his head that my little mare might go looking for a drink herself. Any man with any heart for a horse at all would have gone over that paddock and made sure she couldn't get it, the state she was in. Well, I suppose you can guess the rest. She found water all right. There was a dam down at the far end of that paddock, and she got to it and give herself a gutsful. By the time he got back there was nothing anybody could do for her. And people wonder why I'm crooked on the booze. I loved that mare."

I could have liked him for that were it not for Ada. Still knitting, head bowed, the faintest of smiles on her face. I thought of that son-in-law-to-be coming back to tell Roy what had happened. Or had that grim task fallen to her? And how many other times? With three grown girls on the place there must have been a lot of coming and going of young men. What scenes must have been witnessed here! What bullyings and thwartings and intrigues and diplomacies! Something new was coming into the lined face over the knitting. Not malice, smugness rather. It took me back to the girl in the velvet blouse. Strength in the chin—

"Now then, Bob, do you blame me for being hostile on the booze?"

I nodded, cautiously. I wanted to get him back to horses, and keep him there. "Horses are like children, I suppose. Only they don't grow up. We've always got to do a lot of the thinking for them."

"Unless you get one like that little mare!" He thought for a moment, absorbing my idea. "Yes, I think you've got something there. We've got to keep on watching them, putting things out of their way."

A short silence fell. Then, as he began to speak again, I realized that he hadn't really been following me. He'd been deliberately leading into another apt recollection, digging again into the past. Another little tragedy, another stupid suitor, another daughter, more lost horses.

"Right in the middle of harvest it was. I had to put a man on for a few weeks, and this fellow was . . ." another sidelong glance at Ada, "hanging around. I thought I might as well use him. One morning I sent him out to run the team in. And, mind you, it *was* a team! There wasn't a better one for miles around. Pull? I've seen them go down on their knees like bullocks. All right, out this bloke goes. It's a big paddock, and they wasn't in sight from the house, so I told him to jump on an old grey pony that was in the yard.

"Next thing I know—so help me God—he's got that team coming in at a gallop! At a gallop—heavy draughts! I was in the barn when I heard them, and out I rushed just as they come round the bend in the creek, hell for lick. I suppose he wanted to show off for Agnes. All the girls was up in the cow-yard at the time. I couldn't see him and the pony, they was away back in the dust somewhere. I dropped everything and started to run down to have a piece of him as he come in. But it was nothing to what was coming. D'you know what a Mallee gate is, Bob?"

"Yes, it's a short loose panel, just droppers and wires."

"That's right, you foot 'em into loops on the posts. Well, that's what I had on this paddock. Now the one thing you never do when you open one of these so-called gates is—leave it lying on the ground. If you're going away and want to leave it open— as this bloke did, so he could run the horses through—you carry it right round in a half-circle and stand it along the fence-line. I've seen more stock crippled through getting tangled in a Mallee gate left lying on the ground—anyhow, you know what I'm talking about. . . ."

"He ran the team over it?"

"He put the whole team over it! I had a big wall-eyed chestnut as mob leader, and a bit of a rogue when he was off the bit. There wouldn't have been any trouble at all if they'd been brought in quietly. But you know how it is when you push a mob of horses —something gets into them. And this Red, out he goes in the lead, thumping along like a big rocking-horse. I'm watching him, and I know he's going to break. You get that way you can read horses' minds. I knew what Red was thinking, the way he was slewing off-course and back again and throwing his head about. He was feeling good—to hell with work this morning! Out he lights for the creek again, and the whole mob after him.

"Well, that still didn't break any bones. They wasn't exactly race-horses, and the grey had no trouble turning them. But by the time they're headed for home again they're not lined up for the opening, they're coming down the fence-line."

"And the gate on the ground . . ."

"The gate on the ground. I could see it lying there, but I'm too far off to do anything except give a mad yell. I'm helpless." Roy closed his eyes and shuddered. For the first time he had my full sympathy. "Four wires—all barbed! Fair dinkum, I couldn't bear to look. I shut my eyes. I only opened them again when I heard the first thump, and a scream, and them wires twanging like fiddle-strings. Red's in them, plunging on, and every plunge brings them bloody wires further up his legs. And the rest of the team jostling up in a tight bunch. Two more went down, two others trampled over the top of them, only one cunning old mare managed to sheer off in time." Roy stood up in his excitement. "Bob, you got no idea what it was like. By the time I got over there one of them was up again and running round in circles, blood streaming from it backside to breakfast. The other two just kicked and tore themselves to bits. Four barbs—it was like a butcher's block. First thing I did was sing out for somebody to fetch me a gun. I had to shoot them both, and the other one as soon as I'd had a look at him. I never got a team like it together again."

He sat down again. He was trembling.

"And the young bloke?" I asked.

"Lit out for the scrub. Turned the grey loose in the last paddock and kept going. He knew I had a gun. He left the district, and it was two years before he came back again. I heard he was around, but before I could do anything the constable come out from Weebah and told me he was watching me. Everybody else was too!"

He fell silent. Only the ticking of the clock and the clicking of the knitting needles. It would have helped just then if the needles had stopped. They seemed to be mocking him—a bit of trouble with the girls at the time—I had to put a man on for a few weeks —showing off in front of Agnes. Never threw me a bull calf— everything came back to that, and all three of us sitting there were aware of it.

There was something to be said for Roy this time.

"I suppose you needed the warning, Roy, for your own sake."

He gave me a bitter smile. "Needed it? Yes, I needed it. He didn't stop long. Three weeks, and he was off again. Agnes went with him. Did a moonlight. He'd been writing to her all the time. I knew nothing about it. We've never seen either of them since."

A few difficult minutes followed, but I managed to get him going again, watching the clock, and wondering how long it would be before somebody suggested turning in.

Ada looked as if she was prepared to knit all night. I realized by now that with her also a grievance had eaten in like a cancer. They were fighting over me, had been from the instant I walked in, and for the time being my sympathies had swung a little towards Roy. Ada's sustained silence was becoming suspect. She believed that Roy was digging his own grave with me. The timing of the occasional glances she threw at me was always significant.

Moira—Agnes—what of the other daughter? What did these two talk about when they were alone together and no sound came to them from the road?

Hoping for better luck this time, I asked Roy how many of the horses had recovered, how long it was before they worked again, and how he had treated them. It turned out a good line of inquiry, because he gradually calmed down and became absorbed in something he prided himself on, the healing of sick animals. Every farmer had to be his own vet in those days, but, as in all things, it appeared that Roy excelled. He told me how he had solved not only his own problems, but those of his less capable neighbours also.

"Send for Roy Davison, they say when they're in strife. By

cripes, I've had some queer cases, Bob."

He brought out a set of veterinary surgeon's charts. Beautifully printed in several colours, and with an ingenious arrangement of sliding panels representing the various organs, there was one for each domestic animal. They were worn with handling and obviously very old, but still in usable condition.

"I got them off an old German bloke years ago, he brought them out with him. D'you know what, that man could take a cow to pieces and put her together again, just looking at these cards."

Perhaps he could, too. They showed where everything belonged.

"A fellow sent for me once to come and have a look at a cow with a blind tit. Now that's nothing very unusual, Bob. But this one . . ."

For over an hour I listened to stories of his veterinary exploits. I couldn't always follow them anatomically, but they were fascinating in their revelations of human struggle and resourcefulness. Animals were bread and butter in days when bread and butter were all that a small selector could expect out of life. An incapacitated animal could jeopardize so much. There were unforgettable pictures of anxious families gathered around lame horses, of "staked" sheep-dogs, of Roy riding through the night to a complicated delivery in a cow-paddock.

And never, except once, a sound from the woman. That once was when a click of her tongue silenced Roy and set all three of us listening to the hum of a truck on the road. Apparently this was the only excitement shared by man and woman, the only game they played together. Roy won this time.

"George Mills getting back," he announced solemnly.

Ada gave it a further moment's consideration, then nodded grudgingly and went back to her knitting.

Roy, looking well satisfied, took up again the tale of his sick animals. He was relating his efforts to save a "sanded" colt, and he told the story with all the simple earthiness of a countryman. He had explained to me how a horse in drought country, nuzzling hungrily in the withered stubble, kept taking in sand. And how sometimes the sand failed to evacuate, and kept building up in the bowel.

"Tell you what, Bob, that colt had a lump on his belly like a football." His hands described a circle. "You could move it about, and it was as hard as this board." He thumped the table with his knuckles. "He was down when I got there. Fair dinkum, you wouldn't have given two bob for him. One look at him, and I knew that whatever I did had to be drastic—and quick. Well,

there was two big trees growing just a few yards from where he
was lying, and somehow or other we managed to drag him over to
them. I sang out for some ropes, and we slung that colt from them
trees with his back on the ground and his four legs sticking straight
up in the air. Then I told the woman of the house to go in and
fetch me a rolling-pin. They all wanted to know what for, but I
told them they'd better do just what I said and leave all the thinking to me. So out comes the rolling-pin. Ever heard of anybody
doing this before, Bob?"

"Never!"

"Neither had I—but it worked! Down I got, and I rolled that
lump, that football, just like it was a big chunk of dough. Every
bit of weight I could put into it. It took a long time, mind you,
but once it started to break up I knew I was on the right track.
Grunt? He grunted all right, but there wasn't anything he could
do about it, with his four legs up in the air. I kept it up till the
lump was all gone, broken up and sort of dispersed in his bowels.
Then, while he was still upside down, I give him the biggest
drench I've ever put into any horse, and kept him there till it had
time to work. Then we let him get up. That fetched it!"

All the earthiness of the countryman, and no holds barred. I
don't think Ada minded, though. Another nail in Roy's coffin.
She knew I was watching her and wouldn't miss the disgusted
way she wrinkled her nose and tightened her lips.

"Tell you what, Bob, that colt was working next day. D'you
reckon one of them vets would have thought of that?"

"I doubt it, Roy."

"And even if he'd thought of it, would he have done it? Them
blokes don't like getting their hands dirty, you know."

I let the libel pass, and was instantly sorry, for Roy's next words
took him straight back to the daughters.

"And all I got out of it was a burned haystack."

I could have let that go also, for it was said in the way of a
man capping off a story, not beginning a new one. But before
I could gather my wits it was out: "A what?"

"A burned haystack."

I kept silent, waiting for a clue. Roy's eyes were on his fingers,
nervously drumming the table. Ada was watching him, the peaked
little face full of eagerness. She didn't want him to stop. She'd
forgotten her knitting, and the sudden cessation of the clicking
needles added much to the tenseness of the atmosphere.

"I know that can be a death-blow to a farmer, Roy," I observed.
Somebody had to say something.

"Death-blow?" He drew in a long breath. "Some things is so bad it hurts to talk about them."

"Then don't." I looked at the clock on the mantlepiece, then at each of them in turn. "I don't know what time you good people are in the habit of going to bed. . . ."

"You might as well tell him now you've started," said Ada suddenly. She put down her knitting, lying with the transparency of a child: "To tell the truth, I was beginning to feel a bit sleepy, Mr Johnson. Would you mind if I turned in?"

Roy remained seated as the two of us stood up. I had already gathered from something he'd said that Ada was accustomed to going to bed earlier than he, but there was nothing routine about it tonight. His readiness to keep on talking was as obvious as her determination to give him the opportunity. But the little war between them was maintained to the bitter end. She began to say something to me about being up in the morning to make breakfast, and he instantly roused himself.

"Breakfast, what's special about tomorrow morning? I always get the breakfast, don't I?"

"But there's Mr Johnson. . . ."

"I'll look after Mr Johnston, Ada. . . ."

As for the bone of contention, it was easy for me to take over this time. I did it as gently as possible, and I thought she took it fairly well, but her disappointment came through. Perhaps she'd been looking forward to a short session with me in private while Roy got through some early morning chores.

Her parting smile was loaded with appeal, as was the grasp of her dry old hand. She held on to me.

"It's been nice to have a visitor. It isn't often anybody comes here."

"You've been very kind, Mrs Davison. . . ."

"I hope you get your car out all right in the morning. If ever you're passing this way again . . ."

I promised. I'd made up my mind to send her some little gift, perhaps something to brighten that poor little dressing-table. But the promise was one of those one has to make, regardless of any likelihood of it being kept. I didn't ever expect to see her again. She went out, and all I heard of her afterwards was the scratch of a match as she lighted a lamp.

Nothing could have been more unexpected than Roy's first words when we were left alone.

"You know, Bob, she's not looking too well tonight."

I was astonished, because the remark seemed to have been made with real concern.

"I suppose it's past her usual bedtime," I replied. "She did look tired."

He shook his head. "That wouldn't hurt her." But, rather too casually, he added: "She wouldn't have gone, anyway, if I hadn't mentioned that haystack. It always upsets her."

He pondered, giving me time to throw the ball back to him. Second thoughts seemed to indicate that his anxiety over his wife was merely another device to lead me back to the haystack. It was hard to tell. Odd relationships grow up between two people who live together for a long time. Roy and Ada had probably become as essential to each other, though in a different way, as Darby and Joan.

"Perhaps you shouldn't wake it up," I suggested

"Wake it up?" he scowled. "As far as I'm concerned it never went to sleep. A hundred and fifty tons of hay!—at a time when there wasn't a skerrick of grass in the paddocks. Seven horses to feed, and not a cracker to my name. By jeése, I've gone through it if ever a man did! And d'you know who did that?"

"The fellow who owned the colt?"

"The bloke who owned the colt. And d'you know why he did it?"

I shook my head.

"Because I ran him off the place with a shotgun, as I was entitled to. It was long after I fixed the colt, mind you. To tell the truth, it wasn't his horse, it was his old man's. But he used to ride it, and it was him that come tearing over here one morning, begging me to come and help him. He was a big lump of a bloke, but only seventeen at the time, and I took pity on him. Dropped everything I was doing—you know how it is with a boy and his horse. Well, I saved it for him, like I told you, and the next week-end he rode it over here to thank me. He got asked in to dinner, and that was the beginning of it. He got shook on Rose, that's my youngest daughter."

Roy stopped suddenly, and turned his head towards the door through which Ada had gone. I also thought I'd heard a sound. He hadn't bothered to lower his voice, and must have known as well as I did that she was listening. But all he did was give me a conspiratorial wink and nod—never mind her!—and get on with the tale.

"She was only seventeen, Bob. And I was still sweating it out over Agnes, she'd only been gone a year. What would any father have done?"

"What kind of fellow was he?"

"No good! Irresponsible. His own dad was having trouble

with him. I found out he wasn't as green as he was supposed to be. He'd been away picking-up in the shearing sheds, and he'd learned a bit too much for a boy his age. D'you know what he did one day—but listen, I'll tell you what happened here first. You'll see for yourself what kind of bloke he was. I began by warning him, and I warned Rose. She was as silly as a wheel, too, but a man's got to do what he can to protect his daughters once he's stuck with them. The trouble is I was always kicking against the wind." Another wink, another significant nod at the bedroom door, "It was a battle of wits, believe me. They kept on beating me, no matter how I watched them. I'm not going to go into details, you're old enough to know how it is. One night I caught him. Mind you, I'm not saying they was up to anything real bad, but it was hours after she was supposed to be in her bed. I ran him off the place. I had the gun with me, and I put a charge of shot into the ground behind him as he lit out across the yard. Next night up went my haystack."

"Are you sure it was him?"

"Am I sure it was him—right afterwards he shot himself!"

"Killed himself?"

"Killed himself. Put a bullet through his head. I suppose he hadn't properly realized what he'd done till it was too late. And he'd got scared. He knew I'd be out looking for him. So he beat me to it, very nearly blew his head right off. We found his body days afterwards in one of the back paddocks. You could even see how he'd done it. He's lying alongside the log he'd sat on, and a bit of stick still across the trigger. We'd never have found him if it hadn't been for the smell."

"And Rose?"

"Cleared out. We got a wire from Agnes down town saying she'd turned up there. She stopped with Agnes. Got herself a job and finished up marrying a bloke with the Board of Works. I believe they're living in Geelong now."

I don't think Roy realized what sadness there was in those two words: "I believe". It would have been difficult to tell what his feelings were just then. All the steam had gone out of him. He was sitting with knitted brows, casting back. Moira—Agnes—Rose —and Ada, who wasn't looking so well tonight. It made a cohesive picture, but how he interpreted it I couldn't guess. His face might have been chiselled out of stone.

"You've upset yourself talking about these things, Roy," I said gently. "Why not turn in?"

"I suppose you're right." He stirred himself. "I better go in and see how the wife is."

There were no more stories, and it was left to Ada to round the night off.

At the last minute Roy lit a hurricane lamp and went out, saying he wanted to have a look at a sick sheep. His footfalls had barely died away before I heard a sound behind me and turned to see Ada beckoning me from the barely open bedroom door.

"Mr Johnson—sssh!"

I went over to her, and she instantly reached out and seized my wrist. She was wearing an overcoat over her nightdress and had nothing on her feet. The smell of coconut-oil was strong. Her eyes were bright with anger.

"Mr Johnson, that was a good boy! You hear me—he was a good boy!" She was shaking my wrist in rhythm with what she was saying, dinning it into me.

"Yes, Mrs Davison. . . ."

"And there was nothing wrong going on. I looked after my girls!"

"You don't have to tell me that." I was trying all the time to disengage myself, terrified that Roy would come back and catch us talking.

"They were all glad to get out of the house."

"I understand. . . ."

A gate clashed somewhere across the yard, and I pulled free. She shook a trembling finger at me before closing the door.

"He killed that boy!"

A few minutes later I was lying in the feather-bed, staring over the black iron rail at the firing-squad on the wall. The brothers Davison.

I don't know which of those two people haunts me most, Roy or Ada.

The Crabs

E. M. NOBLET

THIS is the saddest thing I've ever been connected with. It was impossible enough at the time, but now, after more than thirty years, it is so unreal that I've got to take it out of my mind and have a good look at it. It's a haunting thing, and comes back at me whenever I see seaweed scalloped along the shore, or get the taste of sea salt on my tongue or the smell of crustaceans in my nostrils.

It happened in the remotest place you're ever likely to hear about, Cossack, halfway up the nor'-west coast of Western Australia, above the Tropic of Capricorn. Today it's a ghost town, but then it was the port of Roebourne, cattle and sheep town. The coastal vessels couldn't get in there, passengers and cargo came and went by lighter. It was the same all the way along that dreary, desolate coastline.

Sometimes the ships stopped far out at sea and a basket-load of people and cargo was swung overboard to disappear into the night. At other ports, Onslow, Port Hedland, Broome, Derby, the ships waited far out until the tide was right and then came alongside the longest piers you've ever seen and you reached shore via horse trams. Every so often, too often, the piers were swept away by cyclones. But at Cossack you staggered down the gangplank and fell into the bobbing lighter, the *Silver Star* she was, and a most contrary female, given to resting on sandbanks, or plunging headlong into the turtle pen or, when she thought the wool load was too heavy, sinking straight to the bottom of the creek and letting the bales float off. I knew her and her malicious ways almost as well as her own skipper, because she spent most of her time just sitting across the road from my pub, which was practically on the wharf.

In that wretched place, where the silence and the nothingness could drive you crazy, there was the saving grace of constant, though almost imperceptible, movement; constant, almost incredible, change of scene. Sometimes the *Star* sat with her bottom in the mud and sometimes she rode with her mast in the moon. Daily, like a mirage, a bonsai forest of mangroves appeared up out of the creek to clothe the banks and tiny islands, and daily it drowned. All year round until lay-up the clouds harvested heavily on the horizon, shot with incessant sheet lightning and rolls of low thunder.

The little port staggered night and day in the heat, with none of the compensations but all of the pests of the tropics. No refrigeration, no electricity, no good water when the rain-tanks ran dry; but prickly, sweating heat, flies, march-flies, sandflies, and hordes of mosquitoes. In my bar, with its bare board floor, its glassless windows with open-out shutters to let in air or close out dust, with its heavy anchor chains holding it fast against cyclone, we had a big water cooler, the Coolgardie tin and hessian and charcoal safe of the goldmining days, and the bottled beer lay under the counter, heavily rugged in wet blankets. All in the front row, facing the wharf, were the bar, the billiard-room and the drunks' room. We got seasonal visits from the shearers and the Wyndham meat-workers, and weekend descents from the mob working on the new jetty at Port Samson. They were a wild and womanless mob and the police were eight miles off in Roebourne, so we had to operate our own lock-up.

Back left of the bar was a row of walk-in walk-out bedrooms surrounded by a veranda; to the right was a small dance or concert hall; and back of all were my bedroom and the dining-room backed by the kitchen, maids' rooms, showers, and laundry. Up a small rise there was a windmill to fetch the brackish service water, and all around the spinifex sat brooding over us. That was the pub at Cossack. Beyond that, there were merely the general store, run by a Jap, the big hall where the Jap pearlfishers dossed during lay-up, a huddle of tin-roofed crumbling wooden terrace houses where most of the lighter crew hung out, then the wharfinger's cottage on a bit of a cliff with a few high, sprawly-legged beachcombers' shacks below—the Boxer and the Actor lived in one—and there was the fine stone courthouse where the Greeks lived and the long-abandoned turtle soup factory. That was Cossack, and I could tell you many a tale of it.

For women we had my wife, Rhoda; the Irish cook and the Scottish housemaid-waitress, the wharfinger's wife, and the first mate's wife who ran the subsidiary post and telegraph and sang like a prima donna, and we had the second mate's wife, Lissa, who was Norwegian and dying under our eyes.

The lighter went out about once a fortnight to meet a ship, north- or southbound, and from north we might get a supply of tropical fruit and from south we'd get our fresh vegetables. When the Fremantle wharfies were on strike we'd go a long time on tinned stuff, and in drought times our meat would be kangaroo steaks, turtle steaks and whopping big fish from the creek. We weren't a bushwhacker mob, there were still remittance men kicking around, there were adventurous young who scraped up enough to buy a lugger and pearlfished to get a fleet together. Although the pearling industry had long ago centred in Broome, Cossack was where it started, and there were still a few white owners and Jap divers and crews. Top businessmen, bank managers, theatre managers and the like humped their blueys out of the city during the depression; they stayed a while with us, earning their keep and a grubstake as yardmen before they moved on. Young and old, too proud for the dole, came north and got jobs here and there on the everlasting pier building, or fossicked for gold or jackerooed for thirty bob and tucker. We had an old doc who wandered in off the road and stayed with us at the pub. The Boxer was a fine-looking, bright lad who just hadn't been able to get a job after college; and his friend and mentor, the Actor, was just that. Their folks sent them small allowances and they fished and pearlfished and worked on the wharf whenever there was loading.

Rhoda and I had driven out of Perth, out of the youth-destroying depression, and searched every god-blasted little town for work until we fluked it for the managership of this old end-of-the-world pub, the Club.

That was the setting then, for the impossible tragedy that befell Lissa and Lief Jorgenson and Rene and Bill Bolton.

Lief was second mate for the *Silver Star,* and he and Lissa lived at the pub. She lay in her room or sat outside it most of the time. Sometimes she tottered into the bar for a while or sat on a bench outside watching the *Star* come up or go down on the tide. The *Star* brought the Boltons in from the old M.V. *Kangaroo* one day. Bill came ashore in a wheelchair and they booked into the pub, indefinitely, Rene said.

You're friends or enemies right off in the north and no questions asked, and we were friends right off with Rene and Bill. She wheeled him into the showers and into the dining-room and into the bar and up and down the wharf. Knock-off was universal all along the coast, four-thirtyish they all came drifting into the bar, and after what they called tea they all drifted back again. Some evenings the Roebourne mob would drive down to swim in our shark-proof pool beside the wharf, and that usually meant a bit of a dance and sing-song in the little hall. The bar was everyone's living-room, where they could play darts and quoits or poker or wind up the old gramophone.

The old doc took a look at Bill Bolton—people snatch at any hope—but he could only confirm what the doctors south had told Rene, it was inoperable, hopeless, and Bill's time was mighty short. It was the same for Lissa, and they drew together to sit it out. Lief, when he wasn't working on the lighter, was a fisherman. His Nordic eyes were centuries old and stared uncomprehendingly at the world about him. He didn't have a very good grasp of English, so he lived in long silences.

But Rene Bolton could talk. She lashed out at the whole world in her bitterness and anguish. She and Bill had worked and saved hard for a home and a baby and then this evil thing had struck Bill down. The doctor had simply told Rene to give him everything he wanted for the short time left, and all Bill wanted was to get away from everyone who knew him as strong and handsome and brilliant in his law profession. He had great pride and dignity, Bill, he didn't want the pity of his friends, he preferred to sweat it out with a mad mob like us. He picked the isolation of Cossack because he'd been born there, only his folks had taken him away before he could walk. He reckoned where he was born he might as well die.

We were an easy-going mob and we accepted Lissa and Lief and Rene and Bill and what was happening to them in the most casual way possible. Life flowed in and out and up and down like the tidal creek. We didn't see that, along with the disintegration of two bodies, there was also the disintegration of two minds.

You must understand what it was like for Lief and Rene, watching Lissa and Bill suffer and die a little bit more each day. We heard Lissa scream in the night and Bill groan, and we saw old Doc amble into their rooms with his hypodermic, but we weren't Lief and Rene standing helpless watch in the long, long hours, witnesses to unspeakable agony and with only a hell of mourning and loneliness to follow.

The days lengthened and the heat strengthened and it came lay-up. The little pearling fleet came in and now the luggers rode the tide or lay side-on like derelicts in the mud. The Japs shut themselves up in their hall and gambled and drank *sake* and played their gramophone. The black clouds were banked from sea to sky, the incessant lightning was wide and deep, the thunder a constant rumble with sudden earth-shaking bellows. A heat haze shimmered a foot deep all over and it was like living in a steam bath night and day.

One night my Rhoda, restless because she was young and believed there was more to living than this, padded off on her bare feet to the little dance-hall and began to play the old piano. At first she played hard and loud, thumping out her anger and frustration, and we took no notice. But then she became wistful and sentimental, with the sadness of the whole world flowing through her fingers, and we all drifted in to listen.

There was an acetylene lamp stuck on top of the piano, and the light was obscured by the haze of heat and dust. The Boxer began lightly dancing and shadow-sparring a giant wall opponent and the Actor moved in and recited sonorously, dramatically, "The Green Eye of the Little Yellow God" and "Dangerous Dan Mc-Grew", with Rhoda's music-hall accompaniment and the added sound effects of thunder and the spotlight of sheet lightning. And after the applause, the grey-haired postmistress put down her beer and moved into the centre of the hall with a wild trill of notes that Rhoda caught into an operatic aria, and there was this magic, wilderness-wasted soprano filling the hall until it reverberated and chills of exultation ran through us all.

But after the ovation, there was melancholia. We were a futureless, seedy, unkempt, sweat-wet mob, with nowhere to go and nothing to do.

Lief took Lissa's arm in his sombre fashion and she tottered away outside with him. I was struck by their loneliness, these strangers from a far-away snow country, suffering stolidly in our tropic heat, suffering from the language barrier, suffering from Lissa's hopeless fate. Rene wheeled Bill out after them and Rhoda and Doc and I followed. Anyone would mind the bar. There was no faintest hint of a breeze, the clouds were a black awning pressing down on us. We strolled slowly along the wharf, pulling the sweat towels from our belts to mop up and shoo mosquitoes. Yet there was something in the atmosphere up there, unexplainable, indescribable, a waiting, palpitating, promising something that got you in.

We reached the pebbly beach and I took over the wheelchair from Rene and she and Lissa paddled in the squelchy mangrove mud. Then we sat and watched the mangrove crabs come up out of the mud and begin their hideous crawl along the beach. They're good eating, those huge mangrove crabs, but revolting-looking specimens.

"All life came out of the sea," old Doc said.

"Yes," Rene agreed, and after watching a while, she said, "Urk! so that's the sign I was born under!"

"Lief, yes," Lissa said, interested, and Lief nodded—"Yes, Yuly, my sign too—yes"—and he and Rene stared at each other, swallowing the word that nobody ever mentioned. "The process of evolution," old Doc said, "is one of the most fascinating—"

"I wonder," Rene interrupted, "I wonder if some of them won't come back, but are gone off to start the whole process all over again?"

We all stared at the ugly claw-by-claw progress of the crabs, and it began a long absorbing discussion that lifted our melancholy spirits, but we stayed overlong and Lissa couldn't make it back. Lief lifted her and she raised a scrawny arm in anguish. "I never had no sign!" she wailed. "I am so healthy alvays or I don't marry poor Lief, yes."

From the wheelchair Bill snarled, "I never had a sign, either. God knows, I wouldn't have let you in for this, Rene!" It seemed to sweep over him suddenly. "Good God, there was never a man stronger than I, until we were married." . . .

That's when it began to get away from us. We were in a mental and physical torpor or we'd have stopped the thing right there.

We had other serious discussions in the monotonous days that followed.

"Suicide!" Rene told the bar one day, "is a shocking thing."

"Yes, indeed," the Actor dramatized. "It brings a public autopsy on mind and body, a pitiless tipping into the street of the treasure-chest and garbage-can contents of human lives."

Old Doc nodded. "Failure and cowardice are sought, sadness or madness betrayed, and those who are left behind flounder in remorse or scandal and shame." He looked sternly at Rene.

"Bill is much worse," Rhoda whispered to me, "and Rene is queer—hysterical."

"Lissa is worse too," I whispered back, "and Lief hasn't spoken a word in two days."

I went over and tapped the barometer and stared at the wall chart that pin-pointed Cossack as cyclone centre. "We could do with a good blow," I said.

"Yes," old Doc agreed, "the atmosphere is super-charged with electricity. We need the relief of high winds and hard rains."

The Japs in their hall seemed to have only one record and they played it all night and all day, a queer, high-pitched, sing-song oriental tune that got on our nerves.

The postmistress came down to tell us that a storm warning had come through, and I whipped out to check the huge chains that anchored all the bits and pieces of the pub to the ground. Everybody dashed around closing and bolting most of the wooden shutters, and then we sat in the bar, watching the fireworks on the clouds.

The wind came suddenly, with hurricane force. It howled about us and the bar-room shuddered, it lifted, it shifted, and the anchor chains creaked and strained. The ceiling lamps swung madly and the dust gathered into willy-willy coils that ran all over town like crazy great totem poles. We heard the empty water-tanks clamber off their stands and go bowling. We closed the last shutters and the pressure of the atmosphere, the increasing humidity, made us gasp.

When it became unbearable, the rain came.

We opened a shutter and watched it falling in sheets and sucked its sweetness into our lungs. When the first deluge abated we ran out into its steady fall and soaked ourselves through with it, and some of our characters lay flat in its pools, half drowned with delight. The Actor, naked to the waist, suddenly appeared in black bow tie and top hat. He strolled along the wharf with a cane; and the postmistress gurgled, "The Man who Broke the Bank at Monte Carlo", with the rain wetting the notes in her thrown-back throat. The Boxer battled with the rain, hitting with all he had, the cook and housemaid rode around crazily on two-wheelers without tyres and Rhoda played like Paderewski in a puddle. The wharfinger, with native shield and spear, played matador to a goat which butted him into the creek. Then we tin-kettled the town with kerosene tins, frying-pans and the pub dinner gong, and old Doc with bagpipes someone had left in the drunks' room, and the Actor with a one-stringed banjo, and the Boxer with a bugle that he danced with, like Pan.

We saw the *Silver Star* steaming back; Skipper had quick-smart put her out to sea to miss the blow. She steamed straight through the twelve-foot wire enclosing the turtle pen and sat smugly on a sandbank. Skipper went off like a fire-cracker and the crew waded ashore looking like pirates. We went back to the pub. We were a merry, joking band and to hell with the depression. In the bar, Lissa and Rene and Bill seemed to glare at us with hatred, envy. Just waded ashore, Lief was patting Lissa absently, his far-away eyes still gazing out to sea.

The steam came off us and we began to gasp in the increased humidity. That's the curse of the rain in those parts. The Jap record wailed dolorously on.

"Nobody knows the cause!" Rene high-pitched into the night. "All the doctors in the world, and not one knows the cause or the cure of this one thing!"

"No," old Doc agreed, mopping himself desperately. He only wore short shorts, but he was fat and the sweat came out of him like melted butter.

We threw in theories, rough ones, jerked out of our high spirits into their tragedy.

"The crabs!" Rene panted. "With the movement of the crabs!"

"Rene! SHUT UP!" Bill bellowed.

"No I won't, no I won't," she yabbered, and turned her oiled, tortured face on us. "He's alive, you see, and I want to keep him alive. All the time he's alive there's a chance. I'm thinking all the time all the time there must be a cure and it's got to be found now while he's alive. He deserves to be alive. He's good and he's clever and he's done nothing to be young and dead. Except he married me."

"That's a theory that won't hold up, Rene Bolton, so put it out of your stupid head," old Doc rumbled.

"What theory?" my Rhoda asked.

"She has a sense of guilt," old Doc said, wearily mopping. "It's a sort of hysterical state she's got into. She goes and watches the mangrove crabs come up out of the mud and crawl up the beach and she reckons they go off into the mangrove swamp and don't come back because they're starting evolution. She reckons something abominable, something primeval and hideous survives to come down through all the centuries of evolution. She reckons she and Lief are the inheritors, the unwitting hosts, and people like Lissa and Bill are their victims."

"How horrible!" Rhoda shuddered. "But—how fascinating!" We were all for real life drama at Cossack, it was our theatre.

"Anyone's born under any sign," I told Rene, to ease her up. "Me, I'm Taurus, the Bull."

"Me, I'm Capricorn, the Goat," Rhoda giggled.

"Me, Virgo the Virgin," old Doc tittered.

We turned tragedy into comedy, but Rene and Lief didn't relax. The dinner gong clanged, cook had finally got the meal on after the rain dance. Everybody sauntered off. Rene wheeled Bill out, Lissa shuffled off with the sombre Lief. Rhoda, old Doc and I had a warm sherry.

"She said," old Doc told us, "she said, 'What about the married act of love?' She said she has visions of those mindless things that devour their mates during nuptials."

"Could there be anything to it?" I asked, intrigued.

"I dunno," Doc said. "Nobody knows. But her mind's coming unhinged, and Lief—she's pulling the hinges off his. Half the time that poor bugger don't even know what she's gabbing about. Me, I'm unhinged myself."

And that was the night.

Not a night for crawling under the mosquito curtain. Rhoda and I cleaned up the bar a bit. Bedlam broke loose in the Jap hall—there were often fights during lay-up with the all-day, all-night gambling and drinking. Their unholy gramophone record gave a last piercing shriek, it limped awhile and the lute sobbed. Then there was only the sound of the rain.

"Thank God," Rhoda said, and she flung the beer-sour dish-cloth at the huge mirror that backed the bar. It clung to a great bunch of paint-peeled grapes. She giggled, and we went hand-in-hand to sit outside.

The inrushing tide was floating the *Star* off the sandbank, the mangroves were slowly submerging, the luggers slowly righting themselves to float above the drowned forest and suddenly straining their anchors to follow the new creek. It was a bizarre scene, unreal, the heat making it waver, the lightning throwing a ghostly glow over all, and the thunder rumbling, rumbling, gathering itself for another nerve-racking crash.

There was that moment of compensation, of quality, of discovering the incomparable moods in the tide of nature that only the few might witness. We were torpid, dripping with our own sweat and the spray of sweet rain. We didn't realize that soon, when the new, sheltered Port Samson took over, the *Silver Star* would no longer sit outside this old pub, going up and down on the tide, that the old wharf would rot, that the old pub would succumb to cyclone or white ants and be lost beneath the wind-driven sand, along with the Jap store and the Jap hall and the terrace of houses and the shanties that had escaped the road to crouch in the spinifex. The beachcombers' shacks would collapse and go out on the tide to come back, driftwood. The luggers would sail no more and all that would remain of old Cossack, mother of the pearling industry, would be the old stone courthouse and the stone turtle soup factory, both of them grand and mellow buildings.

There was a really dreadful scream. Rhoda clung to me. "Why don't they go away?" she sobbed. "Isn't it bad enough? I can't bear their agony. Why'd they come here, we're all going troppo."

Troppo, they call it, when living on the narrow strip between the sand-blown spinifex and the tidal creeks, hung-over by a mad

moon or scorched by a blazing sun, and the loneliness and the
no-way-out eats into you and sends you crazy.

Then we had a sense of something and we looked round and
there was old Doc sitting by himself in the bar. I went in and he
held up the hypodermic. "I'm out of morphine," he said stupidly.

"I'll run into Roebourne," I said.

"Doc there's away."

"Tomorrow then. They're—well, I suppose they're used to it."

He glared at me and Rhoda gulped. He must have been dedicated once, old Doc. It was pitiful. He'd been important, ambling
in and out to relieve the agony of Lissa and Bill. He wasn't a
doctor any more, never could be again, just for this little while he
had pretended. He was a beaten, useless old man now. We
couldn't help him, so we went off to try to get some sleep.

Some time in the early dawn there was old Doc staring in at me.
I went out onto the veranda because somehow Rhoda had got herself off to sleep. There was the queerest silence all over and the
rain on the tin roofs was a part of it. Old Doc swayed, I had
left him alone in the bar with his wasted life and a thousand
regrets. His shaking hand held out something, a note. His voice
hissed sickly, "There was no morphine, but Lissa and Bill are
sound asleep."

In the dawn light I read the note Rene had left: "Tonight Lief
and I are going to go quietly away and hold hands and walk back
into the sea."

Say to Me Ronald!

HAL PORTER

Good God! thought Perrot, my nose *twitched*. The golf-bag was the biggest he had ever seen. The biggest in the world? Or perhaps it seemed so because it was three o'clock on a Sunday afternoon in 1942, and there was a war on.

In his Adelaide housemaster's study, more oakishly panelled than Sir Jasper's stage library, the golf-bag totemically stood, its effect admonitory. It had, too, the quality of a menhir, albeit composed of a circus-red species of leather, and *fleur-de-lis*'d, gusseted, gored and belted with whitest white. Buckles and nodules of nickel ratified its Maya-like power. From its well protruded uncountable . . . weapons? . . . virile insignia? . . . surely not golf-clubs? . . . of some surely Venusian alloy.

It seemed less to have been lugged upstairs by Wee Soon Wat than to have, like an Aztec archpriest bent on sacrificial mayhem, lugged upstairs Wee Soon Wat. Nevertheless, luggee or lugger, Wee Soon Wat was lotus-immaculate and smooth as sesame-oil.

"My dear Wee!" said Perrot, who felt that he, all over, as well as the nose he felt he had felt twitch, had changed colour. Pinker or paler he could not tell.

"Say to me Ronald, sah," mildly although rebukingly said Wee Soon Wat, seventeen, Sixth Form, Chinese, dressed to kill, and odorous of *Soir de Paris*.

"My dear *Wee*," said Perrot, affecting firmness, feeling older and smaller and unwashed, and—oh, God—changing colour again. "I can't possibly accept this . . . ah . . ." He squinted at the bag as though it were the sort of woman American G.I.s took out, and he his own Seventh Day Adventist Aunt Edith. The bag merely got bigger than Elsa Maxwell. "Wee, I can't *possibly*. It's . . . it's too much."

Wee Soon Wat's face, usually as unmarked as if it were simply portable heredity rather than a private growth capable of illustrating character and emotion, thereupon revealed some sort of character and emotion. It began, moreover, to emit high-pitched sound, courtesan-like, an arpeggio of it. Oriental merriment? It certainly required a fan before it. It ran its course. It petered out. At peace again, its executant seemed purged, and became charming enough to charm a porcupine: "Too *much,* sah! Whai, mai old man are a millionaire, sah!" Upon this Wee Soon Wat's face got rounder than the moon above the autumn bamboos.

"*Is,*" schoolmasterishly said Perrot, schoolmaster, Senior English, Middle School French, *divorcé,* and in love with someone he had no right to be in love with.

"Sah?" said Wee Soon Wat from above the bamboos, most delicately inquiring of the low-born.

"*Is,* Wee. Singular. Is. *Is* a millionaire, Wee."

"Oh, sah, s-u-r-r-e thing *is.* Yiss, *sah*! Singapore millionaire, as you are knowing to date."

Wee glimmered with gladness that Perrot understood. His smile was mother-of-pearl itself. Then, less glimmeringly, for life was really serious, and he insisted on being permitted to live on his own kindness to himself, "Pliss, say to me *Ronald,* sah."

Say?

Say!

Perrot recognized "speechless" as his adjective but, "Ah— Ronald—ah—*Wee,*" he said in a voice nearly resembling his own. "I am—ah—I am grateful for your kind thought. But *not* necessary. Those few extra lessons in English were . . . I thought you —ah—*quite* understood that I was happy to give them. There was no thought of . . ." Payment? Reward? *Pourboire*? Rake-off? No word fitted the overwhelming receptacle and its protrusions. "No thought at all, Wee . . . *Ron-ald* . . . ab-so-lute-ly none."

Slitting his eyes like an adolescent Fu Manchu at the golf-bag, and also in the manner of one who examines another's point of view to disregard it, "To date you are thinking, sah," said Wee Soon Wat, "she are definitely beauteous?"

"*It* and *is,* Wee. I think *it is,*" said Perrot, governess-like. Then stopped dead. What the governess was saying was indubitably not what Perrot wanted said.

"Theah are Scotch within her and Great British cigarettes," said Wee Soon Wat stroking the nickel-barnacled white-and-crimson pockets, his manicured nails and delicate fingers aquiver on their pregnancies, an inward smile suggesting one about to feast on human frailty. "To date theah are this whiskeh and Playah's Please Cigarettes, sah. Oh, gratitude, sah!"

"There *is* . . ." began Perrot.

"No!" cried Perrot. "The plural, Wee. There *are*. Yes, yes."

He resisted tearing hairs or beating breasts. He forbore to wail. Using every effort he manipulated the wires of his nature to simulate forcefulness.

"Wee, I *cannot* accept it. You must take it back to wherever— to whoever—to *whomever*—to the shop—to the man—to . . ."

He ceased, apparently made mad and dumb.

The Oriental moon rose fuller and *blander* above . . . well, the bamboo, the ricefields, the Forbidden City.

"It is impossible, im*poss*ible" suddenly squeaked and gibbered Perrot, dragonfly bamboozled in bamboo, peasant yak-like in rice- fields, witless leper at the city gates. "It is *utterly* impossible, Wee."

"Say to me Ronald, mai *deah* sah," said Wee Soon Wat in his angel-white sharkskin coat, one of his Singapore twenty. It was still only a little after three o'clock, Sunday, 1942, and a war decidedly on.

Perrot knew about the war because the School Matron and the Housekeeper had got crisper and leaner than *grissini,* and wore ration-card-sniping scissors on chains in the manner of 1912 shop- girls. The gymnasium was sandbagged. Lavatory paper was thinner; underwear got more raggedy. Charcoal burners appeared on cars, and tan shoes on boys. All jam had become raspberry. In short, eccentricity was the mode: in becoming more unreal life had become more lifelike.

Of course, vestiges of peace-time past recurred or persisted as no more eccentric than usual: summer, winter, morning hymns, exam- inations. The Headmaster, ever Zeus-like behind rimless spec- tacles blinding with reflected light, remained correct-weight Olym- pian without wane. The leather-aproned school-carpenter, the tuckshop Scotswoman, the nag that pulled the groundsman's roller, the cook floury as a cook, all remained, except for time's imper- ceivably stealthy subtractions and additions, the same.

Elsewhere in the school, the needs and lures of war also effected subtractions and additions, but outrageously, quite without stealth, and in the comic tradition. Maids who had moused about mutch- less, yet with the air of wearing mutches, were now elsewhere, pert and jimp as soubrettes, in one or other war-time uniform. They were constantly being replaced and re-placed by a rout of mock maids with bigger or springier busts, fingernails like dowager Manchu empresses', more make-up, more crystal necklaces, tinier eyes, hairier legs and voices like tawny frogmouths'.

On the same conveyer-belt, stop-gap schoolmasters incredible as creatures from Dostoevsky also moved into and out of view, the

probability of their having habits or hobbies that could shock
trailing them like a reek of burnt stew. The school got noisier
than a zoo. Above all this, that and the other, searchlights slid
about at night finding clouds, no Japanese war-planes and not
even a Zeppelin. However, there were compensating fascinations.

War had side-channelled a number of foreign schoolboys into
the school. Not only were they foreign in tint, profile and accent:
glamour flickered about them like St Elmo's Fire from the fact
that they had been considered sacred enough or costly enough to
be packed up like *objets d'art,* and whisked away from danger.
They were less, it seemed, to be educated than put in storage until
the war whimpered out.

Most fascinating of the many was a selection of princelings:
Batavian, Malayan, Siamese, Balinese—it was impossible to work
out which was which. They gazed with deerlike animal intensity,
as though fevered with sad love, from the bodies of classes. These
gazers were young, yet seemed as ancient as highly-finished statuary
of a remote era in which delicacy was the keynote: their wrists, too
fine for the coarse activities of schoolboys, suggested poetry and
immorality of a jaded kind.

Of the exotics Wee was the most eye-catching. More than his
wealth his own nature made him conspicuous, unless it was that
wealth made him flashier, kinder, more imaginative, fantastically
overflowing with an excess of *noblesse oblige,* and unsittable-on.
Perrot was victim of this florid misconception of the shape of gratitude. Perrot led usually a nicely edited life; his mind usually had
all its lights blazing. Wee Soon Wat and the golf-bag, however,
had caused a dimming and flickering: a fuse could soon be blown.

Perrot cleared his throat as does a character in a short story.

"Wee," he implored brutally, "take the . . . take the bag away,
please."

For the first time an expression approaching human stirred the
Chinese moon, and yet it was no more than a look of butterfly
distress, misty and unattached.

"Oh, sir!" cried Wee, fervently cracking the finger-joints of each
hand with the other. "You have falsed me! To date you are
telling me she are definitely beauteous. And now, 'Take away,
pliss!' Oh, horror! Oh, badly! What shall poor Ronald Wee
believing?"

There was a quarter-second of tragic gloom. Then, victim of
a thought of more splendour, Wee Soon Wat became incandescent
in worldly and enlightened fashion. After all, his father was rich
enough to buy the school, and convert it into a coolie-ridden

College-Tudor godown packed with cloud-ear fungus and tinned water-chestnuts.

"Ah *ha,* sah!" he continued. "You are thinking to date she are definitely beauteous. You have said. But you are thinking she are bad form. Horror and alas! How Ai see! The Awstralian fellohs will be jealousy. Mai sisters have said bad form. How raight Ai see! Su-r-r-re thing: bad form! Ai must thinking. Ai think. To date Ai am thinking raptly."

A Buddha, he put on thought. He cracked anew his finger-joints.

"A golden wrist-watch!" he cried.

"No, Wee—*no.* Nothing."

Perrot might not have spoken.

"A watch *not* for the wrist? A chain-watch of Swissland. But *golden.*"

"No, Wee—no."

"A desk for wraiting? A desk of fashion."

"No, Wee."

"Armchairs with lamps?"

"No."

"Silken shirts!"

Perrot considered screaming. Perrot did not even sigh. He gazed at his pupil as into a crystal turbulent with some lamentable destiny.

A year-long hour later, he heard himself promise to allow himself (in lieu of accepting wireless-sets, crocodile-skin suitcases, concertinas, an aquarium of goldfish, and a variety of pets) to be entertained by his adamantly grateful pupil, in a fortnight's time, at the flat of the Misses Wee.

At the School Swimming Carnival, Perrot had already glimpsed Wee's two sisters. They had been revealingly enclosed in gowns of un-Australian materials and colours. These shape-gripping *cheong sams* had slendered them to elegance. The skirts, ankle-length, but slit to above the knee on each side, had tempered the old-ivory bandiness of their naked high-heeled legs. Their coiffures had been liquorice moulded into convolutions no hand or wind would dare or could playfully budge. On each black miracle a fragile artificial flower had quivered like something recording a delicious feminine undercurrent.

Distinguished and apart as angel-fish, they had each luminously occupied like enchanted growths the luminous and scented area under their sunshades. The Indian-ink-black of their brush-stroke eyebrows, and the lacquer-red of their lipsticks, had caused mothers and aunts, even Botticellian schoolgirls, to feel barbaric and pimpled, to pant like dogs, and wish they had pumiced their legs. Sophisticated agelessness varnished the Misses Wee.

Their apparent fragility had been exported from Singapore to employ safety from war in acquiring a domestic and social extra at an Edwardianly ladylike finishing school. They lived in a flat in one of St Peter's kurrajong-lined streets towards which, a fortnight later, a taxi-cab—no, no, not a taxi-cab, a vice-regal hire-car without a charcoal-burner—conveyed Perrot and his host.

It was, in the saner world, 106 in the shade, even at four in the afternoon. Wee had not a pore, follicle or gesture betraying consciousness of heat: he was so buffed, so blindingly coated and crisply trousered that Perrot, praying to sweat inconspicuously, felt cumbered and furry as an Eskimo. As the hire-car stopped, Wee leapt from it with the grace and elasticity of Lifar, then, in the manner of one tending a lunatic invalid, his curved hand an inch from Perrot's elbow, almost assisted him from the car. Next, he paid off and over-tipped the driver with a note conceivably minted that noon.

Perrot, stroking hopefully over his hair which felt like Struwwelpeter's with a hand that felt like Struwwelpeter's, was encouraged with dove-like murmurs and infinite tenderness through the gate and along the smooth path as over the skulls and rocks of the Valley of the Shadow of Death.

At the door the brother rang, masculinely, as one expressing unequivocally: Sisters, I am without! *Women,* open!

Soundlessness ensued.

There was no brazen gong, no struck zither, no scuttle, slither, squeak, murmur or breath.

No pin was dropped to be heard.

Silence and time continued.

Then, suddenly, swiftly, silently, the door retreated and "Good af-ter-noon, Mis-ter Pel-lot," melodiously and pentatonically in duet chanted the Misses Wee, gorgeous as concubines and, in duet, extended lily hands cold as goldfish although the hallway was hotter than outside, infernal, marbled with almost visible blastings of incense, of the Misses Wee's disparate scents, of garlic, gas, and some more disturbing smell like charred mice.

The living-room was small, but the Wees and money had taken every advantage of the spaces left between the landlord's unpleasant furniture. All overhead lights blazed, and four standard-lamps and two large tablelamps suckling current through perilous lianas of flex. Each lamp was of a different design, boudoir jostling military club; each lamp endlessly repeated its image in a mound of many-coloured witch-balls on a fumed-oak refectory table. Vases, containing jammed-in bundles of artificial and tinselled flowers, prevented every flat surface from practical misuse. Fuming incense-burners abounded.

A cocktail-cabinet, so new that a price-ticket string still hung from a knob, displayed its cut-glass vessels and Saturnalian burden of bottles in a white-hot dazzle. Competently, as though he had often rehearsed this important move, Wee approached the shrine, took up station, shot his cuffs, and the formalities began.

"Would you caring, sah, for whisky-sodah, sah?" said Wee, prepared for no nonsense, and stripping the foil from a bottle-top with the decision of a head-surgeon. The Misses Wee flanked him in attitudes of willowy effacement, as though in a cool iris-garden, but with the air of inwardly abiding a moment, every wire tuned, to be played like musical instruments.

"Thank you, Wee," said Perrot thinly as a beggar, blinded with blaze, dizzy with heat and odours and the obligations of ritual.

With the social aplomb of an undertaker, and in blood-curdling quantity, Wee poured two whisky-sodas. The moment the second crystal goblet was abrim the Misses Wee abandoned the iris-pool, and flexuously undulated to their appointed duties. Beneath their brother's unwatchingly watchful eye, one placed the drink on a silver tray, one indicated a great hairy armchair, and piped sweetly, "Pliss to sit with-in arm-chair, Mis-ter Pel-lot."

As Perrot sank sleep-walkerishly into this hot enclosure she disposed several hotter chenille cushions about and behind him, packing him in like a T'ang statuette, while the other sister presented the drink.

Perrot observed that Wee now held *his* whisky in a position that could only be pre-salutation. First, however: "Sit!" said Wee Soon Wat with some sternness.

Perrot started as much as he was able. The order was not at him. Sinuously the handmaidens sat, one on each arm of another shaggy chair. They were like things dreamed. Their postures were divine. The stage was set. All eyes slid Wee-wards. Wee elevated his goblet a gentlemanly fraction.

"Cheer-*ho*!" he said. "Cheer-*ho, mai deah sah!*"

"Cheers, Wee," said Perrot meekly, commending his sanity and sobriety to any gods.

"Say to me Ronald, kaindly, sah, in mai own abode," said Wee Soon Wat, tossing off his giant whisky as though he were a dipso-maniac collier. This done, he shot an invisible message to his sisters. Their eyes became still. They smiled like leading ladies. They spoke.

"Hah-oo kaind you have said to Lon-ald," said the Miss Wee

in gold and red, perhaps the elder. She had more and larger teeth.

"Lon-ald is glate-ful," recited the Miss Wee in silver and green who had the less bowed legs, and smaller but brighter eyes.

"Lon-ald is sad and tlag-ic because goffing-bags are bad form."

"We have said Lon-ald that goffing-bags are bad form."

"Lon-ald admires Mis-ter Pel-lot and not admires bad form."

"Goffing-bags are bad form," intoned the Misses Wee together.

Then, "Bad form," they again said together as though delicately saying "Incest".

Upon that, abruptly, the record ran down.

"Pliss, sah," took up Wee Soon Wat, moderately sternly, hand on bottle. "Pliss, sah, to drink. To date theah are plenty more wheah that are coming from."

As under hypnosis Perrot drank to the ruinous dregs with a sense of Gorki-ing through *Lower Depths*. The goblet empty, the Misses Wee unfolded like exquisite serpents. Gold-and-red, agitating a fan, disarranged the heated air uselessly through Perrot's mop while packing the cushions tighter; Silver-and-green brought on her silver tray Perrot's refilled goblet.

The Misses Wee then replaced themselves as before, each holding this time in fingers curved like chrysanthemum petals a claret glass enriched to the brim with liqueur. Miss Gold-and-red held *Cherry Heering*, Miss Silver-and-green *creme de menthe*.

"Cheer-*ho*, mai deah sah," said Wee Soon Wat heartily. "And sisters," he added with some distaste.

"Cheer-*ho*, Mis-ter Pel-lot and Lon-ald," said the Misses Wee in duet.

"Cheers—cheer-*ho*!" said Perrot.

Perrot was never sure at which moment, at which drink, the ship, as it were, left the firm shores of formality, but certainly some solid safety was sometime wantonly abandoned: there was a feeling of mural dipping and ducking, of undulations and fireworks, the floor became perverse, noise took on extra intonations and ran about like bediamonded cats.

It was at this stage, early in the storm, that Wee cried out, quite loudly and un-Orientally, "Food! Melting Moments! Fastly!"

The Misses Wee, also crying out but in flutelike voices, "Melt-ing Mom-ents, Melt-ing Mom-ents!" arose like flames, and disappeared apparently into the banks of tinselled flowers.

"Mai sisters have cooking Melting Moments," said Wee.

Melting Moments? Ah, Melting Moments! Perrot remembered these delicacies of his boyhood Sunday suppers: half-spheres of crunchy, pale, sweet biscuit clamped together with icing. They scarcely went with Scotch, but the notion of any sort of food now had its interest. He proposed devouring many of these saccharine spheres which the Misses Wee, chirruping like many birds of paradise behind the lamps or flowers or cocktail-cabinet, were doubtless arranging—for he heard plate-like clinkings—on Ming.

Wee poured another drink. Perrot made a pointless gesture of refusal. Wee, who was turning *eau-de-nil,* scorned the gesture. Perrot accepted the drink just as the Misses Wee re-formed, elated with accomplishment and liqueurs, in the spinning and coruscating prison. "Melting Moments," they cried. "We learn to cooking Melting Moments."

"I," gushed Perrot before he could stop himself, before he saw what they tendered on non-Ming plates, "I love Melting Moments!" Then, sustaining a smile for each Miss Wee, and removing an object from each Miss Wee's plate—how could he dare favour one above the other?—Perrot ate each object in a simulation of relish.

The Misses Wee's Melting Moments were flat, greyish circles gummed together by a pale ooze, and flaccid as Dali watches. That smell of charred mice! The sugar (or was it ground glass?) infesting their plasticine-like texture tasted of garlic—oh, a mere connoisseur's whiff!

The misses Wee closely watched him eat six. Then, once again arranged on their armchair, holding their gown-matching liqueurs in the petal fingers that had constructed and conveyed to him the Satanic sweetmeats, they continued to watch him as though he were an accident.

Where, meantime, was Wee?

"Where," said Perrot, "is Wee Soon Wat?" It suddenly seemed important to know.

The Misses Wee instantly removed their gaze from Perrot as from obscenity, and began to giggle, and continued giggling. Their manner suggested that an impenetrable wall of humour separated ladies from fact. They began to talk with melodious speed at each other in a language Perrot presumed to be Chinese. Miss Silver-and-green downed her *creme de menthe* like an amateur actress playing Anna Christie, and lit a cigarette in an involved way.

The Misses Wee's legs were now being carelessly revealed. As they wildly chattered, vouchsafing nothing, they shot many hyphenated glances at Perrot. He had the impression of such a number of these jet glances *dit-dit-dit-dit* from each that, between the two of them and their four assessing eyes, one solid scrutiny was composed. This and the Chinese hullabaloo were becoming disconcerting, and he blushed. He took vulgar steps: he removed two

of the cushions and dropped them callously on the floor; he
flicked ash on the science-fiction Melting Moments; he smiled
like a fox, and spoke again, more loudly than he intended.

"Where is Wee? Where?"

The schoolmasterliness momentarily terrified the Misses Wee to
silence and paralysis. Their eyes raced about like crickets but
could not resist, finally, all four of them, moving in one direction
towards a door which Perrot now perceived for the first time.

It was a door terribly closed.

It was a bathroom door.

From behind it came the rooster-like sounds of Wee making
efforts to avoid being heard being sick. Having faltered in their
sisterly camouflage of chatter and false joy the Misses Wee returned
their eyes to nowhere, and began more vivaciously and noisily their
exchange of . . . of what?

Perrot, in an embarrassment, lowered his lips to his drink.
Meeting people unlike oneself does not widen one's vision; it con-
firms one's notion that one is unique.

He understood now the clamorous smoke-screen of the sisters,
but could not fully applaud it for he was certain that they were not
discussing the weather or hair-ornaments. No, Perrot thought, they
are discussing me, Perrot. Is my hair too mad? Have I Melting
Moments surrounding my mouth like a screamingly funny leprosy?
Is my fly undone? He could do nothing but drink again. The
bathroom door shot open.

"Bad form! Bad form!" cried Wee Soon Wat, paler than the
heart of a lettuce but immaculate and unchastened. His sisters
stopped as though their throats had been cut. "Bad form to talking Chainese for mai deah sah. Pliss, sah, to drink. To date
theah are plenty more wheah that are coming from."

And once more, like a record one hoped would not be played
again, the formalities began. Wee poured. Miss Silver-and-green
circumspectly took up her tray. Miss Gold-and-red plugged
cushions about her victim.

Their duties done, the Misses Wee replaced themselves like
mobile waxworks.

"Cheer-*ho*, mai deah sah," said Wee restraining a shudder to
drink without a shudder.

"Hah-oo kaind you have said to Lon-ald," intoned a Miss Wee,
her eyes still as bullet-holes through which blew a glacial wind.

"Lon-ald admires Mis-ter Pel-lot and not admires bad form,"
said the other, without conviction, and smiling by numbers.

"Lon-ald is sad and tlag-ic because goffing-bags are bad form."

God!

Perrot made an effort. He called up his most dazzling party manners in an attempt to halt the cultured-pearl remarks.

"Too kind, too kind," he said like the dying Florence Nightingale. "You are all *very* kind. I cannot tell you how heartwarming to meet and to . . ."

What *am* I saying? he thought. And what the hell shall I say next? His audience impassively confronted him.

"Wee, do ask your charming sisters what they were saying before in Chinese. It really sounded fascinating," he said.

God is listening to you, you bloody liar, he thought.

"Tell! Tell Mr Perrot!" said Wee, whose face was becoming dewy, in the voice of one about to enter a tunnel.

The Misses Wee imperceptibly stiffened. Their faces stopped at ivory; one could tell that, although their eyes were discreetly directed away from each other's and on some dot in outer space, they were really staring at each other in dismay. Their souls blinked; their spirits winced; their hearts said, "Barbarians!"

Wee, too, stiffened; the dew on his forehead increased and shone in gems above his pistachio-green face. He was visibly wrestling with some inner demon.

"Tell, pliss," he said in a voice attempting severity but in the tones of one already somewhere else.

"Not to worry, oh, not to worry, Wee," said Perrot. The Misses Wee had, however, dutifully begun to translate themselves.

"We say," said Miss Silver-and-green, "that we not understanding Mis-ter Pel-lot, pliss."

"We say," continued Miss Gold-and-red, "we say are Mis-ter Pel-lot laike all Aws-tlalian boy? Are Mis-ter Pel-lot?"

They both stared fixedly and callously at Perrot.

"Yiss, yiss," said Miss Silver-and-green, suddenly very animated, but in a deadly way. "Are Mis-ter Pel-lot laike all Aws-tlalian boy? *Are* Mis-ter Pel-lot?

There seemed nothing to do but try answering.

"Well," said Perrot, "well, Miss Wee and . . . and Miss Wee, I think I may say I'm typical. That is typical enough. Well, *fairly* typical."

The Misses Wee looked at him as if he were a flower arrangement they would like to tinker with. They uttered not a word.

"Tell, tell, tell!" cried Wee, quite strongly. He was less pallid, the will having successfully wrestled the flesh. "Tell! You cannot clap with one hand."

"We say we thinking Aws-tlalian boy . . ." and here Miss Silver-and-green made an insulting shrug of great beauty, and an exquisite denigratory hand movement.

Miss Gold-and-red imitated these sending-up movements to perfection.

Then both averted their eyes from Perrot in a commenting way and, in the next instant, began to giggle. Their giggles multiplied. They clutched each other. They writhed divinely in each other's slender arms.

"Bad form! To date most bad form!" shouted Wee, restored to full voice. "Tell and tell! Fastly tell!"

Entwined and sinuous as salamanders, the Misses Wee gave broken and hysterically bubbling speech:

"Aws-tlalian boy . . ."

"Aws-tlalian boy not . . ."

"Not . . ."

"Mis-ter Pel-lot not . . ."

"Mis-ter Pel-lot . . ."

"Not . . ."

"Not hot stuff!"

"Singapore boy," sang the Misses Wee, "oh, Singapore boy hot stuff, hot stuff!"

They screeched, supporting each other on memory's ecstatic behalf.

From whatever plane of banishment he occupied Perrot heard the voice of his host, as suave as though the party were just about to begin and there were no shame in the world.

"Would you caring, sah," said the voice of one expecting no denial, "for whiskeh-sodah, sah?"

"Oh no, Wee," said Perrot, attempting to stir, to rise. "Oh, please, *no.*"

Wee Soon Wat was already pouring.

"Not to worrying to date, sah," he said. "Theah are plenty more wheah that are coming from."

As Miss Silver-and-green unwound herself from her sister to carry the silver tray, and Miss Gold-and-red prodded the cushions to embed Perrot more hotly and firmly, "No, Wee, no. No, Wee, no," he said.

"Say to me Ronald, mai deah sah," said Wee Soon Wat, and went on pouring.

Possums

KATHARINE SUSANNAH PRICHARD

Gil stood in his tracks. The country road sprawled before him, drenched in moonlight. An old red gum on the high bank beside the road flung deep shadow, but along one of its branches, silvered by moonlight, two possums were running, swinging and frisking together.

"Silver-greys," the lad gasped. "Gosh, a couple of silver-greys!"

He moved into the shadow the tree cast and watched the possums.

The red gum had a thick, rough-barked trunk and dark leaves, though young green dripped from buds on its branches. It stood in a garden, about eight feet from a bat humpy—an old-fashioned cottage of mud bricks.

Gil knew who lived there: Mrs Mews and her two daughters. A cross-grained, elderly woman, Mrs Mews had quarrelled with most of the neighbours, and wouldn't let her girls have anything to do with them, if she could help it. She couldn't, it was said, because the girls were rather flighty and liked going to dances with boys in the township.

Gil was not interested in girls, and he had to get those possums.

He was proud of being a possum-hunter. One of Mac's gang, although he was only seventeen and worked at the timber mill. A husky lad, with guileless blue eyes and crisp fair hair, he looked older than his years because of the responsibilities which had been thrust on him. His father had cleared out and left his mother three years ago, and there were two young brothers and a sister to provide for. Gil had taken on the job of looking after them, and his mother needed all the money he could earn.

His wages at the timber mill were so small that when Jack Mac suggested he could make a few pounds trapping possums in the bush, Gil jumped at the idea. Trapping possums had become illegal because the trappers were cleaning out the forest. But pelts brought a lot of money. Jack Mac said it was a poor week when he didn't make £40, and offered Gil £1 for every skin he brought in. He would pay £5 for a pair of silver-greys.

Mac had shown the boy a run in the hills: told him the risks of the game. There was another gang trying to work the same run. A man had to be a good shot, quick and quiet on the mark: know every twist and turn of tracks in the bush to make a getaway if the Inspector of Game was prowling, or blokes in the other gang were after him. He was a fine bushman, himself, Mac: could tell by the look of a tree in the distance whether it held possums, whether a snare had caught anything, or whether it had been interfered with.

Gil remembered his first day in the bush with Mac. They had put up a flight of wild ducks near the swamp. Quick as light, Mac swung his twenty-two. Crack! Crack! Crack! He hit a bird with each shot: three wild ducks on the wing.

"You got to be able to shoot like that at this game," he said.

Gil blasted-up packets of cartridges practising to improve his aim. Not that he expected to use the rifle except when a trap had bungled the catch, or a possum could not be caught any other way. The sound of a shot might put the Game Inspector or members of Reno's gang on his trail.

The feud between the two gangs was pretty fierce. Mac, himself, went armed when he stalked through the forest on his own, the ends of his trousers wrapped round with pieces of bagging so that they wouldn't catch on twigs when he was climbing. They gave him some protection, too, from snakes. There were plenty of snakes in the undergrowth.

One night when Gil had gone to his house, Mac's wife opened the door to him with a baby in her arms and a small automatic held under the baby's clothes.

Mac scoffed at the idea that men working for him were gangsters of the American type. His men had to be sober and level-headed. But big money was being made and the trappers were hostile to any man barging in on their profits. That was why there was bad blood between Reno, the Italian who lived on the hill outside Jarranup, and Jack Mac.

Reno had threatened to shoot Mac if he caught him poaching on what he considered his ground in the forest. Mac didn't recognize any man's rights in the forest except those his energy and skill gave him.

He warned his gang against starting trouble with Reno, and although shots had been exchanged, on two or three occasions,

no serious brawl had occurred. By mutual consent the gangs kept
out of each other's way.

All the same, Mac said he couldn't afford to let hard drinking
spoil his bushcraft or befuddle his wits. He needed all his nous,
as well, for the marketing of skins; doing business with the dealers
who knew how to evade customs dues and other restrictions.

Gil had managed to keep clear of the inspector and of Reno's
gang. He guessed they would think him a sawney youth and not
suspect him of being a trapper. That was why Mac found him
useful, he knew. He was shrewd and sharp in the bush: trust-
worthy as a go-between when an agent of the skin buyers visited
the township.

Mac was not satisfied with him as a worthwhile addition to the
gang, though, Gil was afraid. He had messed-up a job lately, and
was still sore about it.

Mac knew there were some rare black and red possums in trees
near the river at the bottom of an orchard. The owner of the
orchard, Mick Fogarty, had warned trappers off his land: threatened to shoot the next one he caught after those possums.

Black possums were rare: the fur along their bellies was not
really red, but a kind of ruddy-brown, discoloured by the urine
seeping into it, the trappers said. "Black and reds", as they were
known in the trade, brought a good price, and Mac had set his
heart on getting those little beasts in Fogarty's trees.

He sent Gil to try his luck, warning him that getting the possums
wouldn't be easy. Fogarty would smash-up any snares he found.
It would have to be a hit and run job, brought off by climbing the
tree a possum was "mooning in", getting close enough to let him
have a straight shot in the ear, drop the body into a bag, and make
off.

Mac had lent Gil his dog, Sandy, trained to track possums, for
the night. It was uncanny the way that dog worked. He would
single out a tree where he scented possums, stand beside it, paw
uplifted, without a sound until Mac or Gil saw him and went into
action.

Gil set out on his raid wearing shorts and sandshoes, a sugar bag
over his back and carrying his rifle. Sandy trotted along beside
him. It was about two o'clock in the morning: the moon waning,
but he reckoned there would be light enough to see what he was
doing, and Fogarty would be sleeping soundly.

Among those young gums across the river in Fogarty's orchard,
Sandy quickly located a tree in which a splendid specimen of the
black possums was outlined against the yellowing moonlight. Gil
climbed the tree and watched him hanging by his tail, swinging

from one branch to another, grabbing it with his little black hands and running along a gleaming bough.

He stood in a fork of the tree, waiting and watching until the possum came within reach. Then stretching out along the bough to be sure his shot struck the ear and did not damage the pelt, his bullet flew. At the same instant the bough cracked and crashed.

Gil found himself dazed and bleeding at the bottom of the tree. Sandy had grabbed the possum, and the possum in its death throes plunged its sharp teeth into Sandy's nose. Sandy's training was not proof against such an outrage. He and the possum rolled together squealing and howling.

On the hilltop Gil heard Fogarty blazing away with his gun. His dog barking furiously, Fogarty and the dog pelted down the track through the orchard.

Gil picked up his rifle, wrapped his bag round the possum and Sandy, and dashed away through thorny scrub to the river. He tried to cross by a log over it, overbalanced and fell in. There he lay with his head just above water, Sandy and the possum, who had become unstuck, in his arms, until the shouting on the bank subsided and he could make his way home.

"You got to do better than that," Mac said when he heard Gil's story and examined the shattered black pelt.

Yes, he had got to do better, Gil agreed. He needed those silver-greys, and the fiver they would bring. Needed it badly. His mother had been eating with bare gums for over a year and he was determined to buy her a set of teeth. There was a big demand for silver-greys. Mac had an order for a dozen matching skins, and Gil was sure he would pay gladly for this pair.

He had to get them. But how? If Mrs Mews or her daughters saw him snooping round that red gum, they would guess he was after the possums, and tear down any snare. Women and girls were like that. Couldn't stand the sight of a snare: would smash-up any they saw. Didn't understand trapping was a business like any other, and a man had to make a living as best he could.

Gil thought Mrs Mews ought to have more sympathy with the trappers. Everybody knew she was as poor as a boudie rat, herself, though her grandfather had been one of the early settlers, and owned half the countryside. Which was why she lived in the bat humpy old Harry had built, and was so stand-offish with the neighbours. She wouldn't let her daughters go out to work, but worked like a navvy herself, ploughing, planting potatoes, chopping wood, rearing pigs and milking half a dozen cows to sell cream in Jarranup.

There was nothing for it, Gil decided, but to make friends with

Mrs Mews, or the girls: have an excuse for strolling past the red gum as he went along the garden path. He must have a good look at the tree: see where the possums ran to earth. You could bet on them always using the same track.

Passing after work at sundown next evening, he saw the old woman chopping her wood.

"Heigh, Mrs Mews," he yelled, "leave go of that axe! I'll show you what I can do with it."

"Don't mind if you do," she called breathlessly.

"Young Gilbert, isn't it?" She peered at him with screwed-up eyes, "Mrs Truscott's boy."

"That's me," Gil said.

He split the wood into neat lengths, quite a pile of it, carried an armful into the house, and scouted under the red gum for sticks and leafy branches to kindle the fire easily in the morning. At the same time he saw what he wanted to, the rubbed bark on the tree where the possums ran down for their nightly frolic on the ground.

"That's real nice of you, Gilbert," Mrs Mews said, glancing at the stack of wood he had cut. "You've chopped enough for a week."

The girls crowded behind her in the doorway.

"He's all of a sweat," Poppy, the younger, exclaimed. "Looks as if he could do with a cool drink."

"Come on in and I'll make you a squash," Meg said.

"I'm jake," Gil replied diffidently, feeling bashful and guilty before them.

But he found himself sitting with Poppy on the narrow front veranda, screened by creepers, while Meg squeezed a lemon for his drink. Poppy was plump and pretty, he realized as he shared a wooden form with her. She giggled happily, making conversation about the weather and dances in the township.

"Don't you go dancing?" she asked.

"Sometimes," Gil said awkwardly. "But Mum likes to go to the pictures Saturday night, and mostly I mind the kids." When I'm not in the forest after possums, he thought to himself.

"There now," Mrs Mews remarked grumpily, taking a bag-seated chair near them, as Meg handed Gil his glass of lemon squash. "He's a good boy. Thinks more of his mother than flying round with any Tom, Dick and Harry."

"Do you, Gil?" Meg quizzed.

"Got to look after Mum and the kids," Gil murmured gravely, sipping his drink. "But—" he squinted up at her—"I like a bit of fun, now and then."

It was so pleasant yarning with Mrs Mews and the girls, feeling Poppy press against him; and catching a glimmer of her eyes in the dusk, that he almost forgot why he had come to see them.

Moonlight splintered through the creeper on the veranda and sprayed silverly over the garden.

"Look! Look!" Poppy cried. "There are the possums."

Sure enough, the silver-greys were gambolling gaily along a bough of the old red gum: hanging by their tails, dancing and posing against the disc of the rising moon.

"Aren't they pretty things?" Poppy queried.

"Not as pretty as someone else," Gil breathed in her ear, and Poppy gurgled delightedly.

"They're an awful pest, really," Mrs Mews grumbled. "Nibble the peaches and plums so as they're not fit to eat. But we put up with them because they act so innocent and happy like."

"I couldn't bear that damned Mac to get them," Meg declared hotly. "He's cleaned out all the trees round about, I know. But I'll put the inspector on to him if he touches our possums."

"They've got a nest in that old red gum," Poppy warbled. "You should see them, Gil. When they come out in the evening, she licks him all over, cleans his tiny black hands and feet, and he does the same for her. They play about and feed in the moon-light: then snuggle-up to each other, lovemaking, drop into their nest and sleep until the moon rises again."

"A man'd ought to be a possum," Gil murmured.

"Fresh thing!" Poppy laughed.

She walked with him down the garden path when he thought it was time to be going. He had done what he wanted to: found out how to get these silver-greys. But it was one thing to be friendly with Mrs Mews and the girls, and quite another to let Poppy get too friendly. When she put up her face, in the shadow of honeysuckle at the gate, he kissed her clumsily and ran off, his mind too full of the possums to be greedy for kisses.

Possums and Poppy were oddly tangled in his dreams that night. He found it difficult to plan what he must do. The moon had to be reckoned with. It would be rising an hour later next evening, and the weather was sultry. If a storm blew up the possums would huddle together in their hollow of the old tree. It might be days before he had another chance to catch them.

The dusk was warm and heavy when he crept into the shadow of the red gum, approaching from the far side. He moved quickly and quietly, with an eye on the cottage to see that Mrs Mews and the girls were not about.

He had prepared his snare carefully, bound the running noose

of flexible wire with hemp, and fixed it so that it would slip round
the neck of a possum and grip before the creature could squeal.
It was a simple bushman's device, but Gil knew how to handle
it expertly, and fix it to the possum's track on a tree so that they
would not notice an obstruction.

He went back to the road, intending when the moon rose to
sneak behind the tree again and crouch there, waiting until the
snare did its work. He hoped to grab the possum and get away
with it before Mrs Mews or one of the girls discovered what had
happened.

Later, if all went well, he would return and have a shot for its
mate.

But when he crawled through the grass, under the wire fence,
and went back to the road, Poppy was hanging over the garden
gate.

"H'lo!" she called, coyly. "I wanted to see you."

"See me," Gil stuttered, wondering whether she had seen him
beside the red gum.

"Will you take me to the dance, Saturday night?" Poppy
asked. "Mum makes such a fuss if I go with some of the boys.
But she's taken quite a fancy to you. Says you've got such honest
eyes and good manners."

"Me?" Gil was taken aback.

"Come on," she opened the gate and dragged him towards her.
"Ask her now. She won't be able to say no, seein' what you did
for her last night."

Gil cast a desperate look at the red gum. He thought he must
get rid of Polly before the moon rose, and the easiest way would
be to ask Mrs Mews about the dance, and say good night: explain
his mother was expecting him and he had to go home right away.

Polly clung to him as they walked through the garden.

"Sit down," she said when they reached the veranda. "Meg's
gone to choir practice, and Mum's making jam. She'll be out
presently."

As he sat beside Poppy on the veranda, moonlight began to
filter through the dark creeper. Gil was so agitated he could
scarcely listen to what the girl was saying, or play his part in the
squeezing of hands and cuddling together she expected. He was
afraid of missing that critical moment when there was the thump
of a furry body being caught in his snare.

Poppy thought he was shy, and not used to sweet-hearting. She
leaned against him. Her breath and her hair brushed across his
face, stirring a wild, delicious excitement. It was something new

to him. Trembling and distraught he put an arm round her and their kisses mingled.

The possum fell with a heavy thump into the silence between them.

"Cripes," Gil muttered, tearing himself from Poppy's arms. "I'd forgotten."

"Forgotten what?" Poppy asked.

But he disappeared. Gazing into the moonlit garden she could not see him. He did not answer when she called. Lurking in the shadow of the red gum, Gil had got his first possum.

Detaching the snare, he hid in the long grass until Poppy went indoors. When lights were out at the humpy, he promised himself to come back and have a shot at the possum's mate.

That was what he did. One crack, and the soft furry pelt fell into his hands. If the shot did waken Mrs Mews and the girls they would never know who fired it, he thought. They would blame Jack Mac, most likely. Mac wouldn't mind. He would be pleased with those silver-greys and Gil would get his fiver.

But he couldn't bring himself to pass the Mewses' cottage next day, or for two or three days. When he did swing along the road, whistling to give himself an air of raffish carelessness, Poppy was standing beside the gate.

"H'lo," she called.

"H'lo," he said.

"You're a nasty cruel boy," she cried, "and I hate you!"

Gil was flabbergasted.

"Think I didn't know you were after those possums," Poppy said waspishly. "Saw you set the snare."

"I needed the money for them, Poppy," Gil pleaded. "True, I did. Needed it badly."

"That's no excuse."

"Suppose not," he admitted.

"Mum and Meg think it was Mac."

"Well, my Mum's going to get a set of teeth."

"Oh!"

She smiled at him, and he smiled back at her.

"How about it?" Gil blurted out. "Comin' to the dance with me Saturday night?"

"P'raps—and p'raps not!"

Poppy giggled and ran away from him through the garden.

The Desert Flower

OLAF RUHEN

I NEVER see the parakeelya spread its dainty lace of cool rose-lilac flower-cups over the scorching rust-coloured stones of the Australian inland, or the orange-pink of its desert sand, but I think of Lacey Soak and the family that lived there, gambling their living and their lives against the chance of the waters failing.

I was there just twice, and I have never forgotten them. The tall, gaunt and silent cattleman MacDonnel, his silent, grey and pudding-faced wife, even the crippled ailing child were figures common enough. It was the girl who blossomed like the parakeelya. She was strangely like the parakeelya blossom, with her flower-face and her thin limbs, and the way she was rooted, as the parakeelya seems always rooted, in an alien soil.

And perhaps there was another less physical resemblance too; for the parakeelya spells life, and at the same time it spells death. So succulent are the finger-length leaves that cattle can feed and fatten on them when there is no water anywhere. They can travel miles from the waterholes and never feel thirst; and then there comes a time when the parakeelya is finished, and, panic-striken, they look for water; but there is no water anywhere and they die in the dry lands: big well-nourished beasts, they stumble and fall and perish in an agony mercifully fast.

It happens often. It happens every year; but the sweet drifts of blossoms that paint the whole land in beauty are joy to the cattle-man nevertheless; they spell money in his pocket, and he is only dimly aware of the menace in their impermanence, the menace of unalloyed goodness that has no lasting power. I've eaten para-keelya myself. It carries a poison so they say, and its taste is bitter on a man's tongue; but when that tongue is dry in your mouth, rasping against dry teeth, and your saddle canteen is empty, a few parakeelya leaves can evoke the blessed relief of flowing saliva, and carry you on to the waters.

The first time I came through Lacey Soak it was a season of rain, with pools of water here and there in the normally dry river-beds, and the desert everywhere safe for travelling. That was why I was there. I had delivered cattle in the south, sold most of my plant of horses, and sent the four native stockmen back to their own country by air. Now I was travelling fast with half a dozen horses I didn't want to part with and, because the water was so plentiful, cutting across country away from the meandering stock route. Besides, I like new country. I always want to see the other side of the next hill.

I was riding through a carpet of parakeelya blossoms, and stiff, butter-yellow everlastings; and the whitewood trees were flowering and I could smell the scented white snapdragons of the duboisia blooms, when I saw this smoke go up a mile or so on my right. It faded quickly enough; it was only a spinifex clump; but as soon as it had died another went up in exactly the same place. I thought there might have been aborigines there signalling to one another; and rode on; but when the third fire rose I headed the horses over and went to find out about it; and not long before I reached there I cut the tracks of a single horse.

Alongside the burnt grass there was a man on the ground. He was on his back, propped up on his elbows, watching me.

"A man can be lucky," he said when I got near. "I saw your dust. I've got a broken leg, kid. You'll have to help me in."

"Your horse lit out?" I asked, though it was obvious enough. He must have thought so, for he just grunted.

He was a tall man, but he looked weak, some ways, not frail, but ineffective. I wouldn't have bet on his horse-sense. He was dark-complected, and hadn't shaved for a few days, and his grey hair showed through a tear in the crown of his felt hat. His shirt had patches over the patches, very neatly made; but his boots were worn beyond saving. So he was not a man who could look after his gear, but somewhere, I guessed, there was a woman doing all she could for him. He didn't seem to want to say more, and after I'd waited awhile I asked him straight.

"What happened?"

"Took a shot at a snake. Young horse. Not trained to the rifle. Threw me and bolted." The rifle was there, near him.

He was true to his looks. He'd been acting silly, and I let him know that I thought so.

"This is a hell of a place to train a young horse when you're by yourself."

"A man can make mistakes, kid."

"Bob," I said. "Bob Corcoran." I outgrew that "kid" stuff years ago, but at nineteen I've still got a young kind of a face, I suppose. Some people do.

"You don't like being called 'kid'?"

"Would you? I've been old enough to do a man's work for years. I'm old enough to pack you in to where you're going. Can you sit a saddle?"

"I reckon. If you can strap me up."

When I'd rigged a splint to make his leg easy I put my palomino through one of her circus tricks and sat her down so it was easy to get him in the saddle. I rode a sorrel gelding I had, bareback, for I'd shipped my spare gear with the men. We took four hours to reach Lacey Soak, and he didn't say more than fourteen words the whole way. He was in some pain, but the reason he didn't talk, I thought, was that he didn't have anything to say.

His homestead was like a hundred others I've seen, an unlined shed of corrugated iron with earthen floors standing perhaps a hundred yards from the tank, the windmill and the watering-troughs of an artesian bore. Iron partitions divided the house into four rooms. There were no connecting doors; instead they all opened onto a kind of veranda, a structure of poles supporting a framework that kept the worst of the afternoon sun from the front wall of the house. Iron cots had been pulled out into the open. Such houses were too hot for sleeping in in summer.

This homestead had something else: a pitiful attempt at a garden; but of the flowers that had been planted the survivors had only a pathetic, small hold on life. I supposed that the water with which they had been drenched was carrying too high a concentration of salts; later, when I dismounted and gulped down a pint or so from the canvas waterbag hanging in the shade, I was sure of it. A little distance from the house some athel pines from Arabia and parkinsonias from Africa had been planted for shade, and were beginning to thrive. For half a mile beyond, no other tree had survived the attentions of the cattle brought to the water; the plain was barren, and it, with the pathetic garden plots, made a sorry contrast to the country I had been riding through, with its blaze of native herbage, the cassias and the desert willows and the casuarinas and the high grained heads of the grasses, the spinifex and the neverfail.

There was a dove-grey carpet flecked with rose spread over some acres of the ground near the troughs, and as we rode up and my loose horses made for the water it lifted, changing like a miracle into a sky-filling flock of screaming galahs.

"Bloody parrots," said MacDonnel.

A grey woman was at the doorway, crying out "Mac, Mac" in surprised delight. He did not answer.

"He's hurt, Mrs MacDonnel," I replied. "He's broken a leg."

She released her hands from the folds of her apron and came running.

"It's all right," I said. "Steady a minute. I'll get him down. The horse won't scare, but take it easy."

There was no doubt about it, she was almost in a panic. I led the palomino as close as I could to the doorway, and took the bridle-rein up close and sat her down there. After that it was easy to stand by MacDonnel's bad leg and get his arm round my shoulder.

"This way," his wife said, and opened the second door.

There was a double-bed in there, a blanketed mattress on an iron bedstead. There was one cheap rug on the earth floor beside the bed, a small chest of drawers standing unevenly by the iron wall, two trunks and two kitchen chairs. It was a room that matched the patched and over-patched shirt and denim trousers MacDonnel had been wearing. The partitions stopped short of the roof and there was no ceiling, but the room was like an oven. For that matter there was no coolness anywhere.

"Deborah's in the kitchen. She'll get you something to eat. I'll come in a little while," the woman told me.

The leg was splinted all right. There was little that needed doing, but a woman fussing makes a sick man comfortable, so I went to the room at the chimney end of the house. There was a table set with clean but ragged linen and standing on the floor between two rough benches; there was a bright-coloured grocer's calendar hung against the black iron walls; there was a child lying on his back on a sofa playing with a braid of kangaroo-hide; and there was a girl standing near the stove, with wide and frightened eyes, with spindly arms and legs and a skin as pallid as though she lived in a city cellar.

"MacDonnel's hurt?" she asked. Though it was just a simple question she somehow managed to make it sound aggressive.

"He'll be all right," I told her. "Give him a month he'll be as good as new."

"A month?"

"Broken leg."

"We can call the doctor in the morning." There was a battery-powered transmitter on a bench near the door. Even the poorest homesteads had them.

"Just as well," I nodded.

I don't get to see many girls, the way I travel; I guess I looked at her too much. She was like a fragile scented flower, and she was the only thing beautiful in that bare and ugly house. As soon as my meal was on the table she picked up the child and left the room. He was too big for her to carry, but she did it effortlessly.

The woman offered me a bed that night, but instead I threw down my swag near the water-tank. A tarp and a blanket is all a man needs, and I sleep better on the ground. But she brought out a pillow for my head, and took my roll of clothes inside. In the morning my shirts were hanging on the line, and one or two rips that had been there for a long time were patched, and all the missing buttons were replaced.

I would have pulled out, but I happened to notice that the water-tank was half empty and the windmill pump not working because of a couple of sheared bolts at the top of the shaft. I poked around and found what was needed, and fixed that; but by that time I'd seen a lot of things that needed a man's hand, things that the women couldn't manage, and in the end I stayed three weeks. In mid-morning, that first day, the doctor flew in, piloting an old-fashioned de Havilland. He taxied right up to the house, and he took the patient away with him when he left. So I felt obliged to stay for a day or two.

And I don't mind admitting I had the thought of getting to know Deborah better. So even though I'd imagined myself in a hurry I stayed and fixed the engine that drove the circular saw, and cut enough mulga wood and blackheart to keep the stove burning half the year, and cleaned the tank and troughs—it was a good time with so much surface water and parakeelya about— and fixed a lot of gear that needed it, and tightened down the roof where it had been lifted by the wind. And tried to get friendly with the girl.

But she was like a frightened wild-cat that's found itself in a house and can't get away. She'd accept a good turn as a wild thing will accept food, warily, with a guarded gratitude that kept her still untouchable. I could call her "Deborah", but she never called me "Bob". It was the woman who spoke with me in the evenings and summoned me to meals.

"Why don't you want to be friendly, Deborah?" I asked her once; and she turned to me, surprised.

"I'm friendly," she said.

"Not so much."

She just looked at me with those big eyes dark in her pallid face and said nothing.

"You've never got much to say," I tried again. "We could be real friendly, you and I."

"Men are all the same," she said. "I came here to get away

from them. I could live my life without seeing a man—I'd like to."

"You have to be fond of somebody, though."

"There's Freddie," she said. Freddie was the child.

"He'll be a man someday," I reminded her.

"Maybe. He doesn't stand too much of a chance, poor kid." He was a fretful, ailing child with some weakness in his legs. I never did ask what was the matter with him, but he wasn't well. He played quietly in the house, in the heat; mostly lying on his back holding something in his hands, usually the half-plaited braid of shiny kangaroo leather.

"You've grown though," I said. "And you can't keep running away all your life."

"I'm not running," she snapped. "And it's my life." Her eyes were steady on me with that queer defensive look, bold and hesitant at the same time.

"I've stopped running," she corrected herself after a pause, and she kicked aside a log of firewood that had fallen off the top of the filled box.

"Here?" I asked. "This is no place to stop. There's nothing here. You've run from nothing to nothing."

"Maybe I like this nothing better," she said, and then she didn't talk any more.

"She's had hard knocks, poor thing," Mrs MacDonnel told me once.

"What happened?"

"I don't know. She's never told me. I don't know anything about her. She came to me a year ago. My sister, before she died, sent her on out to me; and she's worked for me ever since without a word of complaint. And she's good to Freddie. But if there's a man comes round the place she stands and shivers like a filly in a yard ablaze. As yourself, for example; not that you'd do her harm, a good lad like you, but you put her on edge. Or any other man. God knows what happened to her, but the one who did it deserves shooting."

"She doesn't mind your husband?"

"MacDonnel? Lord love you, no. He doesn't know she's there half the time, and she likes it that way. He's a good man, that man of mine. He's been unlucky; the luck's against him when it comes to making money, and he's a bit of a dreamer; he doesn't see when things are going wrong. But he's a good man. He takes no notice of her, nor she of him; though she'll do things for him. He never notices. He takes a power of looking after sometimes, but he doesn't know it himself.   She doesn't mind that.   And she likes to look to Freddie."

When the word came through on the radio that MacDonnel would soon be starting for home I rounded up my plant and left. I reined in as I passed the doorway, and the girl came and looked out, the child in her arms where she'd picked him up to take him somewhere.   She didn't let him walk enough.

"Good-bye, Deborah," I called.

"You've been a help.   Good-bye," she said, and she sounded friendly, but she didn't use my name.

She didn't use it the second time I saw her, and that was more than a year later.   I'd been travelling all that time; I'd been travelling some lonely country; and there was many a night I lay back in my blankets and looked at the lake of darkness at the foot of the Milky Way that the natives call the Emu's Nest, and thought I could see the big dark frightened eyes of the girl from Lacey Soak stare back at me.   And sometimes I wondered whether she was frightened of me, and sometimes whether it was that she was frightened of all the world; and sometimes whether it was just her fear that the mirror of her loneliness might be shattered.

You think all sorts of things if you lie down in the sharp-textured air of the desert night to watch its big bright stars, and sometimes the night will draw you up until you'd believe that you'd left the world behind, except that the drifting tang of wood-smoke and the smell of the night-horse nearby and the cattle a little beyond will tie you to reality.   And I used to imagine myself at Lacey Soak, and think about the girl, and wonder if she would ever turn to meet the world waiting for her, and how; and just what her world would be when she'd accepted it, and whether she would find a true friend waiting for her, and how she would recognize him.   I saw her as a kind of Sleeping Beauty and I wondered what would wake her.   In all my wildest dreams I never would have guessed.

For in the end I rode a hundred miles out of my way, one season, to camp at Lacey Soak; and once again I found that I was needed.   This time it was the woman.   She was ill.   She was worse than ill; she was dying; though she was the only one who knew.

I didn't see her when I came, but they must have told her I was there.   The girl Deborah was still the same, silent and frightened.   The child was bigger, but he was still sickly; he haunted the girl, and went after her wherever she moved.   McDonnel was the same silent man I'd found disabled on the plain, and half his gear was out of order again. He didn't say much, even now he was well.

He spent most of his time in the bedroom with his wife, and I tried to talk to the girl, but she was as remote as the face I'd seen in the stars.

"I've been thinking of you, Deborah," I told her, and she looked at me sharply.

"You've had little to do, then."

"No, it's true. I've been thinking of you a lot."

"I dare say I can't stop you."

I wanted to say some more, but how could I? It didn't seem real to sit and watch that fragile beauty move around that harsh and ugly room; to know that though physically she was near, she was otherwise remote, that she walked in an invisible unbreakable shell as impenetrable as star-distance.

MacDonnel came into the room.

"She wants some paper and a pen," he said. He made no attempt to find them for himself, but just stood there, waiting for the girl to hand him what he needed.

"Paper?" she asked, not moving.

"Paper," he said. "Where's that paper I write orders on? And the pen?"

"Oh, yes."

She rummaged in a wooden box, one of a series stacked one above the other against the wall, with the openings outwards so they could be used for shelves, and she brought him a block of paper and a pen and an inkbottle.

"What's it for?" she asked, but he just shook his head as he went out.

He came back in a moment or two and sat with us. We were all silent; I was wishing I was outside, where the stars at least and the horses were company. We sat so long in silence I was ready to go when a knocking came on the partition wall. MacDonnel got up and answered it. He reappeared in a moment and beckoned the girl.

"She wants you," he said.

I was stretching out my legs when he came to the door again.

"You too," he said. "She asked for you."

She was greyer than ever propped up with pillows against the iron paint-chipped railings of the bedhead. She looked grey and tired, no longer pudding-faced, and older than I had remembered her.

"I want you to listen," she said to me and turned her face to the others.

"I want you all to listen. I'm going to die."

"Now, mother," MacDonnel said tenderly. It was the first time I had heard emotion in his voice. "The doctor will be here in the morning. We'll send for him at first light."

"You'd better tell him to bring the parson then," she said. "I'll not last so long."

I believed her. I'd seen men die, more than once; die of accidents, and one of a long illness; but it was an awesome thing to ride to this place from the wide surrounding desert, and to find a woman ready for death, and accepting it.

"But. . . ." MacDonnel was beginning.

"Listen to me," she said again.

"I want a Christian burial. I want the parson to come out here and bury me. But that's not the end. For when he goes there'll be you, MacDonnel, and young Freddie; and you, Deborah, and the lad will ride on. And I've been thinking of it these hours. You need a woman, MacDonnel, to look after you, and so does Freddie; and Deborah has a need for something of her own, a man and a home and the child. So I brought you in here, Mac-Donnel, to ask you if I die tonight, will you marry her?"

MacDonnel was staring at her, his mouth open, his face twisted between astonishment and despair. I looked past him to Deborah; her eyes were so big they seemed to pulse in the lamplight; she had put her hand to cover her mouth. She was sitting bolt upright on the edge of the wooden chair; I'd have expected her to leap up and run away. No one else was looking at her.

"If you want me to go happy, promise me you'll marry her," the grey woman said.

MacDonnel stood up and came to the bed.

"Maisie, dear," he said; and it was the first time I'd heard a name for her.

"You can do this one thing right, MacDonnel. Will you marry her?"

"All right, mother. If she'll have me."

I thought that the girl cried out then; a tiny cry out of a torment, but no one else seemed to notice. The woman on the bed turned to her.

"Deborah?"

She didn't move or speak.

"Will you marry him, Deborah?"

She put her hand down, and there were long seconds of silence while she seemed to struggle for a sound. Her mouth worked. She caught her breath. When she did speak the sound came abruptly, explosively. But it was "yes".

It satisfied the grey woman.

"All right. Then that's the beginning. You've a head on your shoulders, Deborah, and a heart too big for your body. But now I was thinking beyond, and it wouldn't be fit for you two to live here awhile and then go in to get married; so you'll make me this promise: that the parson that buries me shall marry you before he leaves."

We all stared at her.

"That's the way it's got to be," she said, and her voice was weak, but it was determined. "Promise me."

"All right, mother," MacDonnel said soothingly.

"Deborah?"

"Yes."

"Now as for neighbours they're far enough away. But as like as not the parson will never believe you if you tell him that this was a wish of mine," she said. "So I've written it all out here in my own hand and signed it; and you sign to show you agree, and young Bob will sign it for a witness, or else it will be thought to be something arranged between the two of you."

Her voice was clear, but the hand that reached for the paper on the box beside the bed shook and trembled, and MacDonnel jumped forward to help, but she had the paper in her hand before he could.

"Sign it all three of you, where I've written it out, and I'll go happy," she said.

MacDonnel signed like a man in a trance. The girl took the paper from him and put her name to it firmly and quickly, and passed it to me.

It read, "It is my last dying wish that my husband shall marry Deborah Knight, and that the parson that buries me shall marry them without delay, so that they will be married in the same hour and in proof of this their names shall appear below mine and it shall be witnessed by R. Corkran. And this is my dearest wish and they shall do this in honour of my memory."

She had signed it, and the other two names were below. She had spelt my name wrong; but I signed it with my usual "Bob Corcoran" and then put the wrong spelling in brackets beneath.

"You'll wait for the parson," she said to me. "He might take convincing." Her voice was suddenly very weak and halting.

Then she said, "Bring Freddie in," and I slipped out of the room ahead of the girl.

In the early morning I saw MacDonnel carrying a pick and a shovel. I got up and pulled my boots on and went over to him as he started to dig.

"Not here," I said. "It's not a good place. Leave it to me. I'll fix it all."

I didn't ask him was she dead; I knew it would happen the way she had said, and it did. They were married by the parson that buried her; and the doctor who'd flown the plane out stood with me as witness; and the earth was still crumbling down from the pile over the grave I'd dug beneath the parkinsonias, where the cattle wouldn't trample it.

But the last time I went to town I saw Deborah again, and the child was with her, and her eyes were serene and confident. She had grown in some way; she was a woman complete. She didn't see me; she was too full of her business in the town and I thought it better to leave it that way; for there's nothing now would take me back to Lacey Soak.

And I've thought it over with the stars and tossed it this way and that; for I marvel that the weak and awkward man and the even weaker child should furnish the food for her final growth. It seemed an unlikely place to find such food, or love, or safety. It was a place to find nothing, except their need of her.

Perhaps that was it. I had no need of her, anyway. Sometimes, thinking back, I see her face yet in the dark place amongst the stars; and it is a glory and a wonder to see the frightened eyes turn free and confident; and I think, too, of the moment of revelation that was the grey woman's, before she died. As when I ride amongst the blossoming parakeelya I marvel at the way its frail daintiness thrives in the blazing heat, on the harsh and arid sand.

Spoe

HUGH STOREY

I will not venture a description of any length of Mr Spoe. For
if he were to hear one he would be properly astounded. Not
because he would think it inaccurate but because any collection of
a number of facts about himself would scare the wind out of his
decaying stomach. Fancy, he would think, I'm sixty-one years
old, a pensioner who makes money on the sly selling home-made
toys to souvenir shops, live alone, am single, women have always
given me the shits, and why, someone thinks I've got funny ears
and a head like a mantelpiece . . . why can't they leave me be?
In short, he would refuse to recognize any descriptions of himself,
regarding them as ellipses, as attempts to pick on him, to cast
him prematurely into the pluperfect. With indignation he would
confide to his drinking-mates down at the pub:
"Some bloody prick's trying to libel me."
But I must all the same talk about him. For he, too, knew the
girl. Perhaps better than anyone else.
He often thought afterwards, when she no longer lived in the
tenement next to his, that it was an accident that he had ever
noticed her at all. None of the neighbours ever complained about
the din she made or the rowdy parties she had, except the Greens,
and they were a couple of real old women, ask anyone. He just
happened one night to be getting a gulp of fresh air, looking out
of his window over the narrow lane which separated his house
from hers, when he saw her, with some fellow, the two of them
very drunk and rolling all over the lane, she trying to get her key
out of her purse, he trying to screw her on the spot. It was funny
to watch. He remembered telling his friends at the pub about it
the next day. Charlie, one of them, had replied:
"You should've leaned out of yer window and said, 'Give 'er
one for me, mate!' " He hated Charlie for that remark now: what
a tasteless, dirty thing to say. . . .

But he had noticed her. Indeed, from that evening on she had become an obsession with him. For lots of reasons: she had habits he found incredible, like wearing nothing but black, like playing a mouth organ, like cleaning her teeth ten times a day. Night after night he would listen to her, whether she was with company or alone. For she was never silent. The old man was quite fascinated, each day becoming more and more taken up with her. What awed him most was her sounds. She positively vibrated with sounds and noises; she giggled incessantly, she had a soft, penetrating laugh, she sucked her teeth, she tinkled and gurgled like a budgerigar. Every few minutes she had this curious habit of ever so delicately sniffing her nose.

Once in his mind the thought of the girl could not be dislodged. Mr Spoe's ears became imperceptibly attuned to her. He had never heard such a thing, no one had ever delighted him so much; he began to think that she hummed and sang as she did especially for him. She brought through his back door, as he raffishly reminded himself from time to time, forgotten feelings of his youth.

But it had come errantly to the point where he neglected his workshop of toys, sleeping all day so as to be awake in the evening when the girl usually came home, even missing his regular daily trip to the hotel, guiltily drawing to his curtains so as not to be seen. He must not miss a sound she emitted. His presiding over her affairs and conversations made him increasingly anxious and watchful. And then there were the men.

They came quite frequently, never together, of course. There were about six of them altogether, and he fast grew to hating every one of them, begrudging them every second they spent with her. Fools. She told each one of them she loved only him, but she loved none of them. Or so the old man reasoned. Their presence angered him all the more since, with any of them there, her voice would go shrill and coy and lose its sweetness; and worse, their klaxon, toneless braying made it impossible to hear her. So he began to watch them, to scrutinize them, all their comings and goings, marking off the hours each spent with her. Sometimes, he felt the urge, but only an urge, to lean out of the window as one of them walked past and yell out:

"You're not her favourite, you know. You're only one of six."

He was glad she deceived them.

The fellow who came most was a tall, arrogant lag with fancy clothes and a hairless face. But most of them slept with her. Ah, yes, he couldn't help knowing that: she made a hell of a noise in bed; and besides, she always left her window open, like an amplifier. Don't blame me. It was at these times that the old

man became most frenzied. He felt as if a thousand tiny cork-
screws were tickling him and wriggling around in the glands
beneath his skin; he would lie in bed, pulling his dusty old eiderdown over his small, square neck and shoulders, waiting until he
would hear her, them, at which time his body would flush with
shame, with fear that someone would surprise him as he lay there
tensely listening to his pornography of sound coming in through
the window. Her performances ravished his senility. They led
him to imagine that it was he himself in her bed . . . not whoever
it was . . . his thoughts beat wider and wilder wings until, having
masturbated, he would fall asleep.

He was discreeter than he need have been. When Charlie or
any of his friends would ask, "What happened to that little tart
opposite you, Harry . . . seen her at all?" he would lie that no,
he hadn't really noticed her since.

But even he knew it could not go on.

It was the very evening after the first occasion the girl had
actually smiled at him. The day before he had been going out
for a walk and she had been sitting on her doorstep, drying her
hair in the sun. She had looked up at him, her red hair sprawled
all over her face like a show pony. And she flickered a smile at
him, which his retreating eyes had just caught as he walked past
her. He had almost skipped with joy all the way down to the pub.
There was a party that evening which began to end about 2 a.m.
Mr Spoe was feeling very tired, but all the same he was very quick
to establish that only the girl and the tall, black-haired lout were
left. His ears detected that they were in the kitchen; he waited
for them to go upstairs to her bedroom, but they didn't go. He
had lain in bed some time when he realized that they were having
a quarrel; he couldn't catch what it was about, only that it was no
ordinary quarrel, their voices were too loud and cacophonous for
that, becoming louder and more strident each minute. Every second
that elapsed accelerated Mr Spoe's alarm. He got up and put on
his trousers. Why weren't the neighbours taking notice? Surely
the noise could be heard a mile away, or was it just that he was
imagining it, like a drummer who hears drumming after he has
ceased to play? He crept down his own stairs in order to hear them
better. Then there was a lot of grunting and shuffling, then a
scream. It was an awful scream, and it horrified Mr Spoe. He
must be choking her, listen, she's spluttering. . . . He rushed out of
his door, he must save her.

If only he had said the normal thing: something like:
"What's going on in there?"

Something formal, preliminary, guarded, ambiguous. But he had not stopped to think but had cried out:

"What are you doing to her? Stop it. Stop it. Open the door."

His shout was met with an embarrassed silence from within. At the same time neighbours' windows started popping open like buttons. He sensed his error even before he heard her voice. It came through the door as sharply as if the latter were made of rice paper:

"God . . . it's that bloody old perve from next door."

That was all. Mr Spoe wished he could expire on the spot: harsh, derisory voices, neighbours' voices, rang angrily and querulously above the lane:

"What's going on?"

"Go to sleep. Give us some bloody peace."

He wanted to explain to them, to her, that he thought she was being murdered, but they thought he was drunk. And a perve. The girl's voice came incisively through the door again:

"Go away."

He scuttled to the safety of his house. All his senses felt blank and dead, like over-exposed negatives. "The old perve." "The old perve." The words were carved into the tunnels of his ears, installed there like giant gongs forever.

It must have been for several days that Mr Spoe lay stiff on his bed with his eiderdown stuffed, like wet cement, around and over his ears to expunge all sound. But it was useless. Inner and outer voices invaded him all the time. He had at first thought: "Where are the police?" But he came to realize that was silly; he hadn't committed any crime, nor had he said anything that would count against him. But the girl . . . the girl. What right had she . . . he would ring the police and tell them about the pandemonium she had been making for months . . . tell them about all her men. . . . But such intentions receded rapidly. No. Nothing mattered except that she loathed him. Nothing mattered but for his thoughts to become inaudible to him. The old man longed for a catharsis.

The terrible thing was, he found out when at last, after several weeks, he ventured out of his house, that everyone had forgotten about the incident—one of the neighbours had ribbed him about "being on the bottle", but that was all. Perhaps too, he let himself think, the girl had only abused him in a moment of fury: after all, she had been in the middle of a tiff. Perhaps she would even smile next time she saw him, just as before.

But the girl had gone. An old lady with an enormous grey cat had moved in. An old lady who smiled and winked at him all the time. Ugh. He went back to his toys, applying himself with feverish industry. Part of his consciousness had been extracted, he knew that, but it was better that way, he thought, like a block injection that must never wear off.

The neighbours were quite surprised when Mr Spoe, who had not uttered a civil word to any of them for fifteen years, began to take afternoon tea with the new neighbour.

The Idiot Boy

GRIFFITH WATKINS

HE WAS no longer a boy; though the quiet house down below the fort, with all that expanse of untouched sea plain, gave him the opportunity to remain one, always.

Under the flapping brim of his shapeless cotton hat his brown face, calm and full, continually registered wonder as he walked, in all weathers, along the beaches, his knotty legs taking him far down from the surf clubs into the singing of the dunes. He would walk for miles, his bare feet washed by the tongues of the broken waves, stopping from time to time to consult the seabirds in his strange, throaty pronouncements. Sometimes he would trail great lengths of fresh seaweed, then suddenly run up onto the dry sand, his feet squeaking with each thrust. The trophies he found always delighted him: small pine boxes tossed from passing steamers; nail-scarred planks; shining tins and beer cans; un-smashed light globes; huge, brilliantly white cuttlefish bones, and always, the shells.

Once, he tried to catch a large black bream which had been washed up into a shallow pool. Splashing about, his clothing saturated, he had laughed as his strong hands had touched its darting body. After an hour of this, the fish still proved too elusive so he had left it.

Usually he walked to the beaches in the mornings; in the after-noons he sat around the side of the house in the protected part where the chimney jutted out or, if it was hot, he would climb up the steep hill of thirsting gums to the fort and sleep in the shade, the lazy chirping of insects all around him, the palms of his outstretched arms struck by fleeting nails of sunlight. Or, sitting next to the chimney, he would pat the thistles, grasses and the earth with a stick, humming to himself those strange tunes made up from the harmonies of his completeness.

So he would sit through most of the afternoons, busy with his attentions to plant and soil, pausing to watch the busy streams of ants glistening their haste along the groove where the limestone met the bricks, until his father came home.

When the silver-haired metal-worker in his faded blue overalls came riding down the gravel track that skirted the hill, the caged parrots under the vines would begin screaming. So he would know, hurrying in his uneven shuffle around to the side gate, his head nodding with his haste.

Every night his father would say the same thing.

"Hullo, Danny! Been a good boy?"

He would make a reply and then reach out for the machine. With painful care the idiot boy would wheel it slowly along the cracked cement path to the shed. Had it been made of glass, he could not have shown it more care. Gingerly he would lean it up against the posts and work at the straps holding the lunch tin to the carrier. With the small box safely possessed, into the house he would hurry, to place it, with a terrible concentration, upon the ledge of the crockery-clung cupboard. Then he would sink into his chair at the end of the table, facing his father.

"There you are, Son!" his frail, wispy mother would say as she put the milky cup of tea before him, the currant cake bulging luxuriously from the saucer. Taking up the cake, he would mine out the fruit with his thick fingers, placing the particles in his mouth and chewing them with great deliberation, watching all the time his father read the evening paper. They did this every afternoon, his mother never joining them but busying herself with her preparation of their tea.

He would drink his tea sip for sip with his father, always finishing when he did, pushing back his chair the same way. Shuffling out behind him, he would follow him as far as the workshop door, then continue on to the shed where the bicycle was kept. Here was the grain for the fowls.

He liked feeding them. He would fill up the tin by hand, watching the feed slide through his fingers. When the tin was full, he would go over to the yard where the hens pressed themselves up against the wire, struggling against each other as he approached. Opening the gate, he would bend to hold out a handful of the wheat, spilling some. Most of the birds were content to compete for this; the others possessing more bravado, would peck directly at his laden palm, their short beaks exploding much of it to the sand.

The father's workshop was an extension of the grain shed. It too stood on short piles with several wooden steps leading up to the doorway. Though it was a small room, it held much to

fascinate the boy. On the window side was a long shelf attached
to the wall by rusting metal struts, making an inner sill; here
were the clocks; his father repaired them. There would be grave-
faced alarm clocks with black frames; busy looking mantel clocks
with corrugations of polished wood flanking the dial, sometimes
they bore a silver inscription; then, perhaps a delicate travelling
clock, gold coloured, with a green face that glowed.

On the row of brass hooks that had been wound into the edge
of the wood were the wristlet watches, cards carefully tied to
them, spinning slowly in the draughts. High up on the wall, to
the right of the window, hung the dark-wooded cuckoo clock. It
had some ornate scroll work carved into its wooden projections,
and the long chain which spewed from underneath it almost
reached to the floor.

Below the shelf was an enormous roller-top desk, the dark
recesses of which were crammed with neatly labelled tins and
boxes. Along the wall, opposite the doorway, was an old-fashioned
lathe and an electric drill. Against the third wall was a carpenter's
bench above which a great number of tools lay snugly on their
hooks up against the silhouettes painted there. The idiot boy
always sat on the step; he would not enter the workshop because
of the cuckoo. The cuckoo fascinated him and dismayed him.
When the gentle whirring of the mechanism announced its appearance, he would sit bolt upright, his eyes huge in their anticipation
as the tiny doors flew open and the raucous bird sprang into view.
After the bird had retired again, he would stare up at the clock
for minutes on end waiting for its reappearance. When it failed
to do this he would turn his attention to his father.

The idiot boy's room enclosed one end of the back veranda,
behind an asbestos partition. Glass louvres ran down its side.
Only a few books were on the shelves alongside his bed; they were
picture books. The shelves were filled with his treasures. There
were some ruptured red crackers showing black where they had
exploded; four golf balls, cracked and brittle, lay in a small green
plastic bowl; next to this was a huge pine cone, dark with age;
then the cuttlefish bones, a number of pieces of faded coral, and
five enormous, whorled shells. Above the bed was a picture of
Christ and the children, while above the crisp doily on the dress-
ing table, which held a lonely looking brush and comb set, were
the Sunday school pictures, jammed under the mirror beading. In
one corner were the boxes of shells. Still, the room looked strangely
bare. True, his mother kept the trophies he brought home down
to a reasonable number; he never missed them in any case. But

she never threw the shells away; that was why there were almost
a dozen boxes of them.

Some of these he would occasionally carry out to the kitchen
and, sprawling on the orange and black lino, carefully arrange their
contents in orderly rows.   At times, he would pause and begin
turning them over one at a time, as if considering their subtle
designs and their water-drowned histories.   The pattern on the
floor would slowly grow, its original rectangular shape swelling
into an elastic pyramid that threatened to engulf half of the
room's area.   But his mother never disturbed him, stepping
through the room as best she could, leaving him to his musings.

The day the idiot boy died was a windy one: the easterly wind
had the waves working their way back towards the islands, their
ragged throats exploding white.   Inshore, it was calm, the brown
contours of the reef were visible, and the waves fell carefully onto
the shore.   Along the tops of the dunes, the grasses and mauve
cat's-tails hummed and thrashed themselves to the soil; sand stung
the air, vague clouds of it sighing through the bleached tea-tree
thatch of the empty shade houses.   Up from the beach, along the
higher ground, the gums writhed in an ecstasy of energy.   The
sky had a dull film of wrinkled grey cloud over it.

The edges of the idiot boy's hat vibrated wildly in this wind.
He wore his light green army pants rolled up to the knees; the
blue texture of his rolled-neck sweater was filled with sand.

Few had ever noticed his feet; they were almost beautiful.   He
had seldom worn shoes and so they had grown unimpeded into
brown shapes of perfect regularity.   He walked with these swish-
ing noisily through the wash, his wide brown eyes staring vacantly
at a fishing boat, sail bulging, as it swam up the coast.   His face
had that rapt amazement which the sea always seemed to kindle
in him.   This day he had found no trophy, other than the shells.
He wandered through the troves of these, heaped carelessly by
the high surf during the night, brooding at times on hands and
knees at a particular shape or colour, usually throwing it down
again.

The wind pushed him on down the coast.   It was not until he
was half a mile from the lonely red flag, snapping and fighting
at its pulley, that he discovered something which really pleased
him.   It was a large conch shell, its contours merging into orange
along the line that marked the successive chambers.   Carefully he
placed it in his pocket.

Then, with a quick movement, he turned and looked back up
the coast.   The last surf club was a grey blur.   For a few moments

a vague chatter of guns over on the rifle range reached him, then the wind lost it again.   Sand sprang up into his eyes as a large spiny seedcase, its projections scorched to a light brown by the sun, cartwheeled past him.   He turned and rubbed both eyes with the knuckles of his clenched hands.

When he had dislodged the irritating particles, he walked down to the water again.   From where he stood, on the long wave-cut platform, he watched the waves crumble upon its extreme bronze tissues, heavy, gulping masses of water sliding up towards him. The idiot boy walked happily around the pools, the water tugging at his legs, his feet moving easily over the sharp denticles of rock. In the few moments when the water cleared itself from the reef, he would peer into the exposed pools, seeing the darting small fish or the flimsy sponges.   Then the surge of the water would return and destroy the vision.

As he felt the long, ragged piece of weed strike his leg, he bent down and scooped it up, the water soaking his arms to the elbows. It was a dark, ruby red growth, its serrations glistening.   He traced some of these with his fingers, smiling at the pleasure it gave him. After several waves had swirled around him, he slowly lowered its length back into the water, enjoying the tension of its weight and the tug of the current.   Almost reluctantly, he released it, watching it slowly twist as it disappeared towards a cascading crevice.

As he climbed back onto the beach, the sand again began stinging his exposed skin.   Under the heavy motion of his feet, the thin crust of salt-stiff sand crumbled deliciously.   He began walking towards the flag, passing between two high dunes.   Here, there were no footmarks; the sand had been swept into graceful contours. A seagull hurtled down the banister of the wind, screaming.   Pausing, he shaded his eyes to search for it as it was enveloped by the glare of the cloud-veiled sun.   The valleys between the dunes, protected from the direct blast of the wind, were dry and very warm.   He gave an involuntary shiver as he descended into their comfort, his hat brim losing most of its agitation.

So he walked on, following the line of the terrain, plodding through the wrinkled sand, cocking his head from time to time as the blasphemy of the guns drifted and died on the wind.

Gradually the dunes gave way to the stunted salt plants and hardy small-leafed bushes.   A flourishing castor plant, its pods crackling with short, brittle explosions, attracted his attention.   The wind brought him the distant detonations again; he moved on.

The fence was a barbed wire one with four strands.   These were held to the ground by sturdy metal posts.   Something black was hanging from the top strand.   It spun around with savage convulsions. He started towards it. Even as he did so, half a dozen magpies rose into the air, screaming wildly. They swooped up into a tree, the wind whistling through their pinions. The idiot boy approached the bird; it was a magpie. It had become hooked up on the fence by a length of fishing line, firmly entangled around its feet.

As he approached, it stopped its furious attempts to detach itself, hanging quietly, its wings still extended and its plump body swaying rhythmically.

He went straight up to it, catching it fearlessly under the breast and bringing it into an upright position. With the other hand, he dragged at the line. The bird lay perfectly still, the rush of blood from its head calming it.

Finally the line fell free from the wire. Still the bird offered no resistance. But as soon as he attempted to pluck the nylon from the legs, it struck at him and attempted to fly off. He held it with two hands to stop the anxious flailing of its wings. Still it managed to twist its head down and plunge the black lance of its beak into the cleft between thumb and forefinger of his left hand. With a squeal he pulled the hand away, sliding the bird towards his hip with the other hand and holding it there while he brought the wounded hand back towards it in a hesitating gesture. Again the bird lanced his flesh, blood rushing to follow the tip of the beak. This time he made no sound though tears sprang to his eyes with the pain.

When he found that he could not untangle the line, the bird still continuing to strike at him, he held it out in front of him, as if there, it could no longer reach him. He then clambered through the fence, ripping the back of his head on one of the projecting spikes.

He walked on into the range, the bird held before him at arm's length and small drops of blood staining the sand behind.

The idiot boy's appearance in front of the butts caused the sergeant to gape unbelievingly. It took him several seconds to roar out the command "Cease fire!"

Before this had been obeyed, the idiot boy fell.

The bullet which struck him had ricocheted from the cement parapet behind which the target markers worked. It had entered his left side just below the armpit.

When they got to him, he was already dead. He lay on his back, his arms extended, his eyes still wide with amazement. Unharmed, the bird crouched motionless; it was still attached to his clenched, bleeding hand by the fishing line. Beside him were three pink shells.

The Compound

ANNA WEST

FINALLY the boy-friend said, "Out! Out! You do nothing but read Dostoevsky . . . go!"

And so Stella had to look for a job again.

Young woman. Highly confidential. Must live in. Salary commensurate with ability. No experience expected.

The answering service, "Leave a phone number, please. He will call you back in twenty minutes."

She sat cross-legged on the floor. This time she could not say, "It's only for a little while, then I'll audition again."

No, she had not made it. Now she had to submit, maybe even get married. She *could* read, that would help in later years. Next month she would be thirty.

"What do you look like?" the voice said when she answered the telephone.

"Right now?"

"Any time."

"I have on a pair of red leotards."

"Tights?"

"Yes."

She smiled. Great. The man was crazy. No serious possibilities for work.

"What time can you come for an interview?"

"Any time."

"Come now."

"It will take a while."

"How long?"

"Two hours," she told him.

She wanted to wear something that would scare him. Just right . . . a purple peasant blouse and a red tennis skirt, items left over from bit parts in little theatre. Over those she dropped Allan's dirty trench coat. She covered her legs with black and green diamonds, those diamonds being printed on her baggy knee socks. Onto her feet she secured a pair of saddle oxfords that were too big by wrapping the laces around her ankles.

It was the address of a new apartment building by the beach. A black sign with gold letters announced that there were no vacancies. When she touched the door she heard a faint buzz and the glass swung slowly back. In the centre of the lobby on a marble bench just in front of a waterless fountain sat a man in a blue opaque plastic suit.

"Stella La Veck?"

"Yes."

She took off Allan's coat and watched the man look at her.

"Interesting. Please sit down," the man said.

She sat next to him.

"This job will pay you three hundred dollars a month and you will have a five-room furnished apartment. Your duties are almost non-existent."

"What are they?"

"There's the problem. Until you agree to take the job, I can't tell you."

"That's stupid."

"Yes, but necessary. Suppose I said three fifty a month?"

"Really, you can't expect a person to make an agreement without . . ."

"Four twenty-five."

Oh well, she'd agree. If she didn't like the conditions, she'd leave. It was simple.

"Good. After you move in, we'll talk about your, your . . . work. Will you move in tonight?"

"May I bring a friend?"

"Certainly. There are very few restrictions here."

"I'm not going with you," Allan said. "We are finished. If I allow you just the smallest hold . . ."

First, she changed costumes, arranged herself in a lavender Brussle. The Brussle, new in style this fall, meant to accentuate Breast and Motion. The cloth was at the bodice stitched in a circular manner, creating cups, as in the Old World brassière. A band an inch wide held the upper midriff tight. Below that, as said by the fashion writers, "The Brussle Sprouts into a Full Flamboyant Display of Luxurious Free Pleats. Wonderful to Wear . . . Wonderful to Watch!"

Then she packed three boxes of costumes, four boxes of books,

one tape recorder, and a make-up kit containing eleven half filled
bottles of skin tint.

"You'll have to make two trips," the taxi-driver said.

Inconsiderate man. Never mind, I am going to be financially
secure.

The boulevard, on its way to the beach, went through the new
part of the city. The transparent forms stood shadowless. At
night the people who lived in them would push the proper buttons
and curtains would ripple down the walls, filling the rooms with
sounds of sinking things, like the sizzling of pebbles at low tide.
Stella had always wanted one of those apartments, but had never
met anyone willing to set her up in one.

Now she felt rather pleased with herself. She had made a
definite move, unlike anything she had ever tried. The duties
almost non-existent . . . nothing sinister about the man . . .
secrecy, intrigue, perhaps. He was in charge of a government
project . . . that would account.

"I'll get the other boxes tomorrow," she told the driver.

The driver set the costume boxes and the make-up case in front
of the door.

"Could you help me get these inside?"

"No," he said.

She walked towards the door, heard the faint buzz again. Perhaps she could get the man . . . she had forgotten to ask his name.
If he was gone, or would not help, she would ask one of the tenants.

*This is a recorded announcement. Welcome to The Compound.
If you have anything that needs to be transported, push down on
the green lever to set the belt in motion. Set the dial at 101,
the number of your apartment. Your belongings will be conveyed.
The elevator is to your right.*

Well well well efficient. Completely opposite to previous life.
This will be very good. Make thinking easy.

She found the apartment door open. She stepped directly into
the living-room and the door closed behind her.

"Uhf!" she said.

Above her loomed an orange and black striped ceiling. One
wall, *crème de menthe* green, and possessing the same oily quality
of that drink, was focused upon by the eyes on the opposite wall,
those eyes belonging to George Washington, who lay stretched out
beneath three red palms, both the general and the palms done in
mosaic tile. Stella hurried across the turquoise rug and opened
the sliding glass doors that led to the veranda.

As she stood outside, she looked into the other rooms and was relieved to experience no more startling visual effects. Each of her five rooms opened onto the triangular veranda, the dining-room occupying the corner of the L-shaped floor plan, opening into the living-room on the right, the kitchen above, the kitchen, in turn, leading to the delivery-room, and the living-room adjacent to the bedroom and bath.

She walked to the edge of the veranda, to the marble wall, upon which a telescope was mounted. She looked down at the lights of the amusement park, thought it would be fun to focus the telescope on the roller-coaster, thought simultaneously that the telescope might have something to do with her work, and then she realized that someone had said something.

"Good evening, Miss La Veck."

He spoke to her from the living-room.

"Oh, hello. I thought you had gone home, Mr ah . . . "

"Smith. Marvin Smith. Marvin, if you like."

"Yes. I'm used to calling people by their first names."

"Have you eaten dinner yet?" Marvin Smith said.

She had not, nor breakfast, nor lunch, nor dinner the night before. Allan had locked the kitchen.

"I won't spend another cent on your repulsive appetite! But I'll be glad to pay the cab that takes you away," Allan had said.

She had always appreciated Allan's directness. The actress in her, he had said, needed someone to assume authority over it. She supposed that he was right.

"No, I haven't eaten yet," Stella said.

"Come with me then, and while we eat I'll explain your position."

He took her to The New Fish, a place she had never been inside before. It was said that the fish served there were bred by the State Office of Marine Research, which had somehow managed to develop a boneless species. She didn't believe it.

"You like fish, I hope?"

"Love them."

"Good," Mr Smith said.

The restaurant was a glass bell within the ocean. They entered through an underwater tunnel that began just next to the roller-coaster ticket office.

"It's magnificent!" she said.

Mr Smith led her to a glass-topped table. She could see pink water bubbling under the glass.

"Amazing!"

When she sat down, the chair formed itself to the contours of her body. She felt as though she were sitting on water.

"Fantastic! What is this chair made of?" she asked.

"Who knows? They're actually commonplace by now. It has something to do with adjustment of masses, I suppose."

"Commonplace? You should see where I was living! Fantastic! I didn't realize how out of touch I had become."

Now Mr Smith smiled and Stella noticed that there were no spaces between his teeth. In fact, what she saw in his mouth she could not call teeth at all, so much more were they like two ivory bands, perfectly smooth, so gently curving . . .

"You'll enjoy getting in touch, I think. I'll help you as much as I can," Marvin Smith said.

"But I can't eat all that!" Stella said.

The waiter had set before her a fish fifteen inches long and half a foot wide.

"And it's all meat," Mr Smith said. "No bones. I understand that they do have skeletons, but they are on the outside, like shells, but ribbed, just like the old ones."

Delicious, Stella thought, more body than the old fish, something like the most tender veal.

"The vegetables are ordinary," Mr Smith said.

"Peas?" she asked.

Then she wondered why she had asked. It was obvious that they were peas.

"Yes. On weekends they have beetroot," Mr Smith said.

"Only peas and beetroot?"

"Yes. Some eccentricity on the part of management, I believe."

Stella drank the wine, wine pale, almost sweet, gentle. Stella sighed, relaxed, felt tensions from last romance sinking into the silent pink bubbles beneath the glass. And to think she had been avoiding this kind of life . . . idiotic of her . . . pretence, pride, ignorant to judge without experience, narrow-minded.

"Would you like to hear about your work now?"

She had forgotten about it.

"Yes. My curiosity is beyond everything," she said.

"Fine. Other than yours, there are twelve apartments in the building. You are to check them daily, in the morning between eight and nine, and at night between seven and eight."

"I don't understand what you mean. Check them?"

"Just check them. See if anyone has moved in. It's crazy."

Stella smiled at his slip into the old dialect.

"You smile at that word. Since we usually do not have such situations to deal with in our modern society, it is logical that we do not have words to describe such situations. Therefore, it's

crazy. Six months ago, every apartment but yours was rented.
Seven hundred dollars a month. Luxury apartments, every one.
But as far as we can tell, no one has moved in."

"And the rents?"

"We get prompt payment. Checks drawn on the United Dollar
Fund Corporation."

"Then why do you care if anyone actually lives in them or not?"
Mr Smith frowned.

"It is a matter of policy. Would you like a drink?"

"Thank you," Stella said.

"There's just one other thing, the telescope. No set rule about
this, so far as time goes, I mean when you do it, at what time on
the, by the clock. But once or twice a week you should look
through it. It's aimed towards the beach. If you see anything,
let us know right away."

"See what?"

"Anything. It's set to open under certain conditions. Under
other conditions, when you look through it, you'll just see black.
Get it?"

"Certainly."

"Good. Now I'll take you home. You must be tired."

He gave her fifty dollars.

"To hold you," he said.

Alone in the apartment. She had expected him to stay, but he
had made no move towards her. She missed her books, thought
she should have brought at least one box. Well, now what?
Unpack. No, never mind that tonight. Nothing needed except
toothbrush, that, in make-up case. Television? Why not? Not
tired. Haven't been tired in months. Just tired of never getting
anywhere. Now getting somewhere . . . four twenty-five a month.
Won't spend more than one hundred. Have to cover this couch.
It scratches. Like to sit naked at night watching Old Movie. But
this one, *Cream of the Tartars,* too silly. Must get dressed and
go for a walk.

Some minutes later, she descended. She clicked her heels across
the marble floor of the lobby. The door opened.

*This is a recorded announcement. The main door does not
open from the outside between the hours of ten p.m. and six a.m.
This is a routine security measure. If you wish to come in after
ten p.m. go to the side of the building. The Night Man will assist
you.*

Fine. Strange that Marvin hadn't mentioned the Night Man.

She stepped onto the empty boulevard. She walked. In the

planes of glass fronts she saw her reflection, the only reflection. The night light came from lamps suspended high above the door-ways. From building to building she saw her image keeping pace, visible and having no property of its own. She saw the Brussle skirt swaying lavender, billowing now and then from sudden puffs of hot wind that came up from the gratings along the sidewalk. She walked forty blocks, to the boulevard's end, where, from a circular plaza, radiated the seven main streets of the Old Town.

The Old Town, backed by the Eastern Mountains, had to itself the entire Northern Beach. New Town took a strip forty blocks long and twenty wide between the Southern Plains area and the docks to the north. She had always lived in the Old Town.

First count to a hundred, then learn the alphabet. Now you must recite the names of the Seven Streets and their important intersections.

> "*Skipping down in Old Town*
> *Name The Seven Streets*
> *Widely, Bridely, Bacon, Crumble, Jason, Mason, Vander-*
> *fleets,*"

the children chanted.

> "*Cross the wide with Pomegranate*
> *Bacon meets with Third. . . .*"

Geography. No travel. She had no feeling for it.

She had to go back to Allan's apartment. Not that she would try to tell him what she had learned, he wouldn't believe her. She just wanted to make sure he hadn't thrown out the other boxes.

Note on door, "Stella: Your things are at Natalie's."

Natalie lived in a flat at the end of Vanderfleets, in the dock district. A cab went by. Stella screamed after it. The red lights backed towards her.

"End of Vanderfleets," Stella said.

"Late."

"Midnight."

"Late," the driver repeated.

It seemed that each year things closed earlier than they had the year before. Her parents had never come in before two. She could remember waiting for them. They always brought her presents, ashtrays with gold letters, stuffed animals, little candies, bright paper hats; they had been happy, but not during the day. Now people were trying to be happy during the day, some of them, and they let the nights end before they had even seen the red moon.

"I had given you up," Natalie said.

Natalie had always seemed older than everyone else. She was twenty-three.

"That's a nice thing you're wearing," Stella said.

It was a green knee-length sweater. Purple tassels dangled from the hem.

"Drink?" Natalie said.

"No, I've had enough for one night. I want to tell you about something. It's not what you expect."

"Pot?"

"No, thank you. But if you could give me a minute . . ."

"Your boxes are here."

"Thanks for keeping them."

"You will take them tonight, won't you. I don't like having pieces of other people around."

Stella watched the shadows cast by Natalie's tassels as they bobbed on the muralled wall, just under the tail of a scarlet goat.

"I have a job," Stella said.

Natalie sank to the floor. On her knees, with the soles of her bare feet exposed to the eyes of the peacock feathers painted on the ceiling, she whispered, "I have a perfectly wonderful idea. Why don't you marry Allan?"

"My job. . . ."

"Yes, all right, go on, what is this awful job?"

"I'm manager of an apartment building out by the Western Beach."

She thought she could describe her position no better than that. Natalie either would not believe her or would be bored. It had nothing to do with her.

"A domestic? You do the funniest things," Natalie said.

Stella phoned for a taxi. She would take her boxes now. Another time she would come back to Old Town, not to Natalie's, but to other friends, people she had known since grade school. She had to tell someone about what was happening at the Western Beach. She was amazed at how much the Old Towners didn't know about life.

"Pull up in the alley, please, I have to go in the side entrance."

"That's extra," the driver said.

"Just do it, will you please?"

On the wooden door, a wide door, like those in Old Town, she saw a brass knocker from which stared the grim face of a woman whose head seemed to sprout antlers, who had for one ear a wheel, and for the other, an apple. To Stella, the face was purely decorative, although she supposed that once it might have meant something. She let the knocker fall against the door three times. The door opened.

"Don't just stand, come in."

The man wore a black cap with a plastic visor.

"I have some things."

"The belt doesn't go on until six."

"Just help me pull them inside the door. I'll get them up in the morning."

The Night Man nodded. They pulled the boxes inside.

"I've been alone for six months," the Night Man said, "Now there's you. But you're up there. Going to keep a check on things, so I've heard. Well, there's nothing wrong with that. It's good honest work."

Between words he cleared his throat. He sounded over seventy. He led her down a corridor and up a ramp. He pushed a door open. Light from the lobby glistened on the oily patches of the Night Man's face. It was a soft, pink-cheeked face, not over sixteen years old. Now he giggled and the age left his voice.

"I'm studying. This isn't bad work. I do voices. You're an actress, aren't you? You look like an actress. My mother was an actress, but she stopped because it made her nervous to leave the stage. She used to forget a lot. I mean, people would ask her questions and she . . ."

"Excuse me," Stella said, "Do you have any coffee?"

"You have coffee. Don't you know? All the apartments have coffee, 'n lots of other things. Haven't you looked? The refrigerator's filled with meat 'n cheese. These apartments are completely furnished."

"I'm going up now," Stella said.

"Good night," the Night Man said.

It was just past one. When she stepped naked from her dressing-room-closet, she saw Marvin Smith sitting on her bed.

"Very nice," Marvin Smith said.

"Thank you," Stella said.

"Where did you go?"

"Just a minute," Stella said.

When the other person was dressed, she found it uncomfortable to converse in the nude.

She stepped back into her closet. It annoyed her to put on street clothes after she had taken them off for the night, but her dressing-gown was packed away. The Brussle would have to do.

"There now, Marvin. Marvin. . . ."

He was gone.

Off with the Brussle. This time she let it sink to the floor.

She felt the smooth sheets and sniffed their faint scent of cinnamon. She pulled them back, stretched herself, found this a perfect bed, a bed that neither gave too much nor offered too much resistance. A good love place . . . well, lovers and places, sometimes one, sometimes other, some day, both, today, what? Today complete change. Orbit. Eyes shut, muscles twitch just a little. Good night, dear self, Jason, Mason, Vanderfleets . . .

. . . *Announcement. Seven o'clock . . . to remind you . . . in one hour . . . the apartments.*

She sat sprightly up. Today she would not wear the Brussle.

She went to the delivery room. She pulled the black tape from one of the boxes. The lids creaked open. Black lace, kilt, wool stole, sari, poncho, rubber boots, pink organdie skirt . . . grey dress, that will do, solid neutrality. Find underwear. Underwear in make-up kit. Green tint spilled making spots on white panties, never mind. Go to the bathroom and take a shower, take a show'r, take a show'r, go to the bathroom and take a show'r, here is the soap for the show-er. But where, oh where, is a towl-y-wowl, a towl-y-wowl, a towl-y-wowl? No towel. What's that box?

To operate this unit press red button. Stand under nozzle. Automatic closing.

She stood beneath the nozzle. She shivered. The warm air gave her goose flesh . . . ah, the wonders of the drying process! What about feet? She felt the floor warm beneath her. Gusts of air blew up between her legs. A red light flashed on the instruction box. She felt her hips. Dry. Dry all over.

Teeth, make-up, hair, smile, underwear, dress, shoes . . . where shoes? In the closet. She stepped out of the bathroom and found that her bed had been made. Excellent. She put her shoes on. Then she smelled something. From the kitchen came the odour of coffee.

Behind the glass doors of the cabinet, she saw the cups, six of them, along with saucers, plates, bowls, a complete set. She thought she would have to give a party. The coffee bubbled within a carafe. She opened the refrigerator, saw eggs ham bacon steak cheese . . .

Two eggs.

She looked for a frying-pan. No pan. She studied the stove.

Eggs here.

She cracked the eggs into the two depressions at the back of the grill. The eggs sizzled. From above, two lids descended. They covered the eggs.

Medium: For well push yellow button beside grill.

The words appeared on a metal slide just above the stove.

"Medium will be fine," she said.

She scooped the eggs onto a plate. She heard a soft buzz. The

left-over bits of egg disintegrated. Was there any bread for toast?
She saw what appeared to be an aluminium breadbox. She opened
it. Inside steamed the toast, buttered.

Seven-thirty, said the clock.

She turned on the radio to get the morning report.

". . . in some respects. In other ways, the problems are over,
said Mr Swanson. A bumper crop of cherries has been announced
by the Bureau of Fruit Production. Consumers are requested to
stock jams beginning next month, otherwise it is feared that there
will be no room on the shelves for the up-coming blueberries.

"So much for the domestic news.

"Abroad, colonies are again complaining of over visitation. This
issue will be discussed in today's Satalon. It may be necessary,
said the Bureau of Travel, to limit stays of over three months to
consumers having no children. Hotels and transportation offices,
particularly in the Eastern Development, complain daily of over-
buy and demand immediate relief. Presumably, travel allotments
will be lowered next month.

"And now for the Daily Plot.

"Believe. Be live. Be sure. The horizon spreads over all. The
vertical has fallen."

She waited, expecting something more, heard only the beginning
of what the announcer called "Fifth Electron in Alpha" on a
program of music from yesterday.

But it was extraordinary! Perhaps she had dialled a radio
play. Just yesterday, in Old Town, there had been news of war,
five thousand troops daily. Blueberries? She would go out after
she had done her checking. Someone would know something.

The twelve apartments, one on top the other, empty of living . . .
she opened them. Each like the other, spacious airy view auto-
clean. Stella sought differences between them. In apartment
404, three floors beneath her own, she counted cupboard knobs.

. . . the people? Where? Rich . . . they must be together on
a cruise. That's it. In time, they'll come back. And then, my
position, what will happen if they come back? Don't worry, don't
worry, anticipating problems, nothing to worry about. . . .

Night.

I do not like being alone. Where are my friends? They were
here. I saw them as I walked by. They were sitting at this table.
Now they are gone. They will not believe that I am loyal to
them. We are what we do? they say. You can not mix with

them and with us. We are people of principle. You are selling
yourself. You have forsaken . . .

"'Spresso please," Stella said.

Gio smiles at me. He has a family. He understands. He
speaks to me, says he would like to see The Compound, his wife
too. Why must they judge? I struggled with them all the years
of my childhood and they never gave me love. I was more true
to them than they were to themselves. . . .

"Closing now, Stella."

"Good night, Gio."

"Good night."

"Again?" the Night Man said.

She followed him.

"You going out every night?"

"What business is it of yours?" Stella said.

He giggled.

"You won't last long," he said.

Now he opened the door to the lobby. She looked at him. He
stared at her and smiled just enough to make her want to slap
him.

"Stella."

Marvin Smith called to her from the marble bench. He
walked with her to the elevator.

"May I go up with you?"

She nodded.

"I want you to be happy here. You must know that. There is
nothing I want more than . . ."

"Yes, Mr Smith."

"Please, listen to me."

He followed Stella to her door.

"In this part of town there aren't any women like you. I don't
understand it. What is happening to me? Do you know? These
terrible impulses . . . I do not understand, I . . ."

"Come in, Marvin."

"Thank you."

Bed.

"You are soft, Stella."

"You are smooth, Marvin."

"I love you, Stella."

"That's nice, Marvin."

"Do you love me, Stella?"

"No, Marvin."

"Tell me how you feel."

"I can't," Stella said.

"Why?"

"Words are aggressive. I want to be passive, with no explanations. Are you melting, Marvin?"

"Yes, are you?"

"No."

"I will make you melt!"

Through sound-resistant walls came bangings, shoutings, buzzers ringing, hysterical laughter.

"What's that?"

Stella sat upright and Marvin fell off the bed. He grabbed for the pants of his plastic suit.

"They've come! They've come!" Marvin shouted.

Stella put on her robe and went to the bathroom.

By morning, the people had taken possession of their apartments.

"If only you had looked through the telescope," Marvin said.

"What good would it have done?"

"We could have put out a quarantine sign," Marvin said.

She knew, he had told her, sadly, that she would have to go. There was nothing for her to do now. Apartment 101 would be converted into a club, as specified in the rental contracts.

"I can't go back to Old Town. Nobody's speaking to me there," Stella said.

"I'm terribly sorry, Miss, ah, Miss, Miss, Miss . . ."

"La Veck."

"Yes, of course. But I can not help you. It is impossible. We have to make our own lives. It is one of those requirements. Oh, what can I say? Good-bye, Miss La Veck."

"Good-bye, Marvin."

Now she sat again in the back seat of a taxi. This driver allowed her to take all the boxes in one trip. Marvin had given her a month's salary.

"I've never been to the Southern Plains area before," she told the driver.

"Not much out there. Just houses. You know someone?"

"Yes," Stella said.

There's Mother now. She's sitting on the front porch. She sees the taxi. Here she comes. Such a pretty yellow dress. Such a pretty sixty-year-old Mother. There is Father standing next to her. His arm rests on her shoulder. He is bald. But such a nice smile he has! I am happy to be home, Mother, Father. I would have come earlier, but they wouldn't let me. I love you very much. I can pay the taxi fare myself. You have been here many years, living in your brick house. The cyclone fence keeps away the neighbourhood children. I am crying, I think, but my face is dry.

"Is it you, Stella?" Mother says.

"It is you, Stella," Father says.

Oh, thank you for recognizing me! Thank you, thank you, thank you thank you thank you thank you thank you thank you thank—

The Full Belly

PATRICK WHITE

Not many months after the Germans walked in, the elder Miss Makridis began to fail. She spoke rarely, which was distressing enough for those around her, but worse still, what she said was to the point. She said to her younger sister: "If only we could go off quickly, Pronoë, there would be two mouths less, but age has toughened us, if anything, and we'll probably spend a long time dying."

Pronoë, pinker, softer, less ascetic than her sister, naturally protested. Raising her furry upper lip, she whimpered back: "Ach, Maro, you speak as though we were no longer human beings, but cattle!"

Miss Makridis didn't contradict. Ladies of perfect hearing liked to discuss Maro's increasing deafness, whereas the family recognized her silences as a kind of curtain behind which she chose to withdraw.

"And I don't want to die!" Pronoë insisted, who all her life had resented the hard corners designed for her hurt and humiliation.

As the two elderly ladies continued standing at the window, in the clear light which often seemed all that was left to them of the city they had known, Costa sat, warming his hands between his thighs, the other side of the folding doors. It was one of those afternoons which congealed the blood in his raw fingers, one of the days, frequent now, when he failed to turn the piano from furniture into instrument. The conversation in the next room might have sounded more ominous, if it hadn't been for his faith in the aunts' permanence. It was as unthinkable that the Parthenon, say, should disappear. The real world must obviously survive even these explosive times, because his will would not allow it not to.

The light was already playing its game of coloured slides with the old ladies at the window. From girlhood it had been accepted that Maro was the intellectual one. Pronoë grew up artistic; there

were the high-lit bowls of fruit, in oils, her *Cypresses against a
Wall* (a whole series of them), there were the yards of crochet
lace she hadn't succeeded in giving away.   While Maro dealt,
rather, in ideas.   She used to exchange ideas, passionately, with
men.   She accepted men as intellects, she admired them as scholars,
as poets, as priests.   Otherwise, the whole thing was inconceivable.
Between the wars Goethe had been her great love.   She spoke
English, Italian, French, reckless Russian, and with the greatest
pedantic accuracy, though her conscience now hushed it up —
German.

After Eleni's marriage, the two remaining sisters had wandered
about Europe with Mother, in search of the kind of employment
nice people expected.   They visited watering places, for Mother's
liver, her asthma, and her gout.   There were museums for Maro.
She had taken courses at some of the universities.   While Pronoë
had her little social flutter, in Greek circles, in Paris and Vienna.
She tried on hats, and sketched the easier monuments.   Mother
had died at Rome, after which they brought her back to Greece,
for Christian burial, and because, they suddenly realized, their
money was running out.

Through the folded doors Costa watched the fading light strew
his aunts' crumbly cheeks with ashes of violets.   Light, it seemed,
turned marble to pumice, flesh into grey pottery.   There was a certain light by which his own genius became suspect, he couldn't
believe in the music congealed in his mottled sausages of fingers.

So he was glad enough when Anna gave him a rough kiss in
passing through the dining-room. (Acquaintances considered Anna
cold, simply because she was too busy, too much depended on her.)
This evening she was wearing her brownest, her most livery look,
which meant she had spent most of the day hunting for food.   On
the whole Costa enjoyed being the practical Anna's younger
brother.   He got up now and followed her sturdy calves, which had
something in common with his own hands.   He was anxious to
see what she had got in the bundle.

Anna kept for her aunts a gentleness she seldom showed to
others, probably not even to Stavro.

"Did you take your tablets?"   Her face changed shape, she
lowered her voice, to indulge Aunt Pronoë's imagined heart.   "Are
you cold, Maroula?"   She touched the other old woman's hand
as though it were the flimsiest material.

Aunt Maro answered: "No.   But if I were, nothing could be
done about it."

It was the kind of realism which had begun to upset ladies of
their acquaintance.

Aunt Pronoë let out a sharp little whine. She couldn't wait to
see what Anna had found.

"What is it?" she breathed, gasped, looking wateringly at the
bundle.

"What have you brought?" asked Paraskevi walking slit-slat over
the honey-coloured parquet.

Springing from such different sources the maid and her mis-
tresses had united far far back. They had aged together
grumblingly.

"It's the same," said Anna, handing over the ragful of uprooted
dandelion.

"Weeds again? It's all weeds. I'm all wind from eating weeds,"
the maid grumbled out of her seams as she went back slip-slop
across the no longer polished parquet.

Aunt Pronoë advised her, through an overflow of tears, to give
thanks to God.

"Poh! If He's feeding the other side?" said Paraskevi crankily.

Aunt Maro recollected: "He sent us the lamb from Vitina. It
wasn't His fault if some pig of a man stole it out of the sack."

It was true. And left a dog's carcass in its place.

Aunt Maro laughed. It still amused her, because it was the kind
of incident which illustrated. But almost at once her face grew
stern, her eyes glittered: she was in love with God.

A smell of moist earth lingered in the room, from the weeds
Paraskevi had carried off to wash and boil. Costa used the prospect of a meal as an excuse to postpone working on the Haydn
sonata. He promised himself that the wad of boiled dandelion
he was going to eat, without oil, without salt, without anything,
would endow him with a strength to overcome physical obstacles
and lift him to pinnacles of understanding.

While knowing that Paraskevi was right; the weeds would turn
to wind in their stomachs, the same thin notes continue to twitter
out of his fingers.

"But we shall eat, at least!" said Aunt Pronoë with a kind of
hectic gaiety.

"Not I," said Aunt Maro. "Not when every mouthful counts.
Remember the children. Who am I to deny them food?"

Possibly everyone had become a bit feverish. Costa's hair was
permanently damp. Old Paraskevi muttered, and repeated; her
eyes burned holes in anyone she looked at. And it was precisely
on that evening that Aunt Maro took to her bed.

From there during the days which followed, she continued to
conjure up those unconvincing, over-idealized children. The flame

she had kept burning under the icons, in spite of shortages, at great expense, was more substantial than Aunt Maro's children.

At first his ailing aunt was the perfect excuse for Costa not to practise. In that small flat.

But she began insisting from her bed: "Play to me, Costaki. Music is more nourishing than food."

So he played for her, and at times the music ascended some of the way towards the heights he was determined to reach.

After they had learnt to admit to the Occupation, and the first knife-thrusts of hunger had developed into a permanent ache of emptiness, he had decided to utilize, to *spiritualize,* his physical distress. (He even made a memo of it, in French, in his neatest hand, at the back of his *Wohltemperiertes Klavier.*) To a certain extent he had succeeded, he liked to think. For instance, a detached, hungry melancholy, arising out of his physical condition, helped his Chopin. Out of the ebb and flow of his altered blood, his own *submergence,* his *Cathédrale engloutie* rose with a glowing conviction he hadn't achieved before. The architecture, some of the austerities of Bach, he had begun to grasp, if not yet the epiphanies. Pronoë suggested these depended on "maturity of soul". He no longer had the strength to feel irritated by his aunt. Instead he was amused to visualize his "soul" rounding out, like a football bladder suspended in air, in a space beside the Parthenon.

Costa Iordanou was a serious stubble-headed boy with broad muscular hands. His hands were surprising to those who could recite his pedigree.

Consider his mother alone: Eleni—so dazzling from many worldly angles, her *toilettes* from Worth, her long sheaths of hands, her judgments, her generosity, her malice, her abandoned hair, her throat, her eyes. Her eyes. It was not so extraordinary that Iordanou, a cold, upright man, should have accepted her without a dowry. No doubt it was Eleni who had helped him to the Presidency. Tragic how leukaemia shortened his term of office, far more tragic that Eleni, driving her own car, should crash at that bend in the Kakia Skala.

For Costa his parents had never been more than photographs and myths. His aunts were what his touch confirmed. Only natural that those good souls should have taken Eleni's Anna and Costaki. (It's always sad for the children.) Anna was a brown sulky girl, Costa an amusing child, making up his little tunes at Pronoë's piano not long after he began to toddle.

Until now, from her bed, under the icon of the Panayia, Maro was reminding him of her favourite.

"Play for me, Costaki, *La Cathédrale.*"

His aunt's voice rising slowly in sonorities of green masonry out of his tremulous belly out of the iridescent waters glowed with the light of rose-windows resurrected.

From the beginning the aunts had decided the children should inherit the brilliance of their parents. Anna would marry an ambassador, on a dowry provided—it was hoped—by Cousin Stepho Mavromati. But Anna the brown girl had thrown herself away on that young doctor, Stavro Vlachos, from Vitina. Months later ladies of the aunts' acquaintance were still putting on their kindest voices, as though to help the poor things over another bereavement, or an operation.

So fortunate for them Costaki was born a prodigy. Nina Zakinthinou, one heard, had grown jealous of her own pupil. At the Odeion Antoniadis had informed Miss Makridis at last that Costa must study with someone able to take him farther. Maro returned looking even more haggard than her usual self. Until it was arranged, with the help of Cousin Stepho, that Costa should go to Paris, to Cortambert.

Then the house of Europe incredibly collapsed.

Costa taught himself not to remember the details of his pretended future. Though he kept the steamer ticket at the bottom of his handkerchief drawer. And his music remained, which nothing could devalue or destroy. Its flow continued, perhaps more uneven than formerly, reduced at times to a stammer of frustration, at others forcing itself with the glug-glug of water escaping through a hole.

If ever in that over-intimate flat the atmosphere of cloying love, of suffocating thoughtfulness, dried the music up, he used to refresh himself in an illusion of property: a studio just large enough to hold his piano, in which, besides, he might occasionally undress some girl, not yet completely visualized, let alone possessed, her buttresses of thighs, her gargoyle breasts, rising slowly out of the oil-smeared waters and sumptuous lights of his imagination. Or discuss with his friend Loukas some of the theories of love over the frayed halves of a come-by cigarette. Fingers smelling of nicotine. Loukas said there was a sexual position in which the two bodies made a kind of boat together. So.

Loukas, who had in his left groin a birthmark like the map of Crete, disappeared on a November night the way people did nowadays. The map of Crete was no advantage; nobody had identified him. Costa found himself forgetting Loukas, not even caring. That, too, was the way it happened now. Mourning belonged to the age of visiting-cards and maiden ladies of sufficient means.

Or was he self-centred, as Aunt Pronoë, in moments of extreme hunger, accused? At least he didn't flinch from the disgust he often felt on recognizing doubts and weaknesses, on seeing his own face in the glass. Or was he mistaking self-indulgence for realism? Did he love the spot on his chin? Of his over-exposed puppy face. He longed to be as old, as wily, as inviolable, as Goethe, say, at the end of his sensuality, when his vice passed for experience, and even his platitudes were accepted as gold.

"It is so *satisfying*," Aunt Maro called, as she got control of her machinery, "to realize that music can be French as well. Thank you, dear Costaki. Your *Cathédrale.*"

And Aunt Pronoë, that elderly baby, gurgled: *"Ravissant, ravissant!"* on her way to disturb Maroula's pillows.

Very briefly as a young girl Pronoë* was engaged to an officer. Nobody knew why the engagement had been broken off. Something mysterious, never discussed, had happened to Maro in Munich. After which, the two ladies gave themselves to Athene and the Panayia. Perhaps their names had designed them for it. Neither of them was in any way resentful of her fate. Each, in fact, would have protested her fulfilment. And her devotion to the other.

"Leave me, Pronoë!" Maro's voice began to grate as she sawed with her neck against the pillow. "You are such a *fiddler!*"

"When all I think about is your comfort!"

Comfort was an immorality Maro proposed to resist.

"Oh, no, no, Pronoë! *Go*, Pronoë!" Her voice moaned and reverberated round the marble peaks.

While her sister remained standing on the plain.

"As you hate me, I shall leave you," Pronoë promised. "All our life you have tried to hurt me."

Then Maro laughed, and called down: "My memory isn't as good as yours."

On overhearing Aunt Pronoë as she passed: "What are we going to do if we lose her? What then?" Costa understood he wasn't being addressed.

Immediately she saw him she said: "When I was a girl I played the piano hoping to give pleasure to others. But *professional* musicians become so egocentric they forget they have an audience. Excepting, of course, when they hear the applause."

Everybody drew a circle Pronoë was unable to enter. Even Paraskevi her maid.

"What are you standing there for?" Pronoë called. "Standing, and standing!" Perhaps it was hunger that made her voice so thin and shrill. "What do you think about," on one occasion she

*Pronoë = Prudence

enquired, "when you are standing?"

"I am thinking," said Paraskevi, her slow thoughts voluptuous
for one so old and dry, "I am thinking how it felt in the days when
our bellies were full."

"Oh, our bell——our stomachs—that is all we can think about?
When they are so low down? And unimportant!"

"Important enough," said Paraskevi.

Answering back made her mistress rush at the *bibelots,* dust the
potiches her maid neglected, the books in which forgotten authors
had written compliments for ladies of distinction, the icons which
deteriorated whatever care was taken of them.

Pronoë used to wear gloves for dusting. Once in her rage for
cleanliness and order she put out the flame beneath the icons,
flickering in the drop of oil Maro had got from the Armenian for
four silver spoons. Pronoë could not blame herself enough; it was
as though she had committed sacrilege.

But Maro opened her eyes and said: "Why, Pronoë, all lights
are extinguishable. Except, apparently, my own."

She only opened her eyes now when there was reason for doing
so. The lids seemed to creak back, uncovering a vision of old
brown, uncommon amber. Time might have passed unbroken, a
long slow empty soporific cold, if it hadn't been for the machinery
of Maro's eyelids, and the shots they sometimes heard after curfew.

That winter Costa Iordanou began to notice the house in which
he had always lived with his aunts. Poverty had blotched, history
pitted the ochreous face under its tiara of terracotta tiles. Dun
shutters on rusty hinges could be forced open to admit the sun,
or dragged shut to bar the enemy. Any pretensions to grandeur
the house ever had were somewhat reduced by the fact that it
was shared, admittedly by members of the same family. Since Dr
Stavro Vlachos and his wife Anna had taken over the ground
floor, there was a hugger-mugger, public air, of patients hanging
about. Scabby old men often sat on the steps, waiting their turn,
under the doctor's plate. But there was no question of billeting
now, and whenever it was thought necessary to slam and bolt the
shutters, one heart could be heard as you listened for approaching
footsteps.

Otherwise, living together didn't make all that difference. Though
Anna could be pretty bossy. They heard her moving about below,
and she came up and organized them. Their flat might have been
a dolls' house when Anna began to move them around. Stavro
was a busy man. Many people depended on him. (Although
they had never known how to exchange more than a few words,
Costa loved his brother-in-law.)

Upstairs the sloping rooms had been darkened by string-coloured net curtains and too much inherited furniture. Some of the furniture was so frail the sisters wordlessly dared strangers to use it. There were the inscribed photographs of gentlemen in starched collars, ladies in *demi-décolletage,* everybody's nose impeccably aristocratic without being ostentatious. President Iordanou's photograph was set apart in a silver frame, which added to the cold distinction of his figure. Costa avoided looking at his father, as though he had been present in the flesh. It shocked him to think he had once been a drop of sperm inside the presidential pants. He preferred the crackled portraits of more distantly related admirals and noble brigands who had fought the Turk. His aunts' conversation had always glittered with words like "independence" and "liberation". They made them sound peculiarly theirs until now, after bartering their other jewels, they brought them out more guardedly.

Over Maro's bed hung the tremendous small icon of the Panayia. As a little boy he used to climb on the bed, to rub his nose against the Virgin's brown Byzantine beak. Once when nobody was looking he had scratched a flake of gold off the nimbus. The gold tasted disappointing, and made him cough. By the time his pimples came, She had grown sullen towards him. He was too conscious of the acne of wormholes in the wooden cheeks of the Mother of God. Their relationship finally settled down, half formal, half ironical. (From visits to the museum he suspected his aunt's icon wasn't a very good one.)

Until on a night of their present winter spattered with bullets smelling of damp cold of boiled weeds of blood his own love or hunger overflowed the eyes of his Panayia he was drawn towards her like one drop of water to another into one crystal radiance.

Aunt Maro opened her eyes and asked: "What are you looking at, Costaki?"

He stood trembling in a shamefully uncontrollable glandular stench of dripping armpits.

"You!" He lied smiling, ashamed equally of his cowardice and his unconfessable experience.

Maro made an almost flirtatious grimace, which did not fit her hewn-out features, or her old hair. He ran at her, and began to work her hands as though they were tokens in plaster or wood, articulated by leather thongs. At the same time he looked into her eyes, the opacity of brown amber he had always known. Although it seemed as though he had never communicated with his aunt, he worshipped her imperishability, if not that same radiance of his Panayia.

In the morning the doctor came.

Most mornings Dr Vlachos, a short stocky man from a village of pine-trees and rock, visited Miss Makridis. His heavy footsteps on the stairs were something Costa took for granted.

Maro would never have admitted to her niece's husband that he was the person she most respected, just as she wouldn't admit she could never forgive him for marrying Anna, thus destroying a design.

As he went through his early-morning scales, Costa couldn't help listening, on and off, to his brother-in-law. If he turned on the stool, he could see the back of Stavro's rather large head, his thick, rather unbending neck.

"It is a matter of will-power," Stavro was explaining. "There is nothing wrong with you, Maroula. Except—where is your will?"

Costa knew that Maro would be sawing at the pillow with her neck.

She said: "I know all about the will. I know all about my own. When to use it. And to what extent. If I decide not to, that is my own business." She began to mumble. "My contribution. To the children."

Anna was always tempting their aunt, for some of the doctor's patients were able to pay him: a couple of eggs, say, a medicine-bottleful of oil, once a goat cutlet, which drove the household wild.

That morning Anna had brought a soup-plate of watery rice. It had been mostly dust from the bottom of a sack, and was particularly glutinous. Mrs Vassilopoulo had got it—no one would have asked how—and it had pleased her sense of vengeful charity to give the little Vlachos a pinch of rice for that old creaking snob, her aunt.

Anna said, blowing on the rice: "Just a little mouthful, Maroula." Then she added, with a touch of the brilliance she hadn't otherwise inherited: "It is so insipid, no one should suffer any moral qualms."

At least they were able to laugh together.

But Costa heard his sister had failed. He heard the dring of spoon on porcelain, followed by Anna's demonstrative sigh.

Presently the Vlachos went downstairs to begin plodding through the stages of their day. The voices of patients floated up from the surgery. Costa could recognize the extra cheerful, while tremulous, tone of those who would not be able to pay.

He willed himself to believe in music. The blood of music flowed through their veins as his hands went splattering through the preliminary scales. If he could only live for music, music would give him life, spirit, as old man Bach had demonstrated so

sensibly.   It was consoling to realize sense and not daemon led to
God.

When suddenly he had to rush, the ways so tortuous, so dark,
in their cramped flat.   He had to rush into the bathroom.   Scarcely
had time to arrange himself.   It was the weeds they mostly had to
eat.   The spirit was finally reduced to a stream of green slime.

Or not finally.

Finally he sat pulling at himself, without an image, scarcely
erect.   So much for sense, for Bach, for Maro and Pronoë—for
the worm-holed Panayia.   He bowed his head at last above his
impoverished stickiness.

And remembered the afternoon Pronoë had begun springing
from room to room, an obscene elderly ballerina inspired by
expectation or fear.   His own heart exploding.   Glad he was only
the young nephew.

Paraskevi had returned upstairs.   It surprised him that anyone
so tough and fibrous as their maid could tremble quite so violently.

"A German officer," Paraskevi had announced.

"Of what rank?" babbled Pronoë.

Although her fingers were performing all the arpeggios of fear,
there were certain formalities to be observed.

But Paraskevi had never been able to learn about rank, and in
any case, a German was a German.

Suddenly too old to react any more, Pronoë let fall: "They have
come for us, then."

All three continued *in extremis* awaiting guidance if the saints
hadn't turned to wooden boards since God withdrew His favour.

Maro got up from her chair.   Everybody realized this was what
they had been hoping for.   Maro of course was their one and
present saviour.

They all went down.   As a mere hoplite, Costa breathed more
easily.

There was a wind blowing.   That winter the wind never stopped
blowing on Lykavittos.   Stavro had been called to a patient, Anna
was out digging dandelion.   So the phalanx faced the whole cold
afternoon opening blue and rainy at them through the doorway.

All four stepped out of the house into the street because of the
mortal gravity of the situation.   Pronoë held her hair to her head,
but Maro's hair blew.   She might have appeared cloudy if it
hadn't been for her features.   Her face was a rock to cut cloud.

The young lieutenant—everyone but Maro afterwards admitted
there was nothing objectionable about the lieutenant—standing
unnaturally upright outside their house in Patriarch Isaïou, was
offering a neat, oblong parcel.

"Miss Makridis," he began composing in timid Greek, "please accept with the greetings of Professor Schloszhauer, of whom I have been a student—in Munich—this small parcel of genuine coffee."

The silence swelled in Patriarch Isaïou.

Then Miss Makridis, in a German stiff from disuse, though still thrillingly accurate, said: "Professor Schloszhauer could not have realized he would force me to commit treason by accepting his parcel of coffee. I am sure the Professor would not wish me to."

Above her marble face, her hair was blowing about in tormented streamers of white cloud.

Paraskevi did not stop grunting and muttering.

Maro was actually wetting her lips.

"Tell him," she began. "*Tell* him," she practically sang. But her rising voice had a flaw in it. It cracked on its highest, purest note. And shattered.

The German lieutenant clicked. Saluted. Turned. Still carrying the parcel of coffee. Routed by the phalanx.

The victorious Greeks went upstairs. It was not an evening to celebrate. Pronoë snivelled on and off; she had a permanent cold since they were without heating. Old Paraskevi kept on wondering to them how many little cupfuls she might have squeezed out of the parcel. Where a scent of coffee should have hung, there was the earthy stench of boiling nettles.

As Costa Iordanou sat in the bathroom mopping at his thighs with a handkerchief on the morning of his shame, there wasn't even the stench of weeds. There was a smell of cold. And excrement. The flat was empty now. Paraskevi, Pronoë, each had gone in her chosen direction—to hunt. One day somebody might kill. In the meantime, it was hoped, they would all survive on weeds.

Costa went into Maro's room. He kissed his cold aunt, hoisted on her high bed. The plateful of tepid rice on the bedside table gave him a whiff or two of old old, human flesh. His aunt's eyelids reminded him of hens he had seen peasants tying by the legs, but her lips had the bluish gelatinous look of old, resigned, human lips. He couldn't look any longer. He went out, he didn't know, or care, where. Slamming their front door. He was the disgusting genius whose shortcomings embittered his throat, and stuck to his thighs.

Even so, the little pure notes of truth trickled at intervals through his eyes into his mind: a sky still tolerated the scurfy roofs of houses, a geranium still burned in a pot, a donkey dropped a poor, but still sweetly-smelling, turd.

He went down Callerghi Street buttoning his jacket. He went

down Thessalogenous. His ankle twisted on a stone, and nearly threw him. He glanced back to curse the stone. In Meleagrou, Mrs Vassilopoulo looked out from the ground floor of the block she owned. She had been putting on her hat, but took it off, and called Costaki in.

Mrs Vassilopoulo explained: "Somebody is giving me a lift. To my sister at Porto Rafti. Where I go if possible once a week. It is from my sister's—at Porto Rafti—that the eggs come."

Mrs Vassilopoulo made a phlegmy noise in her throat, a gesture with her head, to indicate the bowl of eggs. Eggs today had acquired the status of flowers. Their smooth, passive forms disturbed. The sister's hens gave brown eggs. There was a bloom on their porous shells. They were the perfection of eggs, not for eating.

Perhaps for that reason you started to hate Mrs Vassilopoulo's eggs. She had a greasy skin, particularly about the eyelids. She had a slightly noticeable goitre. She smelled of body, and looked like bruised, browning pears.

While she spoke she kept on lowering her black eyelids.

"My sister at Porto Rafti."

Flickering and smiling behind the powder.

"Where the eggs come from."

Then Mrs Vassilopoulo stopped smiling. She drew down the corners of her mouth, her eyeballs straining out of her head, her face darkening as she screwed it up into a tight ball of wrinkles. You would have said Mrs Vassilopoulo was suffering from a belly-ache.

"Costaki," she began to pant in short sharp peppermint breaths, "every day you pass I ask myself what have I done that he never looks. Of course," she said, "I know," she said, "young boys go through a brutal phase. And realize too late"—the teardrops were bounding out of Mrs Vassilopoulo's eyes—"what they have missed."

All at once she took his hand and stuck it right inside her nest of rotting pears. The sweat began prickling on him, and he had never felt so cold, so limp, between his legs.

Mrs Vassilopoulo was smiling again. It was more alarming than her belly-ache. The smell of body lying in ambush under powder shot up his nostrils as she moved in.

"I don't believe," she breathed, "you are all that brutal. Not such an angel. Not underneath."

Just then he succeeded in tearing his paralysed hand out from between her hot pears.

"You and your old eggs!"

Emotion seemed to have swelled the eggs, to have increased

their number, just as he and Mrs Vassilopoulo had grown inside
the small palpitating room.

"My eggs?" she shrieked. "You know there were never larger!
Or fresher!"

Her breasts were bounding between her shrieks.

"But what are eggs?" As though to illustrate, she began picking them up. "That," she bellowed, "is all I care for eggs!" She
threw. "And you!" She threw and threw. "And your stuck-up,
crazy aunts!" Always throwing. "Nasty *pousti* boy! Every sign.
Right from the beginning."

He went out. It was a good thing Mrs Vassilopoulo had worked
herself into such a state she could only hit her own walls.

He walked down the hill, down the narrowing, the almost
deserted streets, which bobbed about under him like gangways
over a rough sea. The clearest mornings were perhaps the bitterest
in their city now, their fragility a constant warning.

In a gutter in Bouboulinas Street an old lady was lying. The hat
she should have been wearing was gone from the nice swathes of
her hair. The shoes had gone from her stockinged feet. Her legs,
sticking out too straight, too wide apart, marked her as a carcass
rather than a corpse, yet her decent black-silk, white-spotted dress,
everything about her except the face, was that of his own, living
aunts.

Death hadn't parted her hand from her handbag. Costa had
a look inside the bag, because nowadays nobody, excepting no doubt
his aunts, let an opportunity slip. Naturally the bag was empty.

He walked on through the labyrinth, between the blanks made
by iron shutters. In the entrance to an empty arcade stood a
German corporal offering a tin of something on the palm of his
red hand.

"*Guck mal!*" he coaxed. "*Fleisch kaloh.*"

The unopened tin was so dazzlingly immaculate it could have
contained the true answers to all the riddles.

Costa was fascinated by the tin.

Then the corporal compressed his voice in a lower, straining,
hopefully seductive key.

"*Seh gamo kaloh, paithee. Ehla! Nimm's doch!*"

The corporal's hand, perhaps once-bitten, was trembling like his
voice.

Never given the time, never, to think of historic replies, Costa
Iordanou simply said: "Go and stuff it up your own arse."

It should have sounded thunderous as it rebounded off the
peeling walls, but came out thin, wavery, schoolboyish, finally a
warning of danger.

So he was running. Running from his own pseudo-thunder.
Through the empty market. Running on his too short, once
muscular, now watery, staggery legs.

The wind and the silence were against him.

He ploughed on till that uneven open space at the Agora tore
into the last of his strength. He fell down, lay panting, grunting,
amongst the earthworks, on the vines of withered capers. There
in past summers he had meandered with Loukas his friend laughing at the lovers, their hips and buttocks undulating, amongst the
twining capers, in the smell of warm dust, under a yellow moon.
Now the capers rustled as the gritty wind tweaked at their husks,
the lovers had vanished with the velvet nights. Of melon ices
dissolving trickling trickling down. Of swelling, bursting golden
moons. This year, all those who pushed with their bellies against
the wind were thin girls tragically loaded.

Where breathlessness had been thumping him against the prickly
winter grass, Costa was lying still. Not from exhaustion, or not
altogether. It was that dish of roasted kid he had eaten somewhere
out Halandri way. Memory had made a museum piece of it: bronze
leaf of skin incised with no particular myth beyond that of suc-
culence, then the streaks of ivory in the melting rosy baby flesh,
the bones not yet cast in their final sculpture. There had been a
little, sweet kidney.

Tears ran out from under his eyelids into the whispering capers.
For the most agonizingly live juices had begun to flow again through
his veins his muscles twining like live green vines his cock fighting
against his flies.

He sat up. Of course he had earned eggs in the past, and a tin
or two of German meat. Bach only tittupped along beside the
need to stuff your mouth with food. Always eventually transformed into that same slobbering beast, the spirit stood grinning
at him in the Agora.

He got up. The German corporal would be less messy, if more
painful. In any case Mrs Vassilopoulo, of bruised pears and
perfect eggs, would already have left for her sister's after mopping
out the *saloni*. It was the German corporal of huge meaty hands.

Costa, they called him Costaki, he saw himself in print IORDA-
NOU, was walking apparently away, uneven ground, a wobbly
intention, or cloudy mind, slowing him up still. In normal times
he would cross the Agora with care, listening for the crunch of
something. Now he ought to hurry, though. He began to hobble.
He might have been lame. A noose set by a weed trapped his
ankle. He jerked. Stumbled. Ran clacking at last where the
street began leading to Monastiraki.

He ran.

Swallowing the air.

He was running past the iron shutters. Flat faces of whores and spivs flickered in the entrances to alleys. It was so important to identify. As if he could ever be anything but theirs. His own smell was married to that of crumbling plaster, damp cardboard, rags not fit to steal, shit. As he searched for the corporal who should have awaited his intentions. He couldn't believe the statue might have melted away. Or the tin of German meat.

That alone had been far too solid. His mouth had become a furry thing, but the gummy buds were swelling on his tongue. Hands throbbing already with cuts from tearing the tin apart. To get beyond the jags. To the marbled meat.

All the while he was running houses shops he had been passing all his life that one dusty divided cypress the monument to Diogenes were rooted in reason a practical life could still be led and was. He, for instance, was only being practical. He could never have swallowed a raw egg. He would have had to carry eggs home, to share, boiled, with aunts whose devotion had made him too vulnerable, and a maid whose man's appetite hadn't been dulled by age. So. Eggs. Meat he could scoff down, face to a wall, on the way up, from behind fulfilled lips ignore the pain of getting it.

Meat.

It was distressing ludicrous as he ran to realize what he was doing looking down arcades up culs-de-sac for the figure of an illusory corporal. If he ever found him he would love him kiss him greedily on his meaty mouth. Force the issue too hard perhaps. But *all* Germans love to talk about Wagner, and no Greek could accuse music of treason.

There, you see, the spirit does survive the shit-pit, and the orthodox faith need not be so orthodox.

While he ran she had begun loping beside him. She had discarded her blue for the short white pleated kilt. Each one of her movements was performed with the utmost grace and ease. Health. She would have lobbed an accurate ball into her opponent's court. His Panayia. He searched her eyes, with a love he had never experienced and perhaps never would, her hair streaming in strands of palest sunlight.

Weakness on his part finally caused the milky dimples in the knees of his Valkyrie-Virgin to thin out to blur.

He was passing the little Church of the Annunciation at the bottom of the hill, a chunky, brown, lesser church favoured by Pronoë: "the poorer saints are always saintlier." He had come there with his aunt during their last Easter of peace. Now he pushed the tottering door, and was at once received into an enclosed emptiness.

He leaned, or flopped, against the stassidion, to get his breath, and the ancient wood did give him support of a kind as he lay spread-eagle, his Byzantine ribs cruelly creaking, while the professionally hungry eyed him out of the iconostasis: dog-headed saviours, lion-happy troglodytes, evangelists in cloaks of cruciform check—the whole luxury of consecrated poverty.

He might have prayed if he hadn't forgotten the language, all but a few burnt-in phrases. In moments of indolence or joy he liked to believe that being was prayer, but this did not help on occasions of guilt or desperation. So now he locked his hands together. He snuffed up the smell of dead incense, he rocked his head, and shuffled with his slanted feet. One anaemic candle was burning amongst the grubby pellets, the sickly stalactites, of last year's wax. The gold liturgies of then still hung carved in the grey fluctuating atmosphere of now. From which his lips were hopefully sucking for sustenance.

And there in the centre stood his own wooden Panayia sternly encased however the wind tormented her orthodox hair her supernal eagle's beak. Until it seemed his familiar Virgin was flowing through the whorls of his ears into the sanctuary of his brain.

Take eat, She said, *this is my body, my mess of watery black-market rice, which is given for you.*

And at once he saw clearly through the cloud of his exhaustion the cloud not of incense but of steam rising out of a plateful of boiled rice.

The heavy lids of his Panayia confirmed her decision.

Costa Iordanou elbowed himself away from the stassidion. He stood himself on his proppy legs. If not exactly restored to strength, he was again distinct, his own will, as he faced the last lap up the mountain, zigzag here, between the staggered cypresses, up up the streets of ochreous houses, through what had once been a good address.

Towards the dish of sacramental rice already gumming up his lips with opalescent goo.

On and off he tried to give thanks to his stern Virgin, but rising slowly higher on this half-deliberate half-mystical ascent, he invoked, rather, Debussy. Another cobby little swollen-headed fellow, Debussy was eaten in the end, he had read, by a cancer. There was a wall to the right on which Costa, long enough ago, had written amongst the scribblings—*Iordanou.* The writing existed still. Death was something that happened to others to Debussy or others. For Iordanou rising in swimming chords on weighted feet

a submerged future must surely emerge out of the slurp of soupy
rice.

He broke roughly into the house. It sounded as though neither
Stavro nor Anna was at home. It made him joyous, if not cocky.
Racketing up the dark stairs.

What would he say if she opened her eyes? But She had already opened Hers. And revealed.

He hadn't realized there were so many doors to overcome before
you reached the innermost.

Then the knob on Aunt Maro's door gave so sweetly. He seemed
to have expended unnecessary breath as he threw the easy old door
open. The long thin old woman was lying as usual nowadays
stretched straight eyes closed the sheet under her cold chin. What
was unorthodox shocking shattering was the chip chip of spoon
against porcelain.

It was Aunt Pronoë guzzling at a wobbly plate of rice.

Pronoë rolled her eyes in her old chalky downy face as she
rammed the spoon into a mouth he had never seen before. She
rammed again. He could hear the metal on her still pretty little
teeth. But *rammed*. Desecrating her sister's room with a clatter.
Obviously Pronoë had never understood the respect due to sanct-
ity.

"*You!*" Though he heard his voice a thin hiss, his tongue felt
shaped like a radish.

As he pounced on the plate.

Then they were wrestling together.

"You don't understand!" She was deafening. "I feel so terribly
hungry!"

In those glimpses he got his aunt's face was that of an aged
greedy girl. The strength in her deceiving hands enraged him.
She was cold as lizards, but her stiff satiny agility suggested a
large bird refusing to give up its prey. Her breath came at him
in waves, sweetly scented with masticated rice. Her ugly tongue
stuck out of her mouth.

"Costaki! No! No!" shrieked his gentle aunt. "Haven't you any
pity—respect?"

As they scrambled and fought, the veins in her eyeballs were
terrible. At least her rings didn't scratch; they had gone to the
Armenian. The spoon fell bouncing on worn carpet finally tinkling into silence over boards.

"No, no, Costa! Cost-*ah*-ki!"

The wire lashed.

"You are really a criminal, then!" Her vehemence made it
sound like laughter.

As for himself, as they fought, he had never felt so convinced
of a mission, so strong, though evidently not strong enough.

The plate fell, Anna's plate. In the absence of a dowry, they
had given her a good dinner service, with a few things besides.
Anna had been very proud of her things.

The plate falling amongst their feet trampling scuffing the last
of the pile from the carpet smashed.

"Costa you will suffer!"

Pronoë the gentle aunt couldn't shriek enough to accuse someone other than herself.

In spite of her age she could hop, like some kind of black-and-
white insect. She was hopping away from him. Out of the room.
Suppressing any afterthought of a shriek because of the maid
Paraskevi, who was shifting the pots around in their empty kitchen.

When his aunt had gone, Costa Iordanou plumped on the carpet. He was intent on stuffing his mouth with rice. If only the
few surviving grains. Sometimes fluff got in. Or a coarse thread.
His lips were as swollen as cooked rice. The grains stuck to the
tips of his fingers, the palms of his hands. He licked the grains.
He sucked them up. The splinters of porcelain cutting his lips.
The good goo. The blood running. Even blood was nourishment.

At one point he could never remember which, his Aunt Maro
must have opened her eyes.

"Eat, poor souls," she said. "Fill your stomachs, children."

He had been too engrossed to look. But continued hearing.

"I only pray you'll know how to forgive each other."

Towards evening Paraskevi came calling through the house:
"Miss Pronoë? Costaki! Can you smell it? Anna was given the
head of a lamb, the lights, and two feet! My God! My little Panayia! There will be a feast."

During the night Costa Iordanou, in his emptiness, went back
into that same shameful room hoping the oracle might reassure
him that none of what had happened had happened. He touched
the bones of her fingers. But her eyelids did not stir. He stood
for a little, gratefully listening to her slight breathing. Otherwise,
there was the sound of silence and furniture.

Fortunately there were distant corners in their rather strait flat,
in which those who needed to, could hide. The funeral, however,
forced them out. It stood them face to face. After which, they
were alone together—the heart, it seemed, of their mortified city.

Odour of Eucalyptus

MICHAEL WILDING

HE MET her on the boat coming out and admired her straight-
forward independence. Besides, they were both travelling first
class. On the four weeks' journey they were quite considerably
thrown together, especially as there were few people, travelling
first class, who were within any range of youth. Once he did go
down to a dance on the tourist deck, with Ralph, whom he had
met on the ship too, but a steward politely informed them that it
was for tourist passengers only and requested them to keep to their
own class, and the next day a notice went up and a circular went
round reminding passengers in the first class not to intrude into the
tourist area. And so after that he and Ralph and Miss Thorn
were more and more thrown together. At first they had dutifully
talked to the travellers at dinner, but they were mostly old, and
after the first few meals of getting to know each other over dinner
jackets and wine, there was little to say. So Peter and Ralph
and Miss Thorn soon ceased to pretend to converse with the others
at their table, and talked at one end amongst themselves, and
would abandon the meal as soon as possible to go to the bar for
a drink.

But, he insisted, it was not a drinking voyage. They would only
drink a little. She had only the one sherry. He and Ralph tried
to make her unbend, but she stuck to the one sherry. She was
very stiff, he groped, emphasizing what was not, it appeared, an
easily definable quality, by hinging slightly at the waist, bowing
his trunk jerkily, slightly, and lifting his arms outwards from his
side a little, a foot's penguin flap, and closing them to him again.

This friend and I tried to, you know—and he flapped his arms,
once, eighteen inches from his side—make her, oh make her—and
he turned then and looked out of the window—less formal.

The lift shafts of unclothed buildings stood in the city, cranes
raised behind them lifting girders around them. The flat was high

and at night the window looked on a whole array of neon signs, turning and swooping and flashing.

She was attracted to his stubby northernness, a sort of blunt clumsiness. It reminded her, perhaps, of Lawrence; but though she had read Lawrence—indeed at the time of their getting to know each other was sitting in a deck-chair reading *Kangaroo,* which she didn't like—she would not have liked to have seen her interest in Peter as that, as belonging at all to that area of literature. Rather he existed in her consciousness as a character from some English television series, new and provincial and colloquial, with speech rhythms difficult quite to catch. She liked the way he liked the Beatles, and associated him with them, though not liking the Beatles herself. Indeed, when they came to Sydney she refused his invitation to go to see them. She could not face the mass of screaming teenagers in the Stadium. But she knew he would not have thought of that.

   She saw him in his dinner jacket, his hands clenched, his shoulders just slightly raised. She detected immediately the unsureness, like the boys who had been asked to tea by her father and were uneasy with the schoolmaster off duty. With Peter though there was nothing so obvious as an ill-fitting dinner jacket or a confusion over the knives and forks; she could hardly have endured that. As far as the conventions went, he was satisfactory. She could bear to sit next to or opposite him. But she knew that uneasiness. She knew his lack of assurance, and felt assured, as she sat in the soft silk dress, her back erect and her elbows in, her hands held calmly in her lap.

They had tried to make her unbend. She was awfully set, closed in, stiff.

   So you tried to loosen her up? suggested Derek, as they sat by the open window, waiting for the cool of twilight and the sudden coming of evening.

   No, it wasn't like that. It was more . . . Well, you know, we told her jokes and things. She didn't . . .

   Know the facts of life—

   No, it wasn't that.

   She must have known a lot to set out alone like that, to leave home and travel with no companion. And the home she had left, in its comfort and seclusion, meant, for him, that her leaving it was all the more admirable. She had set out in bravery, not in ignorance. And that she had set out so late, again was admirable. He had come in his very early twenties, on the well-paid contract job to the full sun. He never said quite how much older she was than him, but she was certainly closer to the thirties. And because of that, her increasing age, her setting stiffness and lack of soft pliancy, to have shot off like that when she did, deserved acknowledgment. That for too long she had been sitting not shooting off, he didn't consider. And perhaps it would anyway have been an unfair consideration. It was her achievement now that impressed him.

It must have impressed him, to make him take her for one sherry every evening after dinner, to offer, even, her another.

Oh no, she said, more or less each time, accenting equally each syllable, oh no, with a pleasured surprise and with an automatic reply, as if embroidered on her bosom were written, for all to see, one only. And that enabled her to be just that slightly knowing, that teeny weeny bit superior, because after all, you ought to have known, oughtn't you, that I don't take another, do I?

They did. And he and Ralph might have another. But not more than one other—just repaying the round, the one repaying the other, and she out of it, the buying back. Not that she didn't pay, no. She would offer. Let this one be on me, boys, she'd say easily and with both her hands crossed over and around her purse, she would bow her head over and probe gently into its secrecies. And she would buy them one, each. But because she never had more than one, not even when it had been one bought by herself and they both stood there beside her, each side of her, offering her, at first, another, because of this, they never had more than two, and often only the one. And anyway by then the bar was beginning to fill after dinner, and as they had tripped away from dinner, so they tripped away from the bar, and sat in deckchairs looking at the sky, the three in a line, on her left hand and on her right. And they would talk. This would be when they would tell her jokes. Of course, there was all day too but then they would be disporting themselves in the swimming pool, on the greasy pole, or just reading. In the evening, though, there would be the soft intimacy of the unlit night, lapping around them, secretively.

For Miss Thorn they at first provided a diversion. Uprooted herself as she was, she had to endure a long delay before transplantation, she would have talked happily to the fellow travellers, and she felt a sharp little shudder of wicked guiltiness that she abandoned them, and had begun to spend her time with the two boys. She was throwing over her conventions, just as she had said she would.

They were pleasant to talk to, too, intelligent, good company.

She liked to have them talking to her, to feel that they sought her out for their companionship. It was for all of them a spontaneous activity, and she didn't feel that the purser's order to keep to your class in any way influenced the choice. It didn't for her. She was glad though, in an unexamined way, that they now couldn't go and wander amongst the noisiness of the tourists, the large families of unpatriotic cockneys or northerners who had only dislike for Britain, and who could never have understood Peter's or Ralph's motives for coming; and certainly not hers. They would not have had imagination.

Peter and Ralph had imagination, understood her, she felt, in her shaking off those inhibiting conventions and breasting the waves as she was. They were intelligent, and she could talk to them because of their intelligence, these two clever, efficient graduates. By their intellectual achievements they were qualified to travel first class. It was part of their contracts. With them she felt she was moving in something of the sophisticated world, not the formal and elegant sophistication of the dull diners at the table, but the new dynamic, dogged sophistication, the technology of the English quality Sunday papers. And she could sip her sherry with them, as they leant against the bar in their dinner jackets, or escorted her to a table, and live in a world she had not lived in before. Her home was not like this new dynamism, and the teachers' training college she had gone to had been for Church of England girls only. But though their conversation was from a world she had not known, and though the liner's bar was new, she did not feel at all overwhelmed. And she listened to the northern vowels of Peter's, attuned to the assured noise of the ship, and held her back straight in the conversations of the first class bar. She felt quite composed and poised, and she felt, from her first noticing these two, more at ease from their subtle discomfiture. She would not be the one to be gauche.

I couldn't stand a long sea voyage so I flew, said Derek, as they sat in the window of a coffee bar in King's Cross, watching people going by. Though I don't know, I sort of regretted it. All the stories of sex life on the high seas. Not much hope in a Boeing.

No, said Peter.

Are you agreeing or saying something?

I mean there wasn't much on ship either.

Much what.

Just no people young at all, they're all terribly old.

So no sex?

He was drinking his coffee so only muttered a grunt. But it seemed that there was no sex.

So this bird was the only one?

The only what? Oh, she wasn't like that. He shook his head with an earnest conviction, lowering it slightly as if he would charge. So what he thought like that had implied wasn't made clear.

She was the only person our age, anywhere near it.

It was a gracious qualification.

Derek had a flat lined up and they moved into it to share it, but Miss Thorn had initially to stay in a hotel. Still, she knew some people in Sydney and despite the single sherries had met one or two others on the boat whom she could visit. For the first week Peter did not see her. He was arranging the obvious details of settling in—collecting his luggage and having it delivered, meeting people he would be working with, and sitting in the Cross wondering why he had decided to come.

Oh, it's good, Derek said. He had so many reservations, so many things for him were not good, so many things were ugly, but he argued he liked it. Girls were prettier, browner, easier.

One thing I was told, a piece of advice a friend gave me, before I came, was never, you know, get married to an Australian girl.

Never thought of it, said Derek, truthfully. Why, anyway?

Oh, because she'll have her family in Australia and you have yours in England and well—

You'll be commuting all your life? He eyed the waitress as they sipped coffee, nostalgic for the same espresso bars of his home. Anyway I don't think I'd particularly want to see my family. And I don't see you need ever get married.

Peter made a noise back in his throat, deep in tone, dissentient or interrogative, dissuasive of Derek's sexual successes being recounted.

The fountain rose and burst and spread and they watched it from their silence.

They turn it off when there's a strong wind, Derek said, because it sprays people.

Bravely stepping on the alien shore, she made for the hotel she had been directed to and visited friends she had letters of introduction to. She had carried these letters carefully in her writing folder, preserved in their envelopes, some from friends of her family who lived at home, others from friends or relations who, living at a distance, had written her these aids for the distant land.

She was fully occupied that first week in meeting these people, and she was even amazed at herself for the quick facility with which she managed the public transport. She even, from the back seat, talked to taxi-drivers about her first impressions.

Peter's accounts of the unsocial drinking must have been wildly exaggerated. Somehow—or perhaps just at the swimming pool— he met other people than Miss Thorn, and Miss Thorn met other people than him. The others though were the same; they were, that is, the same others for both of them. Suggesting, perhaps, it was together that they met these others, lying on a towel on the deck, Peter in his swimming shorts which he had adopted as more decorous than the elastic tight trunks he had worn in England, Miss Thorn abloom in her pink one piece costume, reading *Kangaroo* without enthusiasm. Ralph, no doubt, too, until Melbourne. And so they grew brown, Miss Thorn tanning pinkly at her disclosed extremities, sufficient for her in a dinner dress.

And it was one of these meetings with other people that meant they met again. Which is not to suggest they would not otherwise have renewed acquaintance. They most certainly would. But before the forgetfulness of the last night's party, they were both invited to spend a weekend, the next weekend, at Bilgola.

Some people, he said, I met on the boat. So I'm going up there.

Will you be back for this party tonight? asked Derek who had found a party circuit.

No, I mean I'm going for the weekend, he explained, almost resentful of having to be more explicit.

You must show me round Sydney, she said, pinkly on the beach at Bilgola.

I scarcely know it, he said, I'd need to be shown myself.

Well, we can discover it together.

She didn't even brightly add, can't we. Instead, she smiled, at him and at their hosts. It seems a very sensible idea. Economy of effort, she explained, as if applying a scientific metaphor knowingly to the world.

They didn't sunburn because they'd got over that on the boat. But they felt very tired in the heat.

On the Saturday they went round the Botanic Gardens, smelling the blooms as they walked together down the wide stretching paths, amongst the strange flowers and the high unknown trees. They walked down to the water's edge, the blue-grey water lapping towards them and sparkling, and they looked across at the skinless frame of the opera house, a model brontosaurus under construction, and at the molluscal crouching of Pinchgut. They talked about these things, about how pleasant it was and about the high buildings of the skyline and about the rare scents from the trees, and about this city they were both alone in far from their homes, which they still referred to as their homes.

Sniffing at the scents, then, and inhaling the salt sea breeze, they walked round, talking. And he shuffled around in the gravel, dribbling a lump of rock with his two feet, sometimes nearly falling as he tangled his legs round each other at moments of uncertain balance. She watched, from her not superior height (she didn't possess that) but more dumpily from her leveller walk, the solider set of her shoulders, the measured movement of one stockinged leg in front of the other, her back held, after all those deportment lessons she had not forgotten, too stiffly to allow her to play ball. His was a different stiffness, a sort of robot mechanicalness, a want of consonancy, as it were, with the rhythms of the lapping waves and the sliding gum-leaves. So he bobbed around, like a kelly played with by a budgerigar, beneath the still high trees, dribbling random patterns beside and before her, his arms hanging loosely by his sides, and this way they progressed round the Botanic Gardens, and he did not have to decide whether he should take her arm in his, and make then an initiated series of decisions.

He went out early the next Saturday morning and offered no destination to Derek. And Derek, who held himself a liberal in these matters, asked and said nothing. He was pleased in some way that Peter should have found somewhere to go over the weekend, somewhere so engaging and attractive that he would disclose nothing about it. The horizons for him were obviously widening out, someone must have been telling him jokes.

And when he came back he said nothing, but came with a soggy self-sufficiency that would resist any probing, and sat down in a chair and picked up a book and hardly spoke from behind it, except to grunt a refusal to an invitation to a party Derek was going to and from which, in the early hours of the morning, he brought home a girl to sleep with. He had a separate bedroom from Peter.

It must have been about this time that he brought her back to the flat, once. He didn't tell Derek, who was out, till some time later, so when exactly it was, Derek never knew. And as far as Derek knew, she never came back again.

She didn't really like it. The Cross, after all, wasn't pleasant, wasn't, except for this once, a place she really wanted to see except for her duty of discovering Sydney. Repute and that brief visit were enough for her.

Perhaps Peter had been trying to loosen her, make her bend and unbend, massage, in a manner of speaking, her. The Cross by day was a way in, to walk past the strip clubs, glossy photos of bosomy girls and transvestite men in showcases outside. And as a follow-up, bringing additional support through the opened gate, he mentioned his mysterious flat mate.

At least, Derek felt he must have been mysterious, as he never once met her. He mused amusedly to the girl he had picked up at that party and who now spent as many nights at his place as he did at hers, that perhaps Peter thought he would try to race her (Miss Thorn) off. He relished the phrase, race off. He had not heard it in England.

But what had happened was that Miss Thorn had been shown the shared flat, and Peter had launched into his flow of loosening; either that, or he had tried to explain items of feminine attire; either that or he had thought Derek would be a useful subject for broadening the horizons she had travelled so far towards.

But she only sniffed, inhaling nothing but drawing even her mucus into her, lest it should be contaminated in that air, and said, looking at the white walls that made the flat so cool and clean, Painted that colour for the activities that go on here, I suppose.

At which he picked up a newspaper and submerged in the flow he had released behind a headline of RAPE PACK STRIKES AGAIN. Derek only bought evening papers if they had striking headlines.

She evidently did not wish to engage more deeply in the activities that went on there; to know of them was enough, more than enough. Except for the caustic observation (she had a caustic wit) she was not interested in those activities, or any of the activities of the vicious Cross. And the next weekend they went out to see more places, sites and sights, which on a Sunday had usually few activities. Even the speakers at the Domain she insisted only on watching, out of earshot, there for the visual and pictorial interest alone.

And Peter seemed not to mind. She had been people enough for him on that unpeopled ship, and now she seemed enough again, and they would wander around their new-found land, sniffing the balmy odours and looking clear eyed at the fierce harsh light, through the parks and by the beaches, the sound of the surf drum-

ming in their ears with its racing pulse, the high palm trees rising
from the dry ground and roaring up into the fountain of shooting
spreading dropping live green leaves, the tide forcing itself between
the heads and flowing round the soft and calm untroubled inlets,
clefts and quiet harbours.

And so the weekends went as they discovered Sydney. Sometimes
he tired, in the heat or crush of people, but usually he was attentive and kind. She had never had anyone so attentive before, that
she admitted openly to herself, but whatever she had had before,
she did not inquire into, resuscitate or admit to. And she accepted
his kindness rather than probe into what other qualities there might
be lurking there; there was, after all, no obligation for him to be
kind. One day they noticed at Circular Quay the liner they had
sailed out in. It seemed a long time ago; yet they were amazed
also at how long they must have been there (still it was as "there"
that they thought of it) for it to have returned and come back
again. They went round the zoo, and the chimpanzees rattled
their cages at them, hanging from bars and wood, their legs wide
apart and dangling like priapic puppets. They watched the snakes
crawling and sliding and twining, only briefly. They walked, in
that heat, all round the zoo, safe amongst the rampant animals,
side by side. And the roaring of the lions followed them over the
harbour and once or twice on the ferry she shuddered at the snakes.
   A goose walking over my grave, she explained to Peter, to show
that she had been in touch with a real (if refined) traditional
culture, with the sort of thing that coloured the racy working
class speech of the television shows that she found she could still
watch in Australia.

I can't work out whether he is or whether he isn't, said Derek, and
he was quite sad about it.
   His girl wasn't—sad about it, that is. Sex in the normal channels
was enough for her; but Derek was curious about Peter's possible
northern prudery, methodistical decency, and satisfied those qualities in himself by his speculative voyeurism.

Peter's decency, after all, was a very important factor. The
brusque statement that left no room for and refused to tolerate
further speculation, and the brusque uprightness that considered
no temptation or aberration, were related. He would walk the
straight and gravelly path, stumbling perhaps on the way through
not noticing the hazards, but not erring through looking round
too much. He didn't look round. He'd dribble the rocks of

lumpy solid righteousness along with him, stubbing his toes and
tearing the leather of his shoes, but he'd take them along; and
the only real danger would be that he might fell Miss Thorn by
accidentally kicking some rock too hard, not looking around, so
hard that he'd just lam it into her.

Though she was pretty resilient. Her legs had probably taken
some heavy bashing from hockey sticks. And she wouldn't go
down easily. Perhaps she'd never go down at all. She was built
for stability—some sad aberration on the part of nature, like
giving limpets such staying power. Who would want to aim the
blows she was built to resist? But resist them, whenever they
might come, she would, resist anything she would, so that the
stability might be almost a simply deterrent device. And he might
have been more Lawrentian; or even simply more curious. Like
the people who prise limpets off just to have a look at them underneath and poke their fingers in them. It was a subject for
curiosity, as Derek kept explaining defensively to the girl, who
didn't care either way.

But he poked his fingers nowhere, not even to her hands. They
walked demurely and sat at restaurants, when they ate after their
discoveries, tête à tête indeed, but correctly. She liked that, their
being tête à tête. And at night he would take her back to her
hotel, and say goodnight to her.

I'd ask you in for coffee, she would smile, but you know what
people might think.

She knew what people might think, she wasn't that sheltered and
barricaded, but she didn't think like that herself. She would curl
in her pink nightdress (a sewn blue and yellow flower or two
discreetly across the bosom) and think sweet thoughts, leaving
others outside the hotel, where she last mentioned that people might
think things other than sweet, leave, then, any such thoughts there
where she had last acknowledged their existence, leave them with
him and for him to cope with, as he caught a cab back to the
activities of the white-walled flat, not even, as she curled there,
thinking that she was not thinking of certain things.

But of course, left with those thoughts, he might have been
more inflamed. He might bluntly have wanted this girl from
the soft south east of England, the girl with the elocuted voice and
the straight back, the obviously unplucked rose. Her name was
actually Mary, but at first he'd not mentioned this to Derek, and
so Rose was the name that Derek vicariously fed on, the budded,
full and slightly mildewed Rose, amongst her patronymic briers.

She gave a small party to which she invited some of the people she had met. It was small because she did not want to make too much noise in the hotel in which she was living; it was difficult to get a flat near to where she was teaching; and in the hotel she did not have to cook.

She had bought sherry, and it seemed, as they sat there in the room, waiting for the guests to arrive, just like those single sherries on the ship, before the bar became invaded and they left for the deck.

It reminds me of the ship, she said; and perhaps she also meant, as she might have put it in another way, had that way been her way of putting things, It's as if we're still travelling, recognizing implicitly that they had not yet arrived and, in that hotel room, doubting that they ever would.

The guests at first sat in a couple of chairs and on the bed, a coverlet over it and the pillow hidden somewhere so it didn't look like a bed but a couch for a party, and she offered sherry and told Peter to offer peanuts, and when he stood there, picking at them and eating them himself, abstractedly lapping his tongue around his nut-clogged teeth, she tut-tutted at him—enunciating the tut-tut as if reading it in a book of gentle and tolerantly amused reprobation—and shook her head at him, and made a part joke of it, and he blinked and said, Oh, I'm sorry, northernly, and thrust the bowl to the bosom of a seated girl who was also teaching at the school Miss Thorn was at. And they laughed, and she liked him for his gaucheness, that never exceded its limits and became boorishness. The latecomers sat on the carpeted floor and perhaps with everyone there there were a dozen people, talking together. She had invited the couple they had met on the boat and visited together that early weekend, and some school-teachers of about her own age, and a girl of nineteen who was the daughter of one of those friends of friends Miss Thorn had been told to visit in those letters she had carried with her. Peter talked to her, that girl, quite a bit. She was pretty, with long straight black hair, and a white, still face; she was shy, retreating —perhaps normally she was too shy or her parents were too strict to allow her to go to parties. She had large, dark, sad eyes which she directed at Peter as he talked about Australia and the north Midlands of England, and she listened. She sat on one end of the bed, and every time anyone moved for a nut or a drink, or moved to lean back, she was moved by the mattress, and she would pull down the hem of her dress to her knees, and settle again. And Peter wriggled on the floor, sitting on no cushion, to become more comfortable, and each wriggle seemed to bring him nearer to her, and if it had been anyone else, and had Miss Thorn seen someone like such an anyone else close to such a girl, she might have thought he was going gently to lay a hand on the girl's knee. But he didn't and Miss Thorn perhaps would not have thought of somebody doing that, in a hotel room, in that sort of a hotel. But she did come over to him brightly and say, I must break up this tête à tête and introduce you to some other people and she led him off and the girl sat there, the knees of her thin slender legs white through her stockings.

The ferry came into Manly slowly, silently, and then noisily reversing so that it came to a stop by the pier. And above the noise of the revolving screws came the shrieks of girls whirling in cages on the ferris wheels, shrieking and screaming as the cages went head downwards; and bright poster paints called SHARKS and GHOST TRAIN and FUNLAND.

They went down the gangplank among the shorted plump young teenagers and the shambling youths, amongst them along the pier, and out to the road. He remembered summer holidays, walking disconsolate on the promenade behind his mother and father, mackintoshed in the rain or cold in the wind or sometimes sunny sitting in deckchairs on crowded beaches. She, though, would have spent her summers in the quiet and undiscovered Welsh villages, away from the trippers.

These were hardly trippers. They were there all the time, lived there. It was their place through which they carried transistors distortedly crackling pops and the Austral-American commercial announcers voices, girls fat and waddling or thin and gangling, thonged and shambling along the pavement past shops selling coloured tawdriness, noise and garishness, the sickly sweet smell of doughnuts and greasy food in a hot summer. And in one coffee-bar doorway stood the hoodlums, large, heavy, with heavy side-burns and matted hair, their arms akimbo, wearing thick leather motor-cycling jackets, glowering at the pink and orange and green of the surfies going by.

And they sat on the beach looking at the crashing surf and the surfboard riders like pins on the great heaving mass, and all over the beach the girls with white make-up and small bikinis lay, looking through their binoculars of mascara at the gangling heavy-shouldered boys who ran and punched each other. And behind them a group of surfies, the boys with their hair died peroxide white, thatched, began a dispute over surfboards, and others looked across, mouths open, eyes squinting in the glare from the sun-reflecting sand, and the little girls of fourteen or so huddled up to see what was happening, and soon a circle had formed; but

there was no fight, instead a group chanting began, as they all dug
with their forearms in the sand, scuffing it behind them like dogs,
and looking through their legs, chanting.

For Miss Thorn it was discovering Sydney, and she looked at the
surfies with white zinc coated on their noses, or their backs peeling,
the skin coming away in cancerous, multicolour patches, speckled
like the underbelly of some fish, looked at all this with interest.
She didn't like it; but discovering Sydney was what she had come
to do, whereas for Peter it was where he had come to live; and
this was somewhere he would rather have not known existed, this
beach.   And when they walked back to the ferry, and the wind
blew along the street and her dress swirled upwards caught by
the wind, and some of the youths lounging or walking or driving,
whistled, he felt the derision in the whistle directed also at him.

Yet each weekend, and sometimes in the week, they would go
around, and he seemed not to resist and erected no barriers against
her pressure.   While he insisted nothing, demanded nothing,
pressed nothing.   Yet it couldn't simply have been that he grew
more aware of her unattractiveness as he got to know her; her lack
of physical charms would have been at once apparent, and increasing knowledge of each other would have diminished the strikingness
and importance of that.   And if it was her company, her friendship or whatever it was, that lessened in value for him, why then
did he still escort her?   Perhaps the friendship remained; perhaps
the trouble was that he feared to encroach on that long untouched
virginity, that grew each day longer untouched and less attracting
plucking, a buttonhole he would not want to wear.   Perhaps he
feared to insist on her unbending, on her becoming less stiff, in
case she should snap off suddenly and hurtfully.   Perhaps touching
nothing and forcing nothing they were both happier.   Yet he
wasn't happy on those weekends of discovery.   He would set out
in gloom and return in silence.

He had come to say less and less in way of explanation or extenua-
tion of his activities with Miss Thorn to Derek.   It may have been
to block inquiry, to avoid having to discuss her as Derek would
willingly have discussed his girls, to avoid having to associate in
conversation Miss Thorn with the delicate soon-faded flowers that
Derek ravaged.   But his reticence had grown, too, along with his
resentment in the trips of discovery; it seemed that the weekends
had become a duty, like the weekend gardening at home, and he
preferred to forget that and say nothing.   Yet he still went, still
visited her, still shared her companionship, still made his silent

exits at the weekend. And to Derek there seemed no obvious change in the relationship of Peter and Miss Thorn, no development or retardation, so that he was surprised one morning to find a letter for Peter from Melbourne with the name and address of Miss M. Thorn on the back. But he preserved the silence and put the letter face up on the table, so that it was not obvious that he had seen who it was from, and left. But the next time she wrote he had the letters in his hand, looking only to see whom they were for—when Peter appeared, so there was an explanation.

Oh, it's my English friend. She's gone to Melbourne.

And as he had regularly, dutifully explored, so he must have written, for the letters came steadily back; and Melbourne was eventually replaced by Canberra and Canberra by Brisbane, as she discovered Australia. And whether she found someone else with whom to discover Melbourne—did Ralph oblige?—or he found someone with whom to occupy the now tame weekends, he did not say.

Then, with a day's warning, he went to Brisbane, where his English friend was. He wrote, during his stay there, a usual holiday letter, saying that he had swum and seen places and was enjoying it, except, it added, briefly, suggestively, he was not getting on too well with his English friend who kept expecting him to be an English gentleman.

But there was no more. Nor was more said when he returned, at the end of the week. But the correspondence didn't totally stop, though it was certainly reduced, much reduced. Perhaps she had become bored with the Lawrentian hero, the colloquial Midlander, and tried to make him wear a dinner jacket in the Brisbane hotels. Or perhaps he had tired of treating her as the English lady, pure, unmolested, untouched by human hand, and scattering the rocks and pebbles of morality aside, had lowered his head and charged. Perhaps he had tired of the stiff back and the deportment on the Queensland sands, or perhaps she had wanted to go out discovering in the hot midday sun.

He once did remark, discussing some girl who had unsuccessfully tried to make Derek do something for her, that his English friend had wanted things done for her all the time. But he said no more, although Derek sat expectantly, sitting in a pub in the evening looking at the people and the traffic in the Cross, sitting there relaxed and ready for the exiles' reminiscences. But nothing came. There was no full flow of relieving story, merely that odd, pigeon-holed reference.

The letters still came, as she managed to teach briefly in some cities and holiday in others, travelling over the continent with that solid independence that he had first admired in her, moving from hotel to hotel and place to place and in her own way, perhaps the only way possible for her, getting to know the land and taking photographs of it.   And the letter that came from Perth, nearly a year later, must have told him of her final impressions, before she boarded the liner that would take her back home on her boomerang ticket.